D0261640

THE SILVER LINING

Tessa Barclay titles available from
Severn House Large Print

A BETTER CLASS OF PERSON
FAREWELL PERFORMANCE
A LOVELY ILLUSION
STARTING OVER
A TRUE LIKENESS

THE SILVER LINING

Tessa Barclay

Severn House Large Print
London & New York

This first large print edition published in Great Britain 2004 by
SEVERN HOUSE LARGE PRINT BOOKS LTD of
9-15 High Street, Sutton, Surrey, SM1 1DF.
First world regular print edition published 2003 by
Severn House Publishers, London and New York.
This first large print edition published in the USA 2004 by
SEVERN HOUSE PUBLISHERS INC., of
595 Madison Avenue, New York, NY 10022.

British Library Cataloguing in Publication Data

Barclay, Tessa
    The silver lining - Large print ed.
    1.   Women real estate agents - Fiction
    2.   Love stories
    3.   Large type books
    I.   Title
    823.9'14 [F]

    ISBN 0-7278-7349-0

Printed and bound in Great Britain by
MPG Books Ltd, Bodmin, Cornwall.

One

When her Significant Other walked out on her, Karen Montgomery was too busy to notice.

She was in Cambodia at the time. It wasn't a place she wanted to be, but the turmoil in the travel business after the attack on the World Trade Center had made it necessary. The major airlines seemed to have gone into a flat spin, with a knock-on effect on lesser routes such as that serving the towns and cities of the Far East. Her own journey to Phnom Penh had been beset with delays and diversions. Now she'd just finished rescuing a stranded group of travellers from the further reaches of Cambodia by means of a long, crowded train journey. Stations, with throngs of would-be passengers crowding the platforms, had gone by the carriage windows – Batdambang, Kampong Saom – and at last Phnom Penh, the capital.

Previously arranged tickets for air travel had had to be ditched, partly because their date had gone by but also because flights had been cancelled or re-routed. To say

Karen was vexed was to understate it by astronomic measurements. She prided herself on giving her clients a trouble-free trip and this one, though unusual, had gone beautifully until the group was at the ancient capital of Angkor. Then came September 11th, and everything went into a state of collapse.

Her clients were British Buddhists, on a pilgrimage to visit Buddhist temples. That was the kind of thing her travel firm catered for – unusual travellers with unusual aims. Of course there were problems sometimes, and that was where she excelled – soothing anxious spirits, arranging alternative hotels, finding lost luggage. The personal touch – when anything went wrong Karen was always the one to go out to clear it up.

Affairs in Phnom Penh hadn't been easily sorted. In the first place she had to find her group, who turned out to be sheltering in a Buddhist monastery near Angkor Thom. Then she had to get to them, which entailed a hired car with a driver who seemed to have no idea of geography. Then they had to be brought back to the capital city but the hedge-hopping airline that had taken them north no longer existed; lost in the aftermath of the terrorist attack on the Twin Towers. Hence the long return journey by rail, with eleven distressed, tired and rather unworldly protégés.

'Don't worry, everything will be all right,' she'd assured them. She didn't believe it herself while she said it.

But in the end she was justified. Once in Phnom Penh, she got them all off in little separate packages on diverse days on diverse airlines. She had to use all her negotiating skills to achieve it – feminine charm, argument, bribery.

So now, here she sat in her hotel room in Phnom Penh on a sultry October evening, pleased to have looked after charges and come through the crisis, yet in rather low spirits.

She'd been eleven days in Cambodia. How long would it be before she herself got home?

She'd tried to e-mail Michael regularly throughout her endeavours. At first her laptop had worked, but oddly enough, she'd never had a response from him. Then her machine seemed to be affected by the irregular electricity supply, so she'd turned to batteries. But those she was able to buy were either duds or fakes, because she couldn't even get switched on.

But Michael, too, probably had his problems. He was in the US, trying to bring home yet another stranded group. U-Special Tours had taken them on a trip round the casinos of the Native Americans – that's to say, the new gambling complexes set up on

7

their tribal lands by what used to be called Red Indians. Much research and planning had gone into that trip. Alas, the smaller American airlines – almost branch lines – had been brought to a standstill by the after-effects of September 11th. She imagined he was bringing his charges back to Chicago by road.

She'd of course tried to telephone. The telephone service of Phnom Penh, though limited, did at least work. But all she got at the offices of U-Special was the answering machine.

Well, when she got back to London she'd find either a message or Michael himself. She was longing just to hear his voice.

It was eight o'clock in the evening and not much cooler than day-time temperatures. The water supply being as unreliable as the electricity, she'd been unable to do more than pat herself with bottled water. Her loose silk caftan was sticking to her where it touched, the fringe of black hair on her brow looked damp and lifeless, her skin was wan and her velvet brown eyes had lost their sparkle. She was suffering from a slight case of the miseries.

She eased open the louvered shutters to look out at the thundery sky. Black clouds everywhere promising the evening down-pour. Where, oh where was the silver lining she always expected?

She didn't feel like eating dinner, but a nice cold drink would be good. One thing the Hotel Orchid was good at was cool drinks; the former French colonists had taught them the importance of that, and American reporters during the war had always demanded ice in their whisky.

'Ah, mademoiselle,' murmured Ngen the bartender as she came in.

'*Comment ça va?*' It was strictly against government policy to speak the language of the former occupiers of the country, but Karen and Ngen had a secret pact about it. He was elderly, and in the past had had a splendid education, so he enjoyed an opportunity to use the language he'd come to love. She'd found a lot of the officials liked to air their French when they thought no one was around to report the misdeed. It had helped her in her negotiations for airline tickets.

He made her a long Tom Collins without being asked. His thin face creased in smiles when she sighed in satisfaction after a sip. He insisted on carrying her drink to a table where the intermittent air conditioning might give her some comfort.

She'd barely sat down when a middle-aged man with beautifully barbered white hair and a fine wild-silk suit rose from another table and came to stand at her side.

'Mademoiselle Montgomery?'

Of course she was Mademoiselle Montgomery. She was the only European woman staying in the hotel. Over the stranger's shoulder she caught the eye of Ngen, whose impassive gaze somehow conveyed the message that this was a respectable person. She smiled and agreed she was Mademoiselle Montgomery.

'May I sit?'

'Please do.'

He took the chair across from her. He laid folded brown hands on the marble table top. 'Mademoiselle Montgomery, I am Professor Than Banin.' He brought out a fine leather card case, handed her a card. All it said was: Professor Than Banin Ph.D.

'Am I right in thinking you are trying to achieve a ticket for a flight to Europe?'

'You are quite right.' They were having this conversation in English, although she could tell he would rather have spoken French, the forbidden language of the former conquerors. He switched to French now.

'Mademoiselle Montgomery, I have a proposition to put before you, if you will allow.'

Other well-tailored gentlemen had put propositions to her in the past ten days, which she'd tactfully refused. This one, however, looked more trustworthy than the rest.

'Does your proposition include an airline ticket?' she inquired in a neutral tone.

'It includes two airline tickets, mademoiselle. I am here to ask if you would act as escort to a small boy who should be taken to Paris, if it can be arranged.'

This was a new approach, if he was after romance. 'A small boy?'

'May I explain?'

'By all means.'

He gestured at Ngen for service and, when the barman hurried up, ordered Laudun Côtes du Rhone, well chilled. While he waited for it to be brought, he settled himself more comfortably on the rattan chair. 'The boy is Roland Dartieux,' he began. 'The son of Louis Dartieux, a member of the French diplomatic service. Monsieur Dartieux has been here on a commercial mission with his wife and son. But you know ... the uncertainty in the financial markets...?'

'Yes?'

'He was summoned home three days ago. He and his wife were able to get a flight at once, of course, but the child was unwell and had to be left behind. He was to fly as soon as tickets could be arranged for him and his ... ah ... his nanny?' His tone queried the word.

'Oh yes, his nanny, I see.' Although she didn't. 'How old is he?'

'He has six years. I am told, *hélas*, that the nanny, who is a young Australian lady, has run away.'

11

'Run away?' echoed Karen. 'Where to?'

'That is not known. But she has run away with the boyfriend recently acquired here in Phnom Penh, and one imagines they have gone somewhere by boat. In the end, what happens is, now the embassy has achieved two tickets for the boy to go home but his nanny is absent. So I am asked by the embassy if I know of anyone who could take the place of the nanny, and I have heard that you are trying for a ticket to Paris, so this could be of advantage to you.'

'Perhaps it could,' she agreed, her neutral tone hiding a surge of pleasure. To think of it! Back to cool temperatures, mosquito-free evenings, soft beds – and Michael. But she mustn't show too much enthusiasm because Mr Fixer here would raise the price.

She'd no doubt he'd been paid by the French embassy to find a suitable female escort for the child. He would expect to be paid by Karen for the golden opportunity to travel home. She was used to this by now. She said, by way of opening gambit, 'The child is six but has a nurse. He is sickly?'

'By no means, mademoiselle. He has a nanny because the mama does not wish to concern herself with looking after him too much, being greatly occupied with hostess tasks for the papa. Monsieur Dartieux is an *extremely* important member of the commercial division of his government. I believe the young Roland has recovered from what turned out to be merely an upset stomach. He will be no burden to you while you travel, for the cabin staff will of course be always at hand. And it is convenient that you speak good French, as I was told and now find to be true.'

'In other words, you've looked at other possibilities and I've got the best credentials?'

'You are certainly very well qualified for this little task,' he agreed, smiling at her directness. These Europeans – no finesse. He would reply in kind. 'It is unfortunate that there is no female member of the embassy available to act as escort but I have ascertained that you are reliable.'

His wine came, he sipped it with enjoyment, then they began the haggling. In the end she bought the chance to travel to Paris with this unexpected diplomatic baggage for a reasonable sum. He shook hands, gave her a sheet of paper with the flight details, and agreed that she should hand over the money in cash next day at the airport when he handed over the tickets.

Her appetite restored by the thought of going home, she had a light meal. Upstairs again, she tried once more to send e-mails but her laptop was still unresponsive. She telephoned the French embassy to check on arrangements for next day, but had difficulty in finding someone who knew what she was talking about.

At length, a commercial attaché admitted he had heard of Roland Dartieux and the travel plans. 'I intended to ring you later,' he apologized, 'when the paperwork had been accomplished.'

She heard in his tone the weariness she knew from her own experience. 'Are you meeting with problems?' she asked in concern.

'Well – imagine to yourself – the boy has no passport.'

'No passport?'

There was a shrug implied in his reply. 'So far he has travelled on his mother's passport. Now, here he is in Phnom Penh with no papers. Of course, Paris has faxed the necessary particulars and so on, but it doesn't help that he is of the nation regarded here as oppressors from the days of old French Indo-China ... Well, no matter, we shall settle it all and you will meet Roland at the airport tomorrow.'

Of course, nothing went smoothly at the airport. She didn't expect it to. Years in the travel industry had taught her that if anything could go wrong, it would. First of all Professor Banin didn't come himself but sent a henchman with the air tickets. He, of course, wanted a substantial tip for his trouble. Luckily Karen had expected that

14

and brought extra cash. But when she went to exchange her remaining riels for euro, she was met with stubborn incomprehension. The young man behind the guichet had no intention of handing over precious foreign currency, if he could help it.

So she spent the riels on cooling drinks from the bar and souvenirs for her sister Evie's children, two boys and a girl. Take-off time was approaching, and still no sign of her protégé. Karen's luggage had long gone aboard.

At last, as the first call came for their flight, a sleek Mercedes glided up to the entrance of the VIP lounge. The liveried chauffeur leapt out to get luggage from the boot. The back passenger door opened and out tumbled a white-faced little boy with copper-coloured hair and greeny-blue eyes. He was wearing a white linen outfit of tailored shirt and shorts, and clutching a large flat book. Behind him came an elderly lady in a floral silk dress. She was twittering at him in French.

'Quietly, Roland, quietly,' she was admonishing. 'You'll make yourself sick again!'

So that was the reason for the white little face and the late arrival. Travel nerves probably, bringing on travel sickness. Karen had dealt with it often in her former career as a flight attendant. She had been well-trained.

'There's no hurry, Roland,' she said gently,

15

offering her hand. 'What you can hear is only the first call.'

'I'm all right,' he said, gathering himself together. 'Goodbye, Madame Segur, and thank you for taking care of me.' He gave the lady a little bow in formal farewell.

'Goodbye, my little friend,' she replied. 'Mademoiselle Montgomery will look after you now.' Over his head her eyes met Karen's and her mouth turned at the ends in a smile of amusement mixed with concern. Karen, without quite understanding, smiled and nodded in reassurance.

The chauffeur had taken the boy's suitcase to the departure desk of the diplomatic lounge. It was checked through and hurried away to be put aboard. His papers were now offered by the chauffeur, in a bright plastic folder labelled: *Bureau de l' Ambassade de France, Service commercial*. Madame Segur hovered anxiously in the background.

The official refused to be impressed by this. On the contrary, he insisted on examining every piece of paper with unnecessary thoroughness despite the fact that Karen had discussed the situation already, and knew he'd had instructions by phone.

In the end, as the last call was being announced over the address system, he relented, stamped two of the papers, and handed them to Karen. The chauffeur saluted and ushered Madame Segur away. Karen and

Roland joined the occupants of the lounge in boarding a handsome little mini-bus which took them to the walkway to the plane. They left the mid-morning heat of Cambodia for the cool of the first-class seating.

Naturally the child claimed the window seat. He watched the taxiing and take-off. Below them the Mekong and the Tonie Sap dwindled to thin silver ribbons. 'Goodbye, Phnom Penh,' he murmured.

'Are you sorry to leave? The lady, Madame Segur – she was a friend?'

'Oh no. She's the wife of one of the clerks. When Norah ran away a few days ago Madame Segur looked after me.'

'Norah – that was the au pair?'

He shrugged. The flight attendant came up to ask if they wished for any reading material. Karen chose an English language newspaper published in Singapore. 'You've something for children?' she enquired. 'Comics? Colouring books?'

'Please, don't bother,' Roland put in. 'I have my own book.' He put his thin small hand on the folder he'd brought with him. It looked like a loose-leaf binder.

The attendant smiled and went away, to return with one of the books about Babar the Elephant. Roland accepted it with a polite murmur of thanks, glanced through it, but closed it and put it on the table in front of them.

17

'Don't you like it?' Karen asked, watching him over her newspaper.

'It's rather childish.'

'Oh, I see.' Her curiosity was aroused. 'What kind of book is the one you brought?'

'It's my memoirs,' he replied gravely.

'Your memoirs?'

'Of my stay in Phnom Penh. Of course, I didn't get to see much of the city, but the embassy gardens were interesting. There were fish in the big pool, the gardener told me they were golden carp. I took pictures. Would you like to see?'

'I certainly would.'

He opened the binder. Neatly stuck to the pages were photographs with rather drunken capital letters below, giving in well-spelt French the time and place of the photography. The pictures weren't very good, having been taken with a cheap disposable camera, but there were recognizable shots of golden carp, several magnificent orchids, a cat sunning itself, and various grown-ups playing tennis.

'That's excellent, Roland! Is that your hobby, photography?'

'Not particularly. I only did it to pass the time, really. I mean to write a few comments about the garden and the plants, just to make it more thorough.'

What a strange child, thought Karen. He was what her sister Evie would probably call 'old-fashioned'. But he was looking better than when she'd first seen him; some colour had come into his cheeks although she thought he had a naturally pale skin.

'I expect you'll be starting school when you get back to Paris,' she suggested. 'It's too late for the Return, of course.' In France, everyone left the cities during August and came back in time for the resumption of school in September. 'But I suppose they'll take you into the primary class and you'll be able to take that and show your friends.'

'Does one do that?' he enquired, clearly intrigued.

'We-ell ... I don't know if they do it in France, but in England they call it show-and-tell.' Her elder nephew and her niece were always regaling her with accounts of what they'd taken to class for these sessions.

'So you're English. You speak very good French but you do have an accent.'

'So they tell me.'

'I didn't mean that as a criticism,' he said at once. 'Your accent is very charming.'

Compliments from a six-year-old admirer. She took care to hide her amusement.

'Is school agreeable?' he asked.

'I think it is – my nephew and niece seem to enjoy it and I remember my own school-days as being enjoyable.'

'If my parents hadn't had to leave so suddenly and we'd stayed in Cambodia until

Papa finished his duties, I might have had a tutor.' He said this with a certain pride.

'All to yourself?' she said, half teasing.

'I think so. I went with some other children to something called kindergarten. That's German, you know, it means children's garden, but we had it indoors.'

'Did you like that?'

'Not much. We painted with poster colours and made models with plastic clay. Madame wouldn't let me do writing because she said I hadn't been properly taught yet.'

'But you showed her your book?'

'Oh no, we didn't do show-and-tell,' he said with regret.

'Well, when you start proper school you'll like it,' she assured him. 'But I think they'll teach you a different way of writing.'

'You mean joined up. That will be good. It's easy to learn how to do the big letters because you see them on traffic signs and shop fronts, but you don't see joined up so I've never learned that.'

'You just learned to do capitals by seeing them on billboards and things, Roland?' she said in surprise.

'Yes, of course.'

The attendant came now with pre-lunch drinks and to take their order. For all his old-fashionedness he showed a normal child's taste in food, opting for tomato soup, chicken with frites, and ice cream. After the

20

meal he noticed a children's crossword in Karen's newspaper and asked to try it, but by and by the pencil dropped from his fingers, his head drooped, and he fell asleep. Reaction to disturbed sleep the night before and the effects of travel nerves. She tucked a blanket round him before returning to her newspaper.

The plane droned on above the cloud cover, momentary shafts of sunlight came in from first one angle and then another. Karen put on headphones and watched the film on her screen, a noisy adventure with several car chases.

Aperitifs were brought round with the dinner menu. Roland roused himself. He rubbed his eyes, blinked a little, remembered where he was, and announced he needed to go to the toilet. Her offer to escort him was politely rejected. Of course, she told herself, he's travelled by air before – he knows his way about.

When he returned he'd washed his hands, used moist palms to slick back his straight coppery locks, and pulled the creases out of his linen shirt. A handsome child, perhaps with some Norman blood that had given him the pale skin and bright hair. He clambered back to his place by the window, looked out, and shrugged. 'Nothing but clouds,' he sighed.

'But every cloud has a silver lining.'

21

'Are you sure? If the sun shines on it, surely the lining should be gold.'

'That's true. I never thought of that.'

'Of course, when the moon shines, the lining will be silver.'

'You're right, and do you know, you can see the silver spilling out when you look up at night!'

'Really? I must try to wake up and look out one night, to see that.'

They were both smiling at this nonsense. A nice child, she thought.

'I got you some orange juice, and here's the menu for dinner. What about the pasta, Roland? Do you like Italian food?'

He agreed to *penne ai fungi*, but refused the hors d'oeuvre because it had anchovies. 'Horrid little fish,' he said, making a face. He perused the menu card and decided on melon instead. 'That will probably have a cherry in the middle of the slice,' he explained. 'I like the cherry better than the melon.'

'It's a pity there can't be a starter that's all cherries,' she teased.

'Perhaps I'll invent that when I'm grown up. Maman says well-known dishes can be named after people. Peach Melba is named after a singer, she says.'

'Quite right. So perhaps we'll have Cherries Roland.'

'Wouldn't it have to be my last name?' He

studied her, a smile dawning as he decided to take the game further. 'What should we invent for your dish? Anchovies *à la Montgomerie?*'

'Kedgeree *à la Karen.*'

'What's kedgeree?' he asked in surprise. It sounded strange in French.

'It's a dish made with smoked fish and eggs and rice. From India, I think.'

'It sounds terrible. But then Maman says that a lot of the things the English eat are terrible.'

'Maman knows a lot about England?'

'She was born there. But she doesn't have an English accent. I speak English, of course,' he said, switching to that. 'Do you think I speak it with a French accent?'

'You speak beautifully.' And indeed he did, but in a manner that somehow seemed un-childish.

'Could we name a dish for Maman?' he went on, staying with English to show off a little. 'Strawberries Hélène?'

'Oh, she already has a dish named after her. Pear Belle Hélène.'

'Truly?' He examined her face to make sure this wasn't another tease.

'No, it's true. Pears cooked in red wine with chocolate sauce – gorgeous.'

'Well, that's good. I wonder if Maman knows?'

'You can ask her when you get home.'

'Ah.' He said nothing for a while then announced, 'You can call me Roly if you like.'

'Roly?'

'My father calls me that.'

'You have a poem with your name in it!' she exclaimed, laughing.

'You mean the one about the Chevalier Roland? I know all about that.'

'No, no, a poem in English, about Roly. Let me see – the chorus goes something like, "With a roly-poly gammon and spinach, hey ho says Anthony Roly".'

'But that sounds like nonsense!'

'Of course it sounds like nonsense. It's a nursery rhyme. But you see, you already have a dish named after you. Roly-poly gammon and spinach. How about that, you've been famous for years!'

He giggled, a light, happy sound. 'You're funny! I've never met anyone like you before.'

'That's because I'm unique. And you can call me Karen.'

He accepted with a sudden return to solemnity. 'Thank you,' he said.

After the meal he wasn't ready to sleep, though by rights it was his bedtime. He got out his precious book and on one of the pages without photographs he began to write in careful block letters. When he had finished a line he offered it for her approval.

'Food is named after people. Maman's

24

food is Pear Belle Hélène. Mine is Roly Poly but I don't know what that is.'

'Excellent,' she said, and meant it. Compared with anything her nephew Perry could produce, it was superb. Once again she felt that sense of strangeness – this little boy was really one of a kind.

By and by he became drowsy. She escorted him to the toilet to see that he brushed his teeth and washed his face, then settled him down for what might be thought of as a night's sleep. She knew she would have to wake him when they reached Paris.

But he was deep in the rich, heavy sleep of childhood as the plane touched down. She had to carry him into the arrivals lounge. According to her body clock it was about four in the morning, and according to her philosophy anything that could go wrong would now go wrong. But not so. The Department of Commerce was taking care of its own.

She was whisked through the formalities. A hired limousine awaited them. They glided through the early-evening traffic of Paris, to draw up in front of a four-storey apartment block in one of the most expensive *arrondissements*. A semi-circular drive allowed them to stop at the elegant entrance. She got out carrying Roland. The chauffeur went ahead with the boy's luggage, nodding to the concierge to ring for the lift. They went up two levels, then stepped out in a carpeted hallway where a rich ormolu mirror reflected Karen's rather dishevelled appearance and the sleeping boy huddled in her arms. This was clearly the best apartment in the building, a two-storey luxury appropriate for a financial expert and his family.

A member of the airport staff had telephoned ahead so they were expected. The door opened at once when the chauffeur pressed the bell to reveal an elderly lady in a dark blue dress. To Karen she gave a slight inclination of the head which conveyed that she was some sort of servant. Her imperious gesture ordered the chauffeur to carry the luggage indoors. She was perhaps the housekeeper.

'*Reveille-toi, Roland. T'es chez toi,*' she said.

'Don't wake him,' Karen protested. She tried to hand over the sleeping child, but the housekeeper had turned to supervise the precise positioning of the suitcase. 'Would you inform Madame Dartieux—'

'Madame isn't here.'

'Not here?'

'She and Monsieur have had to go to Stockholm for a conference. Roland, wake up,' she said, shaking the boy by the shoulder.

He roused, raised his head a little. '*C'est toi, Gabrielle?*' he murmured.

'Don't do that,' Karen insisted. 'Take him

26

and carry him to bed.'

She might as well have been talking to the doorknob. 'Come along, Roland, upstairs and into the bath. You look quite unsanitary.'

The little boy obediently uncurled himself from Karen's body and lowered himself to the floor. Still half asleep, he allowed Gabrielle to take him by the elbow and usher him a few paces indoors. There she left him to deal with those she clearly considered mere minions.

'Thank you, mademoiselle,' she said, and closed the door.

'Thank *you*,' said Karen.

'*Une mégère*,' remarked the chauffeur.

A shrew indeed, but it didn't do to say so. Karen smiled and went with him back to the lift and then out to the limousine.

'Where to now, mademoiselle?'

'I left my car in a long-stay garage near the Madeleine. Could you take me there?'

'Of course.'

It was late evening by the time she was driving to Calais and by rights she should have been exhausted. But the little scene with the haughty servant at the apartment had made her angry. She was wired, wide awake.

Although it was still only October and the Hovercraft should have been fully booked, she, as a regular traveller, had friends among the booking staff. She was given a cancelled

27

slot. Once safely en route for home, she relaxed. She was accustomed to snatching rest where she could. She got an hour's sleep during the crossing, enough to be refreshed.

While she was waiting to drive off at Dover, she used her mobile to call her sister. 'Where was it you'd been this time, dear?' asked Evie, who found it difficult to keep track.

'Cambodia.'

'Oh yes.' Evie wasn't sure of its where-abouts. 'Did you have a good time?'

'Oh, marvellous.'

'That's good,' said Evie, missing the irony in the reply. 'Are you coming to stay the night?'

'Not this time, love.' Evie lived only a few miles outside Dover, in a ramshackle old house inherited together with a very sub-stantial sum of money from their paternal grandmother. Evie had always been Grand-mother Montgomery's favourite; her plan to marry and have a lot of children chimed perfectly with the old lady's view of life.

'Oh, do come,' Evie urged. 'It's ages since we saw you.

'No, I want to get back to Michael.'

Her sister couldn't argue against that. She'd always had a soft spot for Michael Ansleigh. In fact last Christmas, capturing him for a kiss under the mistletoe, she'd declared that if only he'd turned up before she married Walt, she'd have married Michael instead – and she was only half joking.

On empty roads and under a sky showing the silvery spill of clouds around the moon that Roly had suggested, Karen sped on into London.

The flat she shared with Michael was above the office of U-Special Tours. She unlocked the side door, noting there was a collection of mail in the letter-cage, which surprised her. She went upstairs quietly, intending to surprise Michael by making a dramatic entrance into the living room. But it was empty, and so was the bedroom.

Still in the States? She was disappointed, but at least she was home where there was a reliable electrical supply and the computer would work. She switched on the one in the living room then went back downstairs to get the letters.

When she came back, the computer was ready. She entered her password. While she waited for her e-mail, she started the shower running; a long, long, hot shower with a gloriously steady supply of water to wash away the double fatigue of her stay in the tropics and the long journey home.

But, before she had the chance to get into the shower, she noticed the Dear John letter on her screen...

Two

She had to read it twice before it made any kind of sense to her.

Karen, hi.

I've been offered a good price here in the States for U-Special Tours and in view of the terrible state of the travel industry I've accepted it. I'll be staying on here. Business opportunities are better than back home. I've e-mailed Kitty not to come to the office any more and mailed her a cheque as separation pay. Re your share of the sale price, see airmail following. Yours Michael.

She was too shocked to feel anything for several minutes. Then she whispered, '*No!*' The sound made almost no impact in the silent room. She looked around, as if hoping someone would appear by magic and tell her it was all a mistake.

Then she rose stiffly, to look for the collection of mail she'd brought upstairs.

Sure enough, there was an airmail from the US. She found a letter opener to slit the edge with enormous care, as if the contents were

30

very fragile and precious.

The date at the top was 1st October and in Michael's hit or miss typing she read:

My e-mail gave the gist. Everybody here in Chicago is terribly scared and upset by the Twin Towers thing. Nobody is flying anywhere if they can help it, so you can work out our chances of survival. A firm called SuperScenes made 'an offer I can't refuse', so I sold up. There was a time limit on the offer so I couldn't spend too long weighing it up.

I've made a bank internet transfer of the equivalent of the money you put into the firm originally. Of course, I've added something in acknowledgement of your stalwart work over the last four years. I hope you'll find the sum acceptable.

The lease of the premises expired at Michaelmas. You'll remember I had to dash to Chicago on the 15th Sep. to rescue our casino-visiting group. Once I'd got them safely off home (no easy task, I can tell you!), I telephoned Grice & Bolder to say we wouldn't be taking up the option for the ensuing year. I made arrangements for just the next quarter so you can stay on in the flat until New Year. Of course, you can't trade in the office and in any case the lease on the hired furniture has run out. I imagine Office Decor Ltd will be coming to cart things away. They may have already tried. The computer hire firm is less urgent because of course those models are old hat now, but they'll want them back. You'd better rescue any personal belongings.

I got one or two e-mails from you on my laptop and gather you were sorting out our Buddhists. I'm sure you did well. I'd already sent you my e-mail about the changed circumstances so didn't try to contact you after that.

We were a great team, Karen, and in many ways I feel bad about its break-up. But the times they are a-changing and we have to move on. Of course, I know you'll soon find something challenging to do and you'll make a success of it as you always have. I wish you all the best, Yours Michael.

Her first reaction was to crumple the sheet of paper and throw it in the waste-basket.

Her second reaction was to hit the desk with her clenched fist. That hurt, so she put her hand to her lips to soothe the bruise. It also served to steady her trembling mouth. Then she got up and walked about the room, shaking her head in disbelief.

How could it be true? This was the man she'd given her life to over the past four years. Her trust, her hopes, her plans for the future – all of them had depended on Michael. He came before her mental vision now, his boyish face all wreathed in smiles, his eyes glowing with the enthusiasm that turned their slaty grey to blue. Alive, alert, full of schemes and dreams – a spirit that had called to her own, even though she was often more practical about life.

She had always taken it for granted that theirs was a relationship that would last for ever. True, he'd never seemed to want to talk about commitment. 'Not yet,' his response had been if she murmured a sentence or two about settling down. But that was because there was something eternally young about him, a footloose and fancy-free outlook that was part of his attraction.

Michael had had several previous attempts at business enterprise when she met him. He didn't talk much about them because of course it was his nature to look forward, not back. But she seemed to recall there had been an employment agency, and a school of performing arts. As she remembered from his occasional comments, none of them had lasted long. 'Couldn't get the right co-operation until I met you,' he'd told her with a grateful hug. The travel firm had survived and begun to do well, until the catastrophe at the World Trade Center brought problems and cancellations.

Four years. And now it was over. The partnership – and that was how Karen had thought of it although she now saw she'd been wrong – had extended into their private life almost at once. They'd been lovers, happy, devoted lovers, or so she'd thought. But now he was staying in America, now he was moving on.

Without her.

She fished the crumpled letter out of the waste-basket. She spread out the creases and found the phrases. 'We were a great team ... I feel bad about the break-up.' How bad did he feel? In the letter's style there was a blitheness, a sunniness that seared her like furnace coals. He seemed to have written it without ever imagining its effect on her. And he announced that he thought she'd find something else to do as if only the business side had any validity. 'Find something else to do' – find someone else to love, to fill your thoughts and be your dear comrade...

Another phrase caught her eye: 'An offer I can't refuse' – no discussion with her, no review of the pros and cons. After four years of being his chief confidante, of what she'd thought of as an ideal partnership, he'd ignored her completely.

It was true that the start-up money had come mostly from Michael. Karen had had only what she'd saved during her career, first as a flight attendant and then as an agent in a large travel firm. But she had contributed something that, in her eyes, was more valuable than money. She was the one with experience, and talent as an organizer, and good contacts, and a level head; in a word, she had the know-how. Michael had known almost nothing about the travel business. It was Karen who had been the guiding hand.

'Stay on in the flat until the New Year.' So she was going to be evicted in a couple of months? But the shock to her was more than that. This was her *home*, the place she'd shared with the man she loved. It held memories, cherished incidents and occasions when they'd celebrated some success, times of pure happiness in each other's arms. He could dismiss all that with a few words on paper?

All at once her eyes flooded with tears and she was sobbing, leaning over the letter, breathless, helpless. Her knees buckled. She fell by the desk, her head against the drawer, her elbows shielding her from the light, stifling, gasping, longing to lose consciousness so that she wouldn't know the things she'd learned.

For a long time the world seemed to go away. Then her crying waned, and she heard a sound. She raised her head, listened – and realized she could hear the shower running.

Let it run. Let it flood the whole world and submerge her and her misery.

A strange laughter rose within her. So she was going to drown her sorrows with the bathroom shower? Ridiculous. Her common sense wouldn't let her.

With enormous effort she dragged herself to her feet. She was unsteady as she found her way to the bathroom, turned off the water, then wiped the mirror to look at herself. Blotched features, tangled hair, all distorted by the moisture on the glass.

Leaning on the rim of the washbowl, her eye lighted on the medicine cabinet. Within, there was true release from her misery. She put out a hand. Then she withdrew it.

She shook her head. So far in her life she'd never given up. Every cloud has a silver lining, she repeated to herself bitterly. Where was the silver lining in this black, dense, all-embracing cloud?

Tomorrow. Tomorrow she might see some glint of light.

She went into the bedroom, threw herself on the bed fully clothed, and fell asleep from exhaustion both physical and emotional.

The train had come off the buffers and the wheels were banging on stones and ruts. The poor Buddhists were being thrown about, calling out for help, while in the background Buddhist bells were chiming from a nearby stupa. She turned over, willing the dream to go away. The banging got louder. She realized after a moment that it was real, coming from downstairs, that someone was battering on the door and ringing the bell at the same time.

Some drunk, she told herself, pulling a pillow over her head to shut out the noise and help in a swift return to sleep.

The noise got even louder. Someone was shouting. The office phone was ringing too. She dragged herself upright. 'Stop it!' she cried. 'Stop it! Go away!'

There was no remission of the onslaught of sound. She got off the bed, rubbed her eyes, then took a hurried course through the flat and out to the little landing. There was someone at the downstairs door, hitting it savagely with his fist, ringing the bell, shouting, and apparently trying to get through to the office with his mobile phone. She switched on the landing light and tottered down. The banging and ringing ceased. Now she could make out what the voice was shouting.

'Wake up! Come on! Tell me where he is! You inside, open this door!'

She was at the foot of the narrow staircase now. Scared, she said, 'Who's there?'

'Open this door! What have you done with him? Open up, or I'll go to the police!'

'What on earth are you talking about? Go away!' She looked through the spy-hole. A tallish, sturdy man in a rugby shirt and jeans was visible. He looked like a thug. 'I'm going to phone 999,' she said.

'Open the door! I want to know what you've done with Roly!'

'What?'

'Where is he?'

'Who are you talking about?' she asked, her wits in chaos yet somehow alerted by his use of the name.

'Roly Dartieux – where is he? I'm warning you, you'd better have him here or—'

'Here?'

'Isn't he here? Has anything happened to him? *Open the door!*'

Roly Dartieux – he knew that name. But why should anything have happened to him? Roly was safe home in Paris. Why should this madman be asking about him in London?

She was used to dealing with troublesome or rowdy clients. She summoned all her calmness to ask, 'Who are you?'

'I'm Roly's father, of course.'

'What?'

'His father, Jeffrey Lynwood.'

'Roly's father is Louis Dartieux—'

'That's his *stepfather!* Open this door!' shouted the man in the rugby shirt, and banged the wood with his fist.

Karen put her hands up to her head. Was she still asleep, still having nightmares? 'Just a minute,' she said. She sat down on the lowest stair, took some deep breaths, got up, and said, 'Who are you, again?'

'Jeffrey Lynwood, Roly's father. I was expecting him at my flat tonight.'

'But ... but ... I was told to take him to an

apartment in Paris.'

'Who told you to do that?'

'Wait,' she said. 'I'll open the door but I have to go upstairs for the key.'

She trudged upstairs again, found the keys on the desk, and took a moment to look up Lynwood in the telephone book. There he was, Jeffrey Lynwood with an address in Highgate.

She still couldn't understand what was going on. It appeared the man was neither a drunk nor a thug.

All the same she wasn't going to let him into the flat. She went down, unlocked the door of the office and switched on the lights, then unlocked the outer side door.

'Come in,' she invited. 'This way.' She led him into the office, retreated to comparative safety behind a desk, and gestured to a chair. 'Now explain what you mean.'

'My son – Roly – left Phnom Penh yesterday. I understand that he was given into your care, though I don't know why. He was to come to me in London. He never turned up. I rang the embassy in Phnom Penh and they gave me your address and telephone number. I've been ringing for over an hour but never got a reply. Now what the hell is going on?'

The words rushed out in a furious, anxious spate. His voice was raw with fatigue. He looked ready for a fight, his wiry auburn hair in a tangle, his eyes glowing with anger.

His eyes, she saw, were like Roly's, a clear greeny-blue. The crop of auburn hair was a darker echo of Roly's coppery tint.

'Have you anything by way of identification?' she countered. It wasn't just that she wanted to ensure he was who he said he was; she knew that the moments it took him to find his wallet would give him time to calm down a little.

He brought out his driving licence. She glanced at it and nodded. 'Yes, thank you,' she said. 'And I'm Karen Montgomery.'

'So they said at the embassy. Where is my son?'

'He's at his home in Paris.'

He gave a gasp of anger. 'That old hag!' he cried, raising a clenched fist as if to hit the absent housekeeper. 'I rang her, she'd put on the answering machine—'

'Well, it *is*—' she glanced at her wrist — 'nearly two o'clock in the morning. I delivered Roly to someone I think was called Gabrielle at about eight o'clock last night.'

'But he was supposed to come to *me*,' he insisted. 'Why did you take him there?'

'Those were my instructions.'

'But why didn't Norah bring him?'

'Norah?' She recalled mention of the name. 'His nanny?'

'Yes, I'd arranged it all with her by phone. She was bringing him to me as soon as she could get a flight.'

'When did you speak to her?'

'Sunday.'

'Ah.' She began to see some light. 'Norah ran away, I think it was probably on Monday.'

'Ran away?'

'With a boyfriend she'd found. The embassy people believe she went with him on some coaster — there's a lot of local shipping.'

'She just left?' he said, astounded.

'According to what I was told.'

'She left Roly on his own?'

'Well, he was at the embassy, of course. An elderly lady was looking after him.'

'But surely it was understood he was coming home to me in London?'

'Apparently not.'

'But Norah knew—'

'But did she tell anyone on the staff?' If she had, the information had got mislaid or was ignored. 'Things are in a mess out there, you know,' she said in mitigation, her tone neutral yet soothing. 'Everything's upside down since the September 11th terrorist attack.'

'Good Lord, surely they're not so upside down that they don't know where to send a six-year-old child!'

'But they did, or thought they did. They sent him home.' Her thought processes were gearing up, as they always did, to deal with a problem. 'You say you rang Phnom Penh and they told you he was leaving. Surely they told you I was taking him to Paris?'

'Yes, but in the state of air travel at the moment I thought they meant that was the only booking they could get. I expected you to change planes there and bring him on.'

'Roly never mentioned being expected in London.' And he never mentioned you, she was saying to herself, then recalled that the boy had said it was his father who called him Roly. 'But then,' she added, seeing the distress in the eyes of the father, 'he'd been a bit under the weather with a sick attack.'

'Yes, he doesn't really like flying. When I fetch him to stay with me we usually go by Eurostar.'

'Then, if you don't mind my asking, why was he taken to Cambodia in the first place? It's a long flight, and the climate there isn't the best I've encountered.' After she'd said this she realized it was none of her business, yet she felt a personal interest in the child.

His expression was a mixture of exasperation and distress 'It was sort of ... Louis was ordered to Phnom Penh in July. Normally he and Hélène would have left Roly with Norah at the flat, with Gabrielle in charge. But you know how Parisians like to leave Paris in August.' He looked at her for her understanding and as she nodded went on: 'Gabrielle always goes to her relatives in the

42

Dordogne for the month. I said I'd have Roly and Norah to stay, but – well, you see – the courts agreed I was to have access but Hélène didn't want to let me have Roly for such a long stint – it was likely to be at least two months.'

She could tell she'd better not ask why Hélène thought that a bad idea. There had clearly been an acrimonious divorce at some stage. Instead, she asked, 'But even if the housekeeper was going away, why couldn't they leave him at home with the nanny?'

'Norah *wanted* to go to Phnom Penh. She's one of those globe-trotting Australians. You didn't meet her?'

'No, she'd disappeared by the time I came on the scene.'

'That's why it's all gone haywire. Norah's good at finding her way about. I suppose when Hélène had to dash off with Louis, she left Norah in charge of getting the pair of them home, but then Norah fell for this chap, whoever he is.' He was shaking his head in weary acceptance. 'I can just see that happening, somebody spinning her a yarn about visiting romantic places along the coast. I bet it sounded better to her than going back to stuffy old Paris.'

'Everybody seems to have been concerned for their own affairs,' said Karen indignantly. 'No one seems to have considered Roly.'

He coloured at the accusation. 'That's all

very well for you to say, but I've no influence over what happens. The French courts agreed with Hélène's wish to bring him up in the influence of French culture. I couldn't stop her from taking him to Phnom Penh...' He made a stifled sound, almost a groan. 'Well, at least he's home now.' At the thought, his angry gaze softened. He said, 'How was he when you handed him over to Gabrielle?'

'Asleep.'

'Poor kid. Hélène phoned from Phnom Penh to say she and Louis had been ordered to Stockholm. I could tell there were problems about getting a flight, she was in a bit of a state and I didn't quite get everything. Roly and Norah were coming straight to me as soon as it could be arranged. And then you know, I contacted Norah and she said she was working on it – tickets, I mean. I admit I was a bit concerned because ... well, they seemed so far away.' He seemed to brighten. 'I'll go over first thing tomorrow and fetch him.'

She was about to say that Roly might need a day or so to recover from his previous travels, but then she remembered Gabrielle. Better for him to be with his father than in the charge of that cold-hearted old woman. 'Well, good luck, then,' she said. 'Give him my love.'

'I will.'

44

She got up to see him out. She saw him examine her now, for the first time seeing her as a woman rather than a threat or a kidnapper. She knew she looked a mess – her blouse and skirt crumpled from lying in them, her short hair sticking up every which way, her eyes still a bit red from weeping. She looked more like a derelict than a respectable travel agent.

They shook hands on the threshold of the outer door. 'I'm sorry about ... you know ... shouting at you and all that,' he remarked. 'I was worried about him, that's all.'

'Of course.'

'Well, goodnight – or rather, good morning.' He gave a sudden grin. 'I can't say it's been a pleasure speaking to you but at least it's been a relief!'

She summoned a smile in response, closed and locked the door, switched off the lights in the office and locked it up, then toiled back upstairs to her flat.

She was bone weary. She sat down in an armchair, sighing and wondering if it was worth the effort to undress and go to bed properly.

She heard Jeffrey Lynwood's car start up, saw the reflected glint of his headlights as they came on. In a moment there came the purr of the engine as he drove away.

A lonely sound in a quiet street in the early hours of a dark October morning.

Three

Karen woke around noon. She had at last dragged herself to bed about 5am, after undressing properly and taking the shower she'd intended in what seemed another lifetime.

She pulled on jeans and sweater, made herself a pot of extra strong coffee, then sat down to deal with the post. There were letters going back four weeks, most of them cancelling arrangements made before the airline chaos. There was an accusatory letter from Kitty, their receptionist: 'How could you treat me like this, what did I do to deserve it, I thought of you as friends.'

She rang her. They had a long conversation, tearful on Kitty's side. They ended on good terms, Karen hiding the fact that she was feeling tearful herself.

She went back to the letters. There were demands from Office Decor and Computers Galore. There was a copy of a lease on the premises, limited to the current quarter, signed in Chicago by Michael and faxed through to the proprietors a couple of weeks ago. There was a collection of odds and ends: bills for utilities, offers of loans at advantageous rates, advertisements.

When she'd sorted these into piles – urgent, reply tomorrow, query, junk – she called up her bank statement on the computer. Michael had indeed refunded the money she'd put into the firm four years ago and had added a bonus. But for U-Special Tours there was a separate account, to which she had no access. So, who was to pay the outstanding bills? She would have sent them to Michael in Chicago except that she had no address.

Well, she told herself grimly, *I'm* not going to pay them. She put the bills in a separate pile labelled: 'Return to sender', while she typed out a slip to enclose with each: 'U-Special Tours has been sold to SuperScenes of Chicago'. She found their address on the web and added that. She nevertheless expected a flood of queries by and by, but, 'sufficient unto the day is the evil thereof'.

These unwelcome chores took her until almost six. She discovered she was hungry, which surprised her because when she started the day she'd been feeling sick.

There was a fashionable coffee bar a few doors away. But it was a mistake to go there because when she sat down and looked around, a wave of misery almost overcame her. It was a place she and Michael had frequented.

She got up and went out again. A hundred yards away, near the taxi rank, she found a little café used mainly by the drivers. There she ordered tea and an omelette, but when it came the omelette was enormous and served with a lavish helping of chips.

The mere sight of it was enough to tell her she didn't want it. She drank the tea, however. When the friendly proprietor asked in consternation what was wrong with the food, she explained she'd ordered something she couldn't manage to eat. When he insisted on supplying her with an alternative, she agreed to have a helping of toast. This turned out to be a pile of six slices, of which she ate two and felt better.

'Look after yourself, ducks,' he admonished her as she was leaving. 'You don't look exactly chipper.'

Somehow it was comforting. She went back to the flat feeling less disconsolate

She worked on until late that night, planning next day's schedule. She must make a lot of phone calls, though none of them would be to family and friends – not even her parents, not even her sister Evie. She still didn't feel equal to explaining what had happened to those close to her. It was better to shield herself by dealing with only the business side.

So, she began on the letters she must write

– to clients accepting cancellations but explaining there could be no refunds unless they cared to apply to SuperScenes of Chicago. Poor SuperScenes of Chicago, she thought with wry sympathy, I don't suppose you expected this sort of backlash from your recent purchase.

She must contact the suppliers to make appointments for them to take away the furniture and equipment. She must send word to their commercial printers advising them there would be no brochure for the coming year. She must cancel advertisements booked in magazines and newspapers.

By watching late-night television until she felt drowsy, she managed to get a reasonable amount of sleep. She woke about eight, went out for some milk and bread, then returned to the clear-up campaign.

And so on for the next four or five days. When at length there was nothing awaiting attention except the post of that morning, she rang her sister in Kent.

'Oh, lovely!' Evie cried, her sweet fresh voice rising in pleasure. 'I was so sorry you couldn't stop on your way home last week. You know your room's always ready here.'

That immediate, kindly welcome. Her eyes were full of tears as she hung up. I've got to stop being weepy, she scolded to herself. But although she needed to leave this flat, to close it up and put it all behind her, she dreaded having to explain things to Evie.

So in the end she decided not to explain. Or at least, when she went to stay with Evie, she offered an edited version of events.

'We decided to close down U-Special,' she announced. 'Because of the backwash after September 11th, you know. Michael's in the States at the moment, looking around at one or two projects.'

'That sounds exciting,' said Evie, her plump features wreathed in smiles at hearing news of her hero. 'D'you think you'll be going out there?'

'Who knows?'

'Good thing you shut up shop,' Walt said. 'I always thought that was a stupid name for a business.'

Evie's husband was a solid type, big, fair, unimaginative, immersed in his own business. He ran a cross-Channel haulage firm, which had its ups and downs but was on the whole successful. Karen had secret suspicions that he'd married Evie so as to have her inheritance to enlarge his enterprise, yet they seemed happy enough. What Walt lacked in romance was more than made up for by Evie.

Evie fell in love frequently. She had had a crush on several stars of film and TV, adding and discarding according to her own scale of values. She loved certain leaders of societies or organizations dealing with causes she

50

supported. She had a leaning towards the headmaster of Perry's school. Adventurers sailing the Pacific single-handed or trekking alone to the Poles, archaeologists uncovering lost Mayan temples, one or two politicians...

There was no doubt she loved Michael. But as one among so many, he raised no real jealousy in her husband. With an inward shrug he seemed to acknowledge that Evie had to be in love, that she wasn't any longer 'in love' with Walt himself although she trusted and respected him. Nevertheless, he took every opportunity of disparaging Michael, in hopes of doing a little damage to the competition.

They were at dinner in the big dining room at Dagworth Farm. The house had once been the home of apple-growers, the orchards spreading out on three sides. But now only a small part of the land went with the house – a couple of acres cleared for a large garden and a paddock for her daughter's pony. The orchards themselves had gone to growers prepared to grub up old trees, plant modern varieties, and comply with the rules of the Common Market.

The place had been restored with part of Evie's inheritance. It had eleven rooms furnished by Evie herself, with curtains and loose covers she'd made and embroideries she'd worked and framed. The kitchen was a blend of the old and the new, the new encompassing the very latest in cookers and food processors; for Evie was a fabulous cook. She used her talents not only for her family but for charity stalls, church outings, and village celebrations.

Karen sometimes felt that this was Evie's way of staying level with her sister. 'We had 104 at the Garden Society's exhibition day,' she'd say. 'Have you ever cooked for 104, Karen?'

'No, never,' Karen would reply, adding some complimentary remarks to help build up self-esteem. She couldn't quite understand why it bothered Evie so much. It wasn't as if Karen herself had done so marvellously well, although Evie had insisted on envying her when she landed her first job as airline cabin crew. 'So glamorous,' she sighed when her sister mentioned trips to Rome or Vienna. She paid no heed to complaints about jet lag, swollen ankles, dry skin due to the air conditioning.

According to Karen's view, Evie had chosen her role in life and had been joyous in doing so. Married at twenty-two without ever having held down anything more than pocket-money jobs, she'd started her family at once. Now she had Perry aged eight, Angela aged six, and Norman, known as Noomie, aged four. They were good-looking, kind-hearted children, happy in a home made for them by their sweet-natured mother and living according to rules laid down by their strict but fair-minded father.

If anyone was to be envied, Karen thought, at the moment it was Evie.

'What sort of business is Michael looking at in the States?' Walt enquired as he fuelled his large frame with a second helping of beef stew made with beer and sun-dried tomatoes.

'Oh, it'll be something fascinating!' cried Evie. 'Michael always does special things. Where is he, Karen? New York?'

'No, Chicago.'

'Can't see anything particularly fascinating about Chicago,' muttered Walt.

'Are you going out to join him?' The mere idea thrilled Evie.

'No, quite the opposite, I'll be looking for a job here—'

'Oh, something temporary, of course, just to fill in until Michael finds what he wants. You'll have no problem, love. You've got so much experience.'

'But only in an area that's in the doldrums, Evie. Tourism's not doing well at the moment, now is it?'

Evie really had no idea. She paid very little attention to the news, even when it reported disasters. 'But that's only temporary – isn't it, Walt?'

'I suppose so. But how temporary is temporary?'

'A few weeks? Until Christmas, perhaps?'
'I'd like to find something before Christmas!' protested Karen. 'Otherwise the kids will be opening presents from Auntie Karen that started their lives in charity shops.'

Evie giggled. 'You're such a joker, Karen!'

Karen caught a momentary glimmer in Walt's eye which told her he'd never thought of his sister-in-law as a joker. Nor had the sister-in-law herself, though she made no comment. It was useless to counter any of Evie's character readings. A few days hence her opinion might be something quite different.

'You could always get a job with Mum and Dad for a few weeks,' Evie suggested, pleased with herself for thinking of it. 'With Christmas coming on soon, they'll have lots of orders to pack, I expect.'

Cedric and Janet Montgomery owned a small nursery outside Guildford, where they raised and sold cacti. It had started as a hobby but now provided them with an excellent income. Nevertheless, Karen had never learned to love a cactus. True, the plants could come out in unexpectedly beautiful bloom, yet that happened rather seldom, whereas the prickles – alas, the prickles – were with you always. The idea of spending several weeks packing these unhandy items for dispatch didn't appeal at all.

Later, when the dishes were in the

dishwasher and Evie was relaxing with a huge embroidery frame holding a pictorial collage, Walt took Karen aside. 'You all right?' he asked. 'You look a bit worn, if you don't mind me saying so.'

'I'm all right. I've been doing a lot of work since I got back, winding up the firm, you know.'

'You serious about wanting a temporary job?'

'I certainly am.'

'Might be able to do something for you here – in Dover, I mean. Pal of mine is having a terrible time dealing with the aftermath of airline downsizing. Got a lot of cargoes that had to be changed over to sea transport, and the records are a bit haywire.'

'Records? Computerized?'

'Mostly, but there's paperwork as well, I think.'

'But it's office work.'

'Yeah. Might be a month, six weeks. Interested?'

Beggars can't be choosers. 'Why not?' she said, although it wasn't the kind of work that she enjoyed. She liked dealing with people, not paper.

'A bit late to contact Scholes tonight. I'll give him a buzz first thing in the morning.'

'Thank you, Walt.'

'No prob.' He patted her kindly on the shoulder then wandered off to smoke an

55

after-dinner cigar in the garden. Evie made it known in her gentle way that smoking indoors made her soft furnishings smell of tobacco.

Karen went to take a look at Evie's latest handiwork. On a floor-standing wooden frame about sixty centimetres by a hundred, she was carefully stitching in place little pieces of cloth, cut from a traced pattern, to represent the ramparts of Dover Castle. When finished, the work would be auctioned for charity.

'That looks good.'

'It'll look better when I put in some colours – trees, and a blue sky, and so forth.' Evie stitched, sat back to consider, snipped a frayed edge. 'I might have an exhibition one day,' she remarked. 'There's a gallery in Deal that might put it on.'

'Wouldn't that be marvellous!'

'But I'd have to hire the gallery and Walt says it would be a waste of money.'

Karen knew very well that if the gallery were ever hired, it would be with Evie's own money. She wanted to say, use it the way you want to. But she was chary of ever giving an opinion that might cause friction. Her sister and brother-in-law were happy in their own way, yet she sometimes sensed undercurrents.

'I think I'll go up to bed, Evie,' she said, yawning. 'I'm—'

'But it's only nine o'clock!'

'I know, but I'm really tired. It's been a long day.'

'It's that trip out to wherever it was – Calcutta?'

'Cambodia.'

'You never seem to enjoy tropical climates. What a shame, it must be so marvellous to sit on a beach under a palm tree...'

'It wasn't a holiday, love.'

'No, of course I know that.' She pondered. 'Next year, when Noomie's older, we might go on holiday to the Bahamas.'

'Now there's a place I've never been. I bet it's lovely.' Karen stifled another yawn. 'I'm falling asleep on my feet, Evie...'

'OK, see you in the morning.' She held up her face and Karen deposited a kiss about two inches away from her cheek. They were affectionate sisters, but not demonstrative.

On her way to her room she looked in on the children. In this great old house, they had separate rooms, appropriately decorated by their mother. Perry, sitting up reading in a bed made to look like a miniature ocean liner, looked guilty and closed his book. Karen waved and passed by to Angela, who was asleep under a frilled muslin canopy. Four-year-old Noomie had a mural showing Dalmatian puppies playing in a green meadow. He'd kicked off all his bedclothes. Karen carefully covered him up, dropping a kiss on his nose.

For a moment her thoughts wandered off to the little boy she'd escorted home from Cambodia. She wondered if he were asleep now in his father's home in Highgate, if he were clutching his precious 'memoirs' in his arms, if his dreams were happy.

As promised, Walt telephoned his friend Herbert Scholes next morning. 'Says if you like to drop by about mid-morning, he'll have a chat with you.'

'Thanks a million, Walt.'

He drew a sketch map of the whereabouts of the office. It was in a business park not far from the docks. She sighed inwardly when she saw it, knowing that it wasn't the kind of surroundings she enjoyed – but needs must.

Mr Scholes wasn't inclined to be difficult when he interviewed her. She was after all the sister-in-law of a colleague. He made sure she could handle a computer by seating her at his desk to find next day's loading schedule and print it out. He handed her a French Customs form and asked her to translate the first ten questions.

Satisfied, he gave her a form to fill in with her personal and social insurance details, informed her of the pay and conditions, and said she could start as soon as she liked. She said she could start next day. He shook hands, told her to report to the office manager at eight a.m., and she was hired. She drove back to Dagworth Farm feeling more cheerful than for many days, yet somehow untethered, insecure.

Evie was preparing lunch when she got there. Perry had his midday meal at school, but Angela was already home. She and Noomie were begging their mother to give them ice cream with hot chocolate sauce for dessert. Karen found herself smiling in admiration. In almost any other household, these things would have come from a supermarket. Here, though, they would all be home-made.

'Well, all right,' said Evie, 'but only if you eat up all your salad first.'

They sat down round the big pine kitchen table. Most of the meal was taken up with hearing about Angela's morning at primary school – raffia and spelling. At the end of the meal the two children rushed out to play. Evie cleared the table while Karen made coffee.

'So, how did the thing go with Mr Stiles?'

'Scholes. He's given me the job.'

'Are you pleased?'

'Of course.'

Evie shrugged. 'It seems to me it's a bit of a comedown for you.'

'It's only temporary, Evie.'

'What did Michael say?'

'Michael?'

'Didn't you ring him?'

'Of course not!' cried Karen, forgetting that her sister was unaware of the break-up.

'Why not? He'll want to know.'

'Because...' The excuse came easily. 'Because it's still early morning in Chicago.'

'Oh. I never thought of that! But you're going to ring him, aren't you? Give him my love.'

'Of course,' Karen agreed, thinking it might be better to tell Evie the truth but unable to face the lamentation that would follow.

In a day or two, perhaps. When she felt stronger.

It was taken for granted that she'd stay at Dagworth Farm for the duration of the job. She was glad of it, for she found being with the children was good therapy. They asked nothing from her except that she should love them and enter into their games. The feelings that sometimes welled up – anger against Michael for his desertion, dismay at the wrath and cruelty on the world stage, envy of even her sister's placid happiness – were soothed when she watched Angela trotting sedately round the paddock on her pony, or when Noomie demanded a bedtime story.

She broke her stay one weekend to spend it with her parents. They were delighted to see her, listened with interest to her fable about Michael's sojourn in Chicago, then took her on the obligatory tour of the greenhouses. She admired the display of plants raised on purpose to be in full flower at Christmas, but avoided picking up anything in case it scratched. When, at the end of her two-day stay, she was packing to leave, her mother came into her room. Her excuse was to look at yet more cacti taking the sun on the window sill.

'You've seemed rather quiet, dear,' she said over her shoulder.

'Really?'

'Missing Michael, I expect.'

'Yes.' How true that was.

'Evie was saying on the phone that you might be going out there – Chicago, I mean.'

'Oh no.'

'So how long is Michael going to be away?'

'That's sort of indefinite.'

Mrs Montgomery tweaked some fluff from among the bristles of an Astrophytum capricorne with a pair of tweezers. 'He is coming back?'

The question was quietly asked, but had great weight.

Karen felt a lump come into her throat. 'I don't know.'

'Ah.' Her mother turned the plant round to let it sunbathe on its other side. 'Everything seems strange since September 11th,' she sighed.

'Yes.'

61

'Troubled times. All we can do is have courage.'

'You're right.' She took her overnight bag and started for the stairs. Janet Montgomery went with her, stood by while she unlocked her car and got in. Then, surprisingly, she leaned in to kiss her daughter.

'You always were the quiet one,' she murmured. 'I'll be thinking about you. And don't work too hard in that fill-in job. You're looking rather thin.'

The work at Scholes Cargo was as boring as Karen had expected. It was also quite demanding, because goods that should have arrived at Calais for shipping were still delayed or entirely missing. She found that it sometimes helped if she made a personal telephone call, which was to her more enjoyable than looking at a computer screen.

Days went by. It occurred to her that if she wanted something better when this temporary post came to an end, she'd better start looking for it. She put herself on the list of one or two agencies, but the muted response was consistent: 'Things are a bit tight in tourism at the moment.' She began studying the appointments pages of the broadsheets, ringing anything that seemed likely. Personal assistant to a fund-raiser? Event organizer? Trainee hotel manager? – but no, that one was based in the Far East where she knew she would never be able to function properly.

Those that didn't want applicants to telephone for an interview often asked for a written application. She tried a few, but either her qualifications weren't right or the post was already filled. Some of those to whom she wrote never even replied. She began to think she ought to brush up her curriculum vitae.

One lazy Sunday evening, after at last finding enough appetite for one of Evie's excellent meals, she played a game of snakes and ladders with Perry and Angela. When they'd beaten her three times and gone to bed, she took herself off to a corner of the conservatory with the newspapers. Her pencil marked a couple of possible jobs.

Then something caught her eye. One of the advertisements began:

Speak fluent French and/or Italian? Good with people? Self-starter wanted to deal with clients viewing property abroad.

'That's more like it,' she said, half-aloud. She prepared to ring the item as she read on:

Please apply in writing, using the language you are offering, to the Personnel Officer, Properties Department, Lynwood Associates, 62 Persimmon Road, Highgate, London N6.

Lynwood? Lynwood? The name rang a bell. She put down the paper, while she tried to dredge up the memory. She seemed to remember looking at it in the phone book. She went to Walt's den, where he kept a shelf of reference books including the London telephone directory. She flicked through the pages.

There it was. 'Jeffrey Lynwood, 9 Harkway Mansions, Highgate N6.'

The same postal area. Roly's noisy father?

She folded up the paper. This needed some thought. Was this Lynwood the same Lynwood she'd met? If so, was it good or bad?

Next evening, her mind made up, she sat down in her bedroom to write:

> *Service du personnel,*
> *Departement de propriété*
> *Lynwood et Collegues.*
>
> *Messieurs,*
> *En reponse à votre annonce parue hier...*

She gave a summary of her experience and abilities. Then her fingers played with the pen, swinging it to and fro in hesitation. Should she tell the personnel officer that she'd met the boss? *J'ai eu l' honneur d' une rencontre*, she said to herself. But it hadn't been much of an honour. Jeffrey Lynwood

64

had told her at parting that it had been no pleasure speaking to her. If the personnel officer actually pointed out her letter to Mr Lynwood, it might not have a good effect.

And anyhow, what was the point of saying they'd met? It didn't prove she had a talent for dealing with people abroad who were worried about the amount of currency they'd got for their travellers' cheques.

She dithered for a few more minutes, then supplied the names of some countries in which she'd worked: *'par exemple l' Italie, la Suisse, l'Allemagne, le Cambodge, le Sénégal, la Grèce.'* More dithering. Then she wrote out the long courtesy that completed French business letters, ending with: *'...l'assurance de mes sentiments distingués,* Karen Montgomery.' She signed it.

There, that was done. She put it in an envelope, stamped it, then walked down to the village to post it. No collection until tomorrow, of course – it was now late evening. Perhaps it was a waste of time – 'dealing with clients viewing property abroad'. What did she know about property? The personnel officer would pick out letters saying the applicant had experience as an estate agent. She wished now she'd never written the letter.

She didn't know how long she should expect to wait for a response, if any. She'd been busy for almost an hour at Scholes Cargo with a computer screen full of shipping timetables when her mobile rang. She picked it up and said, 'Hello?'

'Karen Montgomery?'

'Yes?'

'This is Jeffrey Lynwood, about your application.'

She stifled a gasp of amazement. Ten past nine on a Wednesday morning and he was ringing? He'd probably been in his office for only ten minutes.

She pulled herself together. 'Just a moment,' she said, 'let me save what I'm working on...'

'Is this a bad time? I could ring again if you'd rather.'

'No, this is fine for the moment.'

'I'm so glad to have tracked you down! At least, it's the other way about because you were the one to make contact. You're in Dover?'

His voice sounded quite different. Strong and rather deep, but lacking both the wrath and the perplexity of their encounter in London. 'Yes, I'm in a temporary post, as I explained in my letter.'

'Your letter – I could hardly believe it! I'd been ringing your office number and at first I got something about SuperScenes of Chicago. But then the last week or so the line went dead.'

'Yes, the office for U-Special Tours is closed.'

'And you're looking for a permanent job?'

'Exactly.'

'I'd like us to meet. What's the situation – can you come to London?'

'Not until the weekend.'

'Ah. Well then, what sort of hours do you do? Are you free in the evenings?'

'Of course, but I shouldn't like to do London and back in an evening, Mr Lynwood. The hours here are eight till five and I find it quite tiring—'

'No, I meant, if you're free in the evenings we could meet and have dinner in Dover.'

'What?'

'I know Dover, at least superficially. We could have dinner at the Furnival.'

She laughed in pleasure and surprise. 'Are you so desperate to fill that vacancy?'

'It would be nice to find someone really suitable and you sound pretty promising,' he said. 'But more than that, Roly would never forgive me if I didn't catch up with you as soon as I can.'

Four

That evening she dressed with particular care. When moving out of the London flat, she'd given most of her clothes to Oxfam, because at that moment she'd firmly intended to begin all over again with a new wardrobe. Thus far, she hadn't bothered to buy evening wear so had to make do with a black skirt and a wine-coloured silk-jersey top. Both of those, however, had been bought in Milan and had a certain something. She added a fine chain and earrings of gold. The result was considerably better than the crumpled, tear-blotched frump her potential employer had last seen.

She told herself this wasn't mere vanity. Michael's unexpected desertion had been a terrible blow to her self esteem so the dressing-up was by way of a morale boost. The job at which she was now aiming sounded interesting. She wanted to capture it, if only her ignorance of the property business could be surmounted. She knew from experience that looking good helped towards being a success.

She drove into Dover in good time to scout out the Furnival. It was in Harold Street, through which she'd driven a hundred times without ever noticing the hotel particularly. Had it seemed very four-star, she might have turned around and driven back to Dagworth Farm. But it was an old Georgian building, elegant yet not formidable.

Jeffrey Lynwood was already there. He rose from a bar stool to greet her as she came in. 'Miss Montgomery!'

He looked quite different from the thug in the rugby jersey. He was wearing a dark suit with a blue shirt that might well have come from Jermyn Street.

'How do you do?' They shook hands, then he took up his drink to guide her to a table. The bar had quite a few customers but wasn't crowded. They sat down, the waiter approached and she ordered mineral water.

'I'm so glad to meet you properly,' he said. 'Roly talks about you so much!'

'How is he?'

'Oh, he's fine – he's started *école primaire*. He stayed with me until Hélène and Louis got back the following week and then started the Monday after. I'm told his verdict on his first day was: "It's quite pleasant, as Mademoiselle Karen said, but I wouldn't like to waste much time there." '

She burst out laughing. 'That sounds just like him!'

Jeffrey Lynwood shook his head. 'The trouble is, he had to go back the next day and so on. He tolerates it because he can see he'll learn things there that he won't come by easily anywhere else.'

'Joined-up writing.'

'Did he talk to you about that?' Her drink was brought, together with a menu from the restaurant. As she accepted it, he said, 'I hope you don't mind, but I took the liberty of ordering in advance. You said your day was long so I didn't want to keep you hanging about while they grill the sole. If there's anything you'd rather have, please feel free to change it.' There were pencil marks at the hors d' oeuvre and the entrée.

She nodded acceptance. 'That's very thoughtful. Thank you.'

'So ... You're temporary with this forwarding set-up.'

'Yes, and I've more or less finished what I was hired to do.'

'That might mean that you'd be ready to start with our property department after Christmas?'

'Well, yes...' It had to be said. 'But I must point out that I don't know anything about property. Not even here in England, I mean.'

He was nodding. 'That was clear from your application—'

'How did that get to you?' she put in with curiosity. 'What made the personnel officer show it to you? I avoided mentioning the property-viewing so he or she must have guessed I was an ignoramus where that's concerned.'

He grinned. 'Well, to tell the truth ... *I'm* the personnel officer. And the chief of associates, and part owner.'

'Jack of all trades?'

'We're not a very big team, but we function well. We've got about seven people at the moment out in the field: two in Italy, two in France, and three in Spain who also cover Portugal. When I say "out in the field", I don't mean they're there permanently. They go over when we have clients wanting to look at premises, but at this time of year you'll understand there's not too much going on. So you see, if you joined us in the New Year, while there's a lull, you could go to Paris and learn with our associate *notaire* for a month or so.'

'But ... you haven't asked me any questions.'

'About what?'

'Well ... "good with people" ... that was one of the requirements.'

He gave a little grin. 'I know you're good with people because you handled Roly so well.'

'But he didn't need any handling! We got on famously.'

'There you are, then. A lot of people find

71

him quite difficult.'

'Who, for instance?' she said in surprise.

'Teachers at *l'école maternelle*. Hélène moved him from one to another. They said he was unco-operative.'

She understood there might be a slight problem there. 'He did say he found the kindergarten at the embassy rather silly – but then, at six years old, kindergarten stuff probably did seem rather silly to him.'

'Well, he was only three when he started infant school in Paris and it should have been just right for him, but no...' The father of the recalcitrant little pupil sighed and shrugged. 'He went to four different ones. In the end, Hélène hired Norah to look after him. Norah had nursery school training.'

'And he got on all right with Norah.'

'Yes and no. Norah thought him "a funny little thing" but they seemed to have a working arrangement. Yet you can tell from the way she just dumped him in Phnom Penh that there was no real relationship,' he said with anxiety he couldn't quite conceal. 'And from what I can gather, Roly wasn't shedding any tears because she'd gone.'

'Did they find someone to replace her?'

'Oh well ... no ... after all, he's a schoolboy now. And there are three adults at the apartment who can give him any "looking after" that he needs. Anyhow, as Hélène says, after Norah's desertion she doesn't feel like doing that again. And Roly doesn't take to people easily.'

Karen was comparing this character sketch with the other six-year-old she knew: her niece Angela. Angela built up relationships quickly. She was very fond of her teachers, always drawing cards or gathering flowers to take to school. But then Angela was a girl, and perhaps more likely to be sentimental than a boy-child, an only child, a child of divorced parents.

She said, 'I often had children on my passenger lists when I worked as cabin crew. After that, my job with U-Special Tours was mainly to act as trouble shooter. I can only say that compared with some I've come across, Roly was a piece of cake.'

'And you've dealt with troublesome adults too, of course.'

'Of course.'

'Right. So that wraps up "good with people". Let's go back to the matter of learning the ropes with our *notaire*.'

'Are you offering me the job, Mr Lynwood?'

'Call me Jeffrey. We're very informal in our firm. Yes, I am in fact offering you the job. It would mean a period of training so that you understood some of the basics about French property, but you're not expected to be an expert. It's just so you can talk to local agents with some understanding of the legalities, and of course answer the sort of questions the clients ask.'

'For example?'

'Can I put in a swimming pool? If I'm sharing the parking garage, does it come at a reduced rate? Is this a "heritage" property?'

'Nothing about signing documents in front of witnesses, swearing in front of a magistrate?'

'That sounds as if you speak from experience,' he said, raising his eyebrows.

'Oh, well, in my former job, people got mixed up in accidents, or drank too much and landed in jail ... You know the sort of thing.'

'I have to tell you that the same sort of thing could happen with clients in *this* job! It's extraordinary how people behave when they go abroad, even on serious business. But if there's a problem of that sort, you call in our *avocat*. As to the buying or selling of properties, that's all handled by the agents and the lawyers.'

'So what would I actually be doing?'

'If the clients wished it, you'd accompany them from Britain to France. Often they ask to be met on the French side. Some are business people looking for a flat in Paris or one of the other cities. Some are interested in offices or shops. Some want to look at *gîtes*, some want their dream home in a nice warm spot. I must warn you that the name of the

74

house-hunting department of our firm is Dreamday Properties.' He was smiling as he said it.

'Oh dear. That's almost as bad as the one I've left.'

'Well, we needed a title so as to register it in France, and all the sensible ones seemed to have been taken.'

The waiter came to say their table in the restaurant was ready. They followed him to a quiet niche where there was wine already waiting to be poured and the first course had just been set down.

'Not bad,' said Jeffrey as they sat down. 'I've never eaten here before, have you?'

'No, although I've been passing through Dover for Channel crossings for years.'

'You don't like to fly?'

'Oh, it's not that. I like to travel with my own car if I can. But sometimes of course it's not possible.'

'There will be a lot of driving if you take this job. By the way, can we establish that? Are you accepting the post?'

'Well, yes ... I am, as a matter of fact.'

'That's good. Let's drink to it.' The waiter leapt to fill their glasses but Karen raised a hand.

'Not for me. I have to drive home.'

'Oh, that's a shame. This is a dry rosé from the Languedoc, rather nice. Couldn't you have just a sip?'

'All right, just one.' She tried the wine, agreed it was pleasant, and was pleased when he didn't try to tempt her to take more.

They turned their attention to the food. The first course was melon so Karen said, laughing at the recollection, 'Roly likes to have melon as a starter because he likes the cherry that sometimes comes in the middle.'

'Oh, I heard all about that. *Poire Belle Hélène.* And then Roly-poly and so forth. I had a terrible time trying to explain that to him – mainly because I didn't know where it came from.' He looked shamefaced. 'I had to ask a schoolteacher pal of mine, who found it in a book of nursery rhymes. How did it come about that you know it?'

'I've got a niece and two nephews.'

'Oh, I see.' He stifled a sigh. 'I expect you guessed Roly is an only child.'

'Forgive me for being inquisitive but ... you know ... I remember Roly saying his mother is English.'

'Yes.'

'Yet she has a French name?'

Jeffrey nodded. 'That's since she re-married. She was born Helen Forbes, and always had this thing about the French and their wonderful lifestyle. We met at university when she was studying French literature. So now she's Hélène Dartieux, and Roland's name is pronounced in the French way too.'

He paused, then added. 'That's why I call him Roly. It seems to bring him a bit closer, you know?'

She understood at once. There was clearly the friction of an acrimonious divorce behind his explanation although he naturally preferred not to go into that. She changed the subject back to business matters and for the rest of the meal they chatted about how Dreamday Properties earned its fees, which French firms did the legal work, and how long an escort was likely to stay abroad with a client.

'For the first couple of sorties with clients, I'd like you to go with Mireille. You're her replacement. She's leaving to have a baby.' He grinned. 'You'll find yourself having to stump up for her leaving present almost as soon as your first pay check goes into your bank.'

'What are we giving her?' she inquired with a laugh.

'A baby buggy. Luckily Nancy Sisley is taking care of all that. Nancy covers a region in Italy, and if the applicant who answered the advertisement had offered Italian as a "best language", Nancy would have moved over into France. She speaks both French and Italian.'

'Are all the property escorts women? You've mentioned two and I'm going to make it three.'

'No, no, we have four women and three men but it's a fact that women seem to be better at it,' he remarked. 'Got more patience, I suppose – and we've already said that patience is often called for in this job.'

'You speak from personal experience?'

'Lord, yes! I started up on my own, you see. My father died just after I took my finals, and I emerged, rather dazed, into the real world to find he'd left a heap of debts. Not his fault,' he added quickly, 'he owned a factory making materials for car interiors, and you may remember a lot of the car firms went in for very dramatic downsizing.'

'I remember.'

'Well, his life insurance took care of my mother's future income. She's off in Spain now, in one of those special developments for ex-pats, playing bridge every day and loving it. When I'd sorted out the debts, all that was left was a holiday cottage in Provence. I hired it out as a *gîte* just to have some funds to work with, then had the chance to buy a rundown property a couple of miles away at a bargain price...' He broke off, colouring a little. 'I'm sorry, I don't usually bore people with my life story.'

'I'm not bored. Go on, you stopped at quite a cliffhanger!'

'Well, to make a long story short, the firm still owns some properties, but it dawned on me that there was an opening for a firm where I could help others to *find* places without having to own them myself. And it just took off.'

'To tell the truth, I never realized there were firms catering for that.'

'Oh, there are quite a few now. A lot of people move for business reasons, and of course the great retirement dream is "a place in the sun".'

'People used to be content to retire to the South Coast,' she agreed. 'Now they're more adventurous.'

'Exactly. And why not? That's what gives us our business, after all.'

Karen refused any of the rich desserts brought for her inspection on the trolley, and settled for coffee. That was brought to them in the lounge. Over the coffee cups they made arrangements for her to go to London before Christmas to meet Mireille and any others who might be around at the moment.

'Then we have to settle about your stay in Paris. Could we arrange it to begin on January 2nd? Or do you think you'll have a hangover?' He was laughing as he said it.

'Oh, of course – the result of drinking too much fizzy orange with my nephew. My sister's promised he can stay up to see the New Year in.'

'That sounds great,' he said, with something like envy in his tone. Then, returning to the business in hand: 'We have an arrangement with the Hotel Babette, in the Rue Jollifant – it's nothing special but we can always get a room there at short notice. In this instance I'll let them know you're coming, and I expect you'll be staying until the end of January. Is that OK?'

'I could come home at weekends, could I?'

'Oh, of course! What do you think this is – boarding school?'

'We-ell, I'm going to be taking lessons, aren't I?'

'Yes, I suppose that's true. But all you have to do is smile at Antoine and I bet he'll let you off homework.'

'Antoine? He's your legal adviser?'

'One of them. The firm is Gustave Kloss and there are three or four senior partners as dry as old bread. But the younger members are rather nice. I hope you won't find it boring...'

'Not at all. I'm looking forward to it.'

He hesitated. 'There's something I'd like to ask you.' She waited, and he went on: 'It's a favour.'

'Of course, if I can.'

'Would you ... could I ask you to drop in and see Roly while you're there?'

It was Karen's turn to hesitate. She'd liked the little boy a lot, but he was the child of parents who clearly didn't have an easy relationship. She didn't want to find herself in a no man's-land between those two.

'I'm sorry,' Jeffrey said. 'I shouldn't have asked. But Roly keeps talking about you and ... well ... I wondered...'

'Oh, it's a month to go till New Year. He'll have forgotten all about me by then.'

He was shaking his head. 'Not at all,' he observed. 'In fact, when I asked him what he'd like for Christmas, he said, "It would be nice to see Mademoiselle Karen again." '

'Oh,' she said.

After that there was nothing else to be done but to agree.

Five

Evie was delighted when she heard the news. 'A vast improvement on counting cargoes for Mr Stokes!' She'd always thought it drearily unglamorous.

'His name's Scholes. It was very decent of him to take me on. But yes, I must agree, this is more my kind of thing.'

'And you start in Paris in January!'

'Lovely, isn't it?'

'Hmm,' murmured Walt. 'It's cold in Paris in January.'

'Well, darling, it's cold here in January,' his wife protested. 'You have to admit it's better to be cold in Paris than cold in Kent?'

They went off into a long discussion about the shortcomings of the British climate. Karen tactfully withdrew. She still had to start as usual next day at eight o'clock in the offices of Scholes Cargo. But at the end of this week that job would be over.

The next few weeks passed in a blur of activity. In early December she went to London for the Christmas party at Lynwood Associates. This proved to be a mild affair, consisting mostly of a few drinks and mince pies to accompany a great many anecdotes about exploits of the year just ending. They seemed a friendly crew, her new colleagues.

Immediately after the party, Mireille set about emptying her attic flat north of the Thames, a place quite unsuitable for either the new baby or its soon-to-be-acquired baby buggy. Karen was given a makeshift bed on the sofa, while staying so as to lend a hand. She took the opportunity to find a lock-up garage for her car nearby and discovered that it was an easy commute by Tube to the office. Over a week or so she ferried her belongings, mostly clothes and books, from Kent to London, then returned by train to Dagworth Farm for the festivities.

After a particularly enjoyable Christmas and a New Year party that Perry had slept through, Evie gathered her children to say goodbye to their aunt. There were some tears from little Angela when she discovered her Aunt Karen was going to live elsewhere permanently. Perry was more rugged about it but shook her hand with tremendous firmness. Noomie, infected by something in the atmosphere, burst into loud wails.

'Good heavens, you'll be glad to get away from all this,' groaned Walt as he tried to comfort the toddler.

'No, I won't,' Karen sighed, bestowing a kiss on Noomie's wet cheek.

As the taxi drove her off towards Dover, her thoughts turned to the boy she was going to meet in a day or two. She couldn't imagine Roly Dartieux bursting into tears over anything. Whether that was good or bad, she wasn't sure.

The winter crossing by ferry was blessed with a calm, bright day. Although she was only going to Paris for a month, it was with a sense of leave-taking that she watched the well-loved view of white cliffs fade in the distance.

Jeffrey had arranged they should meet in Paris at the Hotel Babette. This proved to be in a respectable *arrondissement* with pollarded sweet chestnuts on the pavement and the scent from a fine patisserie on the air. The room to which she was shown was near the top of the narrow building, reached by a lift something like a birdcage.

'*Et voilà!*' said Madame Colline, showing her in. 'Modernized when we did the work on the rest of the house last year. Not our largest room, I admit, but it is always available for the companions of Monsieur Lynwood.'

'Thank you, it's charming.' And so it was, with its pale floral wallpaper, its voile curtains, and its Art Nouveau furniture. The view from the window gave a glimpse of the roof of the Lycée Voltaire.

She unpacked, gave her hair a good brush

and changed out of her travel outfit – slacks and a jersey. She felt she must wear something a lot smarter for her visit to the Dartieux household, so she put on a dress given to her as a Christmas present by Evie – heavy dark-blue linen, which needed a bright scarf at the neck to relieve its austerity. She surveyed herself in the mirror: cap of dark brown hair recently cut by a good hairdresser, brown eyes accentuated by a little mascara, compact body given a svelte look by the dark dress ... not bad.

Satisfied that she would do herself justice, she went down for a drink from the tiny bar on one side of the vestibule. The rooms were, to her mind, insufferably hot, so she went out with her glass of Campari to stand on the outer steps, watching the traffic rush by in the Rue Jollifant. While she was still there a tall figure in a leather jacket swung round the corner and presented himself at the foot of the steps. It was Jeffrey Lynwood.

'Well, hello,' he greeted her. 'You found the place, I see.'

'The taxi found it,' she amended.

'Well, what do you think of the hotel?'

'Rather sweet. I expected somewhere more business-orientated.'

'Ah, no, if we're back from a session of hard work in the Vosges or Clermont-Ferrand, we want a few home comforts, I think.' He came up the shallow steps. 'I'll just say

85

hello to Madame Colline.' He passed her, and put his head into the office behind the reception desk. 'Madame? *Me voici!*'

'Ah, monsieur! *Bonne année*, and how nice to see you so early in the year.' A long animated conversation ensued, partly in French, partly in English. She heard herself mentioned once or twice, and hoped it was with approval although she'd arrived with hair tousled by the sea-breeze and a red-tipped nose.

By and by Jeffrey reappeared. 'We've caught up with each other,' he explained. 'She and I have been friends since I first went into business. Well, if you'd like to finish up your drink, we could get going.'

Karen looked at the glass in her hand. 'I'm not really bothered about finishing this. Just let me dash upstairs for my coat.'

In her room she gathered not only her camel jacket but the present she'd brought for Roly. Evie had used her artistic talents in wrapping it for her, an enticing display of gold paper and curling paper ribbons for the moment hidden in a small plastic carrier.

Jeffrey had called a taxi. 'It would be quicker by Metro but at this hour in the afternoon it might be a bit crowded.' As he ushered her across the pavement he added, 'You look nice.'

'It's all done to impress Gabrielle.'

'You're not kidding,' he said with a faint

smile, and gave the address to the driver.

The hall porter greeted him by name, exchanging New Year greetings as he ushered them to the lift. Karen thought she saw a considerable tip disappear into his gloved hand as he closed the lift door. At her glance, Jeffrey shrugged. 'New Year handout. And besides, he sometimes gives me little bits of information.'

That troubled her. Was Jeffrey Lynwood the sort of man who paid someone to spy on his ex-wife? But they were at the upper floor, and as they came out of the lift the door of the flat opened.

'Daddy!' shouted Roly in welcome, hurling himself out. 'I heard the lift coming up! *Bonne année! Comment vas-tu?* Ah, Mademoiselle Karen.' He took her hand to shake in a very formal, grown-up fashion. 'How do you do? It's so nice to see you again. Did you recover well from our journey? I'm afraid I didn't say goodbye to you, I think I was asleep.'

He was pulling her through the hall and into the apartment's drawing room. 'Maman! Maman, here is Mademoiselle Karen at last! And Daddy, of course.'

'So I see,' said Hélène Dartieux, coming forward to shake hands. 'I'm glad to meet you. Roland has spoken of you very often.'

'How do you do,' Karen murmured, a little overcome.

The room, in the first place, was gorgeous. Three tall windows let in the last of the winter afternoon light, which gleamed on furniture of the Empire period – much gold and crimson silk, mirrors surmounted by coats of arms; the only word for it was opulent. Standing amongst this splendour, its mistress wasn't at first so eye-catching. She was small, very fair, and pretty rather than beautiful. But her prettiness was of a heart-catching kind – the soft gold curls and forget-me-not blue eyes of a Botticelli painting.

To add to this perfection, she was wearing a suit of black satin so beautifully cut it could only have come from the House of Chanel. There were diamonds in her ears and a single diamond on a fine chain around her neck.

'My husband will be down in a moment,' she said, with a little gesture towards the staircase. 'He's changing. We're going for cocktails with the *dirigeant* of his party. Politics, you know – they forge ahead, even at Christmas and New Year.' She turned the blue eyes towards Jeffrey. 'So how are you? *Tout va bien?*'

'Yes, thank you. And you? All the political irons heating nicely in the fire?'

'Papa Louis is to get a decoration from the Napoleonic History Society,' Roly put in. 'In reward for a paper he's written about – what was it about, Maman?'

'Never mind, sweetie, it's too complicated for a little head like yours. Ah, Louis, there you are! My dear, let me introduce you to the lady who so kindly cared for Roly...'

'Ah yes, of course, how do you do?' He hurried down the last few steps, hand outstretched, a handsome dark man of medium height clad in black tie and evening jacket. 'That was so good of you! We had to leave Phnom Penh at literally a moment's notice, you see, because I was wanted at a monetary consultation in Stockholm. Just after the Twin Towers attack, financial markets were utterly chaotic—'

'Because the New York Stock Exchange lost its computers,' Roly put in. 'I saved some newspaper articles about that, I'm going to do a project about it in my journal.'

'Yes, yes, Roland, you mentioned that before. My dear, are we ready?' He turned an apologetic glance on the visitors. 'Our engagement is some distance the other side of the Bois, alas. So we must be going. I hope you'll excuse us?'

'By all means,' Karen said, although somewhat taken aback. She'd thought she'd been invited to a drink or a cup of coffee. But no, it seemed Roly had invited her and to Roly the task of playing host was handed over.

The door of the drawing room opened. The housekeeper, Gabrielle, came in. '*Elle est arrivée, la limousine,*' she announced.

'Good, we must go. *À toute à l' heure,*' Louis said in some haste, and taking his wife by the elbow, ushered her out.

'Bye-bye, Maman,' called Roly. '*Amuse-toi bien!*'

Karen couldn't help thinking it odd that the little boy should be wishing his mother a good time while he was left at home at this festive time. Her mind went back to Evie at the farm, where probably at this very moment the children were being wrapped up warm for yet another outing to a funfair or a party. Something of her opinion must have shown, because Jeffrey raised his shoulders in a faint shrug.

'Are you going to show me what you got for Christmas?' she asked Roly.

'Would you like to see? Maman gave me this wristwatch and a satchel with Asterix on it, for school, you know, and Papa Louis gave me a voucher to spend as I like, so I'm going to buy a CD ROM. They're in my room.'

'Ah, computer games! My nephew Perry is into that,' she said, following him towards the staircase.

Gabrielle called as they began to go upstairs. 'If you pull things out, put it all back, now, Roland!'

'Yes, Gabrielle.'

Karen turned to look back at the house-keeper. In a dark brown wool dress and sensible shoes she had the look of a faithful retainer, from the old school of domestic service, hard-working, uncompromising, used to strict obedience.

Jeffrey was addressing her with great politeness and offering her an envelope. She accepted it with a slight inclination of her grey head, slipping it into a pocket.

'Come on, Daddy,' cried Roly from the top of the stairs.

'I'm coming.' He leapt up the stairs two at a time, catching up with Karen as Roly ran into this room.

'What was that?' she asked, despite herself. 'You don't think you can bribe that one?'

He laughed. 'Nothing would entice that old gorgon to do anything to help me,' he said. 'She's been with Louis's family since the year dot.'

'Then why?'

'Because she'd hold it against me if I didn't uphold the custom.' He hesitated. 'I saw your look when I gave Émile his tip downstairs. It's just that he lets me know little things – whether Roly talks to him about the Tour de France, whether he walks to school with friends...'

'Come *on*,' urged Roly, appearing at the door of his room with a CD holder. 'Look, here's my programme for *Seas of the World* – it's got whales and dolphins on it. Shall I put it in?'

'Don't you want to see what I brought you first?'

The little boy gaped for a moment, went pink with confusion and pleasure, then said in a very small voice, 'You brought me a present?'

'Of course. When visiting a handsome young man at New Year, a young lady must always bring a present.'

He recovered his composure a little. 'I thought it was the other way round?' he countered.

'But I make up my own rules. Didn't I tell you I was unique?'

'So you did. And it's true, you're different from everyone else.'

'And that's why I brought you something that's going to keep you busy for weeks,' she said. She gave him the plastic carrier.

He took out the brilliantly wrapped parcel. 'Oh, how pretty!' He sat down on the floor cross-legged to open it. Karen was interested to see that he didn't tear it apart like her nephew Perry but painstakingly undid the ribbons and unfolded the paper.

Meanwhile Karen examined the room. In a way, it was as impressive as the drawing room, but of course in a totally different style – an interior decorator's idea of what the average little boy would like. Disney-patterned fabrics made the curtains and the bedspread. The bedside rug was designed like a racing car. The wardrobe and cupboards were painted in bold primary colours. The desk computer had an area to itself with shelves to house CDs and books, the contents announced on labels shaped like oranges and lemons.

All very wonderful. Yet what struck Karen most was its painful neatness. No toys scattered about, no odd socks discarded on the carpet, no favourite sweaters spilling out of drawers...

She turned back to Roly. He was folding the wrapping paper, loosely winding the ribbons round it, putting the result in the little carrier bag, and placing the carrier in the waste-paper basket. She shook her head to herself. Once again she thought of Evie's children – good children, quite obedient and willing to play their part, but never likely to tidy up the wrapping paper so efficiently.

A rectangular wooden box had been revealed. Roly tried various methods to open it and discovered within a few seconds that the lid could be removed by sliding it aside. He laid the lid on the computer desk.

Inside the box was a plain white surface on which iron filings were arranged in circular patterns around two magnets. Roly stared at it, made a little sound of inquiry in his throat, then looked inquiringly at Karen.

She put a finger on one of the magnets and moved it. The iron filings moved with it, remaining in a pattern.

'Oh, let me, let me!' the boy cried, and put his finger on the magnet. He made scribbling motions, and the filings wriggled about.

'The other one too,' Karen said, and moved the second magnet. It took its followers with it, and partially disturbed the others.

'Oh, they can both do it! Is it magic?'

She made no reply, but picked one of the magnets out and, holding the box in one hand, moved the magnet about underneath with the other. The iron filings fled about on the white surface as if without reason.

Roly burst into giggles. 'They're playing football! Look, Daddy, the little specks are playing football!'

Jeffrey was laughing seeing his son so delighted. 'Rugby, if you don't mind,' he said. 'The men of this family support rugby.'

'How do they do it?' Roly cried. He seized the box again from Karen. 'Do you switch something on?' He sought about, but there was no switch.

'I told you it was going to keep you busy for weeks,' she said. She held up the information leaflet supplied with the toy. 'You've got to prove you're bright as well as handsome, young man. If you haven't worked it out by the time I have to go home to London, I'll give you the instructions so you can read all about it.'

'Let me have them now...' He made a grab for them, but she held them out of reach.

'No, no, that's too easy. You were saying you had a project about the Stock Exchange computers. This is another one. And when you've worked out how it works you can take it to school for show-and-tell.'

His laughter waned. 'Oh, they'd say I was showing off...'

'Nonsense, they'll think it's fun.'

He made no reply, but concentrated sternly on making the filings roam about. Over his head Karen glanced at his father, who gave a faint frown as if warning her to say no more on that point.

For the next ten minutes the little boy puzzled over the toy. They were interrupted by the entrance of Gabrielle, her mouth already open to scold if toys were strewn about. 'Now tidy up, Roland, it will soon be time to wash your hands for supper.'

'Yes, Gabrielle.' His voice was compliant, but he was nerving himself for something more. 'May Mademoiselle Karen and Daddy stay for supper with me?'

'What?'

'It would be nice if they could have supper with me, I thought.'

The housekeeper pursed her lips. 'I had no instructions from Madame about that.'

'It wouldn't be much trouble for you—'

'You're not the one to say what's trouble and what isn't. Besides, Mademoiselle and Monsieur would hardly enjoy milk and sponge cake. Now put away your toys.'

Roly closed the box of magnets, opened a cupboard, and stowed away the gift. 'We could have something better than milk and sponge cake,' he mumbled, barely audible.

'I have a better idea,' Karen put in, seeing the boy's mouth begin to droop at the corners. 'Why don't Monsieur Lynwood and I take Roly out to supper?'

'Take him out?' Gabrielle echoed in consternation.

'Yes, for a piece of gateau and some hot chocolate—'

'I don't think Madame would approve—'

'Come on, Gabrielle, it's New Year. All the other children in Paris are being taken out for some fun,' protested Jeffrey.

'But it will soon be his bedtime...'

'It's two hours till bedtime, Gabrielle. Please, may I go? I'm sure Maman wouldn't mind. Please let me go out for hot chocolate!'

'But this is not one of the days when Monsieur is permitted—'

Jeffrey broke in sharply. 'Madame, this isn't a time to discuss that kind of thing. Mademoiselle Karen has come all the way from London to meet Roly again. We are taking him out for a little celebration.'

'No, Monsieur, those are not my instructions.'

Up till then the conversation had been in French. Roly now said in a low voice and in English, 'It's no use. She'll only get more cross.'

Karen studied him for a moment. Pale calm features accepting defeat, against an enemy he knew only too well. 'Never say die,' she murmured in English, then turned with a friendly, polite smile to Gabrielle. 'I quite understand your reservations, Madame,' she said in her most classical French, 'and of course I respect them. But you know, it is the holiday season and it would be pleasant to spend a little more time with my young friend here. It would be an even greater pleasure to have your company too. Would you be so agreeable as to come with us? You no doubt have a favourite café where we could go? A glass of wine, a little something to eat?'

To say that Gabrielle was dumbfounded was an understatement. She almost gaped at Karen. *'Comment?'*

'Of course, why didn't I think of that?' cried Jeffrey, his voice shaking with suppressed laughter. 'Of course, Gabrielle, you must come with us!'

'Impossible! I have duties here.'

'Nothing that can't wait, I feel sure. Madame Dartieux would understand.'

'No, no, I can't entertain such an idea. I don't go out when Madame and Monsieur have an evening engagement.' The housekeeper was shaking her head and looking very put out. It dawned on Karen that she wanted to stay at home, that it was her custom on such occasions to see Roly off to bed and then, perhaps, enjoy television in her own quarters. An episode of some dubbed soap opera probably awaited her on Sky.

'You really prefer not to come with us? What a shame, another time perhaps. But in that case, show me which coat he should wear?' Karen tried the door of a cupboard but it turned out to hold shelves of shirts and underwear.

'This one,' cried Roly, as if on cue. 'I should wear my padded jacket, Gabrielle, no?' He was opening a cupboard alongside, taking the coat from a hanger.

'We'll bring him back in good time for bed,' Karen said, and began helping him into the coat.

'But ... but...'

'Tell us which café you recommend,' Jeffrey said, cutting off the last objection. 'Something nearby.'

'Well, I don't ... at this hour ... speaking for myself, I don't go out in the evening...'

'Never mind, there's sure to be somewhere nice. Thank you, Gabrielle, I appreciate this.

Until later.'

They went out, the servant in a flutter behind them. They crossed the drawing room, went out into the hall, and Roly quickly turned the lock to let them out. Gabrielle took uncertain hold of the door as if she wished to make some last effort.

'*A bientôt, Madame,*' Jeffrey said politely, and stepping across the landing, rang for the lift. The three merrymakers stood waiting for it as the door of the apartment slowly and reluctantly closed behind them.

Outside, under the lights strung in the plane trees, Jeffrey inquired, 'Tell me, Karen, have you got any famous field marshals in your family history?'

'Never mind about my family history. Where are we going for this famous hot chocolate and cake?'

Roly tugged at her hand. 'Could I have a ... a banana milkshake?' he asked as if it were an enormous favour.

'A banana milkshake – right you are. That means one of the chain restaurants.'

'You mean I can have it?' he said, amazed.

'Why not?'

'Maman says it's junk food.'

'I suppose it is. But it's New Year. Perhaps we should ask Daddy if it's OK.'

'I give my blessing to an evening's junk food,' his father said.

'Does that mean I can have a hot dog too?'

'I think there must be a bazaar haggler in *your* family history, Roly,' she said, laughing.

While Roly consumed his supper he explained that other children at school had told him of these delights. It was easy to tell that his classmates lived a different kind of life: cartoons on television, children's discos, pop music on the radio, milkshakes and hamburgers. 'Now that you've got your hot dog and milkshake, what do you think of them?' Jeffrey asked with amusement.

'We-ell ... I don't think they go together really. But it's more interesting than milk and *gâteau de Savoie*.'

This philosophical conclusion ended the meal. They went out and by a few turnings came out near the Pont de l'Alma. Here they stopped to watch the pleasure boats go by, their masts outlined in lights, music playing from their speakers. Roly was delighted. 'They're so *pretty*! Do they go up and down all the time?'

'Well, they're only lit up at night,' his father said, teasing.

The boy gave him a soft blow with his fist. 'Of course I know they'd only be lit at night! It would be nice to go on one, wouldn't it?'

'Another time,' said Karen.

'We could go on one?'

'If Maman agrees.'

'Oh.' The soft sound was full of hope and longing.

100

As they wended their way home, Karen paused at a patisserie. Jeffrey said to her in alarm, 'You're not going to buy him sweets after that meal?'

'No, this is for Gabrielle.'

'What?'

'Just to make sure she's pleased with us.'

'I think it was Macchiavelli in your ancestry,' he told her, with a shake of the head.

She bought a tiny *gâteau forêt noir* in its own elaborately folded cardboard box and tied with coloured tape. When the housekeeper opened the door to them, Karen presented her with the box. '*Bonne année*,' she said blithely. 'A little late, but I hope you'll enjoy it.'

Once again Gabrielle was left speechelss. She managed a muffled, 'Thank you, mademoiselle.' Perhaps as a result, there was no reproach about the stain from the milkshake on Roly's shirt, nor did she point out that it was ten minutes past bedtime.

Roly shook hands with his father and then with Karen. 'You won't forget about the boats?' he said through an enormous yawn as he was led away.

Afterwards Jeffrey took Karen for a meal. They had had nothing but coffee while Roly demolished his hot dog, and it was now after eight. They found a quiet restaurant near the Opera. To her surprise, he ordered champagne.

'This is to thank you for this evening,' he said, holding up his glass in a toast. 'I never would have thought of handling it the way you did.'

'Oh, I'm used to it,' she said. 'But what bothers me is why that old lady has such a down on the kid?'

He hesitated. 'It's complicated. It's partly because Roly isn't Louis's son. She feels he's been foisted on her beloved employer, whom she remembers as a boy himself. And then of course, Roly is an odd little thing in himself. She doesn't understand him – but then not many do.'

'That's true.' She thought a moment and added, 'You know, when I asked which coat he should wear to go out, he understood immediately that he had to get it, put it on, and start on the way out. He understood it was a matter of ... going with the flow ... seizing the advantage...'

'I think you're right. But it's not often he gets the better of Gabrielle, and nor do I. She really dislikes me. No judge could be more strict about the letter of the law when it comes to my visiting rights.'

She wanted to ask about Hélène. There had been something so single-minded about her as she waited for her husband to come downstairs – as if all that mattered was the cocktail party to which they were going. The arrival of Roly's father appeared to be something of a nuisance.

But it would be unwise to blunder in. Instead she asked about Louis Dartieux. To her mind he had the polished look of the successful administrator, with the fine narrow head and dark eyes of the Latin. 'What exactly is it he does?'

'He's a financial consultant to the government. From a very good family, by the way, but they supported Napoleon and came a bit of a cropper when the Empire collapsed. Louis has ambitions.'

'To be the Chancellor of the Exchequer or whatever is the French equivalent?'

'No, he wants to be an ambassador.' He twisted the stem of his champagne glass. 'I think that's what swept Hélène off her feet – think of it, wife to the French ambassador in Washington!'

She gave a laugh of protest. 'But is that likely to happen? I thought you had to be in the diplomatic corps.'

'It lies in the award of the president. And Louis has a lot of friends in that entourage. Oh, yes, it could happen – perhaps not Washington at first, but some lesser posting, and a few more trips abroad to do good work for his country. That outing to Cambodia, for instance, that was some deal the government wanted to do, something about bauxite, I think he said.'

'Ah ... that's a mineral?'

'Yes, but he negotiates in all sorts of things. It's the money he handles, not the commodity – and of course all in very big numbers. He likes to let me know what he's up to because he thinks I'm terribly downmarket.'

'And Hélène usually goes with him on these jaunts?'

'Very often. You see, no matter where you are, you can still be making good contacts, getting to know who's who and what's what. Hélène is a tremendous asset in that way because, of course – well, she's so lovely to look at. I've never been invited to one of their big parties, but I gather she's a wonderful hostess.'

'Roly went with them to Cambodia. Is that usual?'

'That was because of the problem about Gabrielle and her annual holiday,' he reminded her. 'But Roly has gone with them once or twice, to Zurich, to Istanbul – short trips. If they actually got an ambassadorship, Hélène would certainly take him with her.' He sighed.

'You'd hate that, of course.'

'What I'd hate or like doesn't come into it,' he said. 'Nor does what Roly would like, either. The courts decided his mother should have control of his upbringing and that's that.' He smiled a little and added, 'That's

104

why I'm so grateful to you. Tonight was a bonus for me.'

'I'm glad you were pleased with it.'

They dropped the subject while they ate. There were facts about the lessons from the *notaire* that needed discussion. It wasn't until he was saying goodnight to her at the threshold of the Hotel Babette that he returned to the problem of Roly.

'Did you really mean that, about taking him on one of the *bateaux mouches*?'

'Absolutely,' said Karen.

Six

So much for her intention to stay out of difficult terrain, she thought to herself as she went up to bed.

It was really none of her business whether Hélène and Louis Dartieux were making a good job of bringing up Roly. It was in fact wrong of her to be making assumptions about it. Yet in the brief period when they had all been together in the magnificent drawing room, Karen had been acutely aware of a lack of contact between child and adults.

The little boy had been so eager to take part in the conversation. He'd made two attempts: first when he volunteered the favourable information about the award for his stepfather, and secondly when he tried to extend the remarks about the temporary collapse of Wall Street. On each occasion he'd been brushed aside as a nuisance. The parents seemed to regard him as an intrusive, conceited child – and, Karen said to herself, perhaps he is. Perhaps I've got it wrong.

It was clear he wasn't popular at school.

'They'd think I was showing off.' From hints during their evening together she'd gathered his teacher thought him disruptive. Jeffrey Lynwood acknowledged that Roly was seen as 'difficult'.

Yet Karen saw him differently. It was perhaps due to the hours they'd spent together on the long flight from Cambodia. What she'd seen at that time was a lonely little boy, apparently disregarded by those who ought to have been caring for him – his parents had gone, his nanny had deserted him, even the adults at the embassy seemed eager to get him off their hands.

Karen had thought him brave. He didn't complain about being handed over to a complete stranger. He didn't cry because he felt poorly after a bad night and an attack of travel nerves.

Well, well, she scolded, let's not weigh the scales too heavily on his side. Perhaps he's just a little boy going through a difficult phase. She knew children went through 'phases'. Perry as a toddler had had a passion for biting other children. Angela had been a clingy child. Little Noomie was going through a weeping and wailing stage. Perhaps Roly was going through a show-off period.

All the same, she was going to keep her promise about the pleasure-boat trip on the Seine.

In the morning she presented herself at the office of Gustave Kloss in the Boulevard Haussman. Contrary to Jeffrey's remark, there seemed to be nothing dry or venerable about them. The premises were open-plan although the seniors had offices with doors. Antoine Beranger, her mentor, had a desk near a window, which seemed to indicate a certain precedence. He was about forty, with thinning hair and a frank, jovial manner.

She was asked to sign an undertaking of confidentiality concerning any client details she might learn during tuition. She was given a smart card so that she could come and go at the main entrance, and the key to a locker. She wasn't given a desk. It seemed she was to sit alongside Antoine so as to study the cases on which he was actually working. Antoine held her hand a little too long at their first meeting.

He insisted on taking her to lunch. Luckily others joined them in a neighbourhood café, so that after a while she made her escape to put through a call on her mobile. The call was to Hélène Dartieux because she felt it was necessary to establish a good relationship with her.

'Ah, Miss Montgomery – how nice of you to call.' There was coolness in her tone. Karen guessed the housekeeper had been complaining about the happenings of last night.

'Madame Dartieux, I hope I'm not interrupting your lunch.'

'Not at all. It gives me the opportunity to say again how much I appreciate your kindness to Roland on the flight from Phnom Penh,' said Hélène with exquisite politeness.

'That was nothing. You know of course that I was given a free passage home in return.'

'Yes, of course, but all the same you came to his rescue.'

'I wanted to say that I hope you approved of our outing last night?' She made this a question, and waited.

'Certainly,' Hélène said with a notable lack of enthusiasm. 'But I'm a little uncertain of the reason for it.'

'Oh, put it down to the New Year spirit,' Karen said airily. 'I've got nephews and a niece of my own, you see, and we'd been doing all sorts of things like pantomimes and carol services. It was just a sort of overflow from that.' She gave a hesitant little chuckle. 'I think your servant was a bit put out, though.'

She'd used the word intentionally, and Hélène rose to it at once. 'Oh, Gabrielle is considerably more than a servant,' she objected. 'She's been with my husband's family all her life—'

'Oh, dear, I'm sorry, I didn't realize that. Where I come from, we're lucky if we can get someone to come in and do the dusting. I do

109

apologise.'

Hélène picked up at once on this inexperience in dealing with old family retainers. 'Well, you know, tradition counts for a lot in France. Gabrielle is a very important member of our family. Because Louis and I have to spend so much time on entertaining and being entertained, Gabrielle has had Roland in her care, particularly since that awful girl took off into the blue at Phnom Penh.'

'You haven't thought to replace – what was her name? – Norah?'

'That didn't seem necessary. Gabrielle is thoroughly competent and takes her role as Roland's guardian very seriously. Which is perhaps why she rather took offence last night.'

'Ah! So I was right in thinking she was a bit put out.'

'Let's just say it was a surprise to her. You see,' Hélène said with a sigh that had something like resignation in it, 'most people don't take readily to my little boy.'

'Really? What makes you think that?'

'Well, he *is* a bit ... pushy. He likes to be noticed, which I suppose may be because he's an only child. But you don't want to be bored by all that,' she ended rather hastily. She seemed about to say goodbye, but Karen had a point she wanted to gain.

She said at once, 'I hope Gabrielle enjoyed

the Black Forest gateau.'

'Oh.' Hélène was surprised to have the matter brought up. 'Well ... she mentioned it. It was unexpected but' – with a smile in her voice at acknowledging such a failing in her housekeeper – 'she does appreciate good patisserie.'

'I'm so glad. I might bring her another one next time I come. You won't mind if I drop by now and again?' And here, at last, was where she'd been aiming all along.

'Oh, that's too kind – why should you bother—'

'Because, you see, I more or less promised to take Roland on a river trip. I'd enjoy it myself, you know. I've been in the tourist business for years and never yet managed to go on a *bateau mouche*.'

Hélène admitted that she too had neglected to try the river trip, and after a few friendly remarks on both sides they parted agreeing that Karen would take Roly out one evening soon.

Success. She was fixed in Hélène's mind now as someone who had acted as emergency nanny to her son and who'd been kind enough to visit when the little boy wanted to see her again. Jeffrey Lynwood had no doubt explained that Karen's stay in Paris was for a month only. If during that time she was inclined to keep up a friendship with the child, well, so what?

That was a question Karen couldn't quite have answered herself. All she knew was that Roly struck some chord in her, to which she had to respond. She didn't ask herself if she was drawn to him because she herself needed someone to love, because there was a void in her life due to Michael Ansleigh's disappearance, a void that must be filled.

Over the next few days her mentor, Antoine, tried to make as many little physical contacts as he could. Karen was used to that from her career as a flight attendant. She moved her chair away a few inches, and once, when his hand accidentally fell upon her knee, she picked it up and removed it.

'*Défense de passer,*' she said with a smile.

'Ah, traffic regulations are a nuisance!' But he took it in good part, and they became friendly colleagues.

The work was hard. She understood she wasn't expected to become an expert, yet she wanted to acquit herself well. She spent the evenings of her first week in a café in the Rue Jollifant rehearsing the forms of contract, the rights of ownership, the terms of agreement: *compromis de vente, promesse de vente, indivision, jouissance, acte authentique...*

And all this just in case some British buyer needed reassurance.

During her second week in the office her mobile phone signalled a call. It was the rule that such calls were not allowed so she asked

Antoine to excuse her and went out into the corridor. 'Hello?'

'Mademoiselle Karen?'

'Roly?' She was surprised and pleased. 'How nice to hear from you.'

'Mademoiselle Karen, I wanted to tell you I found out how your present worked.'

'You worked it out?'

'We-ell...' He hesitated. 'I asked Pierre.'

'Who's Pierre?'

'He's one of the porters. I asked him what made little specks of metal rush about and make patterns, and he said it sounded like magnetism. So I looked it up in my encyclopaedia and it says it's two poles of negative and positive attraction. I read a lot about it and I'm not sure I understand it properly yet, but anyway, it's measured by a thing called a gauss and that's named after the man who first measured it, years and years ago.'

The information, poured out in his little boy's voice, came in a breathless rush. 'Good heavens,' said Karen, 'that's amazing.'

'I'd have let you know sooner but I had to get your telephone number from Daddy and he was away on business.'

'Well done. But wait a minute,' she said, 'you weren't supposed to ask anyone. You were supposed to find out for yourself.'

'Well, I tried looking up everything I could think of but I didn't know the right words.

Anyhow,' he remarked with a very rational calmness, 'if somebody can tell me what I want to know, why should I waste time looking in the wrong place?'

She laughed. 'I was only teasing, Roly. I think you've done very well.'

'Can I have the leaflet with the information on it? I want to paste it in my journal.'

'I'll bring it with me.'

'You're coming?'

'Seems to me you deserve a reward after all that hard work, don't you agree? What would you like?'

'The river boat!'

'All right. But first I have to ask Maman. Is she there?'

'She's in the drawing room. I'll tell her.'

There was a delay, and then an extension was picked up. 'Miss Montgomery?'

'Good afternoon, Madame. Has Roland explained?'

'Some extraordinary story about the toy you gave him. I don't quite fathom it – has he been bothering you?'

'Not at all. I asked him to let me know if he found out how it worked.'

'You did? That was very kind of you. And is it something about the toy – did you wish to speak about that?'

'You remember we discussed the idea of taking him on one of the boat trips?'

'Ye-es, that seems to ring a bell.'

114

'May I call for him tomorrow evening and take him? We could go on one of the early evening trips. He'd be home by eight.'

There was a pause. Karen guessed that Roly's mother was thinking about Gabrielle, and how she would feel, if this interfering stranger were encouraged to reappear. She explained, 'I said to Roland that I thought he deserved a reward for finding out about the magnetic fields...'

'The what?'

'The toy – I bought it at the Science Museum – it's intended to help understand the principle of magnetic fields, although it seemed a bit condensed to me!'

'Are you a scientist, then, Miss Montgomery? I gathered you were in the travel business.'

'I *am* in the travel business, you're quite right, and what I know about science would go under a postage stamp. I just bought the toy for Roland because ... well, it's the sort of thing my nephew Perry would like.' She pictured Perry playing with the set for half an hour, then rushing off for a bike ride. 'It was a surprise to me when Roland telephoned to say he'd fathomed it. So I said he deserved a reward. And he chose the boat trip.'

'Well, I ... er ... I see nothing against it if you're sure you want to give up your time.'

'Oh, I assure you, it would be rather fun for

115

me. I told you I'd never done the boat trip.'

'Did you? Well, by all means, if you think you'd enjoy it – but are you really sure you want to do this?'

'Well, I sort of promised, you know. Tomorrow evening? I'll be there about five thirty.'

'Very well. I'll tell Roland.'

Hélène disconnected, but Karen waited. Something told her that the little boy had not hung up the phone on which he'd begun the call. After a moment, she heard his voice.

'Tomorrow evening?'

'About five thirty.'

'I'll tell you all about the magnetism when I see you.'

'Thank you. I'm looking forward to it.'

She went back into the main office smiling.

When the lift deposited her at the upper floor of the apartment block the next evening, Roly was waiting to open the door. There was no sign of Gabrielle. But Madame Dartieux, in the role of concerned parent, was at Roly's side.

'This is good of you, Miss Montgomery,' she said. 'Roland is looking forward to it so much.'

'Can we go?' he put in, without much tact.

'Quietly, quietly, my lamb,' his mother reproved. 'I just want to say a few things to Miss Montgomery. You won't mind,' she went on, turning to Karen. 'A few rules? Roland has had supper so there will be no need to do anything more on that score. He must be back by eight o'clock. Is that understood?'

'No problem.'

'Off you go, then.'

'Bye-bye, Maman!' He was dragging Karen towards the lift. As soon as its door closed he began, 'There's magnetism at the North Pole and the South Pole – did you know that?'

'I think I'd heard it somewhere—'

'Yes, well, that's how sailors find their way about on the sea. Only the North Pole isn't true north, so they have to have special instruments. They used to do very clever sums to find out the direction but now of course it's all computers. At least, not on small ships, perhaps. Not on a *bateau* like the one we're going on.'

The lift deposited them at the entrance hall. The concierge gave them a small salute as they went out. 'What was that about not giving you anything to eat?' she inquired. 'Did you get into trouble over the hot dog?'

He gave a sudden mischievous grin. 'Gabrielle wanted to know what we'd had in the restaurant last time so I told her a milk drink and a sandwich.'

'Roly!'

'Well, it was true. A hot dog is a sort of

sandwich and a milkshake is made of milk.'
He was still smiling, but was a little disappointed by her disapproval.

'Well, look here, here's something to add to
the rules. No more junk food. I don't want
you being economical with the truth in
future.'

'Economical with the truth!' he echoed,
savouring the phrase then looking dashed.
'That's a roundabout way of saying...'

'Yes, it is, and though it's clever it's not
pleasant.'

He gazed up at her, greeny-blue eyes
shadowed. 'All right.'

'So let's get a move on because the boat's
due to go.'

He put his hand in hers and they hurried
along. After a moment his spirits revived,
and he began again about magnetism,
ending with: 'Did you bring the instruction
leaflet?' He stowed it in his pocket as they
went down into the Metro. This in itself was
a delight to him. She discovered he'd never
travelled on the Metro before. 'What, never?
If you go to a museum or a theatre, how
d'you get there?'

'By car, of course. Maman never travels on
the Metro.'

'But when you went out with Norah?'

'Norah used to drive us.' He thought a
moment. 'But mostly we walked to the park
or somewhere – for the exercise. Norah went

on the fitness trails.'

'And you – did you go on the fitness trails too?'

'Of course not! People didn't want a little kid running about and getting in their way.'

'So what did you do while Norah went through the routines?'

'I went on the swings. I liked that and sometimes one of the mothers would give me a push.'

The picture this summoned up was depressing, although Roly seemed to take it for granted. Luckily they'd arrived at their station. In the thrill of boarding the boat, he forgot about Norah.

He wasn't by any means the only child making the trip and it was interesting to Karen to see what happened. At first they all shared the excitement and the pleasure of the illuminations, but after a while she noticed a drawing-away from him.

And it was no wonder. He'd primed himself with information about all the places they would pass, so that when anyone mistook the monument or the bridge name, he was ready with a correction. He even corrected some of the adults.

'Clever little chap,' said an English tourist as they disembarked. But there was no great warmth in the remark.

Roly himself had no idea he'd trodden on any toes. 'That was lovely,' he sighed. 'Did you notice how the sound changed when we went under a bridge? I wonder why that is?'

'Something to do with acoustics, I believe.'

'Acoustics – what are they?'

'I don't think it's a they, I think it's an it.'

He giggled. 'You know, you talk differently from anyone else I ever met. And how can it be an it when you can tell there's more than one because of the *s*?'

'Search me.' she said. 'Did you mention you had an encyclopaedia?'

'Yes, on disk, *Children's World of Knowledge.*'

'Well, look it up. But not tonight,' she warned, 'because by the time we get you home it's bedtime – right?'

'OK,' he sighed. Then he checked himself. 'Oh, I forgot, I mustn't say OK. So all right, instead.'

'Why mustn't you say OK?'

'Because it's slang, and it's lazy.'

'I suppose it is. I never thought of that.'

'Although you know, everybody says it,' he went on with a considering air. 'But when I pointed that out to Maman she told me not to be cheeky, so I try not to use it.'

'I see,' said Karen.

She delivered him home at the appointed hour, having paused to buy him a paper full of roast chestnuts on the way. 'Now you must show them to Maman or Gabrielle,' she admonished, 'and if they say you mustn't eat them you must throw them in the bin.'

120

'Oh, it doesn't matter about eating them,' he said, clutching them in his gloved hand. 'It was so *marvellous* to see all that red glowing stuff in the man's metal barrel. What was that?'

'Charcoal, I think.'

'And why does it glow like that?'

'Look it up,' she said as she dropped a goodnight kiss on the top of his head and rang the doorbell for him.

The following weekend was to be spent in London. There were one or two things to settle with Mireille about leaving furniture in the flat, but more importantly Evie was coming for what she described as 'a lovely snoop round the sales'. Evie liked to buy offcuts of fabric to use in her appliqué work, besides looking for bargains in children's wear.

Since this was a brief trip, Karen travelled by Eurostar on Friday evening. Evie met her at Waterloo, waving a shopping list and chattering eagerly. 'Perry wants the latest football outfit for his team, but *that's* not going to be reduced so I've put that last. But if I could get some shirts for Walt...'

'Well, hello, Evie, and I'm very well, thank you.'

'Oh, well, hello, and you don't look all that well, you look quite tired.'

'I am quite tired. Until the last minute in

the office I was trying to fathom a contract for shared occupancy of a flat in Nantes.'

'Sounds terrible. When do you get to go swanning off to the Riviera and so on?'

'Two more weeks.'

In the Underground, Evie's conversation was hampered by having to shout above the noise level, but she resumed immediately they emerged into the darkness of the January night. 'You're so lucky, Karen, living in London! I was just saying to Walt, couldn't we make an arrangement to spend one weekend a month in London, you can make a deal with some of the hotels, it wouldn't really cost so very much, but he says he has to be on hand in case anything goes wrong at the docks.'

'That's true, Evie. And anyhow, what about the children? You wouldn't want to drag them up to London for a weekend in a hotel.'

'If it comes to that, we could go shares in a little pied-à-terre with someone – a flat in one of those new condominiums at Twickenham or somewhere.'

'Good heavens, love, that would cost the earth!'

'Well, you know, Karrie, I've got money.'

'But you don't want to spend it on that kind of thing!'

Evie pulled up her coat collar against the cold and muttered that it was just lying there in the bank.

'Earning interest,' Karen pointed out.

'I suppose so. But it's so ... so mundane! At first, when Walt was using some of it to get the business going, it was fun. But now he's paid me back, and he doesn't have to ask me for any of it because he can raise what he wants from financial corporations or something.'

Karen's view was that Evie should think herself lucky. But they'd arrived at the house, and now her sister's attention was turned to their surroundings. 'Oh, that's quite neat – pity they've had to give up the garden but the parking area is nicely done. An electronic entry pad, my word – never see anything like that around Dagworth village.' Her remarks faded as she toiled up three flights to the attic. 'Do you *have* to live up among the pigeons?'

But when Karen unlocked the door and showed her into the flat, she was silenced. 'Oh, this is great! Very dramatic!'

'German minimalist style,' Karen said. 'By the time Mireille has taken away the things she wants, it'll be like living on an ice floe. But I intend to brighten it up a bit.'

'You do?' Evie said doubtfully. 'But won't you spoil the effect?'

'I should hope so. This isn't to my taste, sweets. I need some warmth, some colour.'

Her sister moved around, viewing the big

studio attic from various angles. 'I wish I could do something like this at the farm,' she sighed. 'But of course it would be quite out of keeping with the building.'

'You don't really want to change it? You've put so much work into it!'

'But it's finished, Karen. That's the point. I've done everything that needs to be done to make it a perfect country farmhouse. I feel I want to ... to have some effect on it, to see it evolve somehow ... but what I really need is to go somewhere else and start all over again!'

'Good gracious! You're too young for a mid-life crisis so what's all this, sea fever? Fresh fields and pastures new?'

'I don't know,' mourned Evie. 'It's just when I compare my life with yours, it seems so *boring*!'

That was a conversational avenue down which Karen didn't want to go. 'What you need is a good cup of tea,' she said, 'or perhaps something stronger.'

The buzzer rang for the main door downstairs.

'Who can that be?' Evie said in annoyed surprise.

'I don't know – perhaps it's Mireille.' She was on her way to the kitchenette with the carrier of provisions brought by Evie. 'Answer that, will you, Evie? Press the button on that thing by the door, to speak.'

124

She was putting fresh butter in the fridge when her sister appeared at her elbow. 'I pressed the wrong thing,' she said in embarrassment. 'I think I opened the downstairs door.'

'Never mind, it's probably Mireille.'

She went to the door of her flat and opening it, looked out.

The head and shoulders that emerged rising from the steep staircase belonged to Jeffrey Lynwood, holding aloft a bottle of wine.

'A house-warming present,' he announced.

'But how did you know?' she asked, ushering him in.

'Mireille told me. I have news from Mireille. Oh, hello, I didn't know you had a visitor, perhaps I should have phoned...' He had stopped short at the sight of Evie, the wine bottle falling to his side.

'It's all right, my sister is here for the weekend. Evie, this is Jeffrey Lynwood, my boss.'

'How do you do?' They shook hands, Evie intrigued as she always was by the arrival of a new man on the scene.

'Karen seems very keen on her new job,' she ventured. 'And I must admit, it sounds lovely.'

'So it is, full of French sunshine and good food and wine – she ought to be paying me, not the other way round.'

Evie laughed with a little too much enthusiasm. She was flustered. She hadn't quite understood that Karen's boss was on dropping-in terms with her.

'And speaking of good wine, did Mireille leave you any wine glasses?' He held up the bottle.

'I've no idea. Let's have a look.'

In the kitchenette a cupboard yielded a small collection of glasses of various kinds. 'This is a Corbières,' he said of the wine. 'Do you like red wine?'

The question was addressed to Evie, who said she did. The wine was poured, they sat down round the steel dining table on the minimalist metal and leather chairs left by Mireille. 'You said you had news?' Karen prompted.

'Yes, about Mireille. She's not going to be available to act as companion and teacher when you start out with your clients.'

'What?'

'It's to do with the baby—'

'Oh, don't say something's wrong!'

'No, no, nothing serious – she told me to stress that everything's all right really. But her doctor thinks it would be better if she stayed in London for the last couple of months just so he can keep an eye on her.'

'Oh ... then, of course...'

Evie was listening avidly, trying to catch up with these new people in her sister's life. 'So Karen will have to go off on her own, then?'

she queried. 'Sounds adventurous!'

'Don't say that, Evie! If you had any idea how much I don't know about French negotiation...'

'Have no fear,' he said, smiling at her alarm. 'After all, when you've finished at Maître Kloss, it's still only going to be February. Almost nobody is looking for property in February, sad to say. But it's likely we'll have a couple of customers urgently looking for offices in Paris, so Antoine can go around with you to hold your hand.'

'Who's Antoine?' Evie wanted to know.

'My teacher,' Karen said, without adding that he was a flirtatious type. She was flooded with relief at the thought of having his help.

'So,' Jeffrey said, 'Mireille told me to let you know you should use any of the furniture and equipment that's still here in the flat, because she didn't see herself wanting to bother moving any of it in the near future.'

'She really is all right?'

He shrugged. 'I believe so. But the doc says to take it easy and she's being an obedient little girl.' He glanced around. 'Not that there's much here for her to be bothering about. And it's a bit frosty, isn't it? But perhaps you like it.' Karen was shaking her head ruefully. 'She and Bobby always were very avant garde about art and decor and so forth. This chair is very uncomfortable,' he added, getting up. 'The first thing you should buy is cushions because I think you're stuck with them.'

'I can help you find things for the flat,' Evie volunteered. 'It would be fun.'

'My sister is an expert at interior decoration,' said Karen.

'Professionally?'

'No, no,' she demurred. 'Karen just means I did the interiors at my house in Kent. It's a former farmhouse, owned by apple-growers, needed a lot done to it when my husband and I first moved in. But it's quite attractive now.' She went on to describe some of the alterations she'd supervized and the handiwork she herself had contributed. She was unaware that her audience had ceased to listen after the first few sentences.

When there was a gap in the narration, he said, 'I wanted to thank you, Karen, for being so kind to Roly. He rang me to tell me all about it.'

'Glad he enjoyed it.'

'Enjoy is hardly the word. He's inspired by it. You know, next weekend is one of his visits with me, and he's announced he wants to be taken to St Paul's.'

'The cathedral?' Evie cried, amazed. In her world, little boys didn't ask to be taken to cathedrals.

'Yes, the Whispering Gallery.'

'But Karen told me he was only six?'

'Nevertheless. St Paul's on Saturday morning, as soon as it opens for visitors.'

'Acoustics,' Karen said.

'What?'

'You remember, Evie – Mum and Dad took us, you go up to the top of the dome and the guide is at the other side of the gallery and speaks in a normal tone of voice.'

'I don't remember that—'

'Don't you? Where did Roly find out about it?' she asked, turning to Jeffrey.

'In his computer children's encyclopaedia. I don't think I ever went to St Paul's. What happens in the Whispering Gallery?'

'The guide speaks at one side, and the tourists hear him as clear as day on the other side. It's a trick of the acoustics.'

'Ah!'

'It was to do with the change in the sound of the boat when it went under the bridges,' she explained. 'He asked why it happened and I said I didn't know but it had something to do with acoustics.'

'He's thrilled. It was almost all he could talk about when he rang. Except there was something about charcoal but I didn't follow that. He said it didn't matter, he had a book he could look it up in.'

Karen was laughing. 'All that from an evening's boat trip!'

'It's ... it's such a help,' his father said. 'I

thought when he started school it would be a lot better for him, but he finds it dull...'

'Dull?' Evie exclaimed. 'My two find it almost too demanding – they're always asking to be taken to the library for a book with pictures of Vikings or somebody, or dabbling in ponds for newts, ugh!'

'Well, there you are,' he sighed. 'Different strokes for different folks.' His eye fell on travel bags on the futon in the corner. 'I'd better push off, I think. I can see you haven't had time to unpack or anything.'

'Thanks for the wine,' Karen said, escorting him to the door.

Before going out, he took her hand. 'I really want to thank you,' he said in an earnest tone. 'Roly seems so pleased with life at the moment – it means a lot to me.'

'Glad to be a help,' she said.

When she came back to the table, Evie was pouring a second glass of wine from the bottle Jeffrey had bought. 'This is jolly good,' she observed, and sipped. Then, in a considering tone: 'You know, Karen, I think Michael better come back from Chicago pretty soon, otherwise he'll find your boss Jeffrey has stepped into his shoes.'

'Evie!' Karen was completely astounded.

'I mean it. Anybody could see, your boss likes you a lot.'

Seven

Karen knew better than to argue with her sister. When she got an idea into her head, it was very difficult to shift it. She could have told Evie that Jeffrey was grateful to her for taking an interest in his son, and that there was no more to it than that. But the conversation would have involved explanations about Jeffrey's failed marriage, the arrangements for seeing Roly, and all kinds of things that were none of Evie's business.

They spent an action-packed weekend together in London. Then Karen went back to Gustave Kloss, and at the end of the month, having satisfied Antoine that she knew at least enough to recognize difficulties and refer them to an expert, she was declared 'savante'. Champagne was drunk, laughing congratulations were offered, and she was prepared to show her first clients around Paris in search of suitable offices.

The first episode, which took place over three rainy days, was revealing. Not only did she have to find the premises by contacting estate agents, she had to explain everything twice over to the prospective lessees. Once the choice was made, there was then the problem of bringing the offices up to the standard required by the client. This meant conversations about air conditioning, maintenance contracts, window cleaning, parking spaces. Antoine's good nature never failed, even when she almost allowed the client to sign a contract with two sets of office cleaners at once.

'You did well,' he pronounced. 'Besides, Mr Cranton and his partner were in a bad mood because of the rain.'

The second set of customers were easier, so much so that on the second day of viewing Antoine left Karen to deal with them on her own. And so she made progress, and went on a two-day trip to Strasbourg with a newly-appointed Eurocrat looking for a family home. And after that to Lyon with a husband and wife in search of a small factory where they might make silk scarves.

By the end of March, when the house-buying season was about to begin, she had a fair amount of confidence. She had two or three outings within reach of Paris, where she could appeal to Antoine for help, but they went well. The next one was in Normandy, and was almost a failure because the buyer was so fond of French food that she fell asleep every day after lunch. But by getting her out to look at a property at nine

132

in the morning, and closing the day's activities down at one thirty in the afternoon, she achieved a happy ending.

In between these trips, she was either in Paris or London. She had her own transport, a roomy Peugeot which wasn't too new yet not too old. Experience as a travel agent had taught her that cars were apt to go missing in France if they were too good-looking or too fresh off the production line   especially a foreign production line. By the time you'd reported the theft, the car was on a ferry to North Africa and beyond. Moreover, having the Peugeot with her meant that she usually travelled across the Channel by ferry, which she loved.

On two more occasions she'd taken Roly out, once for an evening jaunt to a children's amusement park, and once for a picnic when she happened to be in Paris on a Saturday. The picnic raised the little boy to giddy heights of joy. He thought her car was 'quaint', being more accustomed to a town vehicle. He fell in love with the little riverside spot near Moret to which she took him. He shivered with delight when an angler let him pull up the storage net of caught fish so as to feel the wet scales.

'Things are so *interesting* when I'm with you,' he told her as he munched a baguette spread with pâté. 'What was the name of that fish with the grey stripes?'

'I'm afraid I don't know. The fisherman's packed up and gone home to lunch so we can't ask.'

'Well, I'll look it up. On Monday morning we have sums, so if I finish them quickly I'll be allowed to read a book. They probably have a fish book.' He paused before adding, 'With pictures.'

'It would be difficult to find your fish if it hasn't got pictures,' she remarked.

'No, I meant, all the books have pictures. Pictures of cars, pictures of flowers, pictures of tables and chairs and everything – as if we wouldn't know what a chair was if we couldn't see a picture.'

'But that's to help the children who have trouble reading, Roly.'

'I know that, but why can't I read my own book? Mademoiselle always makes me choose one of the class books, and they're so *boring*!'

'What's your own book about?' she asked, intrigued.

'It's called *Treasure Island* and it's in English. I found it on a shelf in Daddy's living room. It's got a few pictures – pirates and a sailing ship – not like in the silly tables-and-chairs books.'

Karen hesitated. 'Have you ever told Maman that you find school books boring?'

'Well ... yes ... but she says rules are rules and one of the things I have to learn is to be obedient. And Gabrielle says if I want to read something that isn't on the school bookshelf I ought to read a proper French book, like Tintin. But I read Tintin ages ago.'

'What a problem,' Karen said, laughing despite herself at the housekeeper's slant on things. 'What about joined-up writing? How's that going?'

'Oh, that! Mademoiselle's been going on about that for the last week or two, but I can't see why we have to *keep* doing it.'

'How do you mean? You have to practise at it so that it becomes second nature.'

'But that happens once you see how to do the link-ups.'

'Does it?'

'Of course.' He picked up a second baguette, lifting the crust to see what it contained. 'Oh, salmon – lovely.' He took a bite. 'One thing, though – writing isn't so fast as using the computer keyboard. Still, I'm glad I learned it. Did you know, it's called cursive script? I love that word, cursive...' He munched for a moment, deep in thought. 'I sent Daddy a letter yesterday to tell him I was going on a picnic. I sent him one as soon as I found out how to do his name in proper writing, just to let him see I could do it. It wasn't showing off,' he added, defensively. 'He says written letters are nicer than typed letters.'

Karen listened and wondered. Her nephew

and niece, intelligent enough to hold their own at school, were nowhere near reading *Treasure Island*, unless in a children's version, and as to writing and addressing letters on their own, they were a long way off.

April had arrived, and as it neared its end came the first of Karen's clients who wanted to look at country property. She was extremely scared because Antoine wasn't available for such trips. It looked as if she'd have to go on her own. She was relieved yet astonished when Jeffrey himself turned up at the Hotel Babette.

'Well, there wasn't anybody else,' he explained. 'And it would have been unfair to send you so far from any guidance. You don't mind, do you?'

'Of course not! I'm very grateful.' All the same, she heard some faint echo of her sister's verdict: 'Your boss likes you a lot.'

He told her there was nothing to worry about with the married couple joining them for the tour of the Riviera. 'They've got pots of money. I hear they sold a piece of coastal land in Northumbria for a casino complex. They don't need any advice on legal matters, they've got their own lawyers lined up. We're only needed because they can't speak a word of French.'

All this proved to be true, but what he hadn't known was that this couple were going to prove extremely choosy. They had come into a fortune, so they intended to get what they wanted in every particular. A pool – yes, but a pool of a pre-determined size. Servants' quarters – but not too close to the bedrooms of the owners and guests. A wine cellar – but with modern equipment. And so on.

'We comfort ourselves with the thought that the commission on this job will be enormous,' Jeffrey sighed. So it proved. Late on the eleventh evening, after a splendid dinner in a bijou hotel in Antibes, the Gilletts agreed that they'd been shown the villa of their dreams and so were prepared to pay the asking price of a million euro.

'Success!' cried Karen. 'Can we go back to Paris tomorrow?'

'Well,' was the crisp reply, '*I* can, but they want *you* to stay on to help them furnish the place.'

'Oh no!'

'Oh yes. They've taken a fancy to you.'

'But have they asked if I've taken a fancy to them?' she countered, with a wry smile.

He returned the smile. 'That's what this job's about, Karen. Being patient with people who suddenly start acting like little kids who need their hands held. And speaking of little kids, can I tell Roly you'll be seeing him when next you get to Paris?'

'Of course, but when will that be?' she

wondered. 'How long does it take to furnish a villa that size?'

'No way of knowing.'

In the event, it took only three weeks because the Gilletts had a lordly way of dealing with the problem. Karen took them to department stores. They went from one section to the next, picking out sideboards with a flick of the hand, ordering huge sofas for the drawing room and king-sized beds for the bedrooms, cushions and throws and tables and chairs...

'But that won't match the carpet,' she protested when they decided on a dark blue fabric for the dining-room curtains.

'Oh, if we don't like it we can change it later,' said Mrs Gillett, and that, Karen found, was the key. Let them do what they wanted, just interpret their wishes to the sales staff.

To her surprise, Mrs Gillett embraced her on parting and gave her a set of expensive sun creams. 'You must look after your skin, dear,' she warned, 'driving about all over the place in all weathers.'

'But really, Mrs Gillett, I can't accept—'

'Nonsense, you've been *such* a darling!'

Karen found she'd rediscovered something she already knew. No matter how difficult, the client could have something endearing about her.

She drove back to Paris feeling cheerful.

She would have to go back to London to hear the details of her next assignment and to change wardrobe. Soon the temperatures in France would be considerably higher so she must pack summer clothes. She stayed overnight at the Hotel Babette because she had some shopping to do. Moreover, she'd promised to spend some time with Roly.

Next day she carried out some commissions from her sister in the artists' quarter – special water-colours for aquarelles, extra-fine canvas, a special device for making a scalloped edge on cloth. All these were needed for some new hobby that Evie was about to take up. Then, of course, there were the essential presents for the children – familiar candies but in French wrapping and with French names, a cuddly toy for Noomie. While she was about it, she bought a children's version of *The Three Musketeers* for Roly.

By the time she presented herself at Roly's home, he was waiting for her with impatience in the hall of the apartment block. 'Gabrielle said I was giving her nervous indigestion with my fidgeting,' he announced, 'so I asked to come down. It's *such* a long time since you were here.'

'Only a month, Roly.'

'But you know, time is elastic.' He was ready for conversation, bubbling with things he wanted to say. 'I was reading about time in my encyclopaedia last week. Do you know that if some men went on a space ship to a star a long way away, they'd be younger than the people they left behind on earth when they got back!'

'I beg your pardon?' she said. 'That's too much to take in after a hard day.'

'Well, it may not be true,' he replied, pursing his lips. 'I mean to say, how could anybody've proved it? Nobody's gone as far as that in space, now have they?'

'Only in Star Trek films.'

He grinned. 'Norah took me to see one, you know. It was very interesting, but I didn't understand how everybody from other planets spoke French.'

'They spoke French?' Karen cried, pretending to be scandalized. 'Mr Spock speaks only Vulcan!'

The little boy laughed, knowing he was being teased. 'It was made in English – or American, I suppose – but they put French voices in. I think it's called dubbing. Isn't that a funny word?'

During this conversation they'd been going through the business of getting into her car and strapping themselves in. 'Where are we going this evening?' the little boy inquired.

'I thought you'd like to see the fishermen on the banks of the Seine, and then there's a shop in Rue François that's got a special exhibition of toys from the last hundred years. I passed it this afternoon – what do you think?'

'Do fishermen catch anything in the Seine?'

'Let's find out.'

The allotted two hours passed quickly. At an early point Roly announced he was hungry because he'd been too excited to eat supper.

'Well,' murmured Karen, 'we could buy something from one of the stalls, but what would Gabrielle—'

'It'll be all right. I'll explain to her when I get home.'

'Are you sure?'

'Yes, yes, come on.' He was pulling her towards a refreshment stand from which came delicious smells of apple charlotte and caramel waffles.

The goods on offer looked harmless. She bought him an orange juice and two waffles spread with fruit confit. They hurried on to the toy exhibition, from which he had to be dragged almost by force. She was thinking that if only he could pay a visit to Evie's children, he would see toys like that, handed on from her own and Evie's childhood and from their parents.

At the main door of the apartment block she suddenly remembered that she hadn't given him his book. 'Wait a minute, Roly, I bought you something this morning. It's in

141

the back.' She leaned into her car to press the button that would open the back window at the tailgate. Reaching in, she rummaged to find the plastic bag from the bookshop.

He clutched it to his chest when she gave it to him, and in the lift he ferreted around to get the book out. *'The Three Musketeers*! Oh, how fantastic'lly ultra-cosmic! I can take it to school and Mademoiselle won't get cross at me reading it 'cos it's in French, of course. *Thank* you, Karen.' He flung himself upon her in gratitude, hugging her round the waist.

'Next time I'll try to get Mr Spock in French,' she laughed.

Gabrielle opened the door to them. Roly rushed forward, brandishing the book. 'Look, look what Karen bought me! May I read in bed, Gabrielle, may I?'

'No you may not,' she rejoined in a grumpy tone and giving him a push towards the stairs. 'It's past your bedtime. Now go straight upstairs and get into the shower. And not another word out of you tonight!'

The little boy flinched at her vehemence, and scurried away with his head down.

'Oh, madame,' said Karen, unwisely, 'please don't be annoyed with him. It's my fault we're a little late – we tried to do too much.'

'Ah, you don't take it seriously, mademoiselle,' admonished the housekeeper, turning to her and spoiling for a fight. 'But he comes home from these outings over-excited, and then he doesn't sleep well, and in the morning he wakes up feeling poorly and doesn't want to go to school – not that he ever does anyway – so all you do is make my life more difficult. I ask myself why Madame permits it, and the truth is that she gives in to the wishes of Monsieur Lynwood in this, and it's quite wrong!'

This tirade took Karen so much aback that she couldn't think of anything to say. After a moment the other woman seemed to realize she'd gone a little too far. 'I am concerned for him,' she said in tones that didn't sound like concern. 'He is a difficult child and, forgive me for saying so, but you make him more difficult.'

'He's not difficult,' Karen objected. 'He's a perfectly normal little boy.'

'Oh, and you are an expert, perhaps? More so than the teachers at the nursery class he went to, or at his present school?'

'No, of course I'm not, but I never find any problem—'

'And that's because you spoil him! It's as simple as that. Well, I have told Madame what I think, and we shall see what she says tomorrow when I report that he was late home yet again. Good evening, mademoiselle.'

She closed the door. Karen stood staring at

the fine mahogany panels and felt a great desire to kick it. But in the end she turned back to the lift and went down to the hall. What an old fogey, she was muttering to herself. How Hélène Dartieux can let that martinet have charge of her son I'll never understand!

As she manoeuvred out of the small circular drive and into the traffic, she was still muttering to herself. But the journey to Calais required her full attention. Once on the ferry, she made herself relax. The extended trip to the Riviera had been a tiring time. She found herself thinking fondly of her own folk, her parents and their patient tending of plants, Evie and her domestic worries, Walt and his gruff kindliness, the children and their uncomplicated demands.

But before she spent time with her family she must get to London, do the chores at the flat, report at the office, go to see Mireille's new baby...

She had a meal, found a comfortable chair. She allowed herself a little snooze. Then the ship began to come alive, letting her know that they were on the approach to the port. She went down to retrieve the Peugeot, in readiness for the drive-off.

She was in the driving seat awaiting the bumps and clangs that meant the gangway was down when a sleepy little voice came from the rear.

'Is this Dover?' it inquired.

She turned, startled beyond words.

Peering at her from among the parcels and the travel rug on the back seat was Roly Dartieux.

Eight

Her first impulse was to squirm round in her seat, to make sure it wasn't a dream. Her next was to cross-question the boy. Luckily good sense prevailed. If she didn't pay attention to disembarking she might cause an enormous snarl-up.

She made her way decorously in line to the exit, drove at the required speed on to the quay, and then on through the various barriers until she was out on the public highway. Luckily no customs official wanted to check her car. She drove a few hundred yards to the nearest lay-by.

There she drew up. The little boy had dropped down among the parcels again and was fast asleep.

It was after midnight. What should she do? What was the best thing to do?

She had to inform someone that Roly was with her. By rights she should ring his home in Paris, but the idea appalled her. They might be searching the building for a missing child, they might have called the police. Either way, it was a situation she was too

146

cowardly to face.

So she rang Jeffrey. London was nearer, she was going there anyway, she could deposit the boy with his father. Besides, she was almost sure Jeffrey would still be up and about.

She was right. He answered almost on the first ring. 'Lynwood here.'

'Jeffrey, it's Karen.'

'Who – oh, Karen, OK?' Something in her voice alerted him. 'Anything wrong?'

'Jeffrey, I've got Roly with me.'

A little pause. 'At this hour of night?'

'Worse than that. *I've just landed at Dover.*'

'Excuse me?'

'I'm in Dover. I came over on the car ferry. Just as we were docking, I discovered Roly hidden in the back of the car.'

'Hidden? Just a minute. Roly is in Dover with you?'

'Yes.'

'Did you get – no, of course not. You didn't get permission from Hélène to bring him.'

'No. I didn't know he was there until he piped up from behind me.'

'And of course he's still there now.' This was a bewildered man, trying to catch up with events.

'Yes. He woke for half a minute while we were landing but he's gone fast asleep again.'

There was a long silence and then Jeffrey said on an outgoing breath, 'Dear Lord.'

And then, 'Did you ring Paris?'

'Ah ... no ... I chickened out.'

A little sound, perhaps a groan, perhaps a laugh. 'I don't blame you.'

'But someone has got to let them know ... they may be searching the parks and all sorts of places.'

'I'll do it, of course. What will you do now?'

'I was coming to London. Shall I carry on and bring him to you?'

Another pause. 'Yes, I think that's best. He's used to his room here. If we're lucky he'll stay asleep and go through until the morning.'

'I'm terribly sorry about this, Jeffrey. I can't think how it happened.'

'You didn't know he was there?'

'Not a clue. I took him out for an evening jaunt and delivered him back at the apartment about a quarter past eight. Gabrielle was in a bad mood and there was a bit of a scene because we were a few minutes late. Roly was sent up to bed in disgrace.'

'That old harpy!'

'So I just said goodnight and drove off.' She thought for a moment. 'While Gabrielle and I were having a bit of a brawl, Roly must have slipped out somehow. Is there a back way?'

'Oh, of course, through the basement garage.'

'So he must have slipped out there, but

how did he get in my...? Oh, wait! I opened the tailgate window to get his book.'

'He got in through a window?'

'It would be easy, he's so small he could have wriggled in and snuggled down among the shopping. You see, when we got home, I opened the back window, got the book, and then hurried upstairs with him because we were late. I only pushed the button to close it as I was driving away.'

'Well, that's how. But *why*?'

Karen made no reply. She was fairly sure it was because Roly was afraid of confessing to the housekeeper that he'd had 'junk food' during his outing. Gabrielle was in such a bad mood already that facing her with this news was more than he could endure.

'Well, we'd better get this show on the road,' his father was saying. 'You carry on to London and meanwhile I'll ring Hélène.'

'OK. See you later.'

She drove on through the drizzly night. Not a sound from the back seat. Traffic was very light, even the M25 was easy. She was in Highgate before she found any problems, because once there she wasn't exactly sure of how to get to Jeffrey's flat. She opened her A–Z and by pausing every now and then to consult it, she eventually drew up at the mansion block. She rang his number on her cellphone to let him know she'd arrived. He came hurrying out from the ornate white

149

stone entrance to greet her.

She pressed the button to open the car doors. He reached in the back, and she could hear a sort of rummaging sound as he unwound the blanket from around his sleeping son. She could hear packages falling to the floor. Melted candy bars, she thought to herself wryly, because it seemed Roly had been sleeping on them.

'If you'd like to drive a few yards down,' he said, 'you'll see an alley that leads to the parking area. I've made some coffee and stuff. My flat is No. 9, on the ground floor to the right of the entrance.'

She nodded and drove on to park. As she got out she found she was a little shaky. Partly it was the after-shock of finding the child in her car, partly it was simple fatigue.

She found the door of the flat ajar. She went in, hearing kitchen sounds – clink of crockery, fridge door opening. She followed them to where Jeffrey Lynwood was taking cling film off a platter of sandwiches. He was clad in a rugby shirt and looked very much as he had the first time they met: beset with anxiety, his lips in a thin tight line.

'Is Roly OK?' she inquired.

'Never stirred. I put him to bed without undressing him properly – just shoes and jeans.'

'You've rung his mother?'

He drew in a long breath and let it out.

'Yes.'

'And?'

'How do you like your coffee? Or would you prefer tea?' He gestured towards chairs at the kitchen table, and she sat.

'Coffee's fine. Lots of milk, please.'

He poured from a cafetière, pushed a jug of milk towards her. She added enough milk to cool the drink and swallowed several large gulps to do away with the dryness of her mouth.

'Are you going to tell me what she said?' she asked.

He put the cafetière down with a thump, pulled out a chair as if to sit down opposite, but instead went to the kitchen window to pull down the blind. He stood staring at the surface of the blind. Then he said, 'She was in bed and asleep. I had to wake her up.'

'*What?*'

'They didn't even know he was missing. Hélène said I was talking nonsense. She thought I was drunk.'

'Jeffrey...'

'I had to wait until she went along to his room to verify what I was saying.'

'He hadn't been missed?'

He said nothing, but his shoulders rose and fell.

'But ... but ... how can that be? Doesn't anyone check last thing, to make sure he's OK?'

'Apparently not. Hélène said she and Louis got in very late and very tired from some political shindig. They went straight to bed.'

'But Gabrielle? Surely she looks in on Roly before she goes to bed?'

'I'd have thought so, but in fact I've no idea.'

At last he turned so that she could see his face. It was grim. He poured a cup of black coffee, then sat down opposite at the table.

After a moment she said, 'Perhaps she *usually* looks in on him. But tonight she was cross. I was a little late bringing him home so she ordered him upstairs. I think she said he was to get to bed at once and there wasn't to be another word out of him, or something to that effect.'

'Which could have meant she wasn't even going to look in to say goodnight.'

'I suppose so.'

'If I had my way I'd throw her out tomorrow,' he said in a very calm tone. 'She's one of the worst aspects of the poor kid's life.'

She nodded agreement, but asked, 'So what's happening next?'

'Hélène and Louis are coming over by an early flight. She's in a rage.'

'Louis is coming too?' She was surprised. She'd had the impression that Louis was too closely involved in high-stakes finance to

152

want to make unscheduled journeys.

'I think that's a measure of how angry Hélène is. I think there are going to be threats about lawyers and things like that – and Louis has some high-powered friends among the lawyers.'

'But how does the law come into it?'

'Well, you see ... She's threatening to cut off my rights to visit.'

'No!'

'I told you, she's furious.'

Because she's been caught out as an inattentive mother, thought Karen, but didn't say so.

'I'm terribly sorry,' she ventured. 'I can't see that it's my fault, exactly, but I shouldn't have left that window open in my car.'

'Don't talk nonsense! How could you possibly have guessed he would...' He broke off, thinking it over. 'It shows how desperate he felt,' he went on, looking for explanations. 'Roly isn't the kind of little boy who wants to dash off and have adventures. He's the last kid in the world to want to run away. At least, that's what I'd have said until tonight. But something's pushed him to this.'

Karen thought about it for a minute before allowing herself to say it. 'It was Gabrielle,' she pronounced. 'She was really harsh with him because we were fifteen minutes late. And then there was the business of the waffles.'

153

'The waffles?'

'While we were out, Roly was hungry because he hadn't eaten his supper. So I bought him some waffles at one of the stalls near the embankment.'

'I'm not following you.'

'I said he could have them if he promised to tell Gabrielle when he got home. There's an embargo on eating junk food. But she was so cross already that I think he couldn't face telling her about them.'

'Are you telling me,' he said, 'that my son ran away from his home over some *gaufres*?'

'It might have been that.'

He gave a bark of angry laughter.

'I know it sounds silly but Gabrielle is very important in Roly's world,' Karen went on. 'As far as I can tell, she's the person he sees most of, the one who drives him to school in the morning and brings him back in the afternoon. She chooses what he eats, she sees to his clothes, I'm pretty sure she's the one who insists on that extraordinary tidiness in his room. There used to be someone else between them, I suppose – Norah and her predecessors, au pairs, that kind of person – but now Gabrielle is in sole charge and ... forgive me for saying so ... but I don't think anyone is checking on her.'

He was nodding reluctant agreement. 'She can't help being the way she is. She's old – or at least, elderly...' He broke off. 'I'm making excuses for her!'

'She's *cold*, Jeffrey – cold and disapproving. On every occasion I've come across her, she's been telling Roly he's in the wrong.'

'But even so, so what?' he countered, struggling to sort it out. 'She's just a servant, after all – he needn't be so scared of her that he'd run away.'

'Scared? I think scared is the wrong word. I think he's just ... fed up with her. Had enough. Can't bear it any more. This was his way of saying, I'm tired of always being reprimanded, found fault with...'

'But he's never said a word about it to me,' Jeffrey said, and it was a lament.

'Perhaps because he has good times with you, and he didn't want to spoil that.' Karen was trying to put herself in the child's place. 'Perhaps he'd just have put up with it tonight,' she suggested, 'except that I happened to be there, and it was an escape route – so he took it.' She fell silent. She'd felt her version of events made some kind of sense but now it was said, she felt less certain.

'Well,' Jeffrey said, musing, 'it was a safe escape route. He was going with someone he liked and could count on. I think I already said that he's not really a foolhardy type.'

'Not a case of "goodbye, cruel world, I'm off to join the circus" – or going as a stow-away on a windjammer.'

155

He summoned a smile. 'One thing I've learned about my son,' he rejoined. 'His adventures are all in his head. He likes to read *Treasure Island* but would never dream of following the example of Jim Hawkins.' He pushed the plate of sandwiches towards her. 'Eat. You must be starving.'

'Thank you.' She took a sandwich, a man's sandwich lavish with chutney and the bread cut thick. 'To tell the truth, my main need is sleep.'

'Of course! What an idiot I am, keeping you here talking like this – as if it was your problem, anyhow! Look, you mustn't drive any further tonight. There's a spare room, why don't you—'

'No, no,' she said hastily. 'I need to get home for clothes and so forth.' She was thinking that if Mrs Dartieux arrived by an early plane and found her eating breakfast in Jeffrey's flat, it would only make matters worse.

'Let me call a cab for you, at least,' he said. 'You look all in.'

'OK, that would be fine.'

While he telephoned, she laid down the sandwich and tiptoed to the door with a big cut-out of Luke Skywalker pasted on it. The door was ajar. She went in. Roly was fast asleep with one bare foot sticking out from under the covers. She tucked him in, dropped a kiss on his silky hair then tiptoed out again. She went back to finish her sandwich and await transport.

At home she found mail in her letterbox and messages on her answering machine. She paid no heed, undressed, brushed her teeth, set her radio alarm for nine, and fell into bed. When the radio woke her with the sound of Stevie Wonder, she dragged herself upright and staggered to the shower to wake herself up. About an hour later she'd drunk enough coffee to have the energy for the telephone messages, mostly from her parents and Evie.

She was sitting down to deal with the letters when her mobile phone chirped. A small scared voice greeted her.

'Roly!' she gasped.

'Karen, could you come to Daddy's flat? There's a terrible quarrel here.'

'But sweetheart, I can't interfere—'

'Maman's dreffully angry and she's saying she won't let me come to stay with Daddy any more.' His voice was full of unshed tears.

'No, no, she can't do that...'

'She says she'll tell the judge he's deceitful and bad, and Daddy's angry, and Papa Louis is saying he thinks a good boarding school's the answer and Karen, I don't want to go to boarding school, 'cos ordinary school is bad enough.'

'Roly, grown-ups say things like that when they're angry...'

'But they won't listen to me when I say I did it all myself. They're saying Daddy asked you to do it.'

Karen made an effort to get a hold on the conversation. 'Where are you at this moment, dear?'

'In Daddy's study. Papa Louis put me here because he said I was a nuisance, always int'rupting. Please come, Karen.'

'I can't just barge in, Roly.'

'Barge in? Does that mean, be a nuisance? I could tell them you're coming, so they'd be expecting you.'

'You mean you'd go back into the living room when they've ordered you out?'

'I could call Daddy on his cellphone, like I'm calling you.'

Despite the seriousness of the situation, Karen almost laughed. 'No, no, Roly, I'll call him,' she said, and once she'd said it, knew she was committed. She broke the connection and pressed buttons for Jeffrey's phone.

Jeffrey picked up and barked, 'What?'

'It's Karen—'

'Bad timing, Karen. I'll ring you later.'

'Wait! I'm coming to the flat.'

'Not now. If it's for your car, come later.'

'It's not my car, it's Roly. He just called me.'

'Called you?'

'From your study. He's desperate to have someone take his side.'

'Take his side?' Jeffrey said, still trapped in astonishment. 'Good Lord, what do you think *I'm* doing?'

'Well, maybe you need an ally. I'll be there in half an hour.' She switched off before he had time to say no.

She threw the mail on the kitchen table and took off. Mid-morning, the Tube was nearly empty, so she reached Highgate Station in quick time. She almost ran the short distance to Harkway Mansions. She took a moment to make sure she was breathing evenly before she rang the bell of the flat. The door was opened almost immediately.

'Well,' Jeffrey said, with an expression that was half a smile and half a glower. 'I don't know what good you think *you're* going to do.'

'At least I'll be able to say a few words and give you a chance to regain your temper,' she said.

He was about to say there was nothing wrong with his temper, checked himself, and sighed aloud. 'OK,' he said. 'Roly's called you in – let's see what happens.'

She followed him into the living room, unseen last night. It was a pleasant room, with comfortable armchairs, and tables piled with newspapers and books. Louis Dartieux rose at her entrance. His wife was gazing out of the window at the dusty shrubs in the narrow front garden, and only half-turned as

Karen came in.

What struck Karen was that this supposedly distraught mother was beautifully turned out: casual clothes but a careful choice of accessories, make-up on the lashes and lips, a faint fragrance of Ma Griffe.

'You already know Miss Montgomery,' Jeffrey said.

'*Tant pis.*' This was a murmur from Hélène.

'I'm sorry you feel like that,' Karen said. 'I never meant to make things more difficult in your household.'

'Nevertheless you have. Every time you've taken Roly out, he's been unsettled and difficult. I know very well you've been filling his head with ideas about how much nicer it would be if he lived with his father.'

'Excuse me, I've done nothing of the kind,' Karen said, utterly taken aback. 'The only time Jeffrey's been mentioned was when Roly told me he'd got a copy of *Treasure Island*—'

'Oh, yes, very suitable for a six-year-old, full of ideas about leaving home.'

'Let's not waste time discussing Robert Louis Stevenson,' Karen said. 'I'm here because Roly rang me to say you wouldn't listen to him.'

'Would you please not call my son by that ridiculous name? His name is Roland.'

'Very well. A child by any other name is just as upset. Roland wants you to understand that the idea of running away was his alone.'

'I find that difficult to believe, mademoiselle,' Louis intervened. Louis was rather grand too – slacks with knife-edge creases, glossy brogues, Breton sweater. His black eyes were snapping with intelligent appraisal. 'He has always been a difficult child, of course, but he has everything he could wish for: a room to himself, a computer, plenty of pocket money, as many toys and books as he wishes to buy, every care and comfort—'

'And no friends.'

'But whose fault is that, mademoiselle? He goes to a good school, one highly recommended to us and God knows it costs the earth. But he refuses to take part in the activities, he withdraws from the other children.'

'Because he doesn't share their interests. He doesn't want to waste his time reading books with pictures. If you'd just understand—'

'I understand that you've been encouraging him to be disobedient and ungrateful,' Hélène said. 'I can't demand your dismissal but I want it firmly understood you never come anywhere near our home again!'

'Very well. If that's your verdict, of course I have to accept it. But I think you're being very unkind.'

'Unkind?' cried Hélène, her voice high

161

with anger. 'How dare you! You know nothing about our problems, about the discussions we've had with teachers and advisers—'

'I know that Roland is a very lonely little boy. No one seems to spend time with him or—'

'Don't be absurd! Gabrielle is with him almost all the time except when he's at school.'

'Gabrielle is part of the problem.'

'Excuse me, mademoiselle, but Gabrielle has been in the employ of my family since I was a boy. I have a high regard for her,' Louis said indignantly.

'She was your nurse?'

'My nurse?' It gave him pause. 'No, she was one of the parlour maids.'

'But she spent time with you, went out for walks with you?'

Louis frowned. 'But no. I explained she was a *femme de chambre*. And has since grown in ability so that she now manages our household.'

'Then she has no special training in handling children.'

'Good heavens, a boy of six needs no specific handling! He is in process of becoming a man!' he cried.

'So Gabrielle is in charge of him. Who tucks him in at night?'

'*Pardon?*'

162

'Qui le borde dans son lit?' Even as she said it, she was dubious if she'd got it right. It sounded as if she was talking about bed-making. 'Who kisses him goodnight?' she amended.

There was a silence.

Jeffrey had had enough respite to be able to take up the matter. He said, very clipped, 'When I rang you early this morning, you didn't even know he was missing.'

Hélène went red. Louis looked at the ceiling, cleared his throat, then said, 'It appears there was some contention last night so to punish him Gabrielle sent him straight to bed.'

'And didn't look in to see if he was all right before closing up the house after you came in?'

'She was annoyed with him. Generally she assures herself that all is well.'

Karen's mouth turned down in a manner that said she thought little of that. 'So his well-being is left to an elderly maid who dislikes him.'

'Gabrielle doesn't dislike Roland,' Hélène interrupted, coming to stand next to her husband. 'That's an absurd thing to say.'

'If Roland would be more obedient and responsive, there would be no problem,' Louis agreed.

'Monsieur Dartieux, it's very difficult to be responsive to someone who is always disapproving.'

'You say Gabrielle is disapproving, mademoiselle?'

'Have you ever heard her praise Roland?'

Louis pursed his lips and tilted his head – a gesture that seemed to say he'd heard something that deserved thought. Hélène looked at her husband in some confusion. She looked for a chair and sat down. Once again there was a pause.

'Look,' Jeffrey said. 'The kid took off because the housekeeper was giving him a hard time. I'm told he had something to confess about eating food from a street stall while he was out with Karen—'

'But he knows very well that American fast food is forbidden!'

'It was French fast food, Madame Dartieux, waffles and fruit preserve. But he'd promised he'd tell Gabrielle about it and I think he just couldn't face it. So he decided to leave home instead.'

'*Dieu me bénit*,' murmured Louis, quite struck by the thought. 'Could that really be the reason?'

'Oh, I don't believe it for a moment, darling,' Hélène cried. 'That's just a way of shifting blame from herself—'

'Hélène, if we're talking about blame...'

'Now you're going to say it's my fault! That's always your way of explaining things, Jeffrey! You make it all the harder to handle

164

Roland and this is the last straw. I'm going to ask the courts to give me sole custody because all you do is make him uncontrollable.'

'Don't make silly threats, Hélène. You can't justify any of your complaints.'

'Oh yes I can, and this latest escapade just shows how right I've been all along. I'm going to see to it that you don't have any more chances to make life difficult.'

Jeffrey ran a hand through his unruly hair, and for a moment Karen thought he was going to launch a verbal onslaught against Hélène. But he checked himself, drew a deep breath, then very calmly said, 'Well, do what you feel you must. But it might not do Louis's career much good.'

'My career?' Louis said.

'Well, yes. When this "tug-of-love" case gets into the papers, it might be quite harmful.'

'Tug-of-love?'

'That's what newspapers call these affairs, where parents in two different countries are trying to get legal rights over a child.'

'I've never heard the term,' Louis said. 'And the French papers don't give much attention to such things.'

'Not the papers you read, perhaps,' Jeffrey said. 'But the British tabloids love that sort of thing.'

'It is quite unlikely they would ever hear

of it.'

'You think so?' Jeffrey asked, in a tone that made it plain he would see to that himself.

Louis gave him a long stare. Jeffrey permitted himself a faint smile.

'Oh, so that's the kind of thing you'd do!' Hélène cried. 'You really have no scruples!'

'My love,' Louis said to his wife, 'I think perhaps it is time for a little reflection on this matter.'

She turned her anger on him. 'Don't descend to his level! I'm not going to let him blackmail us.'

'That's a very unkind word, Hélène,' Jeffrey said. 'All I've said is that if you go to court to get complete possession of our son, I'd fight it.'

'But you implied...'

'We have to look at this rationally,' Louis intervened. *'C'est pas grand'chose.* The boy ran away. Miss Montgomery says she took no voluntary part in it and I'm inclined to believe—'

'Louis, you can't really think she drove from Paris, on to a ferry, and off at Dover before she knew Roland was in the back!'

'I think it's perfectly possible.'

'I don't believe a word of it! I think *he* put her up to it and *she* did it because he's paying her.'

'Then why did he telephone us immediately he was told the child was in England?'

166

Hélène was checked. She started to say something, stopped, then at last came out with: 'Well, he had to do something because he knows we'd have called the police.'

Louis looked at Jeffrey. 'We would, of course, have called the police. However, you spared us that necessity and I am inclined to accept your explanation of how the boy got here. Have you now some proposition to put, monsieur? Based on the present circumstance?'

Karen saw Jeffrey force himself to show no sign of triumph. 'Only that we should go back to the status quo, Louis.'

'Oh, you're talking like a couple of politicians discussing a peace treaty! A serious crime has been committed.'

'No crime has been committed, *chérie*,' her husband said. 'Look at it without emotion. The boy, for some reason, was unhappy. He hid in mademoiselle's car. I'm prepared to take the word of mademoiselle that she knew nothing of it until she was about to land at Dover. We must admit that Jeffrey got in touch immediately he was aware of the escapade.' He paused. 'If anyone is to blame, it is Roland.'

Karen burst into speech. 'Right! Can we talk about Roland for a minute instead of going on like a judicial inquiry? Roland is a very unhappy little boy who—'

'Not at all, mademoiselle,' Louis declared.

167

'We must not allow our judgement to be clouded. One little prank does not mean a very unhappy child.'

'How often do you see him?' she challenged.

'Almost every day, of course. At breakfast.'

'For how long?'

'Well, I...' He paused. He was irked by her questions. After all, he was who he was, and she was nothing but an employee of the ex-husband. 'I hardly think that is your business, mademoiselle.'

'Ten minutes? Fifteen?'

'Really, your manners are deplorable!' Hélène intervened. 'How dare you imply—'

'I'm not implying anything. I'm trying to find out how much attention you give him.' She gazed at Louis. 'You listed all the benefits he enjoyed but they were all about possessions.'

'Ah! I begin to understand your position. You think Roland has been neglected. I assure you, you are wrong. I grew up in a household much like ours, and I never once thought of running away from home. It's only that poor little Roland has these character defects – these difficulties.'

'Which you,' Hélène broke in, 'think you understand better than his own mother! You're nothing but an interfering outsider.'

'*Mon amour, mon amour,*' soothed Louis, 'let us not use harsh words. On the contrary,

168

we should be grateful to mademoiselle—'

'Grateful!'

'Grateful for her concern. We know she is wrong in her views, nevertheless we appreciate her interest.'

Hélène's blue eyes flashed icy fire. She shook her head, jumped from her chair, and walked to look out of the window with her back to them.

Louis was fully involved now in his role of diplomat. He decided to pay no attention to his wife's gesture of disagreement. He said to Karen, 'Understandably, Hélène is indignant. For myself, I believe I understand what has been happening here. You've grown fond of Roland, so much so that you misinterpret our rapport with him. But I do assure you, we have his best interests at heart—'

'That's not the way I see it...'

Jeffrey was shaking his head at her. She faltered and fell silent.

'OK, Louis,' said Jeffrey. 'You agree that Karen wasn't abducting Roly and that it was all the kid's idea. Now that's settled, can we go on to look at the future? I don't want any more threats about cutting off my access to him. Can we take that as read?'

Louis went to Hélène, put an arm about her, and spoke gently into her ear. She shook her head, but after some moments relaxed into the comfort of his embrace. He turned her to face the room. She drew a deep

169

breath.

'All right,' she said to Jeffrey.

'Thank you,' Jeffrey said in what seemed like genuine gratitude.

'But Miss Montgomery doesn't bother us any more,' Hélène said mutinously.

'Now, Hélène! All Karen did was take the kid out now and again.'

'But I don't understand why she's interfering in the first place.'

'Because Roly asked her to.'

'No, he didn't!'

'He did, Hélène. When I asked him what he wanted for Christmas he said he'd like to see Karen again.'

Dumbfounded, Roland's mother stared from Jeffrey to Karen. At last she breathed, 'But why?'

'He likes her.'

'But ... but...'

'You and Louis have just been declaring that Roly doesn't get on with people. Well, he gets on with Karen.'

A silence developed during which Karen felt herself going red with embarrassment. She was all at once aware that she'd rushed out in jeans and an old jersey, and that she'd done nothing to her face or her hair. She knew Hélène was trying to understand why her son should have any affection for this vulgarian.

It was Louis the diplomat who ended the

170

standstill. 'I believe we've reached agreement. The boy was overtaken by some strange impulse but that's behind us. We go on as before, no?'

'Just a minute,' said Karen.

'Oh, here we go again,' protested Hélène.

'OK, I'm interfering, say it if you want to! But Roly telephoned and asked me to come, and I'm here to fight his corner.' She felt she had some slight moral advantage at this point in the argument, and it was always her way to take advantage of any silver lining that might glint at her. 'I want to talk about Gabrielle. She makes life hard for Roly. I want her told to be more sympathetic, and if she can't be sympathetic, to hold her tongue.'

This time Louis didn't spring to the housekeeper's defence. He pursed his lips and thought about it. His wife waited for him to speak out of respect for his long relationship with Gabrielle.

'My love,' he mused, 'perhaps she is rather set in her ways to be in charge of a six-year-old.'

Hélène said nothing.

'We can't replace Gabrielle,' Louis said, appealing to Karen's commonsense. 'She is essential to the running of our household. You do accept that?'

She nodded, though with reluctance.

'However, there may be merit in what you

say. I do perhaps see her outlook is ... shall we say, old-fashioned? I'll speak to her.'

'She's got to stop making Roly feel in the wrong all the time,' Karen insisted.

He sighed. 'I can't agree with your view of my old friend and servant. But I see that you genuinely believe in it, and so I will give instructions and – be assured – Gabrielle will listen.'

'Thank you, Monsieur Dartieux.'

He gave her a little bow then made a little gesture towards the clock on the mantelpiece. 'My love,' he said to Hélène, 'we shall have wasted an entire day on this *sottise*. May we now regard it as settled?'

'But Louis?'

'The de la Framesses are coming to dinner this evening, *tu t'en souviens*? We must get back, or else telephone now to put them off.'

'But I feel we haven't—'

'My angel, surely you are emotionally exhausted? We should take Roland home and forget this whole affair.'

'I'm sure you're both tired,' Jeffrey said, waking up to his duties as a host. 'Let me give you lunch.'

'No, thank you, Jeffrey. We'll eat on the plane.'

'Excuse me,' Karen said. 'Roly doesn't like flying.'

Louis threw up his hands and said, 'Ha!' in exasperation. Hélène gave a bitter smile.

'Well, he doesn't,' Karen insisted. 'And it's just as quick by Eurostar.'

'Very well. Then his mother and I will take Roland home by Eurostar and we will have lunch in the restaurant car. Any other requirements, mademoiselle?' But now his good humour had returned, and he was laughing. He was a man used to negotiation, used to winning some points and losing some. His main interest here was to smooth things over and, above all, have no antagonism from Jeffrey.

Roly was brought from his banishment in the study by his father. He came looking unexpectedly calm. He gave Karen a little smile, almost of complicity, and she all at once understood he'd been listening at the keyhole.

Little rascal! But she could only sympathize. He'd felt his whole life was in danger, so how could he resist the temptation to eavesdrop?

The Dartieux family were now eager to be gone. Jeffrey summoned a taxi, they piled in, and they were off. Karen watched from the window while Jeffrey waved goodbye to Roly.

He came back into the room, swept her up in a tremendous hug.

'You were marvellous!' he cried.

Nine

She was glad to leave London for her sister's home. She was tired, almost exhausted. The scene at Jeffrey Lynwood's flat had been no fun for her even though Jeffrey had been in high spirits when she left.

'A famous victory!' he'd rejoiced.

She couldn't join in his celebration. True, Hélène and Louis Dartieux had agreed to go back to the former situation, and she could only hope that they would live up to that agreement. But how had she got herself involved in this fracas? What did she think she was doing?

Well, she was trying to help Roly. Something about the child called to her – he had claimed her as a friend and she'd responded. She didn't regret her part in the contention that followed: she was of course glad they'd won.

But she didn't want to be hugged by his father. She didn't want to be more than an employee to Jeffrey Lynwood. She liked him, he had her sympathy in the dilemma in which he found himself where his ex-wife was concerned. But she was still too hurt and confused by Michael's desertion to have any confidence in affectionate embraces.

Evie had said, 'Your boss likes you a lot.' And he did. And he had good reason to. She was the rescuer of his little boy, the champion who'd stood up to the she-tiger. Her intervention this morning had given him a chance to cool down, to think of some weapon that he himself could use.

Blackmail, there was no other word for it. He'd used blackmail to get the better of Louis. But she didn't blame him for that because Hélène was being quite unreasonable. Unkind, unloving to her son.

Yet now Hélène, never more than cool towards Karen, would be downright hostile. If Karen were to keep contact with Roly she would have to negotiate each visit, or perhaps ensure she went to the apartment when Hélène was out or away. It would make each contact with the child more difficult but she couldn't withdraw from them. She'd had a demonstration that morning – he needed her, because it seemed that his own mother simply didn't understand him.

Gabrielle too. The housekeeper had always disliked her and the after-effects of the row would only increase her dislike. To be reprimanded by her employer for neglect would not make her like Roly the more. Nor would it endear Karen to her.

She sighed inwardly as she drove. 'Sufficient unto the day is the evil thereof,' she quoted to herself. She'd always had favourite tags to help her in difficult times. 'Every cloud has a silver lining', that was another, but for the moment the silver wasn't exactly forcing itself on her attention.

Come, come, she reproved herself. What's all the misery about? You've got an interesting job, a good-hearted boss, a place to live, family, friends ... What's all this depression about?

Well, it was about Michael Ansleigh. The feeling of being engulfed in a warm embrace had brought back the longing for Michael's touch, Michael's voice, the male scent of him, the whispers of love.

More than six months had gone by. During those months she'd had occasional bouts of self-torture – what had she done, what had she failed to do? How could their relationship have just dried up and blown away? But these moments had gradually diminished to the extent she'd thought herself cured.

Now, just because Jeffrey had given her an affectionate hug, she was blinking back tears as she drove. Fool, she told herself, and stopped for coffee at a motorway restaurant.

She called Evie. 'I'm on my way, might make it in time for dinner.'

'Great! How long are you staying?'

176

'A couple of days. How's everything?'

'Same old, same old,' Evie said with a sigh. 'It'll be *so* nice to see you and hear all your adventures. Nothing ever happens here.'

There's one adventure I'm not going to tell you about, thought Karen. The scene at Jeffrey's flat this morning wasn't for publication. 'Tell the kids I'm coming,' she said. 'I'm dying to see them.' Yes, to have the comfort of their normality, to be able to play with them and take them out to the seaside without anxious planning and painful explanations...

'I hope you're bringing prezzies,' Evie remarked. 'Much though they love you, duckie, they love the contents of your travel bag even more.'

'Cynic!' But they were both chuckling as they hung up.

A traffic tangle delayed her so her arrival was later than she intended. But even Noomie had been allowed to stay up to greet her, and there was a happy half hour while they hugged and kissed and opened packages. Next came an excellent dinner for the grown-ups, then a little chat with Walt while he smoked his after-dinner cigar in the garden.

'Glad you're here,' he told her as they paced idly along a tulip-bordered path in the last remains of daylight. 'Evie's a bit down at the moment, it'll do her good to have you to chat to.'

'Anything wrong?'

'Aw, nothing serious. This new painting gimmick isn't going well. The thing she asked you to get the paints for...'

'The aquarelles?'

'That's them. She'd been having a go at it with paints she got from her usual art shop in Dover, but somehow it all seems to go wrong. Let's hope the stuff you've brought will make all the difference.'

Karen nodded agreement. Evie took up art forms and discarded them quite regularly. She'd made beaten-copper plaques, dried-flower pictures, corn dollies ... She told Karen she *knew* she had talent, it was simply a question of finding the right technique. But she was largely self-taught, for there was no art college close at hand and even if there was, running the house and bringing up the children meant it would be impossible to attend full-time.

Walt was sympathetic but unable to help. He was the first to admit he had no artistic leanings. When Evie showed him the results of her latest endeavour he always told her it was great. So Karen knew she was going to have a session with her sister in which Evie would show what she'd done so far and explain why it wasn't a success, and Karen would be expected to make helpful comments.

So it proved. When she went indoors, Evie took her to the old conservatory which was given up to 'Evie's art stuff'. There she'd laid out four aquarelles on the table with the overhead light full on them. 'You see?' she demanded. 'They don't have that *luminous* look.'

What Karen didn't know about aquarelles would have filled a large book. She nevertheless entered into the critique as best she could. At last they switched off the lights and headed back to the living room and as they made their way along a dimly-lit passage, she said, 'What's really wrong, Evie?'

'Oh, it's all so *boring*!' her sister muttered. 'The school run, the church flowers, drinks parties for Walt's business pals...'

'Sweetie, you always get like this in the spring,' Karen said, trying for a light tone. 'Wait till you have to start organizing the summer fête. You won't be bored then.'

'Oh, don't! The village fête! Is that going to be the highlight of my life from now on?'

They came into the hall. From the living room came the muted roar of the crowd welcoming a goal: Walt was watching football. Evie, with her hand on the doorknob, turned away from the door with a grimace. She led the way into the kitchen where she began stacking the dinner crockery in the dishwasher with unnecessary vehemence.

'It's all right for *you*,' she grumbled as she

worked. 'You've got this lovely job where you float around France and get to Paris regularly, and you've got a gorgeous boyfriend and a wonderful future, but here I am, stuck here for the rest of my life with nothing but more of the same...'

'You don't know that, Evie. Things can change so unexpectedly.'

'I'd like just *something* to happen! I'm not asking to be discovered as the new wonderwoman of British art, or even to have this famous one-woman show in Dover...'

'Why don't you go ahead with that, love? If you think you have enough to put on view?'

Evie switched on the dishwasher. 'I just might,' she announced. 'After all, it *is* my money. I can do what I like with it, can't I?'

'Of course you can.' I'll have to warn Walt that something's in the wind, Karen thought as they finished tidying the kitchen. He was already aware his wife was going through one of her periods of divine discontent, so perhaps he'd reconcile himself to the idea of spending money on hiring a gallery.

Next day was Saturday. Evie wanted the children off her hands while she made preparations for that evening's dinner, a special affair for the bigwigs of a local charity, so Karen took them to a nearby gymkhana.

They were thrilled, especially Angela, who had a pony of her own but wasn't yet at the

180

gymkhana stage. They stood behind the rope watching other youngsters take low fences, cheered and applauded when small silver cups were awarded. They had a picnic lunch with all the usual mishaps – ants marching into the sandwich box, the orange juice tipped over. They visited a special section set up as a pets' zoo. Around five o'clock they went home, Noomie already falling asleep in his special child's seat after such a series of marvels.

At the farmhouse, they rushed to their mother with reports of their exciting day. Evie said, 'Yes, dear,' and 'How wonderful!' at the appropriate points in the narrative yet Karen had a feeling her attention wasn't entirely with them. When at length they'd talked themselves out, had washed their hands and were seated round the kitchen table for an early supper, Evie took Karen aside.

'Darling,' she said, taking hold of her sister's hand and holding it close to her breast as if to prevent her running away, 'I've got a marvellous surprise for you.'

'You have? What?' Karen asked, unnerved by the fervour in Evie's voice.

'Go up to your room and you'll find it.'

'Evie, what have you been up to?'

'Nothing. It's not me. It's something very special but I didn't do it.'

'What? What?' Now Karen was worried.

Evie's face was flushed with a strange emotion – a mixture of delight, triumph, and envy.

'Go on, off you go, and don't bother about coming down for dinner if you don't feel like it.'

'Evie!'

Now her sister was taking her out to the hall, urging her towards the stairs. It was best to give in, to obey instructions and find out what all the excitement was about. With misgiving but tremendous curiosity, Karen climbed the old staircase.

She opened the bedroom door.

Michael Ansleigh was sitting on the end of her bed.

Ten

Her heart gave a great lurch. The breath left her body. She felt deathly cold. It was like losing the world, icily astray in no-man's-land.

Then Michael's arms were around her, and she had what she'd been longing for yesterday.

She relaxed into the embrace. She was happy, oh so happy. Delight, relief, reassurance surged through her. It had all been a mistake, he was back and all would be well.

Then her brain seemed to come to life again, and with it, memory. She began to push with her fists against his chest, trying to free herself. 'Don't, no don't!' she gasped. She was trying to drag herself away, to avoid the kisses he was bestowing on her neck, her cheek.

He let her go a minuscule distance. 'Darling,' he murmured, 'if you knew how I've longed for this...'

'Let me go! Take your hands off me!'

He obeyed, backing away a little, staring at her with hurt grey eyes. 'Karen! Please...?'

'Don't dare,' she said. 'Don't *dare* speak to me—'

'But darling, you must let me explain—'

'No, you explained everything in your letter.'

'That letter,' he groaned, and sank down on a nearby chair as if his legs gave way. 'If you only knew how I regretted it...'

'Oh, really? When was that? Next day? Next month?'

She was studying him as if he were a complete stranger. His clothes advertised a holiday mood: Ralph Lauren corduroy shirt, Dockers, trainers. His soft brown hair was cut in a fashionable crop, he had the beginnings of a summer tan.

There was a deeply pleading note when he tried to reply. 'Karen, Karen, dear heart, you don't understand...'

'No, I don't, and I never will. So don't even try.'

'Let me just say I'm sorry. I'm sorry, my love, I've lived through hell for weeks, wondering how to make things right again...'

'You wasted your time.'

'I've tried over and over again to write to you. But every word I wrote down seemed so feeble ... so petty...' He shook his head. 'I knew I had to *say* it to you, but when I tried to ring you, I couldn't get any reply.'

'But don't you remember, *my love*, you cancelled the lease of the flat?'

'But as soon as I got to Heathrow and thought I was in range, I tried your mobile, and I kept on trying until it dawned on me it was out of action.'

'Oh yes, things have changed since last we were in contact,' she said, her voice hoarse with anger. 'I moved out of the flat before they could throw me out, and started a new life. A life that's got no place in it for an insect like you!'

'Karen, you've got to understand! At that time and place, everything was in chaos – a mess. We all thought the world was coming to an end – and you know the airlines were downsizing.'

'So, it was just a matter of business, is that it?'

'Of course not!' He jumped up, throwing his hands in the air in denial. 'But I was almost broke, Karen, what with finding a way home for my group visiting the Indian reserves...'

'But you made money, of course, when you sold out the firm.'

'It was a tremendous offer, darling! And it wasn't going to be open long because firms in the travel business were going down like ninepins, so they could have had any other firm they wanted. So I signed on the dotted line. I know I should have consulted you but I couldn't contact you in Phnom Penh – I did try, honestly I did. There was a deadline on the sale, so I took it up and then there were funds to support me in trying something else. But—'

'But not if you had to drag me along too, is that it?'

'No, no, I just saw myself starting all over again. Try to understand, sweetheart, I felt I had nothing to offer you. I'd decided that it was better to try in the States because they're more sympathetic to start-ups than here in the UK. And I admit it, Karen, I was in an emotional whirlwind. Everything over there was so, so strung-out, so intense after the Twin Towers thing. And I thought it was best just to ... to say goodbye, to leave you free so you could find someone with a better life ahead of him.'

She was unable to answer that at once. There was enough in it to make her falter, even to feel some acceptance. Had he really been thinking about what was best for her?

At that time, in that place, perhaps it hadn't been easy to stay clear-headed. All around him were people in shock, people afraid of the future. Had it been infectious?

Yes ... perhaps ... But the way it had been done, the cruelly bright letter he'd sent?

He began again. 'I know I was a fool, Karen. I regretted everything I'd done almost as soon as I'd done it. At the time, I thought I was acting properly, setting you free to find someone better. But I look back

186

on it now and see I must have been mad.'

'You hurt me,' she said.

'Oh, don't you think I know that?' He almost clasped his hands together in entreaty. 'That's why I've been trying to find you, to say to you face to face that I was a barbarian – but I ask you to forgive me. I can't live with myself if you don't forgive me.'

'I forgive you,' she said, and motioned him towards the door. She wanted him to leave. It was hard to breathe while she was in the same room as him.

'Thank you.' His voice sounded muffled. She could see that he was suffering, and for a moment was almost sorry for him. But then the cynical part of her asked herself, What's he suffering from? Is it remorse, or embarrassment? Because it couldn't be any fun to have to admit he'd been a selfish weakling.

'I'd like you to go,' she said, eager to be rid of him.

'Very well.' He moved slowly towards the door but as he came close, he paused. 'You never told Evie that we'd split up, did you? She welcomed me with open arms.'

'I didn't want her lamentations.'

'You sure that was why you didn't tell her? Wasn't it...? Be honest, Karen, wasn't it the hope that it was all a mistake?'

'No!'

'But it was, darling – the biggest mistake I ever made. I can't go unless I can make you understand that I didn't know what I was doing.'

'I accept that. Please go.'

'Don't do this to me, Karen. It's taken me a long time to find you, and if you send me away now I'll know you don't accept my poor attempts at explanation...'

'What do you *want*, Michael? Did you expect me to throw my arms around you and tell you it was all forgotten?'

'Well, I ... I thought you might listen to me?'

'I've listened to you. I don't think I want to listen any more.'

'But what we had was so special! We had everything – we loved each other, we were a perfect partnership in every way.'

'But that's all gone now...'

'No, no, we could have it all again. We could make a new beginning.'

'But I don't *want* to.'

'Without even talking about it? Karen, that's not like you. We always used to talk things through.'

She sighed in frustration. 'Talk, talk, talk. You're sorry. I forgive you. What more is there to say?'

'I want to talk about the future. Our future.'

Beguiling words. They made her catch her

breath. It was a long time since she'd thought about her future. She'd just been going along from day to day, dealing with problems as they arose but never making plans.

Did she have a future? Something to share with someone she loved?

She turned slowly, putting distance between them, and sat down on the end of the bed.

'Say what you have to say. I'll listen.'

The grey eyes lit up with hope. For the first time she saw something of the old Michael, of the days before her world went awry. He smiled, made a movement as if to hug himself in reassurance, then began to speak with enthusiasm.

'I came back to England to carry on with a project that could put us back on a firm business footing. I'm looking for property, business property, for a conglomerate with big construction plans. I got in on this with the money I made from selling our little old firm, you see. You and I could do well on this, Karen – you've got the trick of handling people and I could look after the financial side.'

So it was a business project after all. That faint stirring of hope seemed to die in her. She said nothing, and as if catching something from her expression, Michael hurried on.

'I wanted to come home anyway, sweetheart, to explain myself and make everything right between us. When I couldn't find you I nearly went mad! I asked all our friends and business contacts what had happened to you but they said you hadn't been in touch for months. So I came here – I thought you might be living with Evie – it was just a chance. And when she gave me a big welcome I *knew* there was still something between us, and I want us to start again, and I know you'll agree, because you still love me, Karen. You do. I know you do.'

'But you wouldn't have come back to England if there hadn't been a career opportunity.'

'How could I have come back to find you if I didn't have a life to offer you?' he cried. 'Once I got a bit of a foothold in the States, I began to think I ought to contact you, ask you to move to Chicago, but then things turned in my favour and I had the chance to come home and find you and sort it all out.'

He came to her swiftly, took both her hands in his, and pulled her to her feet. He looked into her eyes with earnestness, with pleading. 'Say you understand, my dear love. Say you want to start again.'

His mouth was coming down on hers but she turned her face away. 'Wait, Michael.'

'But you can't deny it. You still love me.'

'Do I?'

'Of course you do. You wouldn't have been so overwhelmed when you saw me if you felt nothing for me.'

Always quick to sense her feelings! Once she'd found it endearing, now she saw it made her vulnerable. He'd put her in a spot where she felt she had to explain.

'All right, I was knocked for six. I admit that. But you're taking far too much for granted. It was shock, not passion, that made my head swim.'

'Really? When you melted into my arms, love?' He laughed, almost conspiratorial.

'That was ... that was ... a momentary foolishness.' She freed herself from his grasp, and stepped around him intent this time on leading him out of the room. 'I don't feel like being in a bedroom with you, Michael. If we're to talk, let's go outside.' She needed space between them, fresh air, a chance to keep hold of common sense. Yet she felt she had to listen to what he wanted to say.

He followed her downstairs. Evie put her head out of the kitchen.

'We're going out,' Karen said.

'I quite understand, duckie,' said her sister, all smiles.

They went out into the garden, around the side of the house and along the path that led to the paddock. Angela's pony, Popcorn, grazing the late spring grass, scarcely raised her head at their coming.

They leaned elbows on the fence. Karen wanted to start on a different note, to make things more polite and impersonal. 'When did you get here?'

'About mid-afternoon. Evie was doing her thing in the kitchen, sixteen different pots on the stove. Is some big event looming?'

'Dinner tonight for some charity committee, I think.'

'She won't want us. We can have a meal somewhere.'

'You think we're going to spend the evening together?'

'Yes, I do, because I recognize your tone of voice,' he said, laughing. 'You're in your let's-be-sensible mode. We're going to talk, and I'm going to explain what I've been doing in the States and how I got hold of this opening here at home, and you're going to point out the problems I'm going to have and tell me how to solve them.'

'You really think I want to spend my evening giving you helpful advice?' She put astonishment into her words, but he was nodding and smiling.

'I know you so well, Karen. You feel concern for me. And that's good, because it tells me you haven't made yourself destroy every bit of feeling.'

'You're so *self-centred*! You want me to talk about you, to help you – hasn't it occurred to you that I've got a life of my own?'

'Well ... of course ... you haven't been in hibernation, I understand that.' His head was turned towards her so that he could catch every flicker of response. 'Evie said something about how lucky it was, you being here for a few days' rest from your job. What did you go in for?'

'My job. Right. Don't expect me to throw up my job and devote myself to helping you with this whatever it is you're going to do. In the first place I don't want to be your colleague again and in the second place I like what I'm doing now.'

'But that's just a job, Karen. If you come in with me it would be a partnership.'

'Like the last one? One you can run out on when you feel like it?'

He had no answer to that, and for a time they stood in silence, staring off at the fresh green of trees at the far side of the paddock. A breeze from across many fields, but bearing the tang of salt, ruffled Karen's hair. She could hear the song of a yellowhammer, and beyond it the scream of seagulls. All around her, the natural order of things. Inside her, turmoil and unhappiness.

Why was she still speaking with him? She looked back and recalled how many other great projects he'd wanted to be involved in. Lack of funds had always prevented him. Some small remains of concern for him, perhaps even some curiosity, had trapped

193

her into wanting to hear what he'd got himself into. But it was really none of her business. She should just say goodbye and walk away.

But before she could do it, Michael summoned some new strength, a mental squaring of shoulders. 'I understand how you feel – that you can't trust me because I was a fool last year. I've tried to apologize, to explain how I was knocked off balance. Perhaps it was idiotic of me to come with all sorts of plans and expect you to fall in with them.' He paused, waiting for a yes or a no, but when she said nothing he pushed on.

'All I ask is that you don't shut me out of your life. Let me prove to you how much I regret what I did, let me show you we still mean a lot to each other.'

'I don't think so, Michael.'

'But we were such a good team,' he protested. 'It can't all go for nothing. Can't we at least be friends, Karen?'

'Friends?'

'I need a friend, dear. I'm starting on a big project and I admit, I'm a bit scared. Every penny I have is invested in it, and I feel sort of alone ... out on a limb. I need someone to talk to, someone just to ... to be in touch with...' He faltered off into silence.

This was a change. Never in her life before had she ever heard Michael doubt himself. He'd always been buoyant, confident, optimistic and in charge.

'What *is* this scheme?' she asked.

'It's ... well ... As I was saying, I have to look for suitable sites for a construction company. In fact it's a big conglomerate, an American firm looking for property here in the UK. It's pretty hush-hush but I was allowed in on it because I was willing to invest – not that it got me a big slice of the action but at least I'm in on the ground floor.'

'What's the name of this firm?'

'I'd rather not say for the moment. There'll be a press conference, fairly soon, but the whole thing is going to be *big* and I feel I'm lucky to be in on it ahead of the competition. That's important, you know, Karen.' They were face to face now and he was examining her reaction as he talked. 'I did some preparatory work before I left the States, and I've looked at a few places, with more to come. But I'm feeling it grow sort of heavy on me, you know? So far I'm their only representative in the UK – I feel a bit like a scout sent far out in front of the troops.'

There seemed to be real anxiety in his voice. She frowned. 'What sort of a deal is it? Are you on salary, or is it commission on successful purchase, or what?'

'Well, I'm acting as agent, so I get expenses and a basic rate, but the real money comes with the signing of contracts, and when the buildings are up and the business is eventually launched I get share options.' He smiled, confidence returning at his own words. 'This is big money, sweetheart.'

'But what is the land going to be used for?' she asked.

He shook his head 'That's confidential. But I can tell you, it's something that can put us on easy street.'

'Us?' she quoted. 'Don't get too sure of yourself, Michael. I've got a job I enjoy and I'm not prepared to give it up just to tag along with you, holding your hand.'

'No, but ... you're not shutting me out completely? I can come to you for your friendship, at least?'

'I'll think about it,' she said.

But even as she said it she knew she was starting to give in. And Michael knew it too.

Eleven

As if he knew he'd gained as much as he could for the moment, Michael fell silent. From the far side of the house came the sound of a car on the farm road.

Michael heard it too. 'One of the dinner guests?' he asked.

'It's probably Walt, getting home a bit early to bathe and change.'

'Let's make our getaway before the drive's choked with cars.'

She shook her head. 'I don't want to go out with you, Michael, and besides I'm needed here to make up Evie's numbers at table.' The latter was quite untrue.

He sighed but she could see he was agreeing. Perhaps he was thinking that it was best to retire from the field with a victory, however small. 'I'll ring you tomorrow,' he said. And then, at her lack of response: 'May I?'

'Do we need to be in touch?'

'Well ... I thought I'd ask you what you thought of some of the properties I'm looking at.'

Well, why not, she said to herself. She gave him the number of her mobile, the one supplied by Lynwood Associates. He scribbled it down on a scrap of paper. Perhaps he'll lose it, she thought, and wondered if she wanted him to.

He would have kissed her goodbye but she leaned away. They shook hands. He walked off to where his car was parked under the sycamores – she realized she'd seen it as she came home with the children but had paid no heed, thinking it was one of Evie's visitors. If only she'd known it was Michael's car ... Would she have taken the children into the house and then walked out and driven away, just to avoid him?

For a long time she stayed where she was, watching Popcorn cropping grass, head down, a happy pony. Presumably ponies never fell in love. Was that a better way of life? She smiled wryly.

Footsteps. She turned to find Walt, all dressed up in collar and tie and dark suit. Clearly these charity people were top drawer so Evie was trying to impress.

'I'm sent by the missus,' he told her. 'It's time you came in and got togged up, she warns.'

'Oh, Walt ... I don't think I want to stay and have dinner.'

'Ah.' He grinned. 'Evie said you might have better plans.' He didn't inquire if she

198

was going to meet Michael, but she knew that was what he thought. She didn't enlighten him.

He said, 'Have a good time then.' Blew her a kiss, and went back to the house.

Some time later, when a couple of the guests had driven in, Karen set off to Dover. She supposed she was going for an evening meal, but wasn't the least hungry. She left the Peugeot in a car park then set off through the town centre. Nothing appealed to her, not fast food, not Chinese, not *cuisine nouvelle*. She ended up in a High Street pub because it seemed a friendly place.

She bought a glass of wine at the bar and took it to a quiet corner. All around her was happy conversation, Saturday night laughter and conviviality. She took a sip or two, trying to empty her mind.

It proved impossible. She found herself going over the scene with Michael, although parts of it seemed to be missing because at the time she'd been too much in the grip of emotion.

Why had he come in search of her? That was the question that kept nagging at her consciousness. Was it love? Or was it perhaps need – of approval, of support?

He admitted he felt insecure over starting this new business enterprise. When she'd asked him outright if it was the business deal that had brought him back, he'd been quick with a fervent protest. She couldn't deny she'd been moved when in self-exoneration he said he wanted to offer her something firm and substantial as the basis for a new start.

But, she asked herself, why she should care – for she did care. The hurt he'd inflicted, the grief of those first days and the subdued misery of those that followed seemed somehow less important when he said he needed her.

So yes, she felt concern for him. She was anxious for him. Was that love? Did she still love him?

Yes. No. The answer within herself seemed to vary from minute to minute.

He was asking her to be his friend. She should have refused. Yet it was touching, because she'd seen that he was very apprehensive about his chosen path. She had found herself unable to refuse a helping hand.

Well, you're an idiot, she told herself. But at least try to be a careful idiot. Don't let him talk you into anything more.

Very good advice. When she at last left the bar, her wine almost untasted, she wondered if she were capable of following it. Because no matter how rational she might be in moments of reflection, she remembered that the mere sight of him had almost sent her into a faint. Even now, hours afterwards, she was thinking about him, worrying about him. Which seemed to mean that he still had a hold on her affections. She asked herself why, but could supply no sensible answer.

When she reached home, the last of Evie's guests were just leaving. They paused a moment to chat with her and say goodnight, then she went in with Walt. They all three went to the dining room to clear up. Evie soon suggested that her husband should go upstairs just to glance in on the children.

The moment he left the room she turned to Karen. 'Well?' she said in conspiratorial tones.

'Well what?'

'How'd it go? I could tell he had something important to say to you.'

Karen tried over two or three different versions of the truth in her mind. She decided on: 'He wanted to tell me about a new business venture that he's embarking on.'

Evie grinned roguishly. 'Oh, come on, Karrie! You haven't seen each other for months and all you talked about was business?'

'What did you think we'd talk about?'

Her sister was put out. 'I thought he was going to ask you to marry him.'

'Michael and I have never discussed marriage...'

'But taking you out to dinner – I thought it

201

would be candlelight and roses and a little velvet box with a ring...'

'Evie, Michael and I didn't have dinner. I went out on my own.'

'*What?*'

It was time to tell Evie enough to end her romantic visions. 'When I said he and I were talking about financial affairs, I meant it. Evie, Michael and I aren't close any more.'

'Don't be silly, you've always been in each other's pockets since the day you met.'

'But that was nearly five years ago, dear, and things have changed a bit since then. Michael's been abroad a long time, and we don't feel the same about each other.'

'It's that Jeffrey Lynwood, isn't it! I *knew* it!'

'No, Evie, no, no! Please, don't run off with an idea like that. I like Jeffrey and he likes me, I think that's true. But it has nothing to do with how I feel about Michael.'

'You can't do this to him, Karen! You don't really know what you're doing! He comes home to you absolutely dying to see you again, and you go cold on him? I never thought you'd be so cruel!'

'Evie—'

The dispute ceased abruptly as Walt came back into the dining room. 'Angela's awake. It was the Johnsons driving off, I think. She heard your voice, Karen, and wants Auntie

202

Karen to come and give a proper goodnight kiss.'

Glad to escape, Karen hurried out. Her niece was lying with an aged cloth doll against her cheek, half-asleep and ready to be soothed back to dreams. Karen tiptoed out, leaving the door ajar as usual. As she did so she was debating whether to make for her own room so as to escape Evie's accusations. She was too late. Her sister was already at the top of the stairs, intent on more.

She took Karen by the arm, urging her to a bench on the landing. 'I want to know what you think you're doing,' she began in an urgent whisper. 'You say you don't feel the same about each other but that can't be true, at least on Michael's side. He was in a tremendous state when he got here this afternoon.'

'Evie, back off. Michael's got a lot on his mind, I don't deny that.'

'Well, why are you being so unkind to him?'

'I haven't been unkind.'

'Are you seriously telling me that he didn't ask you out this evening?'

'Why do I have to tell you anything?' Karen cried, goaded to anger. 'What business is it of yours?'

'Good heavens, I'm your sister! I don't want to see you breaking up a relationship with an absolutely marvellous man just because you've somehow got yourself involved with your boss!'

'Evie, stop trying to live my life for me! Do something to improve your own if you're not happy with it but stop meddling in mine!'

'Oh!' gasped her sister. Her plump features crumpled in distress.

From the little girl's room a sleepy voice called, 'Mummy?'

'There! You've woken her up! I don't know what's got into you, Karen,' Evie hissed, and hurried to settle Angela down.

I don't either, thought Karen as she made her escape back to the dining room where Walt was stacking plates and humming tunelessly to himself.

'Everything OK?' he inquired as she joined him.

'She's a bit restless,' she said. 'Evie's sitting with her.'

He nodded acceptance. They finished the clearing-up. Together they stacked the dishwasher. 'How'd the charity thing go?' she asked.

'Not bad. They decided to run a farm-produce fair in the autumn and a personal greetings card boutique at Christmas. Evie and her artistic chums are going to make the cards, the committee are going to provide the money for the materials. Have to plan far ahead on these money-making schemes, you know.'

'I know,' she agreed with a sigh, thinking of Michael and his stage fright over the new career.

Evie still hadn't come downstairs when they'd finished tidying the kitchen. Walt went outside to smoke his cigar. Karen crept up to her room, washed her face and cleaned her teeth, and was already drifting to sleep when Evie tapped on her door. Karen made no response. Evie cracked open the door, enough to see that her sister was in bed.

'Are you awake?' she called in the soft tones that are supposed not to waken a sleeper.

'Mm...?' said Karen drowsily.

'Karen, I want to speak to you.'

'Can't it wait till the morning?'

'No, it can't. I want an apology.'

'Oh, for heaven's sake, Evie!' She sat up. Evie came to the end of the bed. In the faint light from the starlight coming through the window, she was a vague, imposing figure. Arms folded, head up, ready for a fight.

'How dare you say that about me, about not having a life of my own!' she began in a rush of high indignation.

'I didn't mean it, Evie. I was annoyed, that's all.'

'I've got a wonderful life – a loving husband, three wonderful children, neighbours who respect me, all sorts of activities that involve me in my community.'

'Of course,' agreed Karen. She didn't remind her that earlier Evie had been wailing about having nothing to look forward to except helping to run the village fête.

'And your attitude to what I was trying to do about you and Michael was very unkind,' Evie went on. 'I was only trying to warn you that you'd lose him if you didn't watch out.'

'Yes, I know.'

'Well, I'm glad you've got the decency to admit you were in the wrong.'

'I admit it, Evie.'

'We-ell ... I'm glad you see my point. About Michael. You know I've always thought highly of Michael.'

'Yes.'

'You'd be an utter fool to let him go.'

'You're quite right.'

Nothing is as perplexing as trying to have a quarrel with someone who won't fight. Evie sighed loudly. 'All right then,' she said. 'We'll forget all about it. But let me tell you, Karen, there was a hardness about your manner that really hurt me.'

'I'm sorry.'

'I accept your apology.'

'Thank you. Good night, Evie.'

'Goodnight.' She turned, turned back, then remarked, 'Of course, you can invite him to tomorrow's barbecue if you like.'

'I think he's gone back to London, love.' Although she'd no idea where he'd gone.

'Oh. All right then. Goodnight.' This time she went out, rather slowly, as if wondering what she was doing in her sister's room in the dark on the losing end of an altercation.

Karen didn't wonder. It was all a part of Evie's growing frustration. She wondered if she should have a word with Walt about it, but shrank from the idea. Walt was so down to earth. The subtlety of feminine dreams and longings was probably beyond him.

She fell asleep with the problem unsolved.

Next day was the usual long breakfast, the getting ready for church with the children mutinous, the purchase of Sunday papers on the way home, the arrival of grandparents from Guildford and from Canterbury in time for a quick drink before the barbecue was lit. Evie, of course, had all the food pre-pared ready in the fridge: tiny lamb cutlets sprinkled with rosemary, special Italian sausages mail-ordered in advance, chicken marinated in lemon and mint, tuna fish steaks, salad in a huge bowl, hot rice in an electric pot.

In the midst of the long hurly-burly, Karen's mother drifted up to her holding a plate of food. 'Have you and Evie had a falling-out?'

'What makes you ask?'

'She seems kind of huffy.'

Karen pondered a moment before saying very quietly, 'Did she tell you Michael was here yesterday?'

'Ah, yes, she mentioned he'd come back,' said Mrs Montgomery. Then, after a moment: 'I wish she'd get over that.'

'It's nothing serious, Mother. But he's been away a long time and seeing him has made her restive.'

'Ye-es.' She studied her daughter. 'You didn't speak to me about that?'

'I haven't had a chance to say a word to you until now.'

'True. So how is he?'

'Full of plans.'

Mrs Montgomery gave a rather sad smile. 'The eternal optimist,' she sighed. 'What's the plan this time?'

'He's going into property development.'

'What?'

'Not for himself. Acting as representative or something.'

'Representative for who?'

'I don't know. He isn't allowed to say.'

'Dear me, why not?'

'He says big money is involved.'

'Dear me,' said her mother again. After a moment she said, 'Are you joining up with him in this?'

Karen shook her head. 'I like the job I've got.'

'Are you ... er ... moving in with him again? Or he with you?'

'That's not on the cards. He's going to be

travelling, and so am I – in different directions.'

'Auntie Karen,' called her niece, 'there's a fly in my orange juice.'

'Duty calls,' she said to her mother and was moving away.

'Before you go,' said Mrs Montgomery, catching her by the elbow. 'Are you all right?'

'Absolutely fine,' Karen said and knew she'd sounded far too emphatic.

The long afternoon stretched towards evening. As always, Evie cleared up efficiently so that the garden looked tidy for anyone who wanted to stay outside in the mild June sunshine. The men went in to watch a grand prix on some continental circuit. Karen took the children for a walk to a nearby pool where dragonflies might be emerging.

Her cellphone warbled. She took it out of her pocket, and pressed the button. It was Michael. 'Karen, how about if we meet this evening? I'm in a hotel in Folkestone, we could have—'

'I'm sorry, I can't. It's a family reunion day, my parents and Walt's.'

'Oh.' He sounded dashed. 'It's just that I looked out some stuff I wanted to show you – brochures and information sheets from some estate agents.'

'Some other time, Michael.'

'Tomorrow? I could come out to the farm?'

'I'll be in London tomorrow.'

'Well, I have to get back to town myself. Can I see you there?'

'Sorry, I'll be at the office, getting my next assignment.'

'Your next assignment?' he laughed. 'What on earth does that mean? Are you a secret service agent or something?'

'I take people to look at houses.'

'You never told me that!'

'It didn't come up.'

'So you know quite a lot about property, then.'

'No, I don't. The houses we look at are in France, and any negotiation is done through French solicitors.'

'You'll be going to *France*?'

'That's it.'

'Oh, for heaven's sake! When's that likely to be?'

'Tomorrow evening, perhaps.'

'Karen, that's rotten timing! I really was hoping to see you.'

'Well, I'm sorry, but that's the way it is.'

'But how long are you going to be away?'

'Who knows? Depends on the client.'

There was a silence in which she could hear him trying to think of a way to alter her plans. Before he could offer one she said, 'I have to go, Michael, or the kids will be falling into the pond.'

'No, wait! I'll ring you tomorrow. When

will you know about your assignment?'

'Some time tomorrow.'

'You wouldn't really travel tomorrow evening?'

'I might have to. The clients decide when they want to be met, and where.'

'If I ring you about fourish, will you know your plans?'

'Oh, really, Michael, it can't be so urgent to show me these papers...'

'But I want to take a look at these places before the end of the week, and I'm a bit confused about their possibilities...'

He really sounded extremely nervous. She sighed inwardly. 'I'm sorry, but I'm tied up for the rest of the day.'

'Well, I'll ring you tomorrow afternoon.'

If you must, she thought. 'OK,' she said.

Back in the house there was the usual battle to get the children to bed. One set of grandparents bathed Noomie, the other pair divided themselves between Perry and Angela while Evie prepared the refreshments she felt necessary for the homeward bound travellers. Karen helped Evie, and thought she felt a lessening of the previous friction. She thought her mother had perhaps had a word with her.

Around nine the visitors, including Karen, began to take their leave. Karen was last to go. When she kissed Evie farewell her sister suddenly put her arm around her for a hug.

'Mum told me to stop being cross,' she whispered in her ear. 'I'm sorry I got in a snip, Karrie.'

'No problem.'

'I'd apologize for spoiling your weekend but I know nothing could do that, with Michael coming home.'

'Right.'

'Are you OK? You seem a bit down.'

'I'm a bit exhausted, that's all.'

'Of course – I understand. Well, drive safely. Give my love to Michael.'

'I will.'

She tumbled into her bed around midnight, reflecting that the rest days intended to refuel her energy had done just the opposite. She slept like a long-felled log and was late getting up. The weather looked set to be fine so she put on a short-sleeved silk blouse and a linen skirt – businesslike yet relaxed. Even after two cups of coffee, she still felt tired. She couldn't make herself hurry to the Tube. It was mid-morning by the time she got to the office.

'Sorry,' she said as she came in.

'It's OK, he hasn't been asking for you,' said Alexis, secretary and receptionist.

The premises in Persimmon Road weren't very imposing. They consisted of a fair-sized outer office where there were four desks – one for Alexis, the rest for staff members if and when they were in London. She deposited her handbag on the nearest one, then went into the inner office. Its door always stood open. Her boss, in shirtsleeves, was shifting papers about on his desk.

'Morning,' he greeted her. 'Batteries all recharged for another safari? I've got your folder here, it's fairly straightforward. Mr and Mrs Siddinford are looking for a house in the south of the Dordogne with at least three bedrooms, which will probably translate as a former farmhouse. We haven't quite established whether they want a place that needs renovation, or one they can move right into. There's some talk of putting up the family when they come on holiday, that kind of thing.' He handed her the folder. 'They don't seem to be short of funds.'

He went on to discuss possible prices then pointed out the local estate agents with whom Lynwood Associates had dealt before.

'Have you been in touch with them?' she inquired.

'No, I leave that to you. You should spend some time today ringing them for some possible addresses, that's just for starters. You're meeting the Siddinfords in Calais tomorrow. They've been in Paris for the last week or so, museum hopping.'

'What's the transport situation? Have they got their own car?'

'No, you'll be chauffeuring them. I've booked ahead, rooms at Clermont-Ferrand

and Sarlat, but of course you can alter that if you want to. The hotels are in the file with everything else.'

'Thank you.' She paused. She wanted to touch on something more personal. 'What's the word on Roly?'

The response was an uncertain grin. 'Well, you caused a bit of an earthquake, I think. Hélène's hiring another girl to help with the work, but I think Louis is behind it and I think she's to take care of Roly.'

'But didn't Louis say Roly didn't need anyone to look after him?'

'Right. But maybe Louis thought it over and felt there ought to be a sort of buffer zone. Nothing remarkable, she's not living-in, she's only coming by the day.'

'And how's Gabrielle taking that?'

'Who knows?' Jeffrey said with a sigh. 'I can't ask Roly outright because that would be like asking him to criticize the set-up. Sort of like snitching on them, you know?'

'I bet Gabrielle's mortally offended,' Karen murmured.

'Well, yes. If *she'd* suggested it, it would be OK. But to have this new girl imposed from above...'

She'll blame Roly, Karen thought to herself. Aloud she said, 'Is the new girl on the scene yet? What does Roly think about her?'

'No, she's starting this very morning.

214

Yvette, she's called. I promised to ring him this evening to hear how he feels.'

'Well, it's an improvement, don't you think?'

'I hope so.' He hesitated, then said, 'I'm extremely grateful to you, Karen. If I was a bit over-demonstrative on Saturday morning, I apologize.'

'That's OK.'

'I mean' – he was half-laughing – 'I hope you didn't think it was sexual harassment between employer and employee. It was just gratitude.'

'You never know, I might decide to sue you.'

'I better take out insurance.'

She shook her head at him and went to the other room to use the next hour on planning for the tour with the Siddinfords. There was, of course, no use in continuing during the lunch break, when all self-respecting French citizens would lock up their offices while they either went home or sampled the cuisine of a favourite café. She herself slipped out for a snack and to do some necessary shopping.

But by five thirty she'd crossed off the last number on her list of calls. Alexis was logging off on the computer and switching the phone to Jeffrey's home number. He himself had put on his suit jacket and was coming through to the main door carrying an armful of folders. Karen got up and accompanied them out to the street. They paused while he locked up, exchanging end-of-day remarks.

At the kerb, a car horn beeped. They all looked round.

Karen gave a little start of surprise. The car driver was Michael.

'Friend of yours?' Jeffrey asked as she made a move to cross the pavement.

'Oh ... yes...'

'So long then. Ring me from Calais tomorrow when you've met up with the Siddinfords, OK?'

'Sure.'

She went to the car. Michael said blithely, 'Give you a lift home?'

'How did you know where I worked?' she demanded.

'Evie told me.'

Of course.

'I've brought this stuff I wanted to show you.'

'Michael, this isn't convenient! I'm off to France first thing in the morning.'

'It wouldn't take long,' he coaxed. He was patting a thick satchel that lay on the passenger seat.

'That looks like a huge pile of papers.'

'But you only need to look at a few, the ones I need to visit this week. Come on, Karen, be a pal! Half an hour over a cup of coffee, that's all.'

She sighed. There was something woebegone about him.

'Come on, sweetheart. I've just driven up from Kent and it's been a battle with the traffic all the way. I'm bushed. I need a cup of coffee and a bite to eat before I head for my digs.'

'Where's that, exactly?'

'Watford.'

'Watford?' That would involve him in yet another battle with traffic to get out through north London. 'That's not very convenient, is it?'

'The firm owns some property there – I've got free use of a service flat. But it's not exactly homey.'

She gave in. Better to do what she'd said she'd do, take a look at the brochures, and get it over with. Otherwise she might be here on the kerb arguing until sundown.

'All right,' she agreed.

At once he unlatched the passenger seat door for her. As she went round, he hefted the satchel over to the back seat. She got in, and they drove off. 'Where?' he inquired.

So Evie hadn't given him her home address? But then she realized Evie thought he knew that. As far as Evie was concerned there was no breach between them. And Michael, understanding that, had asked for her office address. It was a nice piece of strategic thinking

217

In the evening traffic it took much longer to get to her flat than it had to go to the office by Tube in the morning. Michael was impressed by the place but not enthusiastic. 'Kind of cold?' he murmured as he glanced about the big room, taking in the stainless steel kitchen on the far side and the few comfortable items she'd installed in the living room.

'I haven't really had time to do much to it,' she replied, taking her shopping to the kitchen area. Over her shoulder she added, 'I haven't got much in the way of food.'

'That's OK. Let's just dump this stuff–' he threw his satchel on the day-bed – 'and go out for a meal. Then we can come back to it in a fit state.'

'Well, I...'

'We can go somewhere handy. Have you got a favourite restaurant?'

'No, I haven't really had time to—'

'We passed a nice-looking place just down the road on the corner – Italian, wasn't it?'

'Well, I've been in, it's not bad.'

'Come on, then.' He strode into the kitchen, enfolded her in an affectionate grasp, and hurried her back to the door. 'Got your keys? Right. Here we go.'

They were going downstairs before she had time to prevent it. She thought about putting up a struggle, but then that was making too much of it. She went along, thinking that she was in any case quite hungry and the rolls and milk she'd bought would do for breakfast.

The bistro was a popular place, offering mainly Italian food. At this hour it wasn't too busy so service was immediate. Karen ordered pasta and salad. Michael opted for a steak with all the trimmings. The meal took some time, more than she would have wished. Michael talked about Evie and her family, explaining that he'd had a long phone conversation with her before setting off for London.

'She says this job of yours is pretty glamorous.'

'Nothing of the kind! She's just a bit envious, that's all, a bit fed up with family routine and that sort of thing. What I'm doing strikes her as more fun.'

'But you travel a lot? You said you were going to France.'

'Yes, on the ferry at crack of dawn tomorrow.'

'Evie said something about having friends in Paris, some posh family?'

She gave a dismissive shrug. 'It's just some relations of my boss. I suppose they're posh – Louis is a consultant to the French government. But I really don't have much to do with them.'

'Your boss – that's Lynwood, is it? Lynwood Associates?'

'That's right.'

'He's connected with someone in the French *government*?'

She gave an inward sigh. 'Michael,' she said, 'you know Evie likes to make a big fairy tale of everything. Jeffrey Lynwood has no influential connections in the French government. He runs a firm helping British clients to buy property there, that's all. And if she's been building up my part in it, all I really do is act as courier to the clients.'

'OK, OK, I was just taking a friendly interest, that's all.' He turned the conversation to himself and his immediate plans. 'I'm off to Newcastle-on-Tyne tomorrow. These places I'm going to look at, they're on the coast near there – Whitley Bay, Newbiggin. Ever been up there, love?'

She shook her head. Like most people, she always thought of the north as industrial terrain. Were his employers American industrialists? Despite herself, she was intrigued. This was something entirely new for Michael, whose previous efforts in business had always been on the recreational side.

The dinner clientèle had come in. Service in the café became less brisk, so they had to wait a long time for their coffee and then for the bill. Karen didn't demur when Michael insisted on settling it. Coming out for a meal had been his idea in the first place.

Once back in her flat Michael produced

papers from his satchel. She was surprised by the number, and then by the variety – it appeared he was going to look at all kinds of properties. Hotels, blocks of flats, even a former holiday camp. 'What's the aim in all this?' she wondered aloud. 'What are the criteria?'

'Well, the place has to be reasonably near a large urban area. It has to have good access by road. It's got to have big grounds.'

'Big grounds? For re-development?'

'Yes.'

'What about planning permission?' she queried. 'And this lovely old hotel here in the hills – that looks as if it might have a preservation order on it.'

'Good heavens,' he said, quite awestruck. 'I'd never have thought of anything to do with a preservation order!'

'Some of the properties I've been showing in France have been in heritage areas. That makes a difference to the client's considerations.'

'How do you find out about that kind of thing?'

'I don't know about here in the UK. The nearest county council office, I'd imagine.'

'Is that what you have to do in France?'

'I leave all that to the lawyers,' she said, and explained some of the legalities of the work.

Well over an hour went by while she looked

at the estate agents' information and answered Michael's questions as best she could. She kept saying that she was no expert, and he would reply that she was being very helpful and that he was very grateful, and she grew more and more worried. He was a total innocent when it came to property; he'd said the money involved was 'big', so what if he made a mistake?

At last he began to gather up the brochures. 'Thanks a million,' he said with a sigh. 'The lesson is, don't take a step until I've thought it over for twenty-four hours.'

'And get a good solicitor.'

'Right.' He slung his satchel to his shoulder, went to the door, and dropped it there in preparation for leaving. 'Lord, I'm tired,' he said, stretching.

'Wait, Michael, you've left one of your folders.' She went to him, holding it out.

He took it, dropped it on top of the satchel, then took her in his arms. 'Just a goodnight kiss,' he murmured, and brought his mouth down on hers.

She would have avoided the kiss but it was too late. He held her close, imprisoning her arms. His lips caressed her cheek, her throat. She felt the warmth flaring at each touch, and when he unbuttoned her blouse to kiss her breast there was a pulse of fire. He was murmuring her name, hoarse with desire. So well-remembered, that voice, rich with the undertones of a passion that had been their greatest joy.

He was holding her with a grasp that made it a bruising, almost a wounding, encounter. The breath seemed to be leaving her body. She should resist, she knew, but memory was surging through her veins. They had always been happy lovers, and he had been dear to her, dearer than her own life. Here was a taste of it again, that delight that had gone out of her world with his going.

All she wanted was the moment. She gave herself up to it. And soon, when they had moved, locked in each other's arms, to the day-bed, there was that transcendent wave that carries lovers to the haven where nothing in the world can intrude.

Twelve

The Siddinfords proved to be elderly but extremely active – one of those couples who don walking boots and backpacks for a weekend of clambering over Lakeland. They'd walked over every inch of the Bois de Boulogne and the gardens of Versailles from all Karen could divine. They intended to walk all over the Dordogne once they were settled in their new home.

About the buying of that, they were less certain. 'We want something we can feel at home in,' said Clarice. 'Lots of room for bookshelves – we've got a large collection of travel books and maps.'

'And for our computers,' added Gilbert. 'We're doing a study of Cro-Magnon cave paintings, thinking of producing a book. We've got lots of stuff on disk.'

'Great,' said Karen. But it wasn't perhaps quite so great, because any time they passed a sign by the roadside mentioning a cave – of which there are many in the Dordogne – they wanted to stop and explore. However, the silver lining was that they didn't demand gourmet restaurants for every meal. French bread and cheese on the banks of a stream pleased them more.

She began by showing them five properties. By their reaction she learned that they wanted a capacious house which needed very little done to it, that they'd be quite content with a patio rather than an extensive garden, and that the most attractive point for them was plenty of good footpaths for walks. She accordingly altered the requests that she put to the local estate agents.

The Siddinfords went to bed early. By ten o'clock at the latest she was always on her own. This was advantageous in making plans for the next day's jaunt, but even so she was left with plenty of time to herself.

It was at those times that she thought about Michael Ansleigh.

How could she have been so weak? She was appalled at her own folly.

Immediately after the episode of sexual surrender she'd managed to blot it all out of her mind. She'd been busy – the drive to Dover had needed her full attention, then there was the fuss of boarding, and after that disembarkation at Calais and finding the hotel where the Siddinfords were staying. Naturally she had to give her attention to them; they were clients, in her care from now on.

But over the next couple of days things fell

into a routine, and she found she was alone more than expected. She couldn't then prevent her mind from going back over what had happened. She couldn't avoid the judgement of her own intelligence. She was weak and foolish.

Why had she given in? That was the question that tormented her. Because now that she looked back on it she found she wasn't happy, she wasn't in a warm glow of pleasure. She was angry. Angry with herself, and with Michael.

Some famous author – Hemingway, perhaps – had said something to the effect that a good action was one that you felt good after. Well, she didn't feel good. She'd made love because she'd let herself be overwhelmed by the sheer pleasure of being loved. It was physical delight that had tempted her.

Michael had known she would be tempted. He'd used that as a weapon.

Their love-making had been almost violent at first. Later there was less ardour and more playfulness until at last they fell asleep. She woke in the wee small hours to find him gone, and on the coffee table, a page torn from his notebook. 'Darling. Must get to far-off Watford! Thanks for everything. Here's to our next merry meeting.'

Thanks for everything. The phrase was like a dash of cold water in her face. Thanks for your company at the restaurant, for your advice on my business problems, for the sex afterwards ... An enjoyable package deal. And here's to our next merry meeting, when we'll have more talk about my problems and I'll reward you for your help by sleeping with you because you seem to enjoy it so much.

Later she wondered if she was being too critical. Michael was never good at expressing himself. He hadn't meant his note to sound superficial.

Yet each time she went through a review of the memories, she felt herself shivering in revulsion. Her reason kept on murmuring the same message: he knows your weaknesses and he's using them.

First of all he'd asked merely for her friendship. He needed a friend, he said. So she'd agreed to be his friend. It would have seemed ungenerous to refuse. Then when he came to her with the business documents, he smoothly led the encounter from friendship into love-making so as to bind her to him again. She, like a fool, had fallen for it every step of the way.

Did she still love him? Had she given in because she still felt incomplete without him? Was it love, or mere desire for a lost paradise? A kind of nostalgia for what had been...

I've got to get the better of this, she told herself. It's like an illness – I've got to cure myself of it. How it was to be done she didn't quite know. Another phrase came into her mind: 'absent thee from felicity a while'. Just stay away from him. Don't get into situations where you lose your head with him.

Good advice. The difficulty was, would she take it?

Luckily Clarice and Gilbert seemed unaware of her mental debates. She drove them from Sarlat to Perigueux, to Rocamadour, to Figeac and Decazeville. At the end of sixteen days they saw a house near Aubin that pleased them – good walks in every direction, a cave with paintings only a short drive away, a stream nearby that joined the Alignon, and the asking price within their means.

'Let's visit the agent,' Karen suggested. 'The owner may be open to offer...'

'Oh, let's not haggle too much,' cried Gilbert. 'Ring your law firm and tell them we want someone to represent us, so we can get on with it.'

She obeyed, so that matters went on with some speed. By the end of June she was driving the Siddinfords back to Paris for a session with one of the *notaires* at Gustave Kloss. The following day she saw then off home on Eurostar. She stood in Paris-Nord in her travel gear of jeans and sleeveless T-shirt feeling oddly alone, out of kilter with the rest of the world.

From the Hotel Babette she rang Jeffrey to

keep him informed. 'The Siddinfords have a lot of stuff to move once they own the house,' she told him. 'I gather they have shelves full of books and cases of drawings and photographic slides, besides the usual furniture and stuff.'

'No problem, of course we can help them with that.' One of the 'associates' in the firm was a removal specialist. She and Jeffrey discussed dates and possibilities; Jeffrey said he would contact the Siddinfords with suggestions in a day or two. 'Now, you take a couple of rest days,' he went on. 'There's a business client arriving in Paris on Tuesday next – I'll fax through all the details.'

'OK by me.' She paused. 'I could catch up with Roly, if that would be all right.'

'I don't see why not. Roly would love it.'

'I was thinking more of the grown-ups,' she explained. 'Don't you think I'll get a bit of frosty reception after ... you know ... that dust-up?'

'Oh. Well, yes ... I suppose that's true. Look, I'll telephone and sort it out beforehand. When do you think of seeing him?'

'Sunday?' she suggested. That was the day after next. 'I thought of taking him to try his hand at fishing.'

'Fishing?'

'Well, I thought I'd buy him one of those little nets on a pole, like Perry and Angela use when they're after tadpoles. He was interested when he saw some old chaps getting a nibble or two with proper rod and line.'

'Karen, think what Gabrielle would say if he came home with a jar of tadpoles!'

'Oh, we'll throw them back,' she promised, laughing. 'But kids love that kind of thing – I know I did when I was his age.'

'That's true,' he agreed. 'It's a good idea.' He paused for a moment, and she thought she heard a sigh. 'When he's with me, I tend to take him to indoor things – museums, or ice-rinks, or cinemas...'

'Oh, he loves all that,' she said in reassurance. 'He was telling me about Pocahontas a while ago. But in this fine hot weather I thought it would be nice to be out of the town for a bit. Could you say I'll call for him Sunday about ten thirty? Don't tell him about the fishing – it's a surprise.'

There was a hesitation. Then he said, 'Thank you, Karen.' The words were simple but the tone was heartfelt.

When she got to the building at the appointed time, Roly was waiting in the hall. He ran towards her with his arms out. 'Karen! It's *ages* since I saw you.'

'Nearly a month,' she acknowledged. 'I'm sorry, I've been busy.'

'Yes, of course. Daddy explained that. What are we going to do today?' He was all eagerness, expecting her to suggest something new as she always did, quite outside his usual routine.

'I'll show you when we get there,' she said.

He could hardly bear the suspense. He strained against the safety strap as they drove out of Paris, craning to see where they were headed, and soon was recognizing the road they'd travelled before to the riverbank. 'Are we going to watch the fishermen?'

'We'll see.'

When they'd parked, she produced the fishing net. 'We're going to look for tadpoles,' she told him.

'Tadpoles?'

'*Têtards* – tiny little baby frogs, more like little fish.'

'Frogs aren't like fish.'

'No, not when they develop properly. But at first they don't have legs and they don't croak or sit on lily pads like in the picture books. They wriggle about in the water and swim like fish.'

'Are you sure?' he said doubtfully.

'Quite sure.'

However, despite her certainty, they caught no tadpoles. The stream flowed too fast, the environment was unsuitable for spawn to develop into tadpoles. But they caught some minnows, which pleased Roly just as well. He cried out in delight when the tiny silvery things slithered between his fingers and back into the water. At once he was full of questions, 'They look a bit like anchovies but they're not anchovies, are they? I'm glad, because I hate anchovies. Do they grow into fish as big as that one I looked up, that the man caught last time we were here? How long does it take them to grow up?'

She didn't know the answer, but she'd bought a book. Alas, when she brought it out so they could look up the facts, it came on to rain. So they dabbled their hands in the stream to clean them, then repaired to the car for their picnic lunch.

An hour later it was raining even more heavily. Roly was all for going back to fishing, but she could just imagine the reaction if she brought him home soaked to the skin. 'I'm afraid we'll have to give fishing what the Americans call a rain check,' she said. 'That means we can come back and do it some other time.'

'Promise?'

'Of course. Now, what shall we do?'

'Let's go home so I can look up about minnows on my computer.' She was surprised that he was ready to part from her so quickly. She must have given some sign because he went on quickly, in a conspiratorial tone: 'Everybody's out, you know. Gabrielle's gone to spend the afternoon with her cousin in Batignolles and Maman and

232

Papa Louis are at a weekend conference in Helsinki. I could show you my chess game on the computer, it's very interesting.'

'But how would we get in?' she countered. 'Is Yvette there?'

'Oh, her – she only comes on weekdays. She could have agreed to weekends too, but I think she's scared to death of Gabrielle so she said no.' He shrugged. 'One of the porters will let us in.'

She hesitated but could see nothing wrong in it. It was absurd to think that they must stay out in the wet rather than go home and be comfortable. So they returned to the apartment.

The porter, Fredi, was perfectly easy about giving them the key. Once in the apartment Roly dragged her upstairs. 'Here's a hanger for your coat in case the shoulders got wet.' He hung up his own, hooking the hanger on the open door of the wardrobe so that it could dry off. As Karen did the same she was telling herself she couldn't imagine any of Evie's offspring ever bothering about such things.

Roly was pushing a chair up to the desk so that she could look at the computer. 'My chess game,' he began. 'It's a version of Deep Fritz.'

'*Deep Fritz?*'

'It's awfully good. The real one – the difficult one – Kramnik played it in Bahrain, you remember? Look, that's the game I'm in at the moment but I'm not doing well – my bishop's got in a fix, I see now how I let it happen. Stupid of me, but Fritz is really clever.'

'But who is Fritz?' she demanded, at a total loss.

'It's the chess program. The one invented by Frederic Friedel?'

He looked at her, waiting for her to say, 'Of course.' But all she could say was, 'Who's Frederic Friedel?'

Roly was surprised. 'You don't play chess?'

'No, I'm afraid not.'

'Not at all?'

'Not at all.'

He frowned, as if he wanted to say that he found that strange but thought it impolite. Then he brightened and said, 'Well, then, I'll teach you.'

Karen didn't really want to learn. The only board games she played were such things as snakes and ladders with Evie's children, and those she enjoyed because the children loved them. For herself, she always thought she'd better things to do than sit at a table agonizing over which move to make.

But it was still raining heavily outside, so she submitted to being taught chess. Roly said, 'It would be no use trying to teach you on computer because the opponent's moves come too fast. So we'll do it with my pocket

234

set.' He produced a little wallet which un-folded into a small chessboard. A pouch provided a set of miniature chessmen. He set them out, fitting them into little holes in the board. 'Neat, isn't it? It's for travelling,' he explained. 'On planes and trains – if they get jolted they stay put.'

They sat down at the corner of the com-puter desk, with the board between them. 'Right, you be black, I'll be white, 'cos white goes first.' He moved a pawn. 'Your move.'

'What do I do?' she asked.

'Move one of your pawns.'

'These are the pawns?' she said, indicating the front row of pieces.

He smothered a laugh. 'You don't know the names of the pieces?'

'Er ... no ... I think this is the bishop,' she said, touching a little figure with a mitre.

'Good! And this is the castle, and this is the knight.'

'Oh, yes, I recognize him from the illustra-tions in *Alice*. And the queen, although she doesn't have a frowning face.'

'Be serious,' he scolded. 'Well, the pawn moves two paces forward at first so pick one and move it.'

She obeyed. What he was taking her through was the Ruy Lopez opening but she was quite unaware of that. When he moved his knight, she did the same, and so on like a mirror image of his moves in a way that soon took them astray from the classic game. He suddenly moved a knight and captured one of her pawns.

'How did you do that?' she cried.

'Simple. Your pawn was open to attack so I took it.'

'But that piece you moved was nowhere near my pawn!'

'Yes, it was.'

'It wasn't,' she protested. 'It wasn't next door on any square!'

'But the knight moves across three squares,' he said, surprised.

'Three squares?'

'Yes, like this.' He demonstrated.

'Well, I don't call that fair.'

'But it's how it moves.'

'You horrible little boy,' she moaned dramatically, 'you've inveigled me into this game just so as to make me look like a nincompoop! Do any other pieces do this sort of jig across the squares?'

He giggled. 'You're *hopeless*! You really don't know how the pieces move?'

'Of course not. And if you aren't going to tell me, I can see you're going to win every game.'

'Well, I didn't know you didn't know how the pieces move. I'll explain.' He made a rapid course through them, touching each piece and explaining their use. Karen had no idea which did what even when he'd finished.

'Please, teacher, I didn't understand any of that.'

He sat back on his chair, deep in thought. 'P'raps I'm not the right person to teach you,' he admitted. 'I can't sort of understand how little you know.' Then he brightened. 'I know, we'll go and ask Pierre.'

'Who's Pierre?'

'He's one of the doormen, he's on nights mostly. Come on!' He leapt up and was out of the room before she could prevent it.

They went along the outer hall to a door at the end labelled *Sortie de secours*, which led to a flight of concrete stairs quite unlike the luxury of the main entrance and with a service lift alongside. Roly went into the lift and pressed buttons. At sub-ground level they emerged into the garage which in the twenties had replaced stabling for horses and lodgings for grooms. They went behind a couple of expensive cars, to a one-storey block of more recent vintage. Roly went in, leading the way into a small vestibule. He tapped on a door opening off it. He called in French, 'Pierre, it's me, Roly. Can I come in?'

After a moment in which Karen could hear a slight coughing and shuffling, as of someone getting up from an armchair, the door opened. 'Roly, my boy. How are you?'

'I'm fine, thanks, and you?'

'Not bad, not bad. And is this the friend you've told me about? Good afternoon, mademoiselle.'

'Good afternoon. I hope we didn't disturb you?'

'No, no, only a little catnap. Well, so here you are. I thought you were going on a picnic?'

'Oh, Pierre, it's pouring with rain!' But out of the basement window, Pierre probably couldn't see the rain. 'We came home and I tried to teach Karen how to play chess, but I don't think I'm any good at that. Could you tell her one or two things to help her?'

Pierre looked at Karen, a friendly half-smile on his lips. He had a high colour, perhaps due to overindulgence in certain beverages, and the grey-white stubble on his chin showed him to be in late middle-age. He was wearing the trousers of his porter's uniform but instead of the jacket there was a worn brown sweater.

He gestured to them to come in. The room was small but well-equipped with built-in furniture. A door on the far side suggested sleeping quarters. She realized this was a slightly modernized version of the concierge system.

'Coffee?' he inquired, nodding at the hot-plate.

'Oh yes, please!' cried Roly.

'Are you allowed coffee?' Karen protested.

238

Pierre gave her a wink. 'It's my special coffee,' he said. 'You too, mademoiselle?'

'I'd like that.'

He made coffee with the quick dexterity of the man accustomed to living alone and catering for himself. A jug, a kettle of hot water, and in two minutes he was pouring the liquid into cups. She noted that Roly's cup was three-quarters milk, so she relaxed.

'So,' said Pierre, 'you're here for a chess lesson, mademoiselle?'

'I'm afraid so, monsieur.'

'My fees are very high,' he warned.

'Oh dear. Then Roly will have to pay you out of his next pocket money.'

Roly giggled. 'I'll pay you thousands and thousands,' he cried, delighted with the joke. 'Anything, if only you'll show her that a knight moves over three squares.'

'Now, that is very, very difficult,' said Pierre. 'Please, mademoiselle, sit down. You see the game already on the board?' It lay on a small table so as to get the muted light from the window. 'This is the final stages of a game Roly and I are engaged in. Can you see what should happen next?'

She stared at the board. There seemed to be about a dozen and a half pieces dotted here and there. She shook her head.

'White to move and mate in four moves,' Pierre prompted.

'No. I'm afraid I'm clueless.'

'In that case, we take the pieces away and we set out the board as if we're going to start a new game. Roly, don't forget where we were with the old game.'

'OK,' the boy said nonchalantly.

Karen glanced at him in surprise. Pierre caught the glance and raised an eyebrow, but said nothing. He set out the pieces, and for the next half hour he tried to guide her through what she should be doing against his play. Roly stood by, occasionally giggling when she made some move even more ridiculous than the last.

In the end she shook her head. 'I'm afraid it's no use,' she said, 'I just can't get the hang of it.'

'No, I see you can't. It doesn't matter, mademoiselle, some people have the knack and some don't.' He glanced at his watch. 'If you'll forgive me, I have to shave and change for my evening stint. Roly, will you take this little collection of rubbish to the *poubelle* for me?' He handed over a plastic bag, which Roly accepted with enthusiasm, running out at once.

'He loves to do the dustbin,' Pierre said. 'He likes to make it clang.' He drew a deep breath, studying her for a moment. 'Mademoiselle, have you any influence with the parents of that child?'

'Me? Good Lord, no!'

'Ah, that's sad. I hoped you might come to

his aid.'

'Well ... I've tried to, in a way. What is it? What's troubling you?'

'Mademoiselle, Roland is a very, very clever little boy. Exceptional. He is one of the best chess players I have ever come across. He beats me more than half the time although I try to hold my own.'

'I know, of course, that he's bright – beyond his age, I would say.'

'He's *exceptional*. I've known him for more than three years, and I can tell you he never ceases to amaze me. I have grandchildren, mademoiselle, but not one of them could compare with that boy. So you see ... I was wondering ... I can't undertake to speak to his parents. But a child like that needs special help, and ... well ... he's not getting it. So I was hoping perhaps you could...?'

'Me?' said Karen, with a sad shake of the head. 'No, I'm the last person, I'm afraid.'

'But you visit the apartment. He goes out with you. The family see you as a friend.'

'No,' she said. 'Quite the reverse.'

Thirteen

Pierre's appeal returned to trouble Karen often during the next few days. Her conclusion was always the same. There was no way she could approach Hélène Dartieux on such a matter. She was very definitely persona non grata in that household.

This had been demonstrated once again before she took leave of Roly on Sunday. She felt she couldn't go until someone came home and that someone, of course, had to be Gabrielle. The other servant didn't come in at the weekend, and the parents were in Helsinki.

Gabrielle's greeting was civil but cool. Karen explained at once that they'd come in to get out of the rain. This was acknowledged by a faint inclination of the neat grey head. Roly said, tentative but urged by the rules of hospitality, 'Could we offer Mademoiselle Karen something to eat before she leaves?'

'I think not, Roland. Mademoiselle doesn't wish to waste any more of her evening, I'm sure.'

He looked hurt at the use of the word 'waste'. Karen said quickly, 'Oh, it's always a great pleasure to spend time with Roland. But I shall be having dinner soon, madame. So I wish you good evening.'

'I'll see you out,' he said, and went down with her to the hall despite a slight movement on the housekeeper's part to prevent him. Pierre had come on duty downstairs, so he opened the heavy outer door for her, touching his cap as he did so.

Outside it was still raining hard. She bestowed a quick kiss on the little boy then ran for her car. As she drove off she could see him in her mirror, still standing in the ornate doorway looking after her, the uniformed man at his side.

This picture returned to her inner vision time and again.

But then it was Tuesday, and she had to meet her client. His name was Frobisher, he was an antique dealer, and what he wanted was a warehouse on the perimeter of the city where he could store purchases until he could ship them to clients in America or Japan. There were plenty of premises to show him. The problem was that he expected modern facilities such as lifts and air conditioning for the kind of money that would get him an old barn.

Verrieres le Buisson, le Port Marly, Ruell, Houille ... She was resigning herself to her first failure. At the end of the second week they parted, her client tucking a folder of properties into his briefcase but shaking his head. She rang Jeffrey to report defeat. 'Never mind,' he said, 'you can't win 'em all.'

That wasn't exactly a new thought, but she felt bad about it all the same. She spent two days at Gustave Kloss clearing up some problems and explaining on the telephone to the local agents that her client had been unresponsive. June was coming to a wet and dreary end. Even Paris looked depressed, the pretty summer clothes of the girls hidden under umbrellas and the cars throwing up plumes of water as they passed, soaking the pedestrians.

Her mobile rang on a Wednesday evening when she was contemplating taking a little time off to visit Evie in Kent. 'He's back!' Jeffrey Lynwood told her.

'Who – a gremlin?'

'Emlyn Frobisher. He wants a re-run of some of the premises you showed him. Are you on for that, or do you want some time off? I could get Roger to do it if you need a break.'

'No, it's OK,' she said. 'But this time he either says yes to something or I throw him in the Seine.'

'Please ensure he has a lifebelt if you do that,' he countered, then gave her the time and place to pick up the choosy Mr Frobisher next day.

She soon realized that in the interim her client had tried elsewhere without success. He now wanted to revisit three of the offers he'd turned down. Friday morning he asked to be taken to the *notaire*, and began negotiations to lease one of the sites.

'You never can tell,' Jeffrey said when she reported it to him. 'People are funny about making decisions. I bet he'd really picked out the place he wanted, perhaps subconsciously, but he just needed time to acknowledge it.'

'But he goes round France and Italy looking for furniture and statues – if he doesn't bid for them when he sees them, how does he get enough antiques to need a warehouse?'

'That's one of the mysteries of psychology. Well, what about some time off? I think you've earned it.'

'It would be nice,' she acknowledged. 'But before I go, I thought I'd drop in on Roly...'

'Would you? He'd love that.'

'This weather puts a damper on outdoor activity. OK to take him to a movie?'

'Well ... I'll check with Hélène. It ought to be OK. I'll ring you back.' When he did, about half an hour later, he was subdued. 'Hélène says it's OK so long as you take him to something suitable. I've looked it up on the Internet and the only thing seems to be a Hungarian cartoon version of *Hansel and Gretel.*'

'What, no *Pocahontas* or *Jungle Book?*'

'Hèléne doesn't approve of American cartoons. She thinks they're vulgar.' He sighed.

'Oh. Well, all right, we'll go to *Hansel and Gretel.*'

'Good Lord, Karen, it seems such a ... an unamusing thing to do!'

'Who knows?' she said. 'Maybe when I ring the cinema there won't be any tickets available.'

'Oh, I see,' he said, and laughed.

She didn't actually lie when she collected Roly at the apartment building. 'Things didn't work out about the film,' she told him, 'so I thought instead we'd go to a shopping mall, if you wouldn't be bored by that.'

'A shopping mall?' He was intrigued. 'Some of the kids in my class go to a shopping mall with their mothers ... They say they get frozen yoghurt, and giant cookies, and there are balloons in all kinds of shapes – like Asterisk, or R2 D2 – is that true?'

'You mean you've never been to a shopping mall?' she asked, astounded.

'Well, no ... When we go shopping for clothes, Mama likes special little shops, and if Gabrielle has to take me with her we generally go to the street market for fruit and stuff. Norah...' He paused to think about Norah, who seemed distant and vague these days. 'Norah took me to a shopping mall once,' he remembered, 'but she left me in the kiddies' place with bouncy balls and things while she tried on trainers. I didn't see any giant cookies.'

'Let's see what we can find.'

The time flew by. Roly was enchanted with everything – with the toy shops, the kiosks selling hot snacks, the tiny carousel on which he had two rides, the giant television screen showing clips from adventure films, the clown on roller-blades who glided about distributing advertising leaflets. He enjoyed himself so much that in the Metro on the way home he fell asleep clutching the string of the balloon she bought him.

She hated to wake him at their stop. They walked rather slowly along the tree-lined avenue to his home, the cuddly form of Winnie the Pooh sailing along beside them. She said to him, 'I'll explain to Gabrielle that we couldn't get into the cinema, OK?'

'Yes,' he said sleepily.

Gabrielle was taken aback at the sight of the balloon. Karen said at once, 'We didn't have any luck at the cinema, so I just took Roland to look at the toy shops.'

'I hope you didn't buy him any of the junk food they sell there, mademoiselle.'

'Not at all. Only the balloon. That's a character from one of the British children's books – a classic, you know.'

'Very well,' said Gabrielle, eyeing it dubiously. 'Thank you and good evening, mademoiselle.'

'Good evening.'

As she made her way back to the Metro, Karen was thinking that the child seemed to have almost no connection to ordinary life. He was driven to and from school on weekdays and to church with his parents on Sundays. School friends didn't visit, nor did he go to their homes to play with them. He'd told her the recently hired Yvette was 'no fun.' The other servants at the flat were part-time cleaners who came while he was at school. His teacher seemed to find him 'un-co-operative'. As far as she could gather the only run-of-the-mill Parisians he met were the hall porters.

When he was with Jeffrey, of course, things would be different. She gathered they went to cinemas and cricket matches, shopped for food in supermarkets, drove to leisure parks. But that was only once a month. It wasn't enough.

As July began, with the rain still coming down over the French countryside, she took an elderly widow on a search for a suitable flat in a suitable country town. It had been a leisurely trip because Miss Grimshaw didn't enjoy the best of health. As they began their return journey to Paris, Karen got a phone call from Jeffrey.

'Listen, Karen, I'm going to ask you an enormous favour. You're due back in Paris tomorrow, yes?'

'That's right.'

'Could you meet me there and take Roly from me? And then bring him to London?'

'Of course, but what's going on?'

'I've got to go to Spain – the firm owns a couple of holiday villas there, in the foothills of the Cordillera Cantabrica, and because of this confounded weather, the two houses have been engulfed in a mud slide. Our clients are in a dreadful mess and the local authorities aren't being too efficient. So could you...?'

'That's no problem, Jeffrey. I can take Roly over. But what happens then?'

'Well, I've got some decent neighbours who say they'll keep an eye on him till I get back...'

'Keep an eye on him?'

'They're OK, Karen. A bit elderly, but—'

'And how long are they supposed to act as nursemaids?'

'Well, with luck I might be back in time to get some time with him—'

'Jeffrey, I know you're doing your best in an emergency, but you can't really let the poor kid be stuck in a block of flats with neighbours! Why don't you let me take him to Evie's with me?'

'Your sister's?'

'Yes, that's where I'm going. I generally try to catch up with her when I can.'

'But what would she say to—'

'Oh, they live in this big rambling farmhouse with a dozen rooms and enough outbuildings to accommodate an army. Roly would hardly be noticed. And besides, he'd be with other children. Don't you think that would be better?'

'It would be great! Are you sure your sister wouldn't mind?'

'Not at all. In fact she'd love to meet Roly because she's heard me talk about him so much. But what about Roly? How does he feel about it?'

'He doesn't know so far,' he confessed. 'I was in such a dilemma I didn't want to phone him until I'd got something worked out. But I bet he'd be thrilled.'

So it proved. Jeffrey brought the little boy to the Hotel Babette early on the Saturday morning before leaving almost at once for a flight to Bilbao. Flushed cheeks and too much chatter showed that Roly was in a high state of excitement.

'Daddy says we'll be going on the ferry! Is it true the ship's so big it's got shops and things? Can I see the anchor going up?'

'But you've done all this before,' Karen teased. 'Only you were fast asleep last time.'

Roly made a face. 'Oh, in your car ... It was uncomf'table among all those parcels! Can I

250

sit in front with you and see everything when you drive on and off?'

'Only if you promise to behave and keep your seat belt fastened.'

'Of course, Daddy's said all that already.' His tone held some of the impatience children always feel at the way grown-ups go on about safety and good behaviour.

The ferry was crowded because the tourist season was in full swing. To most people the crossing would have been tiresome because of the queues and the hubbub, but Roly was enraptured. He loved the cavernous hold with its patient rows of stationary vehicles, the cold stairways leading up to the passenger decks, the array of communications masts above the bridge, the white wake behind them in grey water over which swooped gulls hoping for titbits. Holding tightly to Karen's hand, the little boy drank it all in.

He was equally delighted by the English service station at which they stopped soon after disembarking. 'All-day breakfast,' he read from the signs over the serving tables. 'How can you eat breakfast all day?'

She laughed. 'It doesn't mean that, sweetie. It means you can order the things we eat for breakfast at any hour of the day because people like them so much. Somebody once said you can eat well in Britain so long as you always order breakfast.'

Roly puzzled over that for a long time. But soon he was asking to visit the games machines at which he saw other children playing. 'No, Roly, I don't want to hang about, and besides, I'm sure your parents would disapprove.' His rather shamefaced glance told her that this was so. She gave him a grin to let him know she was quite accustomed to the wiles of children.

His attention was drawn to the fields edging the roads on which they were soon travelling again. 'There's Charolais cattle!' he cried. 'Fancy that! We have those in France too, you know – they're in the picture books at school.'

But as they turned on to side roads and drew close to Dagworth, he fell silent. He was apprehensive, she could tell. He was going to meet new children, and his experience with his schoolmates led him to expect a less than friendly response. She longed to say, 'Don't worry, they're nice kids.' But that would only bring out into the open the fact that he wasn't good at making friends.

Since it was Saturday, Evie's children were at home. As Karen drove up they surged out of the front door to greet her and the new guest. 'Hello, had a good trip? Which is your bag? I'll take it up. No, let me! Look out, you're pushing Noomie over! I say, you've got a TinTin backpack.' And so on. In the midst of this clamour the fact that Roly was

252

silent and shy went unnoticed.

In the hall, Evie was smiling a welcome. She rescued Noomie from the pack then led the way upstairs, her children trying to get ahead of her, to show the visitor his room. Karen took Roly by the hand. He said nervously, 'This is Mrs Felton?'

'Yes, my sister Evie – we'll do introductions in a minute when everybody's calmed down. My brother-in-law – *mon beau-frère* is at his office.' She gave a little laugh of encouragement. 'How do you like it so far?'

'It's ... it's very informal.'

'You can say that again!' Then she added, seeing his puzzlement: 'That's an Americanism, it means "How true". Don't worry, Roly, it's not usually such a brawl. They're glad to see you, that's all.'

He looked sceptical but said nothing. He was ushered into the spare bedroom, where the rather formal decoration had been softened by Evie's addition of some toys from Perry's collection. 'That's mine really,' Perry said at once on seeing a Tonka truck, 'but I'm giving you a lend while you're here. Angela wanted to lend one of her Barbie dolls but I told her that was soppy.'

'Thank you,' said Roly in a faint voice.

'Do you want to unpack now, Roly?' Evie asked. Noomie, set down by his mother, immediately sat on the floor and began to unzip the backpack. 'No, no, Noomie, that belongs to Roly,' scolded his mother.

'Noomie?' Roly repeated. 'Is that an English name?'

'No – when he began to speak he called himself that because he couldn't say his real name, that's Norman.' Perry gave a shrug. 'He's only little.'

Angela had said nothing to the newcomer so far. Now she announced, 'I can speak some French.'

'Oh, what a lie!' Perry gave Roly a knowing smile. 'She can only say *bonjour* and *bonsoir* – she asked Mummy this morning. Auntie Karen says you speak French all the time at home?'

'Ye-es – Maman sometimes speaks English with me.'

By this time Noomie had pulled out pyjamas, a T-shirt, toilet bag, a pair of slippers, and one pair of trainers. Evie scooped it all up to deposit on the bed. 'We'll leave all this until later. Come along downstairs for elevenses.'

'Elevenses?'

'D'inks and bickies,' said Noomie, and taking his hand, began to pull Roly towards the door.

Karen watched it unfold and was pleased. Her niece and nephews had accepted Roly as naturally as they would have accepted any other child. She hoped nothing would happen to mar the camaraderie, although in the natural course of events there would be some bickering. Perry, she knew, liked to be leader. She was interested to note that Roly seemed already to accept that, perhaps because Perry was clearly the eldest child.

After elevenses, Perry declared that even though it was dull and rather drizzly, they must all go out to show Roly the lay of the land. Karen went with them merely as watchdog – she needed to make sure that nobody fell in the pond, for instance. There were promises of playing 'Return of the Jedi' among the hideouts in the shrubbery, and fishing for late-stage tadpoles in the pond, but then they came to the paddock.

'A horse!' cried Roly.

'It's a *pony*,' Perry corrected in a lordly tone. 'It's Angela's.'

'Your pony? You ride it?'

'It's a she, her name's Popcorn,' Angela said. The pony was already making her way from the far side of the paddock at the sound of an approach by those she thought of as her friends. Angela, from her pocket, produced a biscuit purloined from the kitchen for just this moment. She gave a piece to Popcorn, who snuffled it up with her soft lips and nodded appreciation.

'She took it from your hand!' Roly cried.

'Of course, she loves bickies and mints – but she mustn't have too many 'cos they'd make her fat. Would you like to give her a piece?'

'Me?'

'Yes, d'you want to?'

'But ... but ... wouldn't she bite me? She doesn't know me.'

'Oh, Popcorn wouldn't bite anybody,' Perry declared.

Well, if Perry said it, it must be true. Roly looked at Karen for confirmation and permission. She nodded. Breaking off a piece of her mother's home-made chocolate chip cookie, Angela placed it on Roly's palm.

He approached the fence, held out his hand between the bars, Popcorn bent her head, and the gentle lips picked up the gift.

'Ohhh,' sighed the little boy. When he turned to follow the others Karen glimpsed tears in his eyes. She was about to ask if there was anything wrong but he blinked then gave her a starry smile.

She realized he'd just fallen in love.

The rest of the morning went by in a certain amount of showing-off on the part of the Felton children and a complete acceptance of his secondary status from Roly. Karen, reasonably certain that things would go well, left them to play. She went indoors. She needed to change out of the jeans and T-shirt in which she'd travelled, and to wash and freshen up. Clad in a cotton skirt and sleeveless top, she went to gossip with her sister. Evie had started preparations for lunch.

'He's a quiet one,' she said as she cut strips of carrot on a mandolin.

'Not always. But he seems to be fitting in very well.'

'Don't let Perry boss him about too much.'

'Let's just leave them to get on with it.' Karen was opening cupboards to find the crockery for a kitchen lunch: thick mugs for milk, big plates for salad, a platter for home-made bread.

'Michael will be here for dinner,' Evie remarked.

The cutlery Karen was placing hit the table in a jangle. 'What?' she gasped.

'For dinner,' Evie said over her shoulder. 'I thought it wouldn't be any good inviting him for earlier because you'd have to give your attention to the kiddie, of course, until he seems settled in.'

'Michael's here?'

The consternation in her voice made her sister turn from the worktop to stare. 'What's the matter?'

'I thought Michael was in Northumbria!'

'Oh, that trip ended last week. He's been in Kent three or four days, looking at property in the downs behind Deal and Havant.'

'And he's been in touch?'

'Of course. What a funny thing to ask. Naturally, if he's coming to Kent, he'd be in touch.' Evie paused. 'You really didn't know he was here?'

'No.'

'But haven't you – I mean, surely you've rung each other?'

'No.'

Evie frowned. 'What's going on, Karen? I know you said when he first got back that you and he weren't as close as before, but ... he said...' A brighter colour came into her round features. 'I got the impression there had been a kiss-and-make-up night.'

A mixture of anger and confusion surged over Karen. She couldn't think of anything to say. Quite true, Michael might actually believe there had been a reconciliation. That night at her flat, the note he'd left had been full of nonchalant self-confidence. Contrary to his expectation, it had filled her with self-blame.

Since then, he'd rung her once on her mobile. At the time she'd been in a hotel in Pontivy. She'd lied, saying she was driving on a busy auto-route and didn't want to talk. 'I'm with a client, Michael. Please don't ring me on this line.' The last thing she wanted was to have to deal with him during business transactions.

After that there had been a silence. She'd put him out of her mind. But that had clearly been a mistake. He still remained in her life, a problem she still had to deal with because

258

in her own weakness she'd given him power over her.

'We haven't been in touch,' she told her sister. 'While I'm shepherding people around in France, it isn't helpful to get personal calls—'

'But *you've* rung *him?*'

'No I haven't.'

'Karen, you ought to show some sense, you know. Getting involved with your employer is a very bad idea.'

'I'm not involved with my employer.'

'Oh no? Hanging around in Paris to visit his kid, and now bringing the boy here...'

'Surely you don't mind putting Roly up for a couple of days?' Karen exclaimed, startled.

'Of course not, he seems a nice enough lad, but all the same, it's a big step in your relationship with this Lynwood character, sort of taking on the responsibility for him – it's like a try-out to see how you and the boy would get on if it came to ... well ... to hitching up in some way with his father.'

'It's nothing like that, Evie. It was just that it was Jeffrey's turn to have the boy with him and he had to go to Spain—'

'Oh, ha-ha! And there's nobody else he could have called on, of course...'

'Well, there wasn't!'

'If you believe that, you believe in the Tooth Fairy.'

'Evie,' Karen said, trying to keep her

temper, 'even if what you're imagining were true, that's no reason to invite Michael here.'

'Yes, it is a reason!' Evie snapped, her voice rising. 'Michael's a super person and it's just so *rotten* of you to let him down now, when he's got such a lot on his mind with this new business venture—'

'Evie! *Evie!* Stop it! You sound like the Michael Ansleigh fan club!' By speaking very loudly she managed to drown out the rest of what her sister was trying to say. Evie faltered into silence, colouring up as she turned back to her lunch preparations.

After a moment Karen said, 'I know you think a lot of Michael, and you're trying to do what you think is best for me. But I'm a big girl, and I don't need any help from you or anyone else when it comes to my private affairs. Do we agree on that?'

'But you're not saying I have to ask your permission before I invite him to dinner!'

'Of course not.'

'And let's get it clear – are you trying to avoid him?'

'We-ell...'

'And it's true, isn't it, what Michael says, that although you'd drifted apart a bit, you and he got together again before he went up north?'

'I really don't want to go into that. From my point of view we haven't "got together". And whether we have or not has nothing to

260

do with Jeffrey Lynwood.'

'Well, what has it got to do with? That's what I don't understand.'

'It's a long story, and to be candid I'm not clear why I have to make explanations about it to you.' Karen broke off, making a big effort to control her temper. 'You've got four hungry kids outside wanting their lunch. Can we just be sensible and get on with things?'

Evie shrugged and began to put the salad ingredients into a bowl.

After the meal, Noomie had to have his afternoon nap, while his mother began preparations for dinner. Although it was only a small affair, the chief guests being one of Walt's business friends and his wife, it seemed Evie was determined to make it special. Karen decided not to offer any help. An hour or two of separation seemed a good idea. She took the children out for a walk.

They took a footpath along the Dagget, the local stream where the bird-watching was good. Karen let the children look through her binoculars. Roly was enthralled. 'But they're so close! And what's that one with the white *gilet*? Oh, look, he's going into the water ... oh, where's he gone?'

'That's a dipper,' said Angela importantly. 'We often see him. I 'spect you don't have them in Paris.' She gave him a rather muddled lecture about the difference between a dipper and a wagtail, to which he listened with respect. It occurred to Karen that it was seldom he found children who knew more about a subject than he did.

They arrived home tired and hungry, and quite ready for children's tea, children's television, bath and bed. Roly was clearly surprised to witness the argument about going to bed. He took no part, and when at last Karen went into his room to say goodnight, he asked, 'Is it all right for them to disagree when it's bedtime?'

She laughed. 'Their mother would say no to that.'

'But she didn't get cross.'

'No, Evie seldom gets cross.'

'I see.'

She dropped a kiss on his forehead. 'Goodnight, Roly.'

'Goodnight, Karen.'

Downstairs, the guests had arrived for pre-dinner drinks. While the children were having their meal, Karen had showered and changed into a pale print dress, and had put on some make-up and brushed her dark cap of hair. She now went downstairs, bracing herself to greet Michael.

He was engaged in a close conversation with Mr Scholes, while Walt poured sherry for Mrs Scholes. Evie was offering canapés. Karen contented herself with a wave in the general direction of everyone then fetched herself a glass of wine.

'Everything OK upstairs?' Evie asked.

'Yes, fine.'

'You know Mrs Scholes? Marion, this is my sister Karen.'

'Oh, yes, the one who has this marvellous job travelling all round France! Lovely to meet you. Do you know Antibes? Herb and I went there last year for our hols, it was gorgeous. Very chic, which I love.' And Mrs Scholes had the dress to prove it.

Sitting beside Marion Scholes, Karen answered her questions while trying to eavesdrop on the conversation between Michael and Herbert Scholes. As far as she could make out, Michael was getting information about property development around the area where Mr Scholes lived. Good, she thought. If he keeps thinking about business prospects, it'll keep him occupied.

By and by Evie worked her way round to a spot behind Karen's shoulder. 'I can't put you next to him at dinner,' she murmured. 'You'll have to be next to Herbert.'

But with only six people at the table, it was impossible not to be in close proximity. Karen and Herbert were on one side of the table, Marion and Michael the other, with Walt at the head, and Evie at the end closest to the kitchen. Michael held Karen's gaze and gave her a big smile that meant: I know you understand I'd rather be next to you.

She gave a brief smile in return, thinking he looked thinner and with perhaps more of a frown line between his brows, but handsome and bronzed from his journeying around the countryside.

If she'd thought there might be difficulties in dealing with dinner-table conversation, she was quickly disabused. The men talked business, the women talked about family and local events. Karen's part was limited to hearing about the new conservatory at her parents' home in Guildford and giving information about cross-Channel shopping. After the meal the men begged to be allowed to watch cricket. Karen cleared the table and stocked the dishwasher while Evie took Marion to admire the aquarelles which, a failure or not, she felt were worth showing off.

Left to her own devices, Karen went out into the damp coolness of the late-night garden. Far off she heard an owl, and beyond that the faint drone of the holiday traffic heading for the seaside resorts. She was scolding herself for getting panicky over Michael. At the next opportunity she was going to make it clear to Evie that the relationship between them was over no matter what had happened that one foolish night in her London flat.

Whether Evie would understand was another matter. But one thing must be made plain: there was to be no more match-making, no more allowing her to act the affectionate go-between.

Not until it was time for the chief visitors to leave did she have to be alone with Michael. Everyone walked out to see the Scholeses get into their Audi.

'Haven't seen much of you this evening, sweetheart,' he sighed taking her hand and holding it close to his side. 'You understood, of course – two guys like your brother-in-law and Herbert Scholes – I mean, they know the coastal district like the back of their hands. I had to take advantage of the chance.'

'Yes, I understand.' She disengaged herself from his grasp, turning away to wave good-night to the others as they drove off.

'I'll see you tomorrow,' he said.

'Tomorrow!'

'Oh, Evie didn't tell you? I've got some acreage to look at tomorrow. Got the info from an estate agent in Maidstone who deals in greenfield sites, but on my way back I'll be dropping in and then we can have a good long talk. See you, sweetheart!' He got into his rented car; Walt came to remind him of road repairs at the next junction, and he was gone in a flurry of gravel.

So now was the time to get hold of Evie and have the necessary explanation, Karen told herself. Walt had begun the process of

265

putting the house to sleep, bringing in discarded toys, locking doors and windows. Karen and Evie could be alone in the kitchen.

'Evie,' she said, 'I want to tell you something. Before I begin, promise to hear me out and not start an argument.'

'What?'

'Do you promise?'

'Promise what?'

'To *listen*! Will you do that?'

'Well, what a funny thing to say! I always listen when you talk to me—'

'Evie! Pay attention!' She drew a deep breath. 'You are not to invite Michael here on purpose to meet up with me. He and I are no longer friends. I don't telephone him or try to keep in touch with him, I've asked him not to phone me. I don't want to happen upon him every time I come to visit you. If you're inviting him in the future, let me know so I can stay away.'

Her sister, her hands holding a box of freezer film, stood staring at her.

'Is that clear, Evie?'

'But what ... what...?'

'Is it clear? Michael and I are no longer an item.'

'But that's not true! Last time you were here you had a long, long talk out there by the paddock so I knew that if you'd drifted apart you—'

266

'We didn't drift apart. Michael sent me a letter from Chicago telling me we were through—'

'No, he didn't!'

'I found it on the doormat when I got back from Cambodia,' Karen forged on, shaking her head at Evie's interruption. 'He said he was going to start a new life in the States, so goodbye and good luck.'

'That's not true! He mentioned to me about how hard things were after the Twin Towers thing and he couldn't get home at first, and how after a bit he got this chance with this big firm that wants him to find land in England, which of course is so marvellous, to be in on the ground floor like that—'

'*Evie*! I got a letter. I had it in my hands. He told me it was all over. He didn't even give me an address to write back to—'

'Oh, you misunderstood it all, Michael would never—'

'Why are you defending him? Are you saying you'd rather believe Michael than me?'

That gave Evie pause. She set aside the box of film as if making a decision to concentrate. 'Of course I believe you, Karrie. But it's all a misunderstanding, don't you see that? Your new job and the sort of ... glamour, I suppose it is ... that goes with it. I can understand that it would make you feel an attraction to this Jeffrey Lynwood, but you know, dear, a lot of it is sympathy over that funny little boy of his.'

'Michael and I broke up long before I ever went to work for Jeffrey.'

'But that's what I was saying, love, all that about breaking up is just a mistake. I dare say he wrote something silly when he was in a bit of a muddle out there in Chicago in the midst of all that misery and confusion and, if you want to know the truth, I'm surprised at you for being so hard on him.'

'Whether you're surprised at me or not, I want it understood. I don't want you setting up little encounters between him and me. That's what I'm telling you at this moment. Evie? Do you understand?'

Evie frowned and shook her head. 'But I've invited him to drop in for a snack supper tomorrow. I can't cancel that, it wouldn't be civilized.'

'Give him a ring on his mobile. Tell him something's come up.'

'Oh, Karrie, you don't mean it.'

Karen gave a great sigh. 'I asked you to listen before I even started. Have you heard what I've been saying?'

'Of course I have, and what I can see is that you're overreacting to something that's come up between you, and it's not like you, Kar, it's not like you at all!'

They stood looking at each other as

antagonists. For a moment Karen's mind seemed to be telling her to give up the struggle. Her sister was fond of Michael – perhaps too fond. She didn't want to be convinced that it was better not to have him at her house. But then, that very thought urged her to try again. Evie's affection for Michael had its dangers. It was in itself a reason to persist against her baffling arguments.

'If I seem hard, it's because it's imperative to get you to understand. I went through a bad time at the end of last year.'

'Well, of course you felt low. But you wouldn't tell me why...'

'No, I didn't want to talk about it. I knew you'd find it hard to believe Michael had done anything wrong.'

'Well, there's always ups and downs in love, Karrie, you know that as well as I do. And from what Michael's told me—'

'But it's what *I'm* telling you that matters at the moment, Evie. I don't feel anything for Michael any more.'

'Oh, Karen dear, come on! If that's true, how did it come about that he spent a night at your place? He told me that any problems were completely washed away by—'

'By what? By the fact that he got under my defences and helped me make a fool of myself? I don't call that—'

'There you are! You've said it yourself. You don't need "defences" against a man you don't love, now, do you?'

Karen sat down on a chair by the table and put her head in her hands. It was useless. Evie was determined not to believe that Michael could be in the wrong. Evie, surprised, came to her side and put an arm around her.

'I'm sorry, sweetheart, I can see you're in an emotional muddle. But after all, I've been married for a long time now and I know things go wrong and then come right again. You just have to weather times like this. Trust me, whatever it is that's caused this silly fight will seem a triviality in the morning.'

'No, it won't, Evie. You just won't understand what I'm saying.'

'I'm saying you need a good night's sleep to get over all this. So, off to bed with you and, as I often say to the kids, it'll look all better by daylight.'

With this piece of motherly wisdom Evie paced in a regal manner out of the kitchen, calling to Walt that she was just coming and had he unplugged the television?

Karen had trouble getting to sleep that night. She went over her conversation with her sister, trying to see how she could have made it clearer. In the end, she concluded that the only way to stay out of contrived encounters with Michael was to limit her visits to Dagworth. She hoped that by and by Evie would see that she meant it when she said she didn't want to meet him.

Next day was the usual Sunday routine except that the children were quite keen to go to church. Perry had learned that Roly belonged to a different denomination, which meant he was able to explain events in a loud, important whisper. Roly accepted all this as perfectly appropriate. Perry was the eldest, this was his home turf, he owned the largest share of the toys at the house, therefore he was entitled to be bossy.

After Sunday lunch and a session with the newspapers, Karen took the children out to the paddock. It had been agreed that Roly could be given a ride on Popcorn. He was lifted astride, given the reins to hold, while Karen took the pony by the bridle to lead her in a sedate saunter along the inside perimeter.

Roly was white with a mixture of terror and delight, although cheered by cries of encouragement from the others. Even Noomie waved his arms and shouted, 'Good Roly, good!' When, after about fifty yards, he discovered he wasn't going to fall off or be run away with, he began prodding with his heels to get the pony to trot. Popcorn disregarded all that. Angela was the human who gave orders, and only Angela was going to get her to trot. Later, when Angela exchanged places with Roly and actually gave the order, Roly watched with enchantment.

'D'you think Maman and Papa Louis would let me have a pony like Popcorn?' he asked in an unhopeful tone.

'Difficult in Paris, don't you think?'

'I s'pose so.'

'Perhaps on school holidays?' Karen suggested.

'N-no ... Generally we go to somewhere like the Riviera, unless Papa Louis is sent on business somewhere else. Then we'd go there – Berlin, perhaps, or Lisbon.'

It didn't need to be said that the chance of pony-riding in any of those venues was small. 'You'll have to come back here and get Angela to give you another go.'

'Yes.' But he sounded as if he didn't expect it to happen.

They were making their slow way back to the house, the bigger children playing tag through the remains of the apple orchard and Karen carrying the toddler, when her cellphone twittered. She almost decided not to answer, thinking it was probably Michael. But Perry said, 'I'll take Noomie,' so she had no excuse for not getting the phone out of her skirt pocket.

It was Jeffrey. 'Hello, is this inconvenient, Karen?'

'No, no, I was surrounded by children,' she said as explanation for the delay. 'How did it go about the mud slide?'

'I contacted a firm of builders I've used on previous occasions, they were on the scene when I got to the houses. So they're at work and the tenants are in a good hotel trying to decide whether to stay or go home. I left them to it and flew straight to Heathrow. If they want to come back I'll arrange flights for them in the morning.'

'Where are you now?' she asked in surprise.

'I'm just trying to fight my way off the M25. My car was at the airport, of course. But traffic's heavy, heading out towards Kent.'

'You're on your way here?' she said, surprised.

'Yes, if that's OK? I thought if I could make it by, you know, early evening, Roly and I could get home at a reasonable hour, and anyway he can drop off to sleep in the car. Is it OK if I turn up at your sister's?'

'Of course! But what's your plan? Wouldn't it be better if he stayed overnight and I took him back by ferry in the morning? If there's a time limit on his trips to England...' She glanced about, ensuring that Roly wasn't nearby to hear this.

'No, I've got an extra day's grace with him for tomorrow, Karen. You see, it's his birthday. He's seven.'

'Oh, why didn't you say! We could have had a party.'

273

'It was all too much of a rush, wasn't it? But thanks for the thought. If it's not too much trouble to you and your sister, I'd like to come and get him because of his birthday present.' She heard him hesitate and give an embarrassed chuckle. 'You'll think I'm crazy, but it's something he's only likely to have any fun with if he's with me in the London flat.'

'Don't tell me you've bought him a chemistry set!' she countered, half-teasing.

'No. No ... it's a pair of pyjamas that glow in the dark.'

'What?'

'I knew you'd think I'm crazy! But I thought they'd make him laugh, and it's a cert they'd never let him wear them in the Rue Lacharotte. And, of course, they're at this moment on his bed at Harkway Mansions, wrapped up in birthday paper. So, I'd like to get him home so he can have a chance to try them on tonight.'

'I understand perfectly,' she said, smiling to herself at this mental picture. 'I'll tell Roly you're coming – he'll be thrilled.' She called to the little boy, 'Your Daddy says he'll be here in a couple of hours.'

'*C'est lui?*' He ran up, holding out his hand for the phone.

'He wants to speak to you...?'

'No, I pulled off on a lay-by but I must get going again so I'll sign off. Tell him I'll be there soon.'

Roly was dancing with delight at the news. 'When will he be here? I'll take him to see Popcorn!'

'His Daddy?' muttered Perry. 'From Paris?' He was thinking they were going to have to be polite to someone who spoke a foreign language and that Angela's *bonjour* and *bonsoir* would wear out soon.

'No, this is his Daddy that lives in London. He gets to visit him once a month.'

'Oh yes.' Perry and Angela were quite acquainted with that kind of arrangement. Some of their school friends had divorced parents.

In her way, Evie was as thrilled as Roly when she heard the news of the coming guest. 'Jeffrey? I thought you said he was in Spain?'

'Yes, but he just got back. He thought his problem would take longer but he's fixed something up.'

'He's going to need something to eat when he gets here. What sort of food does he like, Karen? Something sophisticated, I suppose, all that travelling he does.'

'I've no idea what he likes. I've not shared enough meals with him to know, really.'

'Well, I was going to do cold game pie and things because Michael likes my home-made pie...'

They were both silent a moment. It had just dawned on them both that the two men were going to meet.

Karen could see Evie thought it exciting, because she regarded them as rivals. Karen knew better and was proved right. For when Michael arrived, the first of the travellers, he was visibly pleased to hear that Jeffrey Lynwood was coming.

'That's a bit of luck,' he declared. 'I've always thought he sounds a clued-up sort of guy.'

'Clued-up?' Walt said.

'Well, he's the first person I'll have come across socially that's really in the property business.'

'But that's in France, Mike,' objected Walt.

'Oh, sure, but I bet he knows a bit about British conditions. You can see my point, I'm sure. I've got a lot of facts and figures and sheets of information about regulations and permissions and so forth, but it's *new* to me. I find it hard to get to grips with.'

'Well, look here, old man,' said Walt, 'the chap's just made a fast trip to Spain and back, and he's going to drive to London later – hardly seems right to corner him about property values.'

'No ... well ... perhaps not. But, I could sound him out, you know. Make a date to see him some day in London.'

'But you don't know the fellow!'

'Oh,' asserted Michael airily, 'any friend of Karen's is a friend of mine!'

Karen sneaked a glance at her sister. Evie looked quite disappointed that there weren't going to be any pistols at dawn over who had first claim to her hand.

Fourteen

Roly had been allowed to stay up because his father was coming to collect him. Therefore, by some unknown logic, *all* the children must be allowed to stay up.

The result was something approaching uproar. Evie had decreed a buffet supper, which meant people moving about with loaded plates and children having too many helpings of dessert. Noomie fell asleep in a corner of the sitting-room sofa with a spoon clutched in one hand. Angela had made herself a dolls' tea-party on an occasional table with a napkin as tablecloth and flowers in a tumbler.

Jeffrey Lynwood regarded it all with a sort of calm bemusement.

If Michael had hoped to make a useful business contact, he was disappointed because it was impossible to have five minutes continuous conversation. At nine o'clock, even leader-of-the-pack Perry was having trouble keeping his eyelids open, Angela had taken herself upstairs and fallen asleep on her bed without undressing, and Roly was

278

blinking like a baby owl.

His belongings had already been stowed in Jeffrey's car. The boy was put, unprotesting, into the back seat and strapped in. The grown-ups gathered round to say goodbye but he made almost no response. 'Ten minutes down the road and he'll be out for the count,' Walt remarked from his own long experience.

Jeffrey was saying his thanks to Evie. Michael was trying to get him aside for a last word. Karen tucked a rug around Roly. Jeffrey got in, they all stood back, and the two unexpected guests were gone.

'We-ell,' said Walt, sighing deeply, 'let's all have a nice quiet drink.'

It was just the right suggestion. But fifteen minutes later he and Evie had set their glasses aside and were putting their children into their beds. Karen started on the clearing up. Michael followed her around, picking up plates and napkins from odd corners.

'Seems clued-up about business.'

'Jeffrey? Well, he knows what he's doing.'

'Quite a laid-back type of guy,' he suggested.

'Oh yes, he doesn't get in much of a flap about anything.'

'I thought of giving him a ring...'

Karen walked away. She wasn't going to encourage him in an idea like that. Quite soon after, he had to leave, saying he had an appointment to look at a farm in Hampshire early next morning. Even the romantic Evie was glad to see him go, for it had been an exhausting day.

Next morning, Karen took the cross-Channel ferry to meet her new clients, a married couple looking for a *gîte* they could develop for holiday letting. The clouds had at last rolled away to reveal that much-desired silver lining. By midday they were in Chartres, enjoying *un sandwich à l'anglaise* and a cup of coffee, when Karen's mobile rang.

It was Roly. 'Happy birthday,' Karen said.

'Thank you, yes, and that's why I'm ringing. Daddy said I could tell you about it.' The little boy went off in a fit of giggles. 'I've got a skeleton!'

'A what?'

'A skeleton! It's on my new pyjamas! I put them on, and Daddy closes the curtains and turns out the lights, and there's my skeleton glowing in the dark!' Another fit of laughter. 'I'm standing here in my skeleton talking to you! I can see myself in the mirror. When I raise my other hand, the bones go up.' He paused for the fraction of a second, then said in a more serious tone, 'It's very clever, you know. Because the pyjamas are black, you can't see them when the lights go off, only the bones.' Another giggle. 'Oh, I do love them! You must come and see my bones next time you're in London.'

'I'd love to. What were your other presents?'

'Ah ... Well ... Maman gave me swimming trunks with dolphins on them and ... things...'

'Water wings,' came a prompt from his father.

'Water wings to match. So I'll look good at the Hotel Rangouf.'

'The what?'

'It's the hotel we go to in Juan-les-Pins.'

'Oh yes.'

'And Papa Louis gave me a *coupon*...'

'Voucher.' From the prompter.

'Voucher to buy toys so I'll get the new computer chess game.'

'I'd like to give you a present too, Roly. Would you like binoculars?'

'To see birds close-up? Oh, that would be great, I could look at the gulls and things by the shore. Oh, thank you, Karen, that would be really cool.'

Muffled conversation. 'Daddy says I must sign off because you may be on the road.'

'No, we're at a bistro.'

'Well, anyway, I'd better go, because it's nearly lunchtime and I have to confess I'm *still in my pyjamas*.' Peals of laughter, in which his eventual goodbye was lost.

Karen was smiling to herself as she walked back to her clients at the table. It was the first time she'd heard Roly laugh so joyously. And, she reflected, it was the first time she'd heard him make a joke. 'I'm still in my pyjamas' – not bad for a first attempt.

The time that followed was rather fraught. Her clients were business people who knew what they wanted, so they covered a lot of ground. She snatched a moment to visit a sporting goods store for binoculars for Roly, ordering them to be sent direct so he could pack them for his seaside trip. July ended, the roads became cluttered with towns-people heading for their holiday homes. Presumably amongst them were the Dartieux with Roly.

In flying visits to London she cleared up mail, returned phone calls, and received instructions. Everyone was at full stretch: this was the busiest time for looking at property abroad. During their school holidays, parents took their children to see possible holiday homes, sometimes entering into negotiation over a cottage they'd rented the previous summer. Karen found she spent quite a lot of time at the offices of Gustave Kloss, helping clients through the opening stages of purchase.

She welcomed the beginning of September with heartfelt relief. The sun still shone and the Midi, where she was spending a lot of her time, was as dry as dinosaurs' bones, but there was a slight lowering of the temperature. A breeze freshened the air. And she managed to get a four-day break, two of which she spent at Dagworth Farm at Evie's demand, because, though Walt and Evie were building sandcastles in Jersey, they worried for fear their home might be broken into.

She put all her laundry through Evie's state-of-the-art equipment and while it was going through its paces she had a quiet visit with Popcorn the pony.

Popcorn was glad to see her. With the children away, she felt neglected. 'Oh, stop being so greedy,' Karen told her as she stroked her neck. 'I haven't got any more mints.' She wondered if Roly had ever asked his mother for a pony. The answer would have been no, but to be fair that was only to be expected. Town children might long for the thrill of trotting in the nearby park, but the difficulties were too great for most families.

She returned to London after ringing Evie to assure her that her home was quite safe and that the gardener had come to mow the lawn as promised. There were household chores at the flat and she had to review her wardrobe – her summer clothes had been almost worn out over the last three months, and there was the coming of autumn to plan for.

She looked in on the office. Mireille had returned on a part-time basis, and Jeffrey was in his room catching up with paperwork. She took Mireille out to a long lunch so as to hear all about the baby, then after parting from her went back to the office to look at work schedules. Jeffrey came to hover at the door of his room.

'Roly loves his binoculars,' he said.

'Yes, he sent me a thank-you card from Juan-les-Pins. A picture of the hotel – it looked very swish.'

'Oh yes. But they were only there two weeks. They're in Montreal now.'

'Montreal!'

'Yes, a World Trade sub-committee on customs duties.'

'That doesn't sound like much fun!'

'Well, perhaps it's not too bad. Louis has relatives there so Roly has someone to play with – a couple of nephews, I believe.'

'Has he been in touch?'

'Oh yes, he sounds OK on the phone.' He paused, then sighed. He said, as if somehow compelled to explain, 'I know it's not ideal, but that's the way things are. The courts gave Hélène charge of his upbringing and, you know, she means well. She wants him to grow up with a cosmopolitan outlook – she's always thought that France was the source of everything sophisticated and civilized...'

He let the words die away. 'When do you

get to see him next?' she asked.

'They'll drop him off at the weekend on their way home. I get him for three whole days. He'll be suffering a bit from jet lag so I've booked a nice quiet weekend on the canals – do you think that's OK?'

'Oh, he'll love that. You'd better read up about water levels and locks and all that sort of stuff – he's sure to ask.'

They laughed, and then he said, on a new note, 'Could you come into the office for a minute? There's something I want to have a word about.'

Surprised, she rose from the desk and followed him. The door was left half open so she thought to herself, It can't be anything very confidential.

He took his place behind his desk, and she set herself down on one of the other chairs. He said, 'That friend of yours...'

'Yes?' She thought he perhaps meant Mireille, but then, Mireille was his friend as much as hers, and surely he would have named her.

'Who I met at your sister's when I came to collect Roly...'

'Michael?'

'Yes, Michael Ansleigh. He dropped in a while ago, while you were on that long trip in France.'

'What?'

'You didn't know?'

'No, certainly not.'

'Oh. I rather thought you'd recommended him to come for a chat.'

'No, Jeffrey, I didn't.'

'Well, perhaps I got it wrong. He wanted to ask me about land regulations, but I'm afraid I wasn't much help because he was talking about this country and of course my knowledge is mainly about the EU.'

'Yes, of course.'

'He's got some big site lined up, at least that's what I gathered. Has he told you about it?'

She shook her head. 'We're not in touch.'

'Really? But I thought...?'

'I don't know what he's been saying, Jeffrey, but he and I are not often in touch.'

'But didn't he say you and he were partners for quite a time?'

'Yes, that was a while ago. We were in business together for about four years. But that ended last year, just after I got back from Cambodia.'

'Oh, that ... I go hot and cold when I remember that episode. Have I ever apologized to you for the way I roared at you that night?'

She summoned a laugh. 'That was a memorable night for me in more ways than one.'

He studied her in silence for a moment. Then he said, 'This Ansleigh type ... He rather worried me.'

What on earth had Michael been saying to him? She felt herself colouring, and in her embarrassment protested with perhaps too much vehemence. 'Michael's got a talent for getting people concerned about him. But I think he has to be left to deal with his own problems.'

'The point is, though ... I think he's in a bit over his head in this land dealing.'

'That could well be. When he talked about it to me, which was quite some time ago, he was still learning the ropes.'

'New at this game,' he mused. 'But you and he were in business together – four years, you said. He does understand about the law of contract and so forth?'

The question startled her. 'Of course he does.' After a moment she added, 'What makes you ask?'

'Well, this American firm that's hired him ... He has a contract with them.' It was a half-question. She frowned at an undertone of doubt.

'Yes, so he told me. To act as their agent in the finding of suitable sites for ... whatever it is they do.'

He raised dark eyebrows in what was a gaze of concern. 'He hasn't told you what the business is?'

'No, I ... I don't believe that was ever mentioned.'

'Mmm...'

'Why? Did he discuss that with you?'

'No, he didn't, he said it was confidential. But from all the circumstances I thought it was pretty clear he's been hired to find sites for casinos.'

'*What?*'

He waited a moment, taking in her consternation. Then he explained, 'The gaming laws in this country are being changed, so there's a big interest in setting up condominiums with hotels and leisure centres and gambling facilities. You know the sort of thing – sort of a mini Las Vegas or Atlantic City.'

'You're joking.'

'Not at all. You didn't know?'

'Well ... it's not the sort of thing I'd take notice of, Jeffrey. I mean, yes, when we were in the travel business we used to lay on special trips for people interested in gambling but...'

He nodded in understanding. 'Investors across the Atlantic must be looking at this new opening as a tremendous opportunity. They have all the know-how for that kind of thing. What they'd want is a big site with planning permission and easy access by road and rail. From all I could gather, that's what Ansleigh's been looking for.'

'Yes,' she agreed, thinking over the sort of brochures Michael had shown her, 'that's what he's been doing.'

'It's very big money, Karen. And it would not be a good idea to try to play any party tricks with the men who control it.'

She felt a chill of anxiety. 'Are you saying that Michael...?' She paused. 'What are you saying?'

'He's been hired to find suitable venues. When he finds them I imagine he's supposed to pass on all the info to his employers, and if they want to buy, get the deal started with the lawyers they've chosen to represent them in this country.'

'That sounds right.'

'Well, I got the impression that he was thinking of doing some sort of side deal.'

She frowned. 'In what way?'

'I think he's withholding information. And if he is, he's in breach of his contract with his bosses.'

In silence she considered his words. After a long pause, she inquired, 'What makes you say he's withholding information? That's just a guess, isn't it?'

'Not entirely. He ... well, he asked me if I'd like to invest in his scheme.'

She jumped from her chair. 'No, no!' But even as her voice was rising in protest, the force went out of it. She stood staring at the wall behind Jeffrey's head, then turned away so as to hide her dismay. Over her shoulder she murmured, 'It's possible.'

Neither of them spoke for a time, then Jeffrey said rather quietly, 'Let's go and get a cup of coffee.' He led the way out of his room towards the coffee-maker on its corner table in the main office. Alexis the receptionist had come back from lunch and was giving brochures and price lists to a client who seemed to have walked in off the street. Jeffrey hesitated, then continued through the big room and out at the main door. It was a fine September afternoon. They sat down at a table outside a café a few doors down the street, shaded by a sun umbrella and to some extent shielded from pedestrians by an arrangement of bay trees in pots.

'Can we start again?' Jeffrey said when they'd ordered. 'I'd like to be clear about where this chap figures in your life.'

She sighed. In a way it would be a relief to get it out in the open. When she'd tried to explain the situation to Evie she'd been met with something like dismissal. She felt she could put it without emotion to a friend like Jeffrey. And might receive sympathy ... understanding ... something that would help to put it behind her at last.

'To put it bluntly, he dumped me,' she said. 'When I got back from Cambodia, in the wake of the Twin Towers attack and all that upset, I found the equivalent of a Dear John letter waiting for me.'

He stared at her, aghast.

'He said he'd had an offer from an American purchaser so he was selling up the travel agency. He included some business information about the lease of our premises and so on.'

'I'm sorry! I'd never have asked if I'd had any idea...'

'It's all right. I got over it. You know how it is, you wake up one day and you think, I'm not going to spend the rest of my life bewailing the past...'

'Yes, I know.' He put out a hand across the little table, grasping hers in a firm clasp.

'He said in the letter he was going to make a fresh start in the States. He was in Chicago then, he'd just rounded up a special travel group that had been visiting the casinos set up by the Native American Indians on their reservations...' She let the words fade. Then she said, 'Oh, of course. That's how he came to be headhunted by this construction company. A Brit already interested in casinos, who would be able to find them suitable property.'

Jeffrey looked doubtful. 'It might have been like that. Or he might have heard they were on the lookout for someone and talked himself up so that they hired him. Because to tell you the truth, Karen, I don't think he's a particularly top-management type.'

She shrugged.

'*Is* he clever about business? Did you do

291

high levels when you ran the travel firm?'

'We did all right. Though when I come to think of it,' she mused, 'he had a little string of failures behind him when we first joined forces. But you know, he ... sort of got by on charm ... and I had plenty of know-how about the travel world so we were a success. Then came September 11th and the travel scene went into meltdown. He decided to go for something else, and this thing he's doing now is the result.'

'Yes, but what *is* it he's doing now?' Jeffrey queried. 'Ostensibly he's being paid to look for big-scale building sites on behalf of employers based in the States. But from some of the hints he was dropping, I sensed he was thinking of buying the land himself and selling it on to the big money-men.'

'Can he do that?'

'Well, I don't think it's ethical. It doesn't even seem legal,' Jeffrey said. 'It's probably fraud of some kind.'

'Oh, Lord!' That was a terrible word – fraud. She shook her head, and there was a pause while the waitress brought their drinks. Then, when they were alone again, she said with some irony, 'Well, I don't think there's much need to worry about any scheme like that. He's never going to raise the money to buy a big property.'

'I think you may be right there.' He sipped Evian water. 'I was in two minds whether to speak to you about all this. From the way he was talking, I got the impression that...'

'No, no, that's all over,' she said with emphasis. 'I was an idiot, but I've come to my senses.'

'Good for you.'

'The problem is, I can't get Michael to accept the fact. He's under the illusion that ... Well, I've been avoiding him for quite a while now so by and by it should dawn on him...' She summoned a faltering smile.

He let a moment go by, then said, 'If I were you I'd go on avoiding him with some determination. Because he could very well land himself in hot water. Hot enough to scald him and any friends he involves in this scheme.'

They sat for some time, letting the warmth of the day relax them, watching the world go by. It was with reluctance Jeffrey looked at his watch. 'I suppose we ought to get back...'

'I suppose so.'

'Karen...'

'Yes?'

'Would you have dinner with me some evening?'

Fifteen

The dinner date was put off to the following week, because Karen was due in Bordeaux next day to pick up a client. Jeffrey, for his part, would be concentrating on giving his son a good time for the three-day visit.

Karen went home that evening in an unsettled frame of mind. She seemed to recall that at some point she'd told herself she didn't want to be more than an employee to Jeffrey Lynwood. At that time she'd been full of sympathy for him in his difficult situation with Hélène, but was sure it could be nothing more.

So why had she agreed to go out with him?

Part of the reason, she told herself, was that she'd regained her emotional balance. Last time she'd considered this matter, she'd still been uncertain and wounded because of the break up with Michael. That was all behind her now. True, she'd made one blunder with him since he came back, but she'd *known* it was a mistake.

But would it turn out to be another mistake if she were to get on closer terms with Jeffrey? She let the problem flutter in and out of her thoughts as she laid items out on the bed for packing. Autumn, she was saying to herself, it's going to get colder, so I mustn't forget sweaters...

That was why she went unwarily to the door when the bell rang. Once there, she paused. How had anyone got to the threshold without having to use the outside intercom to be allowed in?

She said, 'Who's there?'

And her heart sank when she heard the voice that replied.

'It's me,' said Michael. 'Let me in.'

She stood silent, totally taken aback.

'Hello?' he called. 'Come on, Karen, let me in.'

'No,' she said.

'What?'

'How did you get into the building?'

'A nice lady was coming in. I came in behind her.'

'Go away.'

'What?'

'Go away. I don't want you here.'

There was a brief silence. Then Michael knocked loudly. 'Come on, Karen, stop being an idiot. Open the door.'

'Go away,' she insisted.

'What on earth is the matter with you? Open the confounded door!'

She pressed her lips together, turned, and

walked away. Almost at once Michael began banging and urging her to open up. She went back to her packing, but his voice reached her loud and clear even through the door. 'Come on, Karrie, it's me, Michael, let me in. What's got into you? Open the door, I need to talk to you. Karen! *Karen!*'

She put her hands over her ears. It was no help. She could still hear him. Now he began pressing the doorbell. 'Karen! Sweetie! Come on, don't be like this! What's the matter, baby?'

The clamour was going to bring her downstairs neighbour on the scene. Rather than have a public drama, she went to the door and opened it. Michael had his hand up to ring the bell again but dropped it, staring at her with consternation.

'What on earth's got into you?' he demanded, surging forward so that she had to step back in haste. 'Have you lost your mind?'

'Be quiet!' she commanded. 'You'll have the whole house up here!'

'But what the devil do you think you're playing at, keeping the door shut? You knew it was me out there.'

'Yes, and I wanted you to go away.'

'You're not making sense!' he exclaimed. 'I know we've been a bit disconnected for the last few weeks, but I've been up to my ears in work and so have you.'

'That's not the point.'

'What is the point then? Why are you behaving like this?'

She'd left the door ajar, and from the landing came a quavering voice. 'Is there anything wrong, Miss Montgomery?' It was her downstairs neighbour, an elderly lady and no doubt the one who'd let Michael follow her through the front door.

Quickly Karen went out to her. 'Everything's all right, Miss Martin.'

'I heard some sort of upset...'

'Yes, but it's nothing, really.'

'You're sure? Because if anything's wrong I can call the security people.'

'No, no, that's not necessary, thank you. It's just an argument. It's OK, really.'

'All right then. But if there's any kind of problem, just press the security button, you know.'

'Yes, thank you, but there won't be any need for that.'

Miss Martin nodded uncertainly but was glad to go back to her own flat. It had taken some courage to intervene.

Karen closed the door. When she turned back into the big room, Michael had betaken himself to the kitchen area and was examining the coffee-maker.

'How'd you work this thing?' he inquired.

She almost laughed. It was somehow so typical. He took it for granted that he was in charge, that whatever she'd been saying could be disregarded.

'Michael,' she said, 'sit down.' She pointed to the living area of the room, and when he sauntered back to throw himself on one of the big armchairs she took a place at the far end of the sofa. This was as far away from him as possible. She said, 'Why are you here?'

'To see you, of course. It seems ages since that last time...' He let the words tail off, waiting for the memory of their love-making to soften the stiffness of her attitude.

'Yes, it is quite a while ago,' she said coldly, 'since I let myself get involved with you again. But that's all over. I think you knew very well before you came here tonight that I wasn't keen to see you again. I've put as much distance as I could between us, and you've made no great effort to bridge the gap, because you're only interested in me when I can be useful. So your arrival here tonight means you want something. Just tell me what it is and let's get it over with.'

'Karen!'

She said nothing. There was genuine shock in his voice, but she was sure it wasn't because he was stricken. She'd taken him by surprise, that was all.

'Why are you here?' she demanded again.

'Well, good Lord, that's no way to talk! I came here to catch up.'

'You came here to get something – information, a helping hand, I don't know what. Whatever it is, let's get to it, and I'll say no, and then you can go.'

He was shaking his head in bewilderment which might have even been genuine. 'I've never heard you talk like this before.'

'I've never been bright enough to see through you before.'

'What on earth does that mean? You seem to be accusing me of something!'

'I'm not accusing you. I'm speaking plainly so that you'll stop trying to manipulate me.'

'Manipulate? What gave you that idea? Good heavens, I thought you and I were so close that we scarcely needed—'

'We're not close. Give up that idea, Michael. Once we were friends and lovers, and then for one night we were lovers again, but the friendship was gone. And now we're strangers. So please let's cut this short.'

He sat staring at her in dismay. 'It seems I should have listened to Evie,' he muttered.

Karen groaned. 'Let's leave my sister out of it. She lives in a kind of dream world.'

'But she was right when she said you were falling for your boss.'

'That's not true.' But she couldn't quite say it with the same certainty as she might have used yesterday.

'I'm not going to cry even if it is true,' he said with an unexpected calmness. 'What you and I had going was fine and I'll always be glad about it, princess. But maybe, the way things are, it was a fair bet I was going to lose you.'

She could have said a hundred things in reply. That he hadn't 'lost' her, he'd got rid of her. That it wasn't going to happen in the future, it was an established fact. That she didn't look back on their relationship as 'fine' but as the worst mistake she'd ever made. But she knew better than to start on any of that.

'Good, then. That's settled, so can we say goodnight? I've got things to do.'

'Oh, come on, Karen, you've been biting my head off every time I open my mouth. I came to ask you a favour.'

'Ah.'

If he heard the irony in the word, he chose to disregard it. 'It's good that you're close to Lynwood. I had a very good consult with him, he's got a lot of insight into the property business.'

'Oh yes?'

'I did some research about him, you know, before I got in touch. He's well thought of.'

'Yes.'

'Don't you agree?'

'Of course.'

'You don't seem to be waving any flags for him, though. Isn't he pretty high in the foreign property business?'

'I expect so. I've never made any inquiries.'

'Well, the scuttlebut seems to say he's solid. And from the way he was talking I gathered he knows his way about.'

'Yes, he's intelligent.'

'Right. And knows the right people.'

'That's very likely.'

'And could raise a euro or two if he wanted to.'

'Probably.'

'Karen, I'm trying to find out if he's worth cultivating from the business point of view! Be a bit more talkative, for heaven's sake!'

She said crisply, 'I wouldn't waste any more time on that, if I were you. Jeffrey isn't likely to help you raise any money.'

'Oh,' he said, taken aback at the decisive tone. 'Oh, I thought perhaps...'

'Whatever you thought, give it up.'

'But Karen ... the thing is ... I've got this deal I'm trying to finalize...'

'Jeffrey Lynwood isn't going to involve himself in any deal you might put up to him. You can take that as gospel.'

'Well, so you say, but you can't be sure! And besides, if you were to speak to him...'

'Me?'

'Yes, I mean, if you and he are ... If Evie's got it right and he's got a thing for you ... All I need is a bit of support, and only as a temporary measure, you see.'

She drew in a long breath. 'Are you asking

me to persuade Jeffrey Lynwood to lend you money? Is that what this is about?'

'Well … Evie says he's, you know, really stuck on you.'

Exasperation and foolish pleasure flowed over Karen in almost equal amounts. She quenched it at once with the thought that Evie was wrong more often than not. She had to keep her mind on this trap that Michael was trying to spring on her.

'Jeffrey isn't going to lend anybody money on my say-so,' she remarked in a very cool voice. 'Even if I wanted to talk to him about it – which I certainly don't—'

'I'm not asking you to ask him for an actual loan. I've got some of the money I need, and all I'm saying is that if he'd put in a favourable word for me...' He paused, to marshal his argument. 'He must need to raise money himself from time to time, and from all I hear he's regarded as rock solid. Of course, there'd be something in it for him. All he'd have to do, you know, is drop a word with the right people … guarantee my credit...'

'But he doesn't know you.'

'But you could explain my position to him. It's only a temporary thing, Karen. I've got my eye on a deal where the returns would be tremendous.'

'No.'

'Oh, come on, it isn't much to ask! It's only a word or two from you, but it would make

302

all the difference to me.'

She rose, went to the door, and opened it. 'I'm really very busy, Michael. Goodbye.'

'You mean you won't even—'

'Exactly. I won't.'

He got up slowly, looking bewildered. 'This isn't very considerate, Karen. I'm really up against it here.'

'Too bad. You know how to open the downstairs door, I imagine.'

'I never thought you'd be hard-hearted!'

'Well, there you are. You learn something every day.'

He came to the door. There he paused, and raised a hand as if to caress her on the cheek. She drew back sharply. 'Don't even try,' she said.

They were staring at each other, eye to eye, in a confrontation unlike any other between them. His features moved a little, as if he were trying for a smile. But the muscles wouldn't obey. He blinked, turned away, and moved out on to the landing.

There was no goodbye between them. They both knew this was the last time they would ever willingly meet. She closed the door, stood there listening. There was a long hesitation.

Then she heard him start his descent on the staircase, his footsteps slow and heavy. She counted four steps, five, then the sound faded on the efficient industrial carpeting.

Hard-hearted. He wouldn't have thought so if he'd seen her lean against the closed door, weak with the after-effect of the scene. She'd had to see the man she'd once loved reduced to a beggar, trying to save some tricky little scheme from foundering. She was appalled at how silly she'd once been, to care for him.

Their relationship had begun as a business deal. He had the money to start a small travel business, she had the know-how. She now understood that for Michael it had always been a business deal but with romantic benefits he had enjoyed enough to nurture. While Karen was falling in love, she'd thought it was the same for him. She'd thought herself the luckiest woman in the world, to have a life that was totally bound up, day and night, with the man she cared for. She might never have changed her mind – except that Michael did that for her.

Four years of happiness, founded on an illusion.

Well, that was all over. This was the moment in the comfortable darkness of the cinema when the credit titles rolled up the screen and the closing music played. All she could say to herself was, the film hadn't been very enjoyable from where she was sitting.

Sixteen

Luckily the next three weeks were so busy that Karen had no time to look back on her confrontation with Michael. At Bordeaux next day she found her client awaiting her – Mr Dilliver, an elderly man in tweedy clothes. But with him Mr Dilliver had brought Mrs Dilliver, their daughter Enys with her baby David, and their son Larry and his wife and their toddler, Ralph.

Karen found herself with Grandma and Grandpa in her rented car, while the rest of the family were in Larry's people-carrier. Larry followed on behind her like a big black tank, losing her from time to time when traffic was difficult, but ringing on her mobile for directions to find her again. They were a lively group, enlarged at the weekends by other family members bringing with them their school-age children. They loved everything about France: the food, the wine, the people, the cattle in the fields, the castles on the summits, the streams in the valleys; and they intended to buy a big house where Grandma and Grandpa could live all the

305

year round and have the rest of the family as holiday visitors.

They were looking for something almost impossible to find. For the last three years they'd rented a large house in Lot-et-Garonne with a pool and swings for the children, which they'd tried to buy. But it wasn't for sale, so what they wanted to buy now was 'one exactly like that'.

'In two words,' as Sam Goldwyn once said, 'im possible.'

But the Dilliver tribe refused to believe it, so she persuaded them to let her lead them south from Bordeaux, towards the south of Gascony. They travelled slowly, pausing now and again to look at possibilities. They passed through Labrède, skirted Langon, studied several houses in the neighbourhood of Villandraut. The sun shone, the wild flowers along the banks of the Ciron perfumed the air. The houses were often beautiful but one had no pool and another had only six rooms, whereas they needed at least eight, and a third was on the edge of an unexpectedly steep drop to a stream where a toddler might fall over and be carried to meet the main river...

'Well, we'll have to give up for now,' said Mr Dilliver round the stem of his worn pipe. They were in the lounge of the Hotel des Niaux, weary after a day in which they'd driven through more than a hundred square

306

kilometres and looked at two farmhouses with their barns and grounds. 'I've got to get back for a business meeting in Bristol and Enys has a doctor's appointment for the baby. So can we make arrangements for you to show us some other places in a few weeks? Where are we now ... first week in October. Let's say, end of the month?'

'You'd have to fix that with Mr Lynwood,' she said. She rather hoped some other member of the staff would get them. They were fun, but very tiring.

Next morning they got on the autoroute for Bordeaux where the party caught a plane home. She rang Jeffrey from the airport, while waiting for her luggage, to give a situation report.

'Well, it was a hard one from the outset,' he said by way of comfort for her lack of success. 'Eight rooms, a pool and a playground – they should really look at villas in some of the Mediterranean resorts, but they want countryside ... Never mind, I'll see if I can find a few prospects for when they want to go back. How about you? Are you completely exhausted?'

'I can't say I'm ready to run a marathon,' she acknowledged, 'but it's nothing that a good night's sleep won't cure.'

'Shall you go home, then? Or do you want a few days off at your sister's?'

She didn't say that she'd decided to avoid

307

Evie for a while, until she felt confident enough to tell her she'd finally and completely broken with Michael. Instead, she said, 'I've got household things to do at the flat – laundry, bills to pay, stuff like that.'

'OK, let's start by saying you'll take tomorrow and the next two days off. And I've got something on for Thursday.'

'Is Roly coming?'

'No, I don't get him until the month's end,' he explained, with great regret in his voice. Then, businesslike again: 'No, I've got to go back to Spain to see what's happening about repairs to those damaged properties.' He paused. 'I'll be back Friday midday. How about I pick you up Friday evening and we go out for a quiet drink and that dinner?'

She felt a frisson of delight. 'I'd like that.'

Once home, she pulled her belongings out of her suitcase, put the washables in the washing machine, took the rest to the dry-cleaner, then sat down to listen to phone messages and look at the mail. She rang Evie to report her return to England.

'It's absolutely ages since you were here,' Evie complained.

'I came while you were in Jersey, tidied a few things for you...'

'What good is that? And you know, it's Noomie's birthday in ten days and he's counting on—'

'Yes, I bought his present while I was in

France.'

'But you'll bring it in person? He's dying to see you.'

Karen let a second go by. 'Only if...'

'If what?'

'If you haven't invited Michael.'

'What?'

'I don't want to come if Michael's going to be there.'

'Karen, what *do* you mean?'

'From now on I'm avoiding him.'

A gasp. 'Are you crazy?' her sister cried.

Karen took the plunge. 'I've made up my mind never to be in the same room as Michael again.'

'Karen!'

'So if you promise I won't see Michael, I'll be there for Noomie's birthday.'

There were breathless sounds on the other end of the line, as if Evie were seeking for words and failing to find them. 'What's got into you?' she managed at last. 'What have you been doing?'

'What have *I* been doing? Well, if it comes down to it, I've been acting like a scaredy-cat, avoiding something that had to be done. But that's all over now. I had it out with him before I went away on this trip that's just ended, and I made it plain—'

'Made what plain? What's this about? Have you taken leave of your senses? Karen, if you've fallen for this Lynwood man, OK, that happens, but to be unkind to Michael–'

'It was time to be unkind,' she interrupted in annoyance, 'although I prefer to call it honest. He and I had a big quarrel, and I made it clear I didn't want to see him again.'

'But *Karen*, he's a friend of ours now. Are you telling me we've all got to drop him just because you had some silly fight?'

'It wasn't a silly fight.'

'But why should Michael be made to suffer just because you've fallen for another man?'

'I *haven't* fallen for another man.' But as she said it she wondered if it was true. And Evie picked up on the uncertainty in her tone at once.

'It's very unfair on Michael if you're giving him a hard time while you dither over this Lynwood character.'

'Evie,' she said, rather loudly, 'just believe me when I say that I don't want to see Michael and I don't think Michael would want to see me. So take it as read – if he's invited to the house, count me out.'

Her sister's disbelief rang clearly in her reply. 'I wish you'd explain what's put you in this weird frame of mind! Five years now, Michael's been almost like part of the family. Now you say you don't want to see him?'

'My washing machine's just finished,' Karen said, hearing its signal. 'I've got to take the things out, Evie, or you know how it is, I'll have to iron everything including the non-wrinkles.'

'Oh, stuff and nonsense! I want you to explain—'

'Bye for now, sweetheart. I'll be in touch again soon.' She put the phone down, worn out by the conversation. But something necessary, though difficult, had been accomplished. She'd said out loud to her sister that it was all over between herself and Michael. Some time in the near future she'd have to explain why, but she found that she still shrank from having to tell Evie that Michael was dishonest.

Perhaps she'd summon up the courage when she went to Dagworth Farm for Noomie's birthday. Between then and now, she could imagine Evie reporting all this to Walt, and mulling it over, and perhaps becoming somewhat reconciled to the idea. Walt, never a romantic, would accept the situation much more readily than his wife, and might have some influence on her.

It was Walt who contacted her. That evening, while she was watching a sit-com and thinking about bed, he rang. 'Walt? How nice to hear from you.'

'Yeh, listen, Kar, what's all this about you and Michael?'

'Ah. What's Evie been saying?'

'Not much that I can understand, really, but she says you don't want to be here if Michael's here, and to tell the truth, Kar,

311

he's taken to dropping in on us more or less unannounced while he's on his travels – you know, this property thing he's into.'

'Oh ... yes ... I hadn't thought of that.'

'What's up? She says you've got involved with Lynwood but I didn't see too much sign of that when he was here. I mean, it was clear he thinks a lot of you but I didn't see you showing ... you know ... you didn't give him any melting looks or anything.'

She suppressed a laugh at the phrase. 'No, I don't think I did. And I think I can say that Evie's painting too vivid a picture. Jeffrey and I are good friends and colleagues.' Yes, we are, she said to herself inwardly – at least that.

'OK...'

'And who knows what might happen in the future.'

'Ah...'

'But Evie's letting herself get run away with—'

'Well, that happens, heaven knows. But if it's not this Lynwood character, what's the reason you've had a fight with Michael?'

She hesitated. 'It's not something I'd want to discuss over the phone, Walt.'

'No, I can understand that. It's really embarrassing having to ask you about it at all, but Evie's so upset...'

'All I can say is that I had good reason to break it off.'

'Another woman?'

She shrugged, although he couldn't see her. 'There may be, for all I know. But it was a business thing, Walt.'

'Business, eh?' He seemed to think it over. 'I always wondered, Kar ... You know when he stayed over in Chicago to set up some new enterprise or something ... Was all that strictly kosher?'

He was a shrewd man, her brother-in-law. She always thought of him as unimaginative, yet he sometimes came at the truth by his own form of intuition.

'I'll tell you all about it some time,' she said. 'But it's bedtime and I've got a hair appointment first thing in the morning. So, goodnight, Walt.'

'Yeh,' he said in thoughtful tones. 'Goodnight.'

She was out and about over the next day or so, catching up with a few old friends, visiting Mireille to see the baby, shopping for a winter coat, buying magazines and weekend newspapers to catch up on current affairs, and on Thursday going to the offices of Lynwood Associates to hear what her colleagues might have to say.

She left her mobile phone at home on these occasions, and when she was in the flat she let the answering machine pick up on the land line. Though Evie rang twice on it, she didn't take the calls. She'd be seeing her in the coming week at Noomie's birthday party. By then she hoped to have thought of a kindly way to explain what Michael might be up to.

By five thirty Friday evening she'd put on her make-up with especial care, brushed the new hair-do into place, and donned her favourite evening dress, a two-year-old Armani she'd bought in Italy. It was, of course, black, with long sleeves against the chill of the autumn evening yet with a certain amount of cleavage for glamour. She looked at herself in the glass and thought she looked quite good.

Jeffrey rang her downstairs bell precisely on time. 'I'm coming,' she told him on the intercom, and hurried down. He had a taxi waiting. 'Didn't want to drive,' he explained. 'Can't enjoy any wine if you have to drive home.'

'Right. Where are we going?'

'I thought, La Principessa in Mayfair? Do you like Italian food? I've booked a table for seven so we've time for a drink somewhere first. I thought we'd go to the Fonteyn, but if that doesn't appeal we can go elsewhere.'

'Oh, I'm quite happy with your first idea!' she said. The Fonteyn was one of those sophisticated spots written up in the magazine supplements, the kind of place she'd always wanted to try but never had.

At the Fonteyn they found a little table

looking out over the hustle and bustle of Piccadilly. When they'd ordered, they sat admiring the stylish room with its photographs of ballet dancers, wondering if any of the other customers were celebrities. But Karen was feeling that she herself was a celebrity, she was so happy, so contented.

'How's Roly?' she inquired after a while.

A troubled look passed over the lively features. 'He's not settling down very well at school. Of course he went up a class, so he's got a new teacher and some new classmates, but he doesn't seem to be getting on with them.'

'These things take a little while,' she soothed, calling on her experience with her sister's children.

'Of course, yes, I know that. We went through all this when he first started. I know he's going to sort things out in his own way, more or less.'

Their drinks came. That broke the thread of conversation so when they resumed it was on other topics.

They had drunk about half of their cocktail when someone's mobile chirruped. Karen turned to the evening bag strung on the back of her chair, Jeffrey got his Nokia out of his pocket. It turned out to be for Jeffrey. *'Merde!'* he muttered. 'I thought I'd switched it off.'

He was about to do so when Karen said,

315

'Hang on, it's after office hours, it can't be a business call, do you think?'

He hesitated. 'You don't mind?'

'No, no, go ahead.'

He put the phone to his ear. 'Lynwood,' he said. 'Oh – yes – what?'

He raised his eyebrows at Karen, his dark glance holding her gaze. 'Hélène,' he mouthed, looking unenthusiastic. She nodded, and prepared to study a nearby photograph of Lichine in mid-air when suddenly he said, in a startled tone, *'What?'*

She watched while he listened in silence. Then he exclaimed, 'But where were *you?*' Then: 'No. No, he's not with me ... No, of course not. Hélène, I'm in a bar having a drink with a friend, of course he's not with me ... No ... No, I haven't seen him ... Not at all, no contact since – let me think – Wednesday morning, before I left for Spain.'

She didn't need to ask. He was talking about Roly. He was listening in silence, shaking his head in anxious disagreement She longed to be able to hear the other end of the conversation, and he caught her eye and held up a hand as if to say, I'll explain in a moment.

'Have you called the police?' he asked. 'Well, why not? Yes, but, ten hours, Hélène! That's a long time...'

There was a pause during which he appeared to be hearing a long explanation.

316

His expression began to seem grim. 'Call them, Hélène,' he commanded. 'And I'll make inquiries this end. Of *course*, I'll be in touch the minute I get ... Yes, yes, immediately.' He switched off and sat back in his chair.

'Roly's gone missing,' he said.

She'd been prepared for it by what she'd heard. 'Ten hours?'

'The new maid – Yvette – drove him to school this morning and saw him go in. He seems to have gone straight out some back door, his teacher never saw him. Yvette went to bring him home but he never came out of the school. She thought he was being naughty and had walked home on his own, which he's been wanting to do for some time now. Gabrielle agreed with that. Hélène was out at some afternoon event and didn't get back till now.' He glanced at his watch. 'Gabrielle went up to his room then, and found a note.'

'A note?'

'He says he'll be back in a day or two and not to worry!'

They stared at each other. 'In a day or two?' she echoed, aghast.

'Of course, Hélène jumped to the conclusion that he'd come to me.'

'But surely she knows you'd have rung her if he'd turned up?'

He gave a grunt of disillusion. 'Hélène

hasn't a high opinion of me,' he said. 'Well, I'm afraid I've got to take a rain check on this dinner, Karen. You understand I have to rush off and—'

'I'll come with you!'

'No, no, why should you involve yourself in this fracas.'

'Come on, Jeffrey, you know Roly and I are pals. What's the first step?'

'A phone book for the number of Waterloo Station – if Roly was coming here, he wouldn't fly because he hates it and I don't think he'd try for the ferry even though he loves the sea trip. I think he'd come on Eurostar.'

'That's true, but all the same, we ought to ring the Dover police, he just might have gone for the Calais crossing.'

Jeffrey was on his feet and summoning the waiter. She hurried down to the vestibule, to ask the receptionist for a phone book.

'A phone book?'

'Please, we need to ring Waterloo, there's a child gone missing.'

The receptionist's stiff manner melted. 'Go to the white courtesy phone on the wall, madam, our exchange will find the number for you.'

Jeffrey was at her side just as she got to the instrument. She handed it to him.

'The first thing to do is ring home,' he remarked, 'just in case he's turned up there

318

since I went out this evening.' She explained he had to ask for the number. She heard it ringing without answer. Then he asked for another number.

'Mrs Saunders?' he said. 'Have you by any chance seen my little boy today?' Karen heard a surprised response. 'No, I wasn't expecting him but it seems ... He hasn't come to your door? No, it's nothing to worry about ... No, no, it's some sort of mistake ... Oh, would you? That would be kind. Yes, if you would. On my mobile.'

As he hung up he explained to Karen, 'When Roly's in London he often spends time with the couple next door. She says he hasn't been there but she's asking her husband to check around the building, just in case.'

'That makes sense,' Karen said. While Jeffrey was asking to be put through to the station, she summoned her thoughts and pressed the numbers on her cellphone for the Dover Harbour police. She was on amicable terms with them from having had minor problems with her travel groups in the past.

'Nothing reported,' she was told. 'When would he have been travelling?'

She did mental arithmetic. 'Perhaps around lunchtime today, one o'clockish,' she said. 'He went missing in Paris about half past nine.' She gave a description and her

319

mobile number so that she could be contacted at once if there was any news.

Jeffrey had had no greater success. 'The railway police say they've had no report of a child travelling on his own on Eurostar. Besides,' he added, half to himself, 'if somebody checked on him, he'd give my name, and they'd contact me.'

'How would he do it, Jeffrey?' she asked. 'Has he got enough money for a ticket?'

'Oh, I'm sure he has. He gets quite generous pocket money, Louis is quite decent about that, and he saves up for things like CDs. But would a ticket office sell a ticket to a seven-year-old boy on his own?'

They sat in silence thinking it over. 'Who knows?' he said. He made for the door. 'I'm going to Waterloo to see what I can find out about Eurostar. Let me get you a taxi for home.'

'I'll go with you to Waterloo.'

'But don't you want to—'

'Two would be better than one,' she pointed out. 'While you talk to the police I can speak to the ticket people. Let's go!'

In fifteen minutes a taxi had taken them through the bustle of London at early evening. Audiences were still heading for theatres and cinemas, diners were driving to restaurants, the department stores were closing. The station itself was busy.

The officials of the Eurostar company were

helpful but baffled. 'No one has reported anything about a child, I'm afraid. He could have boarded without a ticket, I suppose. Tagged along with a family, made himself look as if he belonged to them.'

Jeffrey went to speak to the platform manager. Karen went to the ticket office. 'No, I'm sure no one at the Gare du Nord would sell a ticket to a child of seven,' said the young woman who listened to her query. 'We're extremely careful. You know the problems we have with illegal immigration. Our colleagues in France would check just in case it was some crazy scheme to try for a ticket for an illegal.'

When she rejoined Jeffrey, he was walking smartly towards an office door on the opposite side of the station from the train platforms. 'The platform manager recommended the railway police. They keep an eye out for runaways and so forth.' They went through the doorway to find a quiet office with a communications system muttering in the background and a uniformed man at a desk.

'Yes, sir?'

Jeffrey explained, cogently and urgently. The desk sergeant made notes as he spoke, then talked into a hand radio. Crackly, harsh voices responded. Karen presumed these were from men on duty elsewhere in the big precinct.

'Nothing, I'm afraid,' reported the sergeant as he switched off. 'Doesn't mean he's not been here, of course. It's a big place, easy to miss him. If he came on one of the morning Eurostars, as you're suggesting, sir, he'd be here around lunchtime. We've had no reports of any sightings.'

They stared at each other. They were all trying to think of possibilities.

'Have you asked if he was seen at Paris Nord?' the sergeant inquired.

'Well, his stepfather is handling that end.'

At the word 'stepfather' the sergeant sighed. He'd heard too often of trouble over step-parents.

'I should be in Paris,' Jeffrey said, giving the desk a thump with his fist. 'Louis is all right in his way but ... I should be there.'

'The late Eurostar is due to leave in a minute, sir. Why don't you get aboard?'

'Oh, you have to book in advance...'

A tolerant smile came over the sergeant's heavy features. 'I think we could manage a little leeway on that, sir. Would you like me to talk to the ticket office?'

'Oh, could you? Yes, that's it – get me aboard!'

'I'll go too.'

'No, no, Karen, I couldn't ask you.'

'Yes, let me! I know the kind of place Roly might have gone to,' she insisted.

The sergeant shrugged and picked up his

phone. 'I'll ask for two seats,' he said as he pressed buttons. 'You can argue it out between you before train time.'

Jeffrey looked at the sergeant with uncertainty then walked to the door and got out his mobile. 'I ought to check in with Hélène,' he explained.

She nodded, dividing her attention between him and the sergeant. He was speaking quietly, but she caught enough to ascertain he was agreeing points with someone at the other end.

'Nothing this end,' Jeffrey was saying to Hélène. 'We've checked at Waterloo, he wasn't seen on Eurostar and the police at the Dover ferry terminal haven't had any reports ... No, nothing. And my neighbour hasn't seen him at the mansion flats ... the Saunderses ... they're looking now.' He stifled a sigh. 'I have no idea, Hélène. Nothing that he said ... No, well, the only thing was, he didn't like his new teacher. Yes, I know he's always had problems with ... I don't *know*, Hélène!'

Karen longed to slip an arm through his, to offer some comfort as he battled not only with the anxiety of a missing son but with the demands of a near-hysterical wife.

Meanwhile, she'd had a thought. Roly had fallen in love with the pony at Dagworth Farm. Could he by any chance have gone there? She went outside to the concourse,

323

rang the farm, and was relieved when Walt answered the phone. Had it been her sister, there would have been exclamations of concern and woe.

When Walt picked up, he took it for granted she wanted Evie. 'She's out at the church hall, putting up some decorations for the harvest-home party. What? The little French kid? No, not at all, Kar. Why would he be here?'

'Well, he was so tremendously taken with Popcorn...' she ventured.

'Was he? Well, listen, I'll go down to the paddock and see if he's there, though I can't think it's likely. Of course it's no trouble. I'll ring you back. Where are you?'

'Waterloo Station.

'On your cellphone? OK, shan't be long.'

When she disconnected, Jeffrey had finished his call. She explained about her inquiry at the farm. 'That's a good thought,' he said hopefully.

'What's been happening in Paris?'

'Louis has called in some personal security that the Finance Ministry supplies.'

'Not the police?'

'Not yet. He doesn't want the problem to get out to the papers. You know how he was that time Roly stowed away in your car.'

She shook her head. 'But the police have far more scope in a thing like this, Jeffrey,' she mourned.

'I know. I tried to convince him ... You know, when you think about it ... Roly's note says he'll be "back in a couple of days". That implies that he's going somewhere and we've taken it for granted that he was coming here.'

'Well ... Yes.'

'But it doesn't look as if he's come to London.'

Her phone chirped. She switched on the call. 'It's me,' said Walt. 'I've been down to the field and had a good look around. No sign of anybody, and though the grass has been trodden down at the fence, that was Angela when she came home from school, she tells me. So I don't think the kid's been here.'

'No,' she agreed. 'But I thought it was worth a try.'

'Right. And how would he have got here, Kar? He'd have had to hitch, because there isn't a bus or anything that comes anywhere near. And around here, you know, if a kid was wandering about on his own asking to get a lift to Dagworth, somebody would have got in touch with us.'

'Yes, that's true.'

'So I don't think he's around here. But I'll phone around just in case. If there's any sign, I'll be in touch.'

'Thank you, Walt.'

'No prob. Anything I can do, you know.'

She relayed the information to Jeffrey. He nodded in acknowledgement and repeated, 'We jumped to the conclusion that he'd cross the Channel. That was Hélène's immediate conclusion. But what if he's somewhere in Paris? Was there anything he particularly liked when you took him out?'

'Oh, lots of things.' She cast her mind back, and pictured the little boy's glowing face over the simplest of pleasures: the trip to the shopping mall, the banks of the Seine, the picnic by the stream where the anglers were busy.

'I'll make a list.'

The police sergeant had come to the door of his office and was beckoning. They went back. 'If you present yourself at the Eurostar platform they'll supply you with tickets and certification in case the blokes at the other end are huffy about it. They'd like it if you could provide some identification?'

'I've got my passport,' Jeffrey said, feeling in his breast pocket. 'I automatically transferred it when I changed my suit.'

'I've got my driving licence and stuff,' said Karen, touching her evening bag.

'Right. So, I'd get a move on 'cos the train goes in about ten minutes.'

They hurried to the escalator, were borne down to the platform, where the train manager was expecting them. After a brief examination of proof of identity they were

326

shown aboard almost as the doors slid shut.

They found their seats and sank down.

'Well,' Jeffrey said glancing at the black silk of her dress, 'I hope it isn't cold in Paris!'

She was still catching her breath. 'I've got stuff in a suitcase at the Babette,' she said. 'Or I can buy a sweater or something.'

Despite his anxiety, he grinned. 'Never at a loss!'

'Don't forget, my job used to be solving problems for travellers.'

'Let's hope you can solve this problem,' he muttered. 'He's gone off on his own, God knows where, and they haven't a clue what set him off...'

'We'll find him,' she comforted him.

He took her hand, and they sat back for a while to let their thoughts settle. Then she took out a pen from her evening bag. 'Have you got anything I can write on?'

He gave her the drinks receipt from the bar. She began to write on the back of it.

It was quite a long list, but there was nothing exceptional about any of the places. And moreover, some of them would be closed by now – the Museum of the Sciences, for instance. So if he had been there, he was elsewhere now.

She said, with a rising doubt, 'You know, if he wanted to go to most of these places, he could go there and come back in a few *hours*. "A few days", his note says.'

'*Quelques jours* ... Depends how you translate it. A couple of days, a few days, a day or two...'

'I can't think he was going to go anywhere in Paris,' she said. 'He's been on the Metro and the buses with me, he knows he could get to most places in an afternoon. If he was going to the shopping mall, for instance, his note would surely have said something like, I'll be back for supper.'

'So you're saying...? What are you saying?'

'He was going out of the city. I think that's a safe guess. But not to London, at least not as far as we've been able to trace.'

'I'll ring the Saunderses again,' he said. He went to the vestibule outside the carriage to make the call, and she sat studying her list of possible places, shaking her head over it.

Jeffrey was gone quite a time. When he came back, he said, 'I rang the Paris police as well and gave them Hélène's number. They know I'm en route to Paris and they say they'll contact us there if there's any news.'

'But what about Louis and his private investigators?'

'Louis can go to the devil! If he thinks I'm going to ignore any chance of finding my kid just to save him a little bad publicity, he's out of his mind.'

'Should you ... Do you think you should ring them to say you're on your way?'

He stifled a groan. 'I did that too but it was

only a few words. Speaking to Hélène at the moment is useless. She's really not making sense.'

There was nothing to say to that. Karen felt an unexpected sympathy with Hélène. If it was her son who'd run away, she wouldn't be making much sense either.

They fell silent, deep in thought. Neither of them gave voice to the anxiety that was in their minds, unspoken by either of them nor by those to whom they'd turned for help. It was too awful to put into words, that this handsome little seven-year-old was out there in the great world where predators might harm him.

They spent time trying to remember any places in and around Paris to which either of them had taken Roly. Some of them they discarded; Jeffrey had taken him to a rugby match once but it was impossible to believe the boy would have gone to the grounds when nothing was happening there.

After a while they went along to the restaurant car, but, though they were thirsty, they found little appetite for the excellent food. They were in the tunnel and France was rushing towards them. Jeffrey stared at the black windows.

'Where *is* he?' he muttered, and shook his head in apprehension.

'He's all right,' she declared. 'He's a very intelligent little boy. Whatever he's doing, he's thought it out.'

A few minutes before eleven o'clock, French time, they glided into Paris Nord. They were trying for a taxi when Louis Dartieux appeared, waving for their attention. 'Quick, we're illegally parked.' He turned back almost as he was speaking, and they hurried after him. A splendid black Mercedes was awaiting them, with a uniformed driver. They got into the back and it purred away from the kerb.

'What's the news?' Jeffrey asked. 'I rang everybody I could think of back home but he hasn't been seen there.'

'No, we've learnt very little for our part. Gabrielle says he's taken a few things: a T-shirt, his pocket chess set, and the money from what he calls his piggy bank is gone.'

'Is that much?'

'I've no idea,' said Louis with a shrug.

'What do the police say?'

'Ah, that ... I wish you had not done that, my friend. However, they've told me they'll be discreet.'

'But what do they say about Roly?'

'They haven't any information so far. They've been in touch with his teacher and got the names of some of his classmates, but nothing has emerged.'

'We've made a list of possible places he might have gone. Have you a number to contact the police?'

Louis took out an elegant little notebook and opening it, handed it to Jeffrey, who got out his mobile and pressed the digits. A conversation in French ensued, which ended as they were pulling into the little semi-circle of driveway at the apartment building.

They hurried in. The doorman touched his cap to Louis. 'Wait,' Karen cried. They all paused. She said to the doorman, 'Is Pierre here?'

'Er ... he comes on duty soon, mademoiselle.'

'Can you ring him to come up to Monsieur Dartieux's apartment?'

'Certainly, mademoiselle? You mean now?'

'At once.'

Gabrielle had the door open when they reached it. She looked down, unwilling to meet the eyes of the newcomers. Hélène came out of the drawing room with one hand outstretched and the other up to her face as if in defence. She was pale and looked weary. 'What can have got into him?' she cried. 'I thought he'd learned his lesson last time!'

The door bell rang. Gabrielle ushered in Pierre, the doorman. 'You sent for me, madame?' he said to Hélène.

'I?' she exclaimed, astonished. 'Who are you?'

'This is Pierre, on the concierge staff,' Karen explained, surprised in her turn that

Hélène didn't even recognize the man who saluted her as she went out and came in at night.

'A hall porter?'

'I asked for him. He and Roly are friends.'

Louis stared. 'What makes you think so, Karen?' he asked in some disbelief.

'Because Roly took me to visit him in his little den at the bottom of the building. Pierre, have you heard that Roland has run away?'

'I ... I heard something of the kind,' he said, turning his cap in his hands. 'There were people searching the building earlier.'

'Have you any idea where he's gone?'

'Alas, no, mademoiselle, I only wish I had.'

'Have you seen him recently?

'Oh, yes, now and again, you know. And one day last week – I think it was Tuesday – we played a game of chess and he beat me, as usual.' He gave a half-smile that lasted only a second or two, to be succeeded by a grimace of worry. 'He's very clever, of course, but still too young to be off on his own like this.'

'Quite so,' Louis said, waving him away. 'Well, thank you, that will be all.'

Pierre gave a little bow and removed himself. Karen said, 'I hoped he might give us some clue—'

'You can't really mean my son spends much time with a man like that,' Hélène interrupted. 'It's very unsuitable.'

'But they have something in common.'

'Not at all! And, in any case, I still think Roly is in London. It's the only place he'd want to go, and if he went by coach he might not have been seen at the ferry, because I believe the coach passengers don't get out until the coach is on board.'

'I never thought of that,' groaned Jeffrey.

'Yes, well, you see, you rushed about and came all the way here without even consulting me.'

'Hélène—'

'And so naturally Roland has this rosy view of life with his father, because, of course, there are no lessons when he's with you, all you do is spoil him and give him ideas about life that unsettle him and make him even more difficult.'

'My dear, calm yourself,' her husband interposed. 'You'll make yourself ill. And besides, I believe the Calais police checked the coach drivers to see if a small boy had been noticed on his own.'

'But he could have gone by some other port – he might not have gone to Dover.'

'Let's not think what he might not have done,' Karen said. 'Let's try to think of places he was interested in.'

'Well, of course, London is the first place you think of,' Hélène cried. 'The child is always talking about what fun he has in

London.'

'The police there have all the addresses he might go to,' Jeffrey said. 'If he turns up there, we'll hear of it at once. But where else has he wanted to go? Has he been interested in any films? *The Lord of the Rings,* that kind of thing? Or a theme park – Disneyland?'

Louis muttered in French, 'God forbid that he should want to go to any of those pop-culture places...'

They passed ideas back and forth. Louis remembered his duties as a host and poured drinks. Midnight went by, and there was no news. Hélène began to look really unwell, so Louis persuaded her to take a sleeping pill and go to bed.

'There is, of course, the spare room?' he said, looking at Jeffrey.

Jeffrey understood that he was being told they should call it a day. 'No thanks, you know I've got a little *pied à terre* near the Luxembourg. You'll ring me the minute you hear anything? And I'll do the same if I hear anything from London.'

'The spare room, mademoiselle?' Louis said, turning to Karen.

'I think I'll go to the Hotel Babette, thank you. I have some clothes and things there. I'll just check to make sure they have my room available.'

A taxi was waiting by the time they'd said their farewells. Jeffrey took her to the Hotel

Babette then was driven on to the Jardins de Luxembourg. The night porter at the hotel was expecting her, had taken her suitcase out of storage, and welcomed her with the offer of hot chocolate.

'No, thank you,' she said, with an inward groan. 'I'm sure I won't sleep.'

Yet she fell asleep before she had time to be surprised by the fact. She was restless, troubled by dreams of hastening down a long corridor on which the doors wouldn't open.

At fifteen minutes past five she sat up in her bed. A brilliantly clear idea had taken over her mind. 'I think I know where he's gone,' she said aloud.

Seventeen

Although there was urgency, Karen felt it was still too early to waken everyone. So she spent twenty minutes on a fast shower and a general freshening up, after which she pulled jeans and a blue cable-knit sweater from her suitcase. When she was dressed, it was going on for a quarter to six, so she dialled Jeffrey's number on the room phone.

The phone the other end was snatched up: she guessed Jeffrey had spent a sleepless night. 'Lynwood. What?'

'It's me, Jeffrey. I think I know where Roly's gone.'

She heard him draw in his breath. 'Where?'

'To a chess tournament.'

'What?'

'Chess. He loves to play chess.'

'I know that. We have a game now and then,' he said with some weary exasperation coming into his voice.

'Well, think about it. He's gone somewhere "for a couple of days". It could be to watch someone famous play chess.'

'Well, where?' he asked, unconvinced.

'I don't know. But once, when I was with him, he wanted to show me a chess video he'd just bought, and it was in a plastic carrier bag with the name of a shop, and there was some advertising material – a leaflet or something – that fell out, and it was something about chess tournaments.'

'When was this?'

'Before the school holidays.'

There was a silence on the other end. 'That'll have been thrown out by now,' he muttered. 'You know how Gabrielle is about tidiness.'

'But he picked the leaflet up off the floor and set it aside as if it was important. He has a scrap album, or a loose-leaf notebook, or something. He keeps clippings and things. He showed me some stuff he'd printed out from his computer encyclopaedia about fish—'

'Fish?'

'We'd seen an angler land a fish ... oh, never mind all that, the point is, Jeffrey, I saw this file of cuttings and stuff, and that thing about the chess tournament seemed like something he wanted to keep, so it may be there.'

'In the scrapbook.'

'Yes.'

'Have you told the Dartieux about it?'

'Well, no. I thought it would be better coming from you.'

'You may be right. I'll ring. What's the scrapbook like?'

'It's sort of A4 size, red, with a label on it saying something like "Important Things".'

'I'll ask them to look. It's something to try, at any rate. Thank you, Karen. I'll go there as soon as I've called them.'

'Meet you there.'

'OK.'

She disconnected, then rang for a taxi. She had to wait a few minutes outside the Babette for it but through the early morning streets it was an easy ride to the Dartieux's apartment. Gabrielle let her in. She hurried past her with a breathless greeting then ran up the staircase to Roly's room.

Everyone was in there, Louis in dressing gown and pyjamas standing by the child-size writing bureau watching Jeffrey leaf through the contents of a loose-leaf binder. Hélène was sitting on the side of the neatly made bed, looking troubled and confused, as if she wasn't yet quite awake. Her pretty blonde hair was in a tangle, and though her negligée was of the finest Japanese silk it looked untidy puckered around her drooping figure. Karen thought that the sleeping pill she'd taken was still having some effect. By contrast with these two, Jeffrey in rugby sweatshirt and Dockers looked vital and in control.

He looked up at Karen, shaking his head.

338

'Nothing. There's a page with chess stuff in it, but it's clippings and photographs, there's no leaflet.'

The binder had pages of transparent holders, each with a coloured sticky label to identify its contents. *'Les échecs'* seemed to hold about ten or twelve pieces of paper. Karen leaned over and took them out. True enough, they were newspaper accounts of previous match games, and photographs of one or two famous players. But there was no advertising leaflet.

She tried to summon it up in her mind's eye. It had been a folding leaflet, brightly coloured with, in French, an announcement about a tournament or tournaments. *'Concours des Échecs'* – something like that.

'Well, that's that,' grunted Louis. 'A false trail.'

'We don't know that,' Karen objected. 'He may have gone to a tournament, we just don't know where. Is there one this week in Paris?'

They exchanged glances of helpless inquiry. 'Would it be in the papers?' she urged.

'Gabrielle puts the papers out for the dustmen.'

'We could ring one of the newspapers, ask if—'

'Pierre!' exclaimed Karen.

'Who?' said Hélèn, startled.

'Pierre, the concierge, the man who was

339

here last night.' Karen turned to Louis. 'Can you ring down to the hall and ask if he's gone off duty yet?'

'Certainly.' Louis was ready to do anything that might offer any clue.

'But what has he to do with it?' Hélène insisted, summoning up the energy to take part.

'He plays chess with Roly.'

'Plays chess with him?' Clearly Pierre's remarks last night had failed to register.

'Yes, and gets beaten,' Karen said. 'He'll know about chess tournaments.'

'The hall porter?' said Hélène faintly. But it was too much for her to take in. Shaking her head, she fell silent. She followed as they all went downstairs to the drawing room.

Pierre arrived with his tunic unbuttoned, looking anxious. 'Is it about the boy?' he asked as he was being shown in by an iron-faced Gabrielle. 'Is there news?'

'Not yet, but we think we have a place to start,' Jeffrey said. 'You play chess with my son?'

'Yes, monsieur, but there's no harm in it.'

'Of course not, we're just trying to get information. Has Roly ever said anything to you about a tournament?'

'Oh, yes, of course, monsieur, we discuss some of the moves. Only last week we were saying how strange it was that at Palm Springs, Yrionov played his bishop—'

'No, no, not about past games, about games that are on now! Is there a chess tournament in Paris at the moment?'

Pierre rubbed his hand over his balding head. 'Nothing public, monsieur. I'm sure there are little weekend get-togethers going on, but nothing that I know of.'

Hélène shrugged and muttered under her breath that it was absurd to be consulting one of the hired help.

'Is there a tournament anywhere that Roly might have been interested in?' Karen persevered. 'He says in his note that he'll be back in a day or two. Is there a gathering not too far off?'

'We-ell...' Pierre mused for a long moment, then said with hesitation and unwillingly, 'There's Mainz, of course.'

'Mainz?' cried Karen.

'In Germany, mademoiselle. You know? On the river—'

'We know, Pierre, we know,' said Jeffrey. 'But why Mainz?'

'It's the European Junior Championships, that's all.'

'But, wait a minute,' Louis intervened. 'How could he get to Mainz?'

'It's this business about getting a ticket,' groaned Jeffrey. 'Everything we think of, it seems impossible he could have done it because he'd need to buy a train ticket—'

'But all the same, monsieur,' Pierre

341

interrupted, having had a chance to think it through, 'it may be ... Mainz, yes, he might have gone there. He was very keen about seeing Nadejda Frick. He was saying to me that he hoped it would be on the television news, but you know, the TV doesn't pay any attention to chess.'

'Who on earth is Nadejda Frick?' Jeffrey asked in bewilderment.

'Oh, very promising. Roland thinks a lot of her. It's ... you know ... a little bit of a romance in its way, because she's only twelve and rather pretty.'

Louis gave a sudden ironic little laugh. 'Is that what it is? He's gone to Mainz to watch his lady love play chess?'

For a moment there was a lightening of the atmosphere. Then Hélène wailed, 'But he *can't* have gone to Mainz! And if he has, where did he sleep last night? On the streets? No, no, it's too unlikely. I don't believe he's...' She fell silent, and shrank into herself. She was frightened at what might have happened to her son, of imagining whom he might go with if offered the chance to see his favourite chess player in action.

A taut silence followed. Then Jeffrey said, 'We can at least ask the police to contact Mainz and see if Roly's been seen at the tournament. Pierre, what time does the activity start at a thing like that?'

'Oh, about ten in the morning, sir, as far as

I know, but that's only in public, you know. They'll all be up and about by now, playing practice games and thinking about the strategy.'

'Right. Louis, will you ring the police and ask them to get going on the line to Mainz?'

Louis was reluctant. His view was that they should keep the matter as quiet as possible. But Jeffrey had already dragged in the police, and looking at the others he saw he was expected to act. 'And what am I to say?' he asked, a little indignant.

'Ask them if they can find out whether a boy called Roland Dartieux is among the audience. They must have tickets to get in, surely?' Jeffrey said, wondering aloud. 'Tell them, aged seven, green eyes, coppery hair, wearing ... Tell me again what he's wearing, Hélène?'

'What?'

'His clothes, what had he put on yesterday?'

'I ... Let me see...' She sounded dazed, uncertain. 'Gabrielle knows...'

Louis took control. 'Go and ask Gabrielle,' he ordered Pierre, 'and tell her I want her to make coffee and bring it in.'

'Yes, sir.'

The porter went out. Hélène said, 'I don't understand what's going on...'

'Dearest, we think he's gone to watch some girl playing chess,' Louis explained with gentle patience. 'There's a competition going on. You know we were talking about Mainz – that's where the competition is.'

'What girl?' she said, shaking her head, at a loss. 'Why should he want to watch some girl playing chess?'

'He's interested in chess, my love. You know he is.'

'Yes, he plays on his computer sometimes ... Does he watch this girl on his computer?'

'He may, for all know. I think he told me he'd bought a CD-ROM of championship play with his birthday money,' he said, looking back over the last few weeks for clues.

'Champions? Like ... Spassky?' She snatched at this vague memory of a name.

'Yes, like that. But these are just youngsters.'

'And they're in Mainz?'

'Yes, dear, that's it.'

Pierre came back. 'Blue jeans, blue and white trainers, dark red sweatshirt with "Bonnard" on the front. Little backpack with a Tintin picture.'

'Thank you, Pierre. That will be all,' said Louis, uncomfortable with this menial as a witness.

'Coffee and rolls are coming, sir.'

'Yes, thank you.'

Pierre went out, looking reluctant. Karen followed him to the foyer. 'It's all right,

Pierre, I'll let you know when we hear anything.'

'You will? Oh, thank you, mademoiselle. It was no good asking that lot,' he said, with a jerk of the head towards the drawing room. Then, seeing she didn't want to join him in his open disapproval, he said, 'I'll stay around, Mademoiselle Karen. Just a word on the intercom, eh?'

'I promise.'

As she turned back to the drawing room she met with Gabrielle pushing a little trolley on which were fresh rolls, a coffee pot and all the equipment for breakfast. She held open the drawing-room door for her. The maid went past without even looking up at her to say thanks.

Louis was on the phone. He covered the mouthpiece with his hand as she came in, to say, 'They're asking what they should tell the German police to do if he's there. Should they pick him up?'

'No!' cried Karen.

'Well, what then?' he demanded. 'Suppose he makes a run for it.'

'Good Lord, they're not going the storm the building with uniformed police, are they?' Jeffrey exclaimed. 'Have some sense, Louis.'

Louis coloured. 'Well, I don't know what the rules are in a case like this.'

'They'll send a woman officer,' Karen said,

345

from experience of dealing with lost children in her days as a travel guide. 'But all the same, it would be better if they didn't cause a fuss.'

'But after all, they've got to take him into custody.'

'Take him into custody? Does Roly speak German?' she demanded.

'Well, no.'

'It would be lovely for him, wouldn't it, to be arrested and taken away by someone whose language he didn't speak?'

'I don't see why we should be too soft-hearted with him over this! After all, he's been very naughty and inconsiderate.'

'Louis, back off,' Jeffrey interrupted. 'This is my kid you're talking about. I don't want him scared out of his wits just so you can feel he's being paid back for giving you a scare.'

The telephone made protesting sounds. 'Just a minute,' Louis said into it, and then angrily to Jeffrey, 'So, what am I to say to them?'

'If they tell us he's there, I'll go and fetch him back.'

'Ah,' Louis said, with relief and satisfaction. He relayed the substance of their talk to the detective on the other end of the line, nodded once or twice in agreement, said thank you and disconnected. 'They'll contact the Mainz police and ask them to make inquiries. They'll say not to take any action if they find him, just keep an eye on him.' He groaned, softly. 'He's such a *difficult* child,' he said, with his troubled gaze resting on his wife.

Gabrielle had poured coffee for everyone and left the room. As they waited for some word from the *gendarmerie*, Louis tried to coax his wife to drink and eat. 'How are we going to get to Mainz?' Karen inquired, to be doing something practical.

'We?' Jeffrey said.

'Of course.' She gave him a frown, a message that she by no means wanted to wait alone with the Dartieux while he made the trip.

'Best would be by train,' he ventured, thinking aloud. 'I expect there's an air link to Mainz but by the time we got out to the airport...'

'OK, let's ring the station for train times.'

Louis gestured at the wall phone. 'The porter will do that for you.'

The call was answered by Pierre. 'I thought you were off duty?' she said in surprise.

'Oh, might as well be at the desk as anywhere else. Is there news?'

'The police are contacting Mainz and the minute they ring back with information we're going there – Monsieur Lynwood and myself. We need to know the best way to travel, Pierre.'

'I understand. I'll get the station and let

you know in a minute.'

There was a short wait. He rang back with efficient suggestions. 'It turns out the quickest way to Mainz is express train to Frankfurt and then by the local line. It's only about twenty-five kilometres to Mainz. I've got the booking office on the line – shall I order tickets?'

'Yes, two tickets, please. When's the next train?'

'The Rhineland Express leaves at nine o'clock, mademoiselle.'

'Nine? But Pierre, it's only just gone seven now.'

'Yes, mademoiselle, but if you were to go by air to Frankfurt you'd have to get out to Charles de Gaulle, and it's Saturday, so by about eight the road would be one long traffic jam.'

'Oh, I see. You're right.' She broke off to let Jeffrey know the score. He'd done enough travelling to know the concierge was right. Having got his agreement, she told Pierre to go ahead.

A few minutes later the outside line rang. Louis picked up. 'Yes? Yes? Oh, they're sure?' He turned to the others, making a thumbs-up with his free hand, and listening intently. 'Yes, we've been looking up travel arrangements. Wait a minute – Jeffrey, they want to speak to you.'

He took over the phone. Karen heard him

say, 'He's all right? Where is he? Yes, I've got that. No, we're taking a train ... Yes, via Frankfurt ... Oh? Well, yes, that would be great. Thank you. Yes, we're all very relieved. Thank you.'

'So the Mainz police found him?' Karen demanded, a quaver in her voice from the slackening of tension.

'Yes, they've informed the local force he's with a group called the St Ouen Chess Club and they all spent last night at the *auberge de jeunesse*,' explained Louis. 'The tournament's taking place in the ballroom of the Hotel Allemand, so they checked there and his name is on the list of ticket-holders for the ballroom. And then from the people in charge of allotting tickets, they learned he's in a group registered for accommodation at the youth hostel. So, my love–' he turned to Hélène – 'he's been safe and sound all the while.'

Hélène began to cry.

'There, there, my angel, it's going to be all right. Come along now, I think you ought to go back to bed. Come now, sweetheart, let me take you upstairs and you can lie down and everything will be better by the time you wake up.' He helped her up from the sofa, his arm protectively around her shoulders. 'This is all too much for her,' he said in apology to Karen and Jeffrey as he led her out.

Karen stifled a sigh. She said to Jeffrey, 'What was that they were saying to you?'

'They're asking the Mainz police to meet us at Frankfurt Station and drive us to Mainz. I only hope they don't turn up in a marked car with the siren going.' But he was smiling. The relief and pleasure lit up his weary features as clearly as the sunlight now pouring into the room.

'So long as Roly's all right...'

'Wicked little sprat,' said his father, picking up a roll from the trolley and loading it with preserve. 'All of a sudden, I'm hideously hungry. I suppose it's no use asking Gabrielle for an English breakfast?'

'I don't recommend it,' she replied. But she too began to tuck into the food on the trolley. Dinner last night had been abandoned, they hadn't felt like eating on the Eurostar, so this was the first food in eighteen hours or so.

By and by Pierre buzzed on the intercom to say the train tickets would be waiting for them at the *guichets* if and when they wanted them. 'Thank you, Pierre. And the news is that Roly stayed overnight in a youth hostel at Mainz with a group of chess enthusiasts. The St Ouens Club – I never heard him mention it. Has he been to St Ouens often?'

'Oh, mademoiselle, that's the club that meets in St Ouens Avenue here in Paris!'

350

said Pierre with a shaky laugh. 'They adver-
tize on boards at the supermarket and in
local bookshops. I think I've even been once
to a match there.'

'Well, he's on their list in some way. When
we get to the hotel in Mainz where the
tournament's taking place, I imagine he'll be
with them.'

'Little imp,' said Pierre fondly and without
any trace of blame. Karen couldn't help
feeling the same. Moreover, she felt that at
last some vestige of a silver lining was about
to appear in the black clouds of this wretch-
ed affair.

She and Jeffrey got to Paris Nord in good
time to queue for their tickets among the
crush of Saturday travellers. Once on board,
the rhythm of the train had the unexpected
effect of lulling them into sleep; neither had
slept much the previous night. They woke to
hear the train intercom announcing *Frankfurt am Main* and to find they had slept with
Karen's head resting on Jeffrey's shoulder. If
either was embarrassed, they were too busy
to let it show.

A tall girl in a business suit was at the
barrier holding up a placard saying 'Lin-
wald', a recognizable version of Jeffrey's
name. They introduced themselves, and the
young woman said, 'I'm Ahrend, Maria
Ahrend. I'm with the Family Assistance
Department of Frankfurt City Council. I'm

351

to drive you to Mainz, where your little boy is currently under observation by *Polizist* Annabel Schiefer.'

'*Polizist?*' Jeffrey repeated, alarmed. 'Does that mean someone in uniform?'

'No, no, Schiefer is what you would call a plain clothes officer. Good experience, nothing to frighten the child.'

'Is he all right?'

'Fine, fine, sir, he watched the semi-final this morning, quite immersed ... immersed, is that what you say?'

'Yes, that's it, thank you,' he replied, thinking more about his son than about her English, which was excellent.

'We'll go now. Very quickly we'll be at the hotel in Mainz, and my colleague Schiefer will tell me by a little message on my *mobil* whether he's in the ballroom. This way.'

She led them to a Volkswagen parked under the watchful eye of a traffic warden, who gave them a little salute as they piled in. Rather to Karen's surprise, they didn't take the Autobahn, but after crossing the Alte Brücke went off along some residential roads. 'Traffic on the motorway is very heavy,' she explained over her shoulder. 'We'll do good on the back roads.' As she drove, she diverted her attention enough to toss back questions about the runaway. 'Is he in trouble often?' she inquired. 'He's young to be absconding, if I may say.'

'This is the first time – well, there was another occasion but that was different, he didn't go off on his own like this.'

'But he's not alone this time, sir. He's with a chess club.'

Jeffrey was silent for a moment. 'I don't understand that,' he confessed. 'He plays chess, but I can't understand how he can play with a club – unless it's a postal game.'

'Or the Internet?'

'He's not on the Internet,' he rejoined. 'His stepfather doesn't allow it.'

'Ah,' said Fräulein Ahrend, but whether it was about not being on the Internet or having a stepfather, Karen couldn't discern.

'Roly doesn't get out much on his own.' She took it up. 'If he were playing chess at a chess club, someone would take him there and bring him home. So we'd know about it.'

'Besides, would any chess club accept a seven-year-old boy?' Jeffrey asked.

'Oh, that we don't know about,' said Fräulein Ahrend. 'To tell the truth, I didn't even know there were such things as junior championships or that they were being played this week. Chess is outside my sphere of knowledge, although about children and football I could tell you much.'

'But you know, Jeffrey,' Karen said, 'if there are junior championships there must be clubs and things for junior chess players – or how do you get to be entered for a championship?'

'*Richtig*,' said Fräulein Ahrend, nodding.

They discussed the problem and Roly's behaviour throughout the drive. As they came into the outskirts of Mainz, their escort tapped a callback number on her mobile then murmured a word or two. As she disconnected, she said, 'He's having lunch.'

'Lunch!' exclaimed Jeffrey, and Karen could see he was astounded at the idea of his little boy sitting at a table in a hotel restaurant studying a menu.

'At a café, some 100 metres from the hotel. Schiefer says he's at an outdoor table eating a hamburger.'

'Ah,' said his father and Karen in unison. They both knew Roly had been dying to sample a hamburger for ages.

'This is significant?' asked their escort.

'It's ... sort of symbolic,' said Karen. 'He's not allowed hamburgers.'

'Oh, I see, figurative rebellion,' murmured Fräulein Ahrend, calling upon her training in child psychology.

They rolled quietly into Schillerplatz and by a one-way system into a shopping area. Because of pedestrian enclaves, their rate of progress was slow. At a corner they passed a hotel, with the name 'Allemand' on its canopy. A woman in a summer dress stepped off the kerb to speak to Fräulein Ahrend. They exchanged a few words, then the woman turned away and the Volkswagen moved a few yards further.

'We'll have to go round and come back because of the shopping precinct,' said Fräulein Ahrend. 'He's at a café in the shopping precinct, it's called Bei Fritzi.' She manoeuvred to the right-hand stream for a turning. They went down a narrow alley with the backdoors of shops in evidence, turned right again into a street lined with department stores, then at the next corner their driver pulled up. 'You go on foot from here. Turn right along the pavement, Fritzi's is about thirty metres along. I'll find a parking space and come back to join you.'

'Thank you,' said Karen as they scrambled out.

The area was clearly a popular venue for Saturday afternoon leisure. There were casual fashions in the shop windows, pop music was provided by a group of young musicians on a little triangle of concrete steps, and a street photographer was snapping family groups.

Outside Fritzi's there were two rows of tables seating four. At one of the tables sat two teenagers, an elderly lady throwing crumbs to the pigeons, and Roly Dartieux.

He was drinking a smoothie through a straw. Before him there was a plate with the remains of a hamburger bun. He was wearing a baseball cap emblazoned with the

355

words Texas Tigers. He seemed blissfully happy.

Karen and Jeffrey moved towards him. They came between him and the sunshine. He raised his head to find out what was casting the shade.

At first a beaming smile of welcome spread over his features. Then understanding crashed in on him, and he blushed scarlet. He made a move as if to get up from his chair and run, but subsided back into it. The high colour faded; he turned pale.

'Had a nice lunch, Roly?' his father inquired

The child looked with guilt at the empty plate. He set down his drink with a trembling hand.

'And who might *you* be?' the teenage lad asked in French, looking up with puzzlement at Jeffrey.

'Ask Roly,' said Jeffrey in the same language.

'This is my father, Victor.'

Victor stared. 'But he's English!'

'And who are you?' Jeffrey demanded grimly.

'Well ... I'm Victor Chenez, if you must know.' And then in Americanized English: 'But what's with all the heavy-handed attitude?'

'And this is Milly Serrier,' Roly put in hastily, 'and this is Madame Fournier, she's doing a study of plumage vary-atation in urban pigeons for the Académie.'

The elderly lady tore her attention away from the pigeons only long enough to say good afternoon.

'Wait a minute,' Victor exclaimed to Roly, returning to French. 'She's your grandmother, right? If this is your dad, he's got to know her, surely?'

Roly said nothing. He concentrated his gaze on Madame Fournier's pigeons.

'She's not your grandmother?' asked Victor. 'Or he's not your father? Come on, speak up.'

'I just made friends with her on the coach,' muttered Roly. 'You just *thought* she was my grandmother.'

'I don't get it,' Victor said, looking from one to the other in confusion.

'Oh, he's a clever little snippet,' murmured Milly Serrier in admiration, and nudged her boyfriend with a bony elbow. 'Don't you get it? He's not with old Pigeon-Fancier here, he's come on his own without Papa's permission.'

Madame Fournier paid no attention, apparently untroubled by Milly's nickname for her. She was concentrating on the pigeons. It struck Karen that she was perhaps a little deaf.

Victor was about to ask more questions when Jeffrey stopped him with a wave of his

357

hand. 'Where's your backpack?' he said to his son.

'Here,' said the little boy, groping under the table.

'Right, then let's go.'

'No!'

'What?'

'Nadejda Frick hasn't finished her game,' Roly burst out. 'She'll be playing again this afternoon and I want to—'

'Roly, when you skip off without warning and make your mother ill with anxiety, you have to pay. And this is the payment – you're coming straight home with me now.'

The child's face crumpled. Tears came to the rims of his eyes. He fought to stop them spilling over, and Karen's heart went out to him. She was about to intervene, but checked herself. This was between father and son.

'I *didn't* go without warning,' Roly cried. 'I left a note.'

' "I'll be back in a day or two". Seven-year-old boys don't make decisions like that, and you know it very well. Pick up your backpack.'

'Daddy, please!'

'Oh, hey, monsieur—' Victor began.

'Mind your own business,' Jeffrey said in a voice that silenced any opposition. 'Roly, come along.'

Slowly, but obediently, Roly stood up. He took off the garish baseball cap and handed it to the teenage girl, who accepted it with a little grimace of sympathy. 'Goodbye, madame,' he said to the old lady, who turned from her pigeons for a moment to watch with some bewilderment. But as he gathered up the backpack and came round the table, she was already looking at a bird fluttering down to join the group round her chair.

Roly hesitated, looking to see if either of the grown-ups would take his hand. But Jeffrey made no move, and Karen thought it best to follow suit. He walked between them like a very small prisoner of war.

The plain clothes police officer joined them. Together they made their way though the press of pedestrians towards the hotel. There Fräulein Ahrend was awaiting them. The two women had a short conference in German.

'I'll just try to ring Roly's mother to let her know everything's OK,' Jeffrey said to Fräulein Ahrend, and stepped aside to let the others go on.

Roly looked up at Karen, so that she could read in his eyes the consternation he was feeling at the two ladies speaking in German – undoubtedly about him – over his head. She said quickly, 'These are officials from the local authorities who helped us find you, Roly.'

Fräulein Ahrend said to him in her good English, 'We only have a few papers to sign at the office and you'll be on your way home.'

'Papers?' faltered Roly.

'You cause us a lot of paperwork, young man. I'm not pleased with you.' But her voice was kind.

She unlocked her car. They stood waiting for Jeffrey to rejoin them. He came in a moment, and Roly ran towards him.

'Daddy?'

'I got through to Papa Louis. He gave Maman the news, and he says she's very relieved,' Jeffrey told him.

'Is she all right?'

'She's in bed, resting.'

'In bed ill?'

'Under the weather, yes.'

'It's my fault?'

'Who else is to blame?' Jeffrey asked sternly. 'If you wanted to watch a chess tournament why didn't you ask?'

'I *did* ask! I asked twice! Maman didn't even listen!'

'You didn't ask *me*.'

'But all you always say is, you can't disagree with Maman.'

The social worker made a muffled sound which seemed to convey she understood all too well the difficulties between divorced parents. Karen allowed her hand to come into contact with the little boy's, and he grasped it fiercely, feeling for her sympathy by the strength of his fingers.

He said nothing more. In silence they found Fräulein Ahrend's car in the hotel parking lot, the two German officials exchanged a few words of farewell, and the visitors got into the Volkswagen. Karen was in the back with Roly. Jeffrey had chosen to sit in front with their escort. Karen guessed it was so that he wouldn't soften at the closeness of his son in the back seat.

They drove off in silence. After a while Fräulein Ahrend began a conversation with Jeffrey about the paperwork. Karen said quietly to the child, 'You're going to have to apologize, Roly.'

'Yes.'

'You knew it was wrong to go, didn't you?'

'No, it wasn't.'

'Roly!'

'Well, I *left a note*. And I was only going to be away two days.'

'Only two days. While no one knew where you were.'

'But it didn't matter where I was. I *said* I'd be back.'

'You didn't think it was dangerous to be away from home on your own, especially at night?'

'Of course not,' he said, almost crossly. 'I was with the St Ouen Chess Club, all of us stayed in the *auberge de jeunesse*.'

'But we didn't know that, Roly.'

'But if I'd put that in the note you'd have known how to find me,' he said with defiant logic.

'Exactly. So you kept it a secret so you wouldn't be found until you'd seen your chess player either win or lose her match.'

'Yes, of course.'

'But it didn't work because, you see, you made us all so terribly anxious. We had to find you, Roly. We didn't know if you were safe.'

He looked puzzled and exasperated. 'I don't know why you keep going on and on so much about being safe.'

'Why do you think Yvette takes you to school each day and brings you home?'

'Because of traffic, although it's a pain, 'cos I know all about crossing the road now.'

'It's not just about traffic. There are dangerous people in the world.'

'You mean robbers and pickpockets? But the group doesn't have anyone like—'

'Haven't you been told at school that you must never get into a car with someone you don't know? Haven't you been told not to accept toys or sweets from strangers?'

'Yes, but the chess club people weren't *strangers*, at least, they were at first ... It was only – well, I didn't know them when I got on the coach but we soon made friends.'

'How did you ever come to have a ticket for the coach?' Karen burst out in confusion.

'How could anyone actually sell you a coach ticket?'

Roly hesitated, then decided on confession. 'Well, I didn't ackshally buy a ticket at the coach station. I saw an advertisement in the games shop – you know, where I buy CD-ROMS and things?'

'Yes?'

'And it was all about what they called a package deal – the St Ouens Club saying they wanted a lot of extra chess-lovers to make up the numbers so they could book the coach. So, I filled up the form and handed it in at the shop counter and paid with my birthday money.'

'And the shop didn't query it?'

'No,' Roly said, and had the grace to look a little guilty, 'because you know Yvette was with me and I s'pose they thought she was saying it was all right.'

'But did Yvette know what you were doing?'

' 'Course not! I would never talk to Yvette about anything. She's only interested in horoscopes and people like Bjork and Beatrice Dalle.'

'So you were deceitful, weren't you?' Karen said in a very cool tone.

He made no reply. His firmly closed mouth turned down at the corners, but he said nothing.

Karen let the silence endure. After a long

moment the child said, 'Is Maman really ill?'

'She looked very unwell this morning.'

'Oh.'

Another silence. He turned away his head so as to stare through the window. The landscape swept past, the shadows lengthened a little as the sun moved westwards.

'So those two teenagers thought you were the old lady's grandson,' she prompted at length.

He shrugged.

'Did you say you were?'

He seemed shocked. 'No, no, that would have been a lie. No, it was just that when I got on the coach, no one was sitting with her. She's a member of the club, of course ... they know her ... I think they find her a bit of a bore. She plays good chess but she's got this thing about pigeons, she has a degree in onnithonomy...'

'So, because you were sitting with her, they thought you were related.'

'I expect they did,' he agreed reluctantly.

'And you didn't contradict them.'

'Well, nobody actually *said* anything. What we all talked about was mainly chess, you know. And we played more than we talked. Victor has this awfully good computerized thing, like a Nintendo game, you know...'

'And when it came to sleeping arrangements, you just went to the youth hostel and were given beds?'

'Oh yes, very small rooms and the bed was sort of hard, but it was all right. And I didn't take coffee at breakfast, honestly I didn't.' Coffee was forbidden to Roly so far except as a milky drink. 'There was what they call a buffet, and I got a glass of milk. It was a 'normous big jug but luckily it wasn't very full so I didn't spill anything. The only thing was...' He hesitated, about to confess something serious. 'I'd forgotten my toothbrush so I couldn't brush my teeth.'

Karen couldn't prevent the smile that tugged at her mouth. Roly, seeing it, ventured a tremulous one of his own.

As they came into the outskirts of Frankfurt, Jeffrey turned his head to speak to them.

'I have to go through some formalities here. Fräulein Ahrend says it should only take a few moments but they've got to see and speak to Roly to make sure everything's all right.'

'Where are we going?'

'The local cop shop. The Paris force have certified our bona fides, but naturally the locals have to have signatures and so forth. I'm told there's a train in about an hour that we should make.'

The formalities were soon over. Roly, very pale and rigid with fright, was asked through a translator and before a *Jugendbeamter* whether he knew the two people who were to

365

take him home to Paris. He replied that Jeffrey was his father and Mademoiselle Karen was a friend. The magistrate offered a document for signature by Fräulein Ahrend and Jeffrey. '*Sei nicht wieder boöse*,' he said to Roly, wagging a finger as he dismissed them. And Roly looked as if he would indeed never be naughty again.

Fräulein Ahrend drove them to Frankfurt station. As they boarded the train she said in an undertone to Karen, 'At that age they can't really see very far into the future, Fräulein Montgomery. I'm sure Roly didn't understand what would be the resultings of his escape. Tell his Mama not to be too angry with him.'

Karen smiled and nodded. She didn't think it worthwhile to say she could have no influence on Hélène one way or the other. For herself, the first effects of finding the boy were wearing off. All she felt now was a great thankfulness that he'd come to no harm, that their anxiety had in fact been needless.

She could see Jeffrey was feeling the same. The grimness had gone from his features. He too began to relax, and when the refreshment trolley came round was quick to ask his little boy whether he needed a drink or a snack.

'Could I have Coca-Cola, Daddy?'

'I'm afraid not, Roly. You know better than

to ask.'

'But ... this would be the last chance...'

She watched Jeffrey suppress a smile at this cry for the last benefits of freedom. 'Fruit juice?' the attendant offered. 'Lemonade? Tea?'

'Lemonade,' Roly agreed, disappointed but resigned.

By and by he rummaged in his backpack. He got out a travelling set of chessmen and began to play against himself. After watching him for a few minutes Jeffrey took up the opposition and the two of them settled down to a contest.

All signs of asperity had gone. In perfect harmony they played out to the end, with Roly admitting defeat and setting up immediately for the next match.

By the time they drew into Paris Nord, he was yawning. Karen suspected he'd been up till very late the previous night and perhaps up very early this morning, roused by the older members of the chess club party wanting to replay some of the match they'd seen yesterday.

Louis had sent a car and driver to meet them. Karen chose to say goodbye at that point.

'Oh, please come,' Roly cried, tugging at her hand. He saw her as an ally in what he had suddenly realized might be a very unpleasant reunion.

'No, Roly, I think it's better if I say *au revoir* now. I'm tired, and I need a change of clothes and a shower.' She was in fact thinking of the difficulties that might follow if she went up with them to the apartment. She'd plunged into the search for Roly because that was only right – everyone should do all they could to help find a missing child. But the aftermath ... That was a family matter. She suspected that Louis would disapprove of any interference from her, and more importantly, Hélène wouldn't welcome her. Her presence could only acerbate the situation.

'Tell her, Daddy! Tell her we want her to come with us!'

Jeffrey looked at her. She saw he was following her train of thought. 'You'd rather not?'

'I don't think it's my place to be there, Jeffrey. I'm not one of the family.'

'No, but in a way you're...' He broke off. 'I'm sorry, I'm not thinking straight. I can see there's going to be a bit of a showdown now.'

'And my being there might make matters worse. I think it would be better if I bowed out now.'

He gave a reluctant nod. 'You may be right.'

'But you'll let me know what happens?'

'Of course.' He took her hand, pressed it,

then turned to his son. 'Come along now, Karen has things of her own to attend to.'

The little boy looked at her as if he couldn't believe she had anything to do as important as standing by him now. She gently shook her head. 'I'll see you soon, sweetie.'

He hung his head and got into the car as if he were going into the tumbril. Jeffrey smiled at Karen over the boy's shoulders. 'Thanks for everything,' he murmured in a tone that left a million things unsaid.

She nodded, he got in, and the car swept away.

She went back into the station for a cup of coffee and something to eat. She took her time over it, needing to reorientate herself after this hectic day. She took the Metro to the Hotel Babette where she showered and changed into a comfortable jersey dress. Then she sat down in her room to use the hotel phone. She had to report Roly's safe recovery to Walt at Dagworth. But it was Evie who picked up. 'Oh, so he's all right? Thank goodness for that! But what a naughty trick, Karen. I'd be out of my mind if Perry tried that on!'

'Yes, he's probably getting a long lecture from his mother and stepfather at this moment.'

'You know, Walt looked everywhere in the grounds because you said he might have come here, and he asked around, and then this morning he—'

'Yes, please thank him, Evie. I shouldn't have bothered him but at the time I thought it was just a possibility.'

'Well, he was only too glad, dear, because you know how he'd have felt if it had been one of his own.'

'Yes, I know, when I see him I'll tell him thank you myself.'

'Will you be coming soon?' Evie asked, with what seemed like a quickening of attention.

Ah, she's expecting Michael to drop by, Karen thought to herself. Aloud she said, 'I'll let you know beforehand. Won't be for a day or two – I'm really too tired to want to travel for a bit.'

'Oh, yes, I quite see that – London to Paris one day, Paris to Mainz and back the next, although I've no idea where Mainz is, really. Is it far?'

They spent some minutes while Karen described her journey and how they'd found Roly eating a hamburger. 'Oh, kids love all that sort of thing, don't they? Well, thanks for setting our minds at rest, dear, and take it easy for a day or two,' Evie counselled.

Now she felt tired, and after her phone conversation, thirsty. She went down for a drink in the tiny corner bar off the foyer.

She was still there, sipping and glancing

through the *France Soir*, when Jeffrey walked in. One glance told her he'd been having a hard time. He sank down on a chair beside her, sighing with relief. 'I thought you'd want to know. Roly's to get no pocket money for six weeks and has had his computer and TV set disconnected until further notice. But he's not being sent away to boarding school.'

'Good heavens! Was that on the cards?'

'Very much so. Louis has always rather favoured that idea.' He shrugged. 'Not this time, though it might happen if he blots his copybook again.' He glanced about. 'Mind if I join you for a drink?'

'Of course not. Ring the bell on the reception desk.'

But he knew the place better than she did, for he put his head in at the door behind the desk. 'Albert, would you bring me a whisky?'

Muffled assent from the night porter. Jeffrey came back and sat down. She said, 'You look as if you deserve a whisky. You shouldn't have bothered to come all this way, you could have phoned.'

'I wanted to see you,' he said. He paused. 'You look nice. I apologize – I should have stopped to change before I came rushing here. But it seemed more important to get here ... I *needed* to see you.'

'It's all right, Jeffrey,' she said, and laid her

hand on his arm.

He covered it with his own. 'What would I do without you?' he wondered. 'How did I manage before you came into my life?'

He leaned forward, and his lips brushed hers. For a moment she sat still, surprised and yet not surprised, ready for what must come next.

He stood, drew her up to him, and put his arms around her. They kissed, bodies pressed close, thigh to thigh, heart to heart. For an eternity they were lost in each other.

This moment had been coming for a long time. Yet each knew that there was more to come. As one, they turned towards the little brass cage of the lift at the back of the foyer. His arm was about her shoulders. He bent to whisper in her ear, 'If you want to say no, say it now before it's too late.' But there was humour in the warning, and the certainty that she wouldn't say no.

For answer, she pulled open the lattice-work door. They stepped inside, and as the lift bore them upwards they lost themselves once again in a long kiss. Karen had the feeling that her whole life was concentrated now, in this moment, in this little world where her lover held her in an embrace that was the threshold to paradise.

Albert, coming a few moments later with the whisky on a tray, stood in surprise at finding no one in the bar area. Then he heard the wheezing clank of the old lift, raised his head to listen, and smiled as he understood why they had vanished.

Eighteen

The dawn found them still wrapped in each other's arms, still wakeful in the soft tranquillity that follows the ascent to the heights, whispering endearments, exchanging thoughts that until now had remained unspoken. They laughed a little at the memory of their first meeting in the early morning after Karen had brought Roly home from Phnom Penh. 'I was so angry with you,' Jeffrey confessed. 'I saw you as some tattered idiot – perhaps even on drugs – who'd spirited my kid away.'

'And I thought you were a crazy, mannerless lout. You scared me.'

'Forgive me now?'

'I'll think about it. Depends on how you treat me.'

'Like this?' he murmured, his hands caressing her with the reawakening of desire.

'That might convince me.' And she held him all the closer, matching his passion until once more they found the paradise that was theirs alone.

By and by they could hear the sounds that

meant the little hotel was coming to life. They sat up, still in an embrace they would not surrender yet. 'I hesitate to ask because if the answer is yes, I might die of misery, but do you happen to have a man's razor or a spare toothbrush?' he inquired.

'No need to order any wreaths. I haven't either of those things.'

'In that case, I think we ought to order breakfast and then I'll dash to my place and make myself neat and tidy. And while we eat we can think about the rest of the day.'

When the *café complet à deux* was brought up, they ate croissants and drank coffee while they made plans. It was Sunday. They decided to give themselves the next twelve hours. Then they must return to the real world because there were business matters expecting their attention on Monday. They showered together, which led to a delay that perhaps they should have foreseen. But by ten o'clock they were on their way to the Luxembourg.

There Karen investigated Jeffrey's belongings while he shaved and changed. She found he read mainly biography, and books about the architecture and topography of countries in which he had business. In the tiny flat there was no hi-fi equipment, but a small radio was tuned to a music station specializing in jazz. There were photographs of Roly as a toddler and holding a prize from a funfair stall. Otherwise Jeffrey's place was spartan.

It filled her with a longing to bring some comfort into his life. It seemed to her that for too long he'd had very little that was tender and loving. She told herself that she was going to fill that emptiness; she was going to lighten up his world, wrap him around with gentleness and contentment.

He dressed quickly, then they went out to share the pleasures of Sunday leisure. Since the Luxembourg Gardens were nearby, they went there, to find it full of students deep in argument and grown-ups with young children heading for the Punch and Judy show. 'Roly loved that when he was smaller,' Jeffrey remarked, watching the little people dragging at their parent's hands. 'But he outgrew it pretty quickly. He's always been too old for his age, it seems to me.'

'Exceptionally bright, I think,' Karen said. 'That's one of his problems. He's cleverer than most kids of his age but everyone mistakes it for uppishness.' Including Hélène and Louis, she could have added.

'Well, let's leave my family problems behind,' he rejoined. 'I sometimes wonder if you get time for your own family, Karen. They were nice, your sister and her brood.'

'Oh yes, Evie's great, and the children seem nice to me, but then I'm biased. And Walt too; he appears a bit stolid, but in many ways he's the ideal partner for Evie – down to earth and practical, whereas Evie ... Well, my mother used to call her Dreams, short for dreamer, and she still needs someone to remind her that it can't be Valentine's every day.'

'Your mother ... I don't think you've ever mentioned her before.'

'Oh, she's alive and well and living in Guildford, surrounded by my father and a host of prickly cactus plants.'

'I beg your pardon?'

'They grow cacti on a commercial basis.' She gave him a short review of her parents and their life as growers and lecturers. From there they went on to more general topics, strolling to the sparkle of the Medici fountain in the soft October sun. As they were discussing whether it was scary or not to see the sculpture of Cyclops preparing to heave a rock at the lovers, Jeffrey's phone cheeped.

He gave her an apologetic glance. 'I kept it switched on; I thought it might be a comfort to Roly so I told him last night he could ring if he wanted to.' After answering the call, he nodded at her, mouthing, 'Roly.' Then to the phone he said, 'Well, you deserve to be. Don't expect any sympathy from me. No. No, I haven't gone home yet, I'm in the Luxembourg Gardens ... no, of course not.' He murmured to Karen, 'Asking if I was going to the Punch and Judy.' He listened again, then said, 'I'm with Karen. What? I'll ask her. Roly wants to know if you'll speak to him,' he reported to her.

'Of course.'

'She says yes. It's more than you deserve. You should be sent to Coventry. What? No, it's just a saying that means nobody should speak to you for a week.' He held out the mobile to her.

'Hello?' she said. 'How are things?'

'We went to church,' he said dolefully. 'And now I've got to stay in for the rest of the day.'

'You could read a book,' she suggested. 'How about *Treasure Island*?'

'I've read that twice. Will you come and see me soon, Karen?'

'I ... Well ... I'll try.'

She could hear him sigh. 'Let me speak to Daddy again.'

She handed back the phone, and gathered from the rest of the conversation that Roly was putting the case for a visit from her in the near future. When Roly had rung off, Jeffrey looked at her and shrugged. 'I don't know how you rate with Hélène as a trouble-maker,' he said ruefully. 'I'm an evil-doer because I give Roly far too much freedom when he's with me. So I can't ask for any privileges. I don't get to see him again until the end of the month.'

'They haven't cancelled that as a punishment?'

'Let them try!' he growled. 'It's a legal requirement, set by a legal French court.' Then he shook himself as if to get rid of the thought. 'No, Louis is very meticulous about things like that because of his position in the political set-up. He wants calm waters all around him, thank goodness. No, I'll have Roly with me in London as usual at the end of the month.'

'Whereas I have no claim if I want to take him out for a walk or something?'

'Afraid not. Still, if we let a week or so go by, everything may go back to normal again. If Roly behaves himself ... And I think he had enough of a scare not to try any little escapades, for a while at least.'

Poor kid, Karen thought, but didn't say it. He didn't seem to have anyone to turn to at home. Even the members of the St Ouens Chess Club, in the short time he was with them, had become closer to him than the members of his household.

'As a matter of fact, I'll be here again myself at the end of the week,' he said, 'to collect him and take him back to London with me.' He thought it over. 'Look here,' he went on, 'I think it would be unfair to expect you to go back to London now, collect your car, and then set off again immediately to chauffeur clients around France. After a weekend like this...'

She gave a little smile of agreement. It had

been like a ride on the Big Dipper, one emotion rushing in to replace another, and in the end the sleepless night that had just gone by. 'What are you thinking?'

'Seems to me it would be better if you stayed on here and took over Paul's clients – they're looking for premises to start a school of computer training. It would just be Paris and its environs, no great distances, you could do it all by taxi. And meanwhile Paul could take over your customer – that's the Dillivers if I remember rightly.'

'But it's short notice to rearrange things?'

'No problem, Paul would be leaving tomorrow mid-morning, I'll simply redirect him. Let's find a place for lunch and I'll ring Paul to fix it up. And you'll be meeting your computer people at Gustave Kloss, where you know the ropes, so that's OK.'

The sunny day tempted them to the fore-court of a restaurant off the Rue de Bernini. While they were waiting for their meal, he got out his mobile and began to make calls. When he put it away he was nodding in satisfaction. 'Paul's OK about doing the Gascony trip and I told him to collect the Dillivers' list of requirements and our recommendations from the office before he leaves tomorrow. I'll send the stuff you need about the computer guys by e-mail to Kloss first thing in the morning so it'll be waiting when you get there.'

'What about you?' she inquired. 'If you're going to be in the office first thing, when are you going to travel back?'

He sighed. 'I'll have to go back this evening,' he said. 'But–' he glanced at his watch – 'that gives us at least eight hours, sweetheart.'

After the meal they spent an hour or two strolling around Paris hand in hand. Then they went back to Jeffrey's flat to make love during the hours of twilight. They were happy together, their world consisting of only themselves and the joy they gave each other.

As the true hours of night approached, they roused themselves unwillingly. So as to be with her as long as he could, he'd chosen to go back on an overnight ferry and snatch some rest on the boat. She wanted to go on the train with him to Calais but he wouldn't hear of it. 'We'll see each other soon, Karen – I'll be back Friday evening.' She had to wave goodbye on a draughty platform as his train pulled out at ten. Sitting in the Metro on her way to the Hotel Babette, she felt more lost and alone than at any time in her life before.

The next few days were taken up with work. The computer people were a man and wife team, clearly very intelligent but almost naive when it came to ordinary business. Karen escorted them around Paris, explained legal requirements with regard to both leasing property and setting up an educational facility. They were somewhat taken aback, but gathered themselves to face the difficulties.

She spoke to Jeffrey by phone every evening, ostensibly to report business progress but really just to hear his voice. It astonished her how the mere sound of it could fill her whole being with delight. It helped her to fall asleep each night into a land of dreams where she glimpsed him often but could never capture his image for more than a fleeting moment. In the morning she would wake confused, happy yet uncertain. It was because she couldn't quite foresee their future.

By the weekend there were two probable premises for the computer couple. They went home to think it over. Karen waved them off at Paris-Nord, then returned a few hours later to meet Jeffrey off the Eurostar.

He swept her into a mighty embrace that almost crushed the life out of her. They had time for a drink and a snack before collecting Roly from the apartment, and during that she learned that he too had been having mixed signals from his psyche. For years he'd been putting Roly first. To begin thinking of his own needs seemed strange. 'I think I'd like you to move in with me, Karen,' he said. 'That way we can see each other all the time.'

She was shaking her head.

'Why not? It makes sense to me.'

'But what about when Roly comes?'

'What about it? He likes you, you've got this great rapport with him, he'd be happy to find you living at the flat.'

'Are you sure? He's been through a lot in his life already, Jeffrey. Do you think he's ready to find his dad has collected a new live-in partner?'

'He knows divorced people find new partners. Some of the kids he goes to school with are in their second family relationship – sometimes even their third.'

'I know that, darling. I've seen it in my job in the past – little kids being flown here and there to join their blood parents, or being taken on holiday to get to know a new step-father. Believe me, it's never easy for them. And Roly is different from most – he's very quick on the uptake.'

'So ... Are you saying we should stay as we are – getting glimpses of each other at odd intervals?'

'Well, there are degrees of closeness, aren't there?' she said, thinking it through and smiling. 'You could come and stay with me at my place when it suits us. That way, no likelihood of Roly thinking that I'm taking his place in your life, none of my belongings in your bedroom to make him wonder.'

383

He was studying her expression. 'That sounds like a solution for the present,' he agreed, though with reluctance. 'But in the long run, Karen?'

'Who knows?'

They went to fetch Roly from the Rue Lacharotte. It appalled Karen to find him waiting alone in the hall of the building, sitting on a gilt chair by the porter's desk. He held his backpack to him, its contents seeming to consist of books and videos rather than clothes. He sprang up at their entrance.

'You're late!' he accused. But he flung himself upon his father, grabbing him round the waist.

'We're exactly on time,' said Jeffrey, picking him up to hug him. 'And Eurostar is waiting for us, so let's go.'

They had tickets for the six o'clock departure. Karen was beginning to think of the cross-Channel train as a sort of commuter service, she was using it so often these days. She realized what a big part it played in Jeffrey's life, a monthly link with the son to whom he had only minimal access. And that link was so precious, particularly to the child, that nothing must be done to harm it.

That being so, she said farewell to father and son when they reached Waterloo. Roly looked a little unwilling. 'I thought you'd be spending the evening with us?' he ventured.

'The evening's almost gone,' she pointed

out. 'It's nearly your bedtime.'

'But my first evening – Daddy always lets me stay up a bit longer.'

'How much longer?'

'We-ell, half an hour.'

'OK, then we'll spend half an hour together and then we'll say goodnight. What would you like to do?'

'Could we see the boats on the river?'

'All right, but you know there aren't as many of them as on the Seine and they aren't as glamorous.'

They went out of the station and across York Road to the river. There were almost no pleasure boats to be seen, but Festival Hall was alight, and in the glow of its windows they stood looking at the brightness of the Savoy and the Oxo tower.

'It's sort of different, isn't it?' Roly remarked. 'The Seine is sort of ... prettier at night. But I like it here, you know. I brought my b'nocklers. Last time I was here I saw a bird on the mud. I looked it up later and I think it was a curlew.'

'I'm told if you stay on the embankment for the whole day you can see all kinds of birds,' Karen agreed. 'I've a friend who's a birdwatcher and she says she's seen a kestrel hovering. But I'm afraid you see mostly pigeons.'

She felt him go still. After a moment he said, 'I'm not too keen on pigeons.' She

385

knew he was thinking of Madame Fournier of the St Ouens Club and her study of coloration.

She said, 'Pigeons are all right. But if you're not interested in them there are lots of other birds, after all.'

He looked up at her, and in the light from the concert hall she saw there was something like a tear in his eye. She knew that he was truly sorry for that escapade, and that she'd just told him he was forgiven.

Soon they returned to the station to take the Tube to their separate destinations. 'Will I see you tomorrow?' he asked.

'Would you like that?'

'Oh, yes, and we could go to Tower Bridge, and we might see the bridge opening; it does sometimes, you know, and I could show you the place where I saw the curlew, although of course the curlew won't be there now but we might see something else.'

'That sounds like fun.' Jeffrey raised his eyebrows at her over the child's head, in mute protest. 'And we could have lunch at St Katherine's Wharf,' she amended for his benefit. 'How about that?'

Roly's plan was to collect her at dawn next day. 'In case a ship wants to go through the bridge early.' But this was amended before they went their separate ways. In the morning she had time to rush to the cleaners to collect some of her wardrobe and to ring her parents and Evie so they would know she was back.

'Come to lunch,' said her mother. 'It's ages since you were here.' This was only too true, but she explained that she had a date with Tower Bridge. 'Well, come tomorrow, then. We've got some new plants we want to show you.'

She promised she'd let them know first thing on Sunday morning whether she could make it. She donned sensible shoes, slim cords and a light cagoule for late October weather, then waited for Jeffrey to ring from downstairs. Roly was intrigued by the entry-phone at the outside door. 'Let me, let me!' she could hear him cry, until he was lifted up and spoke into the mike. 'Hello, hello, this is me, Karen! Are you on the other side of the door?'

'No, I'm upstairs. Would you like to come up and see the other end of the line?' She pressed the release. Next moment she could hear him thumping up the stairs.

He was pleased with the neat little phone when she demonstrated it to him, but less so with her home. 'It's really only one room!' he cried. 'Where do you sleep?'

'That's the bed,' she said, pointing to the divan.

'And that's the kitchen, but it's sort of joined on.' He made a face then looked at his father. 'Gabrielle wouldn't like *that*, having everyone see how she did her cooking.'

'Well, I don't do much cooking,' she reminded him. 'I'm away a lot, aren't I?'

'Oh, that's true. But even so, wouldn't you like a proper home?'

'Roly!' chided his father.

The little boy had dashed off to see if there was a separate bathroom. Jeffrey said, 'He's a bit above himself with excitement, I'm afraid. I'll have to lay on something a bit quieter for tomorrow. There might be a late-season cricket match somewhere.'

'I suppose you wouldn't like to come for lunch in Guildford, would you?' she suggested.

'Guildford?'

'My mother and father live there, remember? It's months since I saw them.'

'But would they want extra people?'

'Oh, they've got some new variety of cactus they're dying to show off. If you'll say nice things about the cactus, they'd be delighted.'

'Cactus plants?' said Roly, arriving back from his inspection of the bathing arrangements. 'Those are the ones with prickles, aren't they?'

'Quite right. And once, when a very important botanist came visiting my mother and father, he nearly went away with a prickly cactus dangling on the end of his scarf.'

He eyed her. 'Is that true?'

'Absolutely. It was only when the little pot fell off leaving the plant and roots attached that he realized what had happened.'

'Are they the ones that catch flies?' He had that look of frightened delight that children show when considering *Dionaea*, and was quite disappointed when she shook her head. 'Oh, well, prickly plants sound interesting. Can we go, Daddy?'

'Well, I...' Jeffrey looked at Karen. 'We have to be in Paris by bedtime Sunday evening...?'

'That's not a problem,' she said. 'If Roly would agree to fly back, we could use my car and I could drop you off at Gatwick. Mum and Dad will give us lunch and we'll make approving noises about the plants, and then we can go and look at the river.'

'The Thames?' queried Roland, excitement building in his eyes.

'No, it's the River Wey, but it's nice, there are little islandy bits—'

'That sounds lovely.' He tugged at Jeffrey's sleeve. 'I don't mind flying, Daddy. It's only short. What I hate is long, long journeys with nothing to look at outside except clouds.'

Tower Bridge didn't open for them, but he was consoled by a lengthy visit to HMS Belfast. He wanted everything explained to him, borrowed some pocket money to buy a souvenir booklet, and immersed himself in it when they sat down to lunch. Jeffrey gave Karen an apologetic smile as he persuaded

Roly it was bad manners to read when sharing a meal with others. 'Oh, all right,' he said grudgingly, putting the book away.

Karen could see why Hélène and Louis might consider him a difficult boy.

She left them after lunch. Her feeling was that father and son needed time to be together without any interlopers. She did some necessary shopping on the way home, then telephoned her mother to see if it would be OK to bring friends tomorrow.

'Certainly, dear, any time. This is your boss, isn't it?'

'Yes, and his little boy.'

'Oh,' said Janet Montgomery, 'how old?'

'Roly's seven, Mum, but don't be alarmed, he won't damage any of your darlings. He's a very grown-up little boy.'

'All right then,' said her mother, but there was great doubt in her tone.

The doubts were done away with after a few minutes in Roly's company. He shook hands beautifully with Mr and Mrs Montgomery, was quiet and obedient all through lunch, even though it fell short of the standards set by Gabrielle, then produced a sheet of paper the moment a tour of the glasshouses was proposed.

'I made a list,' he explained. 'Daddy let me look up cactuses on his computer. There's this one, the picture on the screen showed it as if it had a beard wrapped round it – is that right? And this one – it's got little sort of worms growing out of it—'

'Oh, that's the Goat's Horn,' interrupted Karen's father, his face lighting up. 'Those aren't little worms, those are spines. We specialize in that and one or two other Astrophytum. Come, and I'll show you.' He held out his hand, the little boy put his in it, and they hurried off together. Janet Montgomery hesitated a moment, looking after them enviously. A smiling nod from her daughter gave her leave to abandon her hostess duties, and off she went to join in the inspection of the plants.

'There,' said Karen, 'everybody's happy – unless you'd like to rush after her and spend an hour looking at Echinolossulocactus zacatecasensis.'

'You made that up,' he accused.

'No, honestly, I learned to pronounce it when I was about Roly's age. My mum and dad have been mad about cacti since I was a baby. But that doesn't mean you have to be polite and go round the entire set-up with them – Roly will keep them happy for an hour or so. Would you like to go for a walk? There's a nice bit of woodland up the road, turning nice autumn colours.'

'Let's go.'

The trees were like a Monet painting, red and brown and lime green against a Nile blue sky. Under their feet was spread a carpet of gold from the beech leaves. They walked with arms around each other's waist, silent most of the time but letting thoughts and hopes rise into speech now and again.

'Have you thought any more about moving in with me?' he asked.

'I've thought about it, yes. But I feel that would be rushing things a bit. There's always the other alternative – you can come to me instead.'

'You feel I was trying to rush you? I haven't scared you off, have I?'

'Oh, Jeffrey!' There was an interval while she gave him a kiss of reassurance which he prolonged into an embrace of physical yearning. But the woods were used by others besides themselves. They broke apart as voices and the barking of a dog warned them of someone approaching.

He took her hand as they strolled on. 'There was this other guy in your life,' he said. 'He hasn't made you wary about ... you know ... committing yourself?'

'Oh, him...' She shrugged. 'Michael ... That's all over and done with. I admit it shook me. Shook me? It was like an earthquake. Because you see, everybody in my circle of family and friends really liked him. I wasn't the only one taken in. But truly, Jeffrey, I look back on it now and it seems to me it all happened to another person.'

'The new person being the one I'm holding hands with at this moment. Well, I understand what you're saying,' he confessed. 'I went through something like that after the divorce. When Hélène said she wanted us to split up, I couldn't believe it. But I look back and I realize she was never really pleased with our marriage. She'd always thought we'd live in France because that was where I did most of my business, and I didn't take that seriously enough. Then Louis came along...'

Karen felt there was no comparison between the two men. Louis was pleasant enough, neat and good-looking but somehow too cool, too lacking in spontaneity. 'He seems to care for her a lot,' she offered.

'Oh, in his way ... yes ... he loves her. And she loves him because he embodies what she's always admired – the culture, the lifestyle. And of course he's extremely rich.' He hesitated and added, 'No, that's a mean thing to say. They're a good couple.'

'But not a good couple to be the parents of Roly,' she countered. 'Perhaps I shouldn't say this out loud, but you're his compensation for the coldness and lack of understanding in his other life.' Jeffrey made a face of distress at the words but said nothing aloud. She went on: 'He only met me last year and I think he's fond of me, but it's a minefield, Jeffrey. He might see me as competition.'

'No, no—'

'I think he might, darling. He would have to share you.'

'But he's doing that today.'

'Yes, but he knows that after he's looked at all the plants and we've had a walk by the river, he's going to have you to himself for the rest of the evening, on the plane and all the way back to the doorstep of the Paris apartment. It's going to build him up so he can bear the next long separation. It's important to him, I'm sure.'

He kicked at a little pile of leaves, making them swirl upwards in a faint breeze. 'So you won't move in with me. Which means I'll bring a spare shirt and my toothbrush next time I come calling on you at your flat.'

They smiled at each other. For the moment, that would have to be the solution to their problem.

Janet Montgomery had wrapped up a Golden Tom Thumb cactus for Roly to take home, together with a little tub of cactus fertiliser and a miniature spray. He burst into explanations at once as they came in. 'This cactus will put out yellow flowers! I'm to feed it once a fortnight when little bumps show – that's the flower buds, you see, and it needs extra help to get the flowers to open. And I'm to clean the bristly bits by puffing air at it – isn't that a clever idea? It's like using a vacuum cleaner only the other way round!'

Jeffrey was about to ask whether Gabrielle would appreciate having a plant in Roly's fastidiously tidy room. Roly sorted that point out by saying at once, 'I'll leave it with you, Daddy. You'll watch for the little bumps, won't you? And give it this stuff – it tells you on the label how much to give. P'raps when I come next time it's going to have flower buds.'

'So I'm to be a gardener, am I?' countered his father. 'You know, gardeners have to be paid – the man who does the plants at my place is on the pay roll.'

'Oh, it can't cost much to get you to put a teeny spoonful of growing stuff in the pot!'

'I'll take it off your pocket money.'

Roly grinned. 'Then I'll ask Karen to look after it. Karen, would you take a look at my cactus every time you visit Daddy and make sure it's doing all right?'

'It would be a pleasure,' she said with gravity.

'There! And because she's a nicer person than you, Daddy, she doesn't ask to be paid. So there.'

This exchange had taken them out to the car. Leaving them amiably bickering, Karen went back to say a few words of goodbye to her father and mother. Mrs Montgomery touched her arm and said, 'Just a tiny moment, Karen – have you seen Evie recently?'

'Not for a few weeks. I've spoken to her on the phone, though.'

'Does she seem all right to you?'

'Yes, just as usual – well, she has her ups and downs, of course. Why?'

'A week ago Saturday she came for the day. Walt was to take Perry to a local football match and Angela was invited to go with the family of one her pony friends to a horse thing, so she only had the baby with her and we talked more than we normally do. She seemed ... I don't know ... She didn't seem herself.'

'A bit in the dumps,' contributed her father.

'But that happens.'

'Yes, but normally she has some reason for it, and she's dying to tell you about it: her flower-arranging club didn't give her a prize, or her charity concert didn't go well – things like that. This time she avoided the point when I asked if anything was wrong.'

'I wondered if she and Walt had had a falling out?' murmured Mr Montgomery.

'About what?'

'Oh, I don't have any facts. It's just a feeling I got.'

'Will you be seeing her soon?' her mother asked.

'I hadn't planned on it.' Karen didn't go into explanations about wanting to avoid Dagworth if Michael was to be there. 'But I could drop in on my way home from my next trip. I suppose, really, it's time I did.'

'That would be nice of you, dear. Let me know what you think.'

'Will do.'

They kissed and parted. She rejoined her passengers, strapped Roly into his seat, and they went to look at the River Wey. A few anglers kept him interested for a good while, then they had tea and a muffin from a kiosk. 'Ooh, *lovely*!' sighed the little boy, sinking his teeth into a cake he knew both his mother and Gabrielle would forbid

When they said goodbye at Gatwick, Roly pulled at Karen's hand until she bent towards him. To her surprise and delight he planted a little kiss on her cheek. 'It's such fun with you,' he whispered.

That remark kept her happy on her way back to London. But thoughts of her sister soon intruded. Her mother had said Evie sounded depressed. Karen felt a little pang of guilt. Was this her fault? By saying she didn't want to be at the farmhouse if Michael was there, had she made Evie uncertain about his visits? Or about hers?

Was it trouble with the children? Were they going through 'a phase' as mothers were wont to express it. Or a problem with Walt? The latter was hard to imagine. Walt was so easy-going that he seldom made a fuss about anything. Except, of course, money. The business might be going through a hard time. That could make him edgy.

Well, she would drop in on her sister at the next opportunity and spend some time with her. She couldn't help reproaching herself for the fact that recently her mind hadn't been on her own family, but on the new-found wonder of being in love again, and on the problems of little Roly Dartieux.

She had to be in Bordeaux on Monday to meet with the Dillivers. Her colleague Paul had failed to find the right place for them last week and, since he was needed else-where, Karen was to resume the search. She decided to use the same system as for her last foray with them. She'd fly early next day, pick up a car at the airport, and have a com-fortable lunch with them so as to put them all in a good mood before starting the trek.

She had to sort out clothes, pack, and have a bite to eat. While she was heating a slimline microwave dinner, she rang Evie.

'Oh, hello. You were at Mum and Dad's today, I hear,' her sister said.

'Yes, very enjoyable.'

'You took your boss and his kiddie.'

'I did. Roly had written out a list of about twenty questions on cacti.'

'Taking them to meet the folks. Sounds serious.'

'Oh! Well, it wasn't quite like that, Jeffrey wanted to have a quiet day because we rather overdid it yesterday—'

'You were with them yesterday, too?'

'Yes.'

'As I said, sounds serious.'

'Evie, talk sense. It can't be serious to the extent you're implying. There's the little boy's feelings to think of.'

Evie seemed to consider this then changed the subject by inquiring, 'Where are you off to next? Somewhere entrancing?'

'Is Bordeaux entrancing? That's tomorrow's target.'

'Better than Dagworth village and the local playschool.'

'Evie, is anything wrong?'

'Nothing at all. Why should it be?'

'You sound sort of ... tetchy.'

'No, nothing's wrong. Everything's peachy. I hardly see anybody interesting to talk to and your mind is totally taken up with this new man and his kid—'

'Evie!'

Her sister seemed to draw in a sobbing breath. Then she quavered, 'Karrie, come and see me soon. I've got something to tell you.'

'What about?'

'I'll explain when I see you.'

'Is it Walt? Is the business in trouble?'

'No, it's nothing like that. Karrie, it's about Michael.'

Nineteen

They sat either side of a low coffee table in Evie's living room. It was mid-morning, a week later. The elder children were at school, the toddler was playing on the patio with a range of plastic trucks and cars. Karen had planned her return journey so as to arrive at Dagworth at this agreed hour.

Evie had put on make-up and one of her going-out dresses. It was easy to see that this was her version of armour, against the disapproval she expected. Karen, on the other hand, felt in need of a hairdressing appointment and in her plain blue sweatshirt was no match for her sister's soignée appearance.

In the intervals of showing her clients suitable properties and being a pleasant travelling companion, she'd spent six anxious days wondering what she would hear. She feared that her sister was having an affair, and yet somehow she didn't convince herself of it. Evie adored Michael, that was true. But the adoration was schoolgirlish, something like a crush on a pop star.

400

In Karen's view, her sister wasn't very interested in sex. She hugged and kissed her family, but she didn't invite long embraces from others. A little mistletoe kiss was enough flirtation for Evie, although many men in their circle found her attractive with her ample curves and her soft dark eyes. There was an innocence about her that was appealing, so that they ended up feeling brotherly rather than amorous.

Trying to view it from Michael's standpoint, Karen could accept that there might be temptations. Evie was always there, welcoming, admiring, ready to comfort him if things didn't go well. And the art of courtship came naturally to him. She could picture the situation; Walt safely off in Dover, Evie all sympathy and affection...

Evie pushed forward the little plate on which she'd set out newly-baked shortbread fingers. 'They're caramel flavoured,' she urged.

'No thanks.'

'It's a new recipe I got from an American magazine.'

'Evie, stop beating about the bush.' She drew in a breath for a direct attack. 'How long has this thing with Michael been going on?'

'A little over a month.' Evie's colour had risen. Her brown eyes were fixed on her coffee cup.

'Does Walt know?'

'Good heavens no! Of course not, Karen. No, and I don't want him to.'

Karen tried not to sigh at this. 'So, where do you see it as going?' she asked. 'What's the future?'

'That's where I need your help, Kar. I don't know what to do.'

'But unless I have some idea of how you feel, I don't know how to help, love. You know how *I* feel about Michael. That's why I've wanted to stay out of his way. If you've got yourself involved with him, my only advice would be to end it.'

'But I can't do that! It will all turn out fine, I know that. It's just that I'd like to hear more from him, and that's the problem.'

'What's the problem?' Karen asked, confused.

'That I can't seem to contact him.'

'Who?'

'Michael, of course.'

'You can't contact Michael?'

'That's what I've been saying, dear. I'm not really worried, you know. It's just that it's gone sort of ... quiet ... I thought there would have been some result or something.'

'Wait,' said Karen. 'Let's go back a bit.' She was holding up a hand like a schoolteacher asking for silence. 'You're in a relationship with Michael?'

'Yes, that's what we've been talking about,

isn't it?'

'What sort of relationship?'

'What sort? Well – friendly but business-like.'

'Businesslike?'

'Informal, I suppose. But quite business-like.'

'You're in some sort of business agreement with Michael?'

'Yes. And I'm not really worried. But time's going by and I still hear nothing—'

'Evie,' Karen cut in, suddenly understanding, 'you haven't lent Michael any money?'

Evie's pink cheeks went even pinker. 'Yes, I have. And I'm ashamed to say I'm getting a bit anxious about it. I've got full confidence in him, you know, but I wish I could get in touch. So I thought you might have an address or a phone number?'

Karen was torn with conflicting emotions. She wanted to laugh at her own mistaken fears of a love affair, she wanted to shake her sister for her naiveté, she wanted to strangle Michael for playing his tricks on poor trusting Evie.

It took her while to get her thoughts in order. She had to dismiss all thoughts of a secret love affair and instead think about finance. And that was bad. Her understanding of Michael was influenced by the events of the past year, which had led her to believe he wasn't to be trusted.

After a long pause, she asked, 'How much did you lend him?'

'Rather a lot.'

'How much, Evie?'

With her head lowered, Evie said, 'What was left of Granny's money.'

'All of it?'

'Yes.'

Granny Montgomery had left a very large legacy to her favourite granddaughter. Over the years, it had dwindled. Some of it had been invested in Walt's business, though that had largely been refunded by allotting a share of profits to Evie. A big chunk had gone in the restoration of their house and its grounds, some was laid aside for the children's education. But a decent amount still had remained, somewhere between twenty and thirty thousand pounds at Karen's rough guess.

She said nothing. She was trying to come to terms with this horrendous confession.

'Well, say something!' Evie muttered. 'Don't just sit there like the Day of Judgement!'

'I'm thinking. You've taken me completely by surprise.' She gathered herself to face the situation. 'Was there some kind of agreement? A contract?'

'Oh, of course. Michael typed it up on the computer, two copies, one each, and we signed both of them.'

'Could I see yours?'

Evie rose to go to the walnut bureau by the window. From it she took an envelope which she handed to her sister. It contained a single sheet of paper which proved to be headed 'Contract' and was dated September 19th.

This statement records the loan of £32,000 by the first participant, Evelyn Marion Felton, to the second participant Michael Stafford Ansleigh, for his use in the purchase of suitable property for re-sale.

On completion of the re-sale, Evelyn Marion Felton shall be refunded her loan together with any appropriate bonus.

Signed this day...

Following this was both their names and signatures.

Karen read it with dismay. She had no legal training but it seemed to her to be full of holes. What was suitable property? By what date should the property have been bought? On what date should the completion of the re-sale be recognized? What was an appropriate bonus?

'What did Walt say to this?' she inquired, tapping it with a finger.

Evie made a little mutter, half annoyance, half distress. 'I *told* you – I didn't want Walt to know anything about it.'

But that had been said when Karen was expecting a confession about passion and longing, perhaps even talk about divorce. The idea of secret loans had never entered her head. Now she had to assimilate the fact that Evie had handed over a very large sum of money without even consulting her husband who, in the normal run of things, was the controller of the exchequer.

'Well ... the next question is, why not, Evie? Was it because you knew he'd disapprove?'

'Walt disapproves of me doing anything with that money! You know he's never wanted me to use some of it to hire a gallery for a one-man show.'

'But this is different! This is such a lot! You've handed over all the money Granny left you to be used in a business deal. Walt's a businessman – surely you should have asked his opinion.'

'He'd only have said no.'

That was a certainty. 'And quite right, too,' Karen sighed. 'Evie, did Michael explain why he wanted your money?'

'Of course, and it was for a very good reason. He'd seen a piece of land that he knew he could re-sell at a big profit but he didn't have quite enough to finance the deal and the banks wouldn't lend him any.'

'Did it occur to you to ask why the banks wouldn't lend?'

'Oh, you know what banks are like...'

'Yes, they like the kind of set-up that will end in a profit. So Michael couldn't convince them that this would bring in a profit.'

'But there will be a profit, Karen. Michael explained he knew where to sell it and get about fifty per cent more.'

'So if it's such a sure thing, why wouldn't the banks respond?'

'Well, *I* don't know. Banks are funny...' She trailed into silence.

'You didn't ask him, Evie. Is that it?'

'Well, I ... It's just that ... You know Michael's clued up about that sort of thing. He told me the banks wouldn't play for some silly reason of their own, wheels within wheels, you know...'

Karen shook her head. 'The fact of the matter is, he couldn't go to them because he shouldn't be buying that land in the first place.'

'Don't be silly. Of course he should buy it if he can make a profit.'

'No.'

'But that's business, Karen. Buying, and then selling at a profit.'

'Evie,' began Karen gently and slowly, 'Michael is employed by a property company. His contract with them requires that when he finds suitable land, he tells them. If they approve, he sets up the purchase with the solicitors retained for the purpose. To buy the land and then re-sell it at a profit to

407

his employers – or to anyone else – is against the terms of his contract. I think it's a form of fraud.'

'What?'

'The development company are covering his living and travelling expenses, and paying him a retainer, on the expectation that he'll spend his time looking at acreage that they would use. He's not allowed to spend his time finding land for himself.'

'But in his free time, Karen...?'

'I think his employers could sue him.'

'Oh, that's nonsense!'

'I don't think so.'

'But all he's doing is—'

'Making money out of the company that hired him by selling something to them they're supposed to hear about in the first place.'

'But that can't be right,' protested Evie, brightening as a good argument occurred to her, 'because if Michael went to them and said, "I've got a bit of land I want to sell to you", they'd have him arrested or something, according to you.'

'But don't you see, Evie, he's not going to go to them out in the open like that. I think he'll have someone else do that on his behalf – pay someone a fee or a percentage or something. Or, he's set up a company in a different name – that's easy to do.'

'Karen, you're absolutely crazy! Michael

would never do anything like that.'

'Then what does he want the money for?'

'I told you. To buy a piece of land.'

'And what does he want the land for?'

'To re-sell.' She pointed to the sheet of paper Karen was still holding. 'It says it on that.'

'But he can't go to the banks for the purchase price because the minute they find out he's got a contract with a big company, they'd want to know why he's acting for himself. A bank manager isn't going to get involved in anything dicey, sweetheart. And he hasn't enough money of his own to complete the purchase because he invested it in the property company to *get* this job.'

'I don't understand all that, Karen...'

'Michael told me when he first came back from the US. He said he'd used most of the money he got from selling our travel firm, U-Special, to get his foot in the door with this big new venture. So he's got nothing now except those shares or stocks or whatever they gave him, and the minute the name of that company comes up with a bank manager he's going to ask the ins and outs. And what he'd hear is that Michael mustn't buy property for his own benefit. I'm pretty sure his contract won't allow it.'

'But I can't believe Michael would be deceitful, Karen.'

'All the basics are there, aren't they? He

wants to buy property to sell to someone else. But the development company are paying him to find property for *them*, not for himself. Since he knows they're looking for that kind of site, the likeliest people he wants to sell to are his bosses. And that would be some sort of a swindle.'

'You're only guessing! And I must say, one thing I've noticed about you recently, Karen, is that you're awfully mean about Michael. Just because you've taken up with someone else.'

'Evie, please don't go off on some side-track. This is nothing to do with any feelings I may have about Michael. This is about the fact that you've lent your legacy from Granny to a man who'll probably never return it and may quite possibly end up in jail.'

'Don't say things like that!' cried her sister, covering her ears.

'It could happen, love. He told me once that it's a big American corporation he's working for, and Jeffrey says such people aren't to be trifled with.'

'You've talked to your Jeffrey about Michael?' Evie asked in consternation.

Karen sighed. 'Not by any choice of mine, I assure you. Michael actually went to see Jeffrey in hopes of getting some backing for this scheme.'

'What?'

She gestured at the piece of paper. 'Jeffrey turned him down flat. He felt that there was double-dealing in it somewhere.'

'I ... I don't see why Michael went to Jeffrey. I mean, he must have seen that Jeffrey and you ... That Sunday when the little boy was here...'

'He'd only just met him here – that one time, when Jeffrey came to fetch Roly. And a few days later he turned up at Jeffrey's office with this proposal about buying a tract of land. He didn't want actual money from Jeffrey, he wanted him to recommend him to his bank or something.' She paused, trying to put the pieces in place. 'I think he's been getting more and more desperate. It seems as if he's put some of his own money in as a deposit, perhaps what he's scraped together out of his salary, or he's raised from one of those firms that advertise easy loans, you know, and now he wants to finalize the deal and can't raise the balance.'

'So he turned to me,' Evie said with a little sigh that still had in it some overtones of her idyllic view of Michael.

Because you're such a soft touch, thought Karen, but didn't voice it. Instead, she read through the contract again. No address or telephone number, no business heading. It was more like an IOU than a legal document.

'You said you couldn't get in touch? You

411

rang him, I suppose?'

'I rang his mobile,' said Evie in a small voice. 'I got a robot voice telling me the number had been closed down. I decided to write, but when I looked in my address book, all I had for him was that flat you used to have above U-Special Tours.' They were silent while they tried to think of other points of contact.

'He said he had to go to Watford,' Karen remarked, recalling the night he'd stayed at her flat. 'I think he said it was a property that belonged to his employers.'

'So if we contact them...?'

'That might be the way to do it. So who are they?'

Evie flushed. 'I don't know. He always said it was confidential, they didn't want the opposition to know they were in the market.'

'The opposition being other companies looking for a good site for a casino,' she murmured.

'For a casino?'

'Well, Jeffrey says that's his assumption.'

'You mean a gambling casino?'

'Is there any other kind?' Karen inquired rather curtly.

'Oh,' said Evie, and began to cry.

At once Karen was overcome with remorse. How could she have been so harsh to her poor unhappy sister? She went to her and knelt by her chair, putting an arm

412

around the shaking shoulders. 'Don't cry, love. Don't, he's not worth it. I'm sorry I sounded cross. We'll try to sort it out. Don't cry, dear, don't, you're making me feel all weepy too.'

It took many more soothing words and the administration of many tissues from the ornamental box on the bureau before Evie could be restored to normality. She sat up, glanced about, patted her hair, and tried to smile.

'I'll make fresh coffee,' she faltered.

'No, I'll do it. You wash your face and put on fresh make-up.'

'All right.' Like a child who has been gently chided, she obeyed.

Karen went into the kitchen to empty the cafetière and start again, and while she waited for the water to boil she went to cast an eye on Noomie. The toddler was sitting on a little plastic tricycle, crooning as he rocked himself one pace forward and one pace back. Satisfied he was safe and happy, Karen filled the cafetière, took clean mugs from the cupboard, and set them out on the kitchen table.

Evie came in a little later, still with reddened eyes and with no make-up, but seeming in control of herself. 'I'm sorry I was such a fool,' she murmured.

'Nothing of the kind. Anybody'd want to weep a bit after being let down so badly.'

413

'Let down?'

'Well, don't you think Michael's let you down?'

'I don't quite see...'

'He's borrowed money from you on a promise that you'd get it back soon. He did say soon, didn't he?'

'Well, yes.'

'What did you understand by that? How soon?'

'Well ... a few days ... a week or two.'

'And how many weeks have gone by?'

'Five.'

'And when did you first try his mobile and find it had been discontinued?'

'Two weeks ago.'

'That's to say, after three weeks had gone by since you gave him the cheque.'

'Yes.'

'And you were told the number was closed.'

'Yes.'

'So what did you do?'

'I thought I'd get him on his house phone so I tried directory inquiries but they told me I had to have an address.'

'Of course. And we don't know his address. Only that some time last year he was living in or near Watford.'

'I didn't even know *that*,' muttered Evie. 'I only ever got in touch by his mobile, and you know he travelled all over the country on this job of his. I never really knew where he was...' She died off into silence. Then she asked desperately, 'Do you really think he's swindling his employer, Karen?'

'I'm afraid so.'

'But he's ... not a crook, Kar.'

Karen said nothing. She was thinking of the small sum of money she'd put into the travel firm at the outset. Not much compared with Evie's investment now, but for her it had been all she had at the time. When Michael had sold the firm behind her back, he'd transferred a sum to her bank account. It had been equivalent to the amount she'd put in at the beginning plus a small extra – very small – in recognition of her four years of faithful and enthusiastic service. Hardly a silver handshake, let alone a golden one.

Had that been the action of a crook? Well, she could say it was the action of someone with scant regard for the feelings of others. And now again, he had behaved without the slightest regard for Evie's feelings or situation.

He might intend to return her loan; she would do him that much justice, to think that he meant no real harm to Evie. But to leave her without any means of getting in touch, to have his mobile number changed, to enter no business or private address on the so-called contract...

Moreover, he was involving her in an act of

bad faith, a very questionable piece of commerce. Insensitive was the least she could say of it. Selfish and egocentric, cruel ... Even if he brought it off, she now asked herself, did he intend to refund poor Evie's money? Pay her back for her trust in him? Using the funds he'd gained by fraud? That would make Evie an accessory...

'We can't be sure what he's up to, Evie,' she remarked, beset by all these unwelcome notions. 'I don't think it's anything good. If it were all above board, I feel sure he could raise the money in the open. I know for a fact that he couldn't go to the banks because that's what he wanted from Jeffrey – help with getting their approval. And I think it's perhaps become urgent so he turned to you, sort of as a last resort. Perhaps he had to close this deal almost immediately.'

'So you think ... he's parted with my money by now?'

'I think it's likely.'

'So I'd have to wait until he re-sells before I get it back?'

'Yes.'

'And you really think he's going to sell it to this American conglomerate...?'

Karen didn't know whether to say yes or no.

'And if he does, it's ... it's a crime?'

'I think it is, Evie.'

'Would he be arrested?'

416

'If he was found out ... Perhaps ... I don't know.'

'None of this can be true,' Evie said, and looked as if she would burst into tears again.

'Now try to be strong, love! Get a hold of yourself, and drink your coffee. You're going to have to start getting a meal in a little while, the children will be home for the lunch break, you don't want them to see you with your eyes all red.'

'Yes ... I won't be silly ... But what am I going to *do*, Karrie?' It ended in a wail of misery.

She took a moment before replying. 'I think you're going to have to tell Walt, Evie.'

'No!'

'Sweetie, you're in such a state, he's going to ask what's wrong. You'll have to tell him.'

'No, by the time he comes home this evening, I'll be all right, I'll have got a grip on things. He won't notice anything.'

'You're not enough of an actress for that, Evie. You look like Ophelia after she drowned herself.'

'Who's Oph—? Oh, you mean in Hamlet. But I'll do my face up, I'll make him something special for dinner, he won't suspect—'

'I was thinking about your expression rather than your make-up,' sighed Karen. 'You look desperately *unhappy*. And besides, you underestimate Walt. It wouldn't take him long to see something's up.'

'I can't tell him, Kar. He's so serious about money.'

'Yes, that's true.'

'And because it's Michael...'

'Yes.'

'He's never been as enthusiastic as the rest of us about Michael.'

'And that's why you didn't tell him you were going to lend Michael the money,' she put in very gently.

'Well, it all happened in a bit of a hurry...' Then she stifled a sob and said it aloud. 'But yes, it's true, I decided not to tell him what I'd done. But you know, he hasn't suspected a thing so I'm not so bad at keeping things to myself as you're trying to suggest.'

'I don't know about Walt, but I can tell you that Mum and Dad asked me on Sunday if something was troubling you.'

'No!'

'Yes. So I bet you anything that Walt's already wondering what's wrong.'

'No, no, he's not, you're just saying that so I'll tell him.'

'Don't you think you ought to? If he asks why you're unhappy, what will you say?'

This time there was no way to stop the flood of tears. 'I *can't*, Karen,' protested Evie. 'You'll have to do it.'

'Absolutely not!' It was an exclamation of dismay. 'This is between you and him, between husband and wife. It's not a thing where I should be standing between you.'

'He'll hate me!' she cried, her voice rising in desperation. 'I can't tell him!'

Karen was holding her and patting her on the back. Noomie came rushing in. 'What's wrong with Mummy? Has Mummy got a poorly head?'

'Oh,' wept Evie, 'my poor little boy, my children. What will Walt tell them?'

'Mummy, Mummy!' cried the toddler. 'Mummy, don't cry, Mummy!'

For the sake of her little boy, Evie made a huge effort and pulled herself together. She wiped her eyes with her hands then picked up Noomie. 'It's all right, I hurt my finger, it's not serious, darling, kiss it and make it better.'

She held out a forefinger. Noomie obediently put his lips to it and gave it a smacking kiss. Divided between smiles and tears, her breathing ragged with sobs, she took him on her lap and rocked him. Karen went back to her chair and picked up her mug of coffee. It seemed that never in her life had she felt so miserable.

By now the coffee was tepid but she drank thirstily. She felt what she needed was a double brandy, but coffee would have to do.

By and by the little boy was satisfied everything was all right. At Karen's suggestion he went to put his toys away in the Shaker storage bench outside. Evie dragged herself to her feet.

'I'll have to get started on lunch,' she announced huskily. 'I promised hot chicken wraps.'

'I'll lend a hand. Do you want a salad?'

'Yes, and there's some fresh coriander to go in it.'

'Righto.'

They went into the kitchen. Evie ran cold water then patted it over her face. Her cheeks were blotched with tears, her eyes were swollen. She dried her face, then sighing, opened the refrigerator door. Karen could see that she felt some slight return of confidence by being here, in her own special kingdom, where she was expert and assured.

Karen picked up a tray so as to clear the crockery in the living room. While she was putting the cafetière and the mugs on it, Evie appeared in the doorway.

'You're right, I can't keep this to myself. I have to tell Walt.'

'Good.'

'I'll do it tonight.'

'Right.'

'But only if you stay so that afterwards you can explain all this about the property being sold again.'

'No, Evie.'

'You've got to. I'm sure to make a mess of it so you've got to be there to pick up the pieces.'

Twenty

The wait was shorter than Karen expected. She heard her brother-in-law crunching along the path to the garden bench where she was sitting, a jacket slung over her shoulders against the chill of the October evening. The moon hadn't yet risen. The thought came that there was no use looking for a silver lining in the sky above, because there was only starlight to paint the autumn anemones with a faint silver. And as for human affairs here on earth, the clouds seemed leaden.

Walt paused beside her, then lowered himself to the bench as if his joints were paining him. 'Is it really true? She's given all her grandmother's legacy to that toad?'

'I'm afraid so.'

'What was all this about property and the banks and your friend Jeffrey?'

She stifled a sigh then set about the explanation.

Dinner had been a strained affair. Walt had glanced at his wife more than once in anxious puzzlement. Karen had avoided his gaze

421

while making bright conversation about her latest trip to France. Neither she nor Evie had managed to swallow more than a few morsels of the excellent duck in cherry sauce. As for dessert, only Walt had accepted the dish of home-made walnut ice cream.

Karen had left them together carrying out the usual after dinner chores of clearing the table and stacking the dishwasher. She tried to imagine how her sister would make a start on her revelation but it defeated her. She'd imagined it would take a long time and many tears, but no, within ten minutes here was Walt and she was trying to put things straight.

When she finished, he sat in silence for a few minutes. Then he said, 'He's a worm. He's a rotten, two-timing rat. She's had him here dozens of times, she's cooked for him, given him a bed overnight, she's treated him like a close friend, almost like a brother. And this is how he repays her.'

'You think then ... You really think he's up to no good?'

He gave a snort of laughter. 'Borrows £32,000 then disappears off the map? Hands her that nonsensical piece of paper as a covenant? Karen, I never thought as highly of him as you and Evie. I always thought there was something ... lightweight about him. But I never set him down as a swindler until now. But this...'

'He may intend to repay the loan?'

In the darkness she could make out the shake of his head. 'No, what he's going to do is sell the land to a competitor of this firm that's employing him, and then make himself scarce. Bought his airline ticket by now, I'd imagine. You see, Karen, the conglomerate that hired him isn't going to be pleased about this. If you're right and the site is intended for a casino complex, it's big money – really big. If they find out he's gypped them, they could make life very uncomfortable for him, to say the least.'

'Oh dear.'

'The man's a fool. If he played it straight, he'd be doing very well out of it. You say he bought into the project to some extent with the money from the sale of your travel firm – well, that would have brought him a very decent profit once the place gets going. I suppose...' He paused and thought about it. 'He didn't want to wait until the land was bought and the complex was built. That could be a year or two. Quick easy money, that's what he wanted.'

She thought he was probably right, but said nothing.

'Evie's devastated,' he said. 'Poor lamb, she's the sort that's not fit to be let out without a keeper.'

'So you're not ... not angry with her?'

'I'm angry with *him!* If I ever get my hands

on him, I'll throttle him! But her ... no, I'm more ... sort of miserable for her. She thought such a lot of him. Prince Charming ... And he turns out to be the Artful Dodger.'

They sat in silence for some moments. Then he said, 'I'm sorry you got landed with all the explaining. I couldn't really make out what she was trying to tell me after the straightforward admission that she'd given him the money.'

'That's all right. I owed you that because, you see, I've suspected for quite a while that Michael was up to no good. I just never thought he'd drag Evie into it.'

'Question is, what should we do about it?'

'What can we do?'

'Go to the police?'

She shuddered at the thought. Yet it seemed to be the next step. As she was about to say so, Walt went on: 'But we can't actually say a crime's been committed, can we? He's borrowed some money from my wife, but he's given her a written promise to repay it, so we can't say he intends to defraud.'

'But it's such an empty thing, Walt. I don't know if it's even legally binding.'

'It doesn't have to be legally binding. He could say it was proof he never intended to swindle her, that's all he needs. As to what he meant to do with her money as regards the property-buying, we don't know that he's actually done it – we're just guessing. Then there's the bit about thinking he intended to trick his employers – we don't even know their names!'

It was all too true. She murmured, 'Perhaps we're being terribly unfair. After all, it's only five weeks...'

'Oh, don't be daft, Kar! He promised to be in touch within a few days, but five weeks have gone by without a word from him. He's closed the mobile phone line she knew. She's got no address, she doesn't know who he's working for. What sort of a businessman behaves like that? I'll tell you – a businessman who's planning to do a flit.'

'Yes.'

'He's gone, and so is the legacy.' He heaved a great sigh, then said, 'Well, she was never going to do anything much with it anyway. Hire a gallery for a one-man show, get a share in a *pied-à-terre* in London. None of that was really going to happen because she needed someone to do it for her, and *I* wasn't going to – I thought it was a waste of money.' He thought about that for a long moment, then said, 'I was wrong. I should have encouraged her. Rather that than let this cockroach have it.'

'I'm sorry, Walt.'

'You've nothing to be sorry for.'

'I brought him here. I believed in him and so I made everybody else believe.'

'Yeah ... Well, I never thought he'd stoop to this sort of thing, to tell you the truth. I just thought he was a bit of a puffball, you know. So he took us all in. And we've just got to grin and bear it.'

He sighed very deeply. She could just distinguish that he was feeling in his jacket pocket. A moment later there was the familiar sound of his leather case being opened, and she knew he was seeking comfort in the ritual of his nightly cigar.

As he applied a match, she rose. 'I'll say goodnight, then, Walt.'

'Goodnight, dear. Thank you for trying to clear things up.'

'Not much help, I'm afraid. Night, then.'

As she came near the house she could make out her sister standing in the patio doorway. 'What did he say?' she asked in a voice muffled by anxiety and the onset of more tears.

'He's furious with Michael. Perhaps it's a good thing Michael's made himself scarce...'

'But what did he say about *me*?'

'He said that he never thought Michael would drag you into his schemes.'

'But that seems to mean he ... always thought Michael was ... no good.'

'Yes.'

'And *you* said he wasn't to be trusted.'

'Yes.'

'So *I* was a silly fool.'

426

'Evie love, you're not the only one who was taken in. It took that letter from Chicago to cure me of being in love with him.'

'I wish you'd shown it to me.'

'I tore it up. And I thought he was safely off on the other side of the Atlantic so that I didn't have to go into long explanations about breaking up.' She put an arm around her sister's shoulder to urge her indoors. 'Come on, let's go up and tuck the kids in.'

They went upstairs together. Noomie, in a stretch pyjama suit patterned with shooting stars, was sweetly asleep. Angela awoke momentarily to give a faint smile and allow herself to be kissed. Perry was playing with his Gameboy, which he guiltily hid under the sheet as they came in.

The absolute normality of it all was solace to them. They parted on the landing with a hug and a gentle murmur of 'Sweet dreams'. Karen went into the guest room but was nowhere near ready for sleep. She found the book she was currently reading, settled in the little armchair by the bureau, and addressed herself once again to Balzac.

Her mobile phone chirped. She picked it up at once, knowing it would be Jeffrey. They kept in touch all the time when they were separated.

'You weren't asleep then?'

'No, I'm reading.'

'What are you reading?

'Eugénie Grandet.'

'Oh dear. That's melancholy.'

'Yes, I think I'll have to give it up, it's too depressing,' she confessed, and immediately regretted it.

'What's wrong?' he asked quickly.

'It's just a family thing, Jeffrey.'

'But it's something serious. I can tell by your voice.'

'Oh, I really don't want to go into it. Let's talk about something nice.'

'All right. Shall I see you soon, or will this family thing mean you're staying on in Kent?'

'No, no.' She was strongly of the opinion that Walt and Evie should be left alone to sort out their problems. She felt that the daily routine, the need to get back to normal for the sake of their children, would put the trickery of Michael Ansleigh into perspective. 'I'll make an early start, get home by lunchtime, then perhaps drop in at the office late afternoon with some information about the the darling Dillivers and their house. Would that be OK?'

'And then we can go out for dinner, and then perhaps ... who knows?'

She laughed, and after they said goodnight she was ready to go to bed and sleep.

Next morning the house was abuzz, as usual, with the children looking for school books and Walt calling from his study that he couldn't find his document case. The good aroma of coffee and freshly baked rolls filled the kitchen. Karen quietly explained that she wanted to get away before the traffic built up, kissed everyone goodbye, and whispered in Evie's ear, 'It'll be all right, sweetheart.'

As she drove off, she was telling herself that this was true. Evie and Walt loved each other, they had a beautiful family, they would weather the unexpected storm that Michael had stirred up in their lives. The trouble was all about money, after all, not about the most meaningful things in their relationship. Thus, she mused as she made her way towards London and the man who was the most meaningful thing in her own life.

When she, at length, reached the office, it had turned cold and rainy. She went by Tube to avoid driving in the rush hour but thinking regretfully that she still needed a hairdressing appointment and that a rainstorm wasn't the most helpful of conditions for looking glamorous. She was wearing heels, an aubergine shift, and a soft beige wool coat that let the raindrops through.

Jeffrey stifled a grin when she came in. 'What you need in quick succession is a towel and a hot drink,' he suggested.

'Very funny. Just let me go and hang my coat to dry off in the cloakroom.' When she returned, having done the best she could with the cloakroom paper towels, she was greeted with a cup of steaming coffee. 'Never say I don't look after you,' he said.

'You're more than kind. Oh, that *is* good.' She sipped gratefully. 'Now, let me tell you about the darling Dillivers. The moving spirit in that clan is Grandma Dilliver, and she can't make up her mind. We hadn't done well in Lot-et-Garonne, so as you know, I persuaded them to look westward to the northern part of Gascony. I took them to four farmhouses, they were in raptures with them all. But then Grandma pointed out that though the first one had enough bedrooms, it had no swimming pool. The next house was big enough but the pool is too small, the next is very cheap and needs a lot of improvement which she says she couldn't cope with, and the last one was great but the pool was on the shady side of the house. Darling Grandma Dilliver is a ditherer!'

'Dear me.'

'I tried to explain how impossible it all was. But she says she has confidence in us and she's sure we'll sort it out for them.'

'How long are they staying in the digs at Bordeaux?'

'Oh, semi-permanently. It's out of season – they're getting cheap rates.'

'Um. I'll have to think about it. And now that you've unloaded such a long complaint

430

– which is quite unlike you – tell me what's really bothering you.'

'Oh dear, have I been taking out my anxieties on poor Mrs Dilliver?'

'So, there are anxieties?'

'It's just a family thing, Jeffrey. No need to bother you with it.'

'If you think it would be a bother, then we're not on the same wavelength here. Anything that worries you, worries me. So tell me.'

'Well, it's about my poor sister Evie.'

He nodded. 'Oh yes, when I came to fetch Roly ... She seemed very sweet.'

'Ye-es ... Sweet and ... well ... silly.'

'Silly? Are you telling me I'm involved with a woman who's got silliness in her family?' When she conjured up only a faint smile he took her hand and went on: 'Tell me.'

'Well ... You remember Michael Ansleigh?'

He frowned at that. 'Your former partner. And ... er ... partner.'

'Yes, him. He came to ask you for help in raising money.'

'He did.'

'And you told him to get lost.'

'Not in so many words, but yes.' A faint shrug at the memory. 'What about him?'

'It seems he's solved his cash flow problem by tricking Evie into parting with a legacy she got from Granny Montgomery.' He waited, and she continued: 'We may all be doing him an injustice. But Walt – that's my brother-in-law, you remember – he thinks Michael's done a vanishing act with the money.' She studied Jeffrey's face and ended: 'You think that's possible?'

'More than possible. I hate to say this since you must once have thought a lot of him, but when he was doing his sales pitch to me, he came over as a complete phoney.'

'Oh, Jeffrey!'

He patted her hand. 'I'm sorry. I didn't mean to upset you.'

'Oh, it's not *him*! I don't care what you say about him. It's Evie. Jeffrey, she's absolutely shattered. She ... adored him. No, that's not the word. She *cherished* him. He represented something romantic and glamorous in her life. And he seems to have made off with all her money.'

'Explain.'

Once more, as for Evie's husband, she went through the story. He listened in silence, a slight compression of the lips showing his feelings on the subject. She faltered to an end then asked, 'Do you think we'll ever get anything back from him?'

'Not if you don't know how to contact him. And that's the signal flag, Karen. A reputable borrower doesn't disappear into the blue like that. He goes to a bank and signs papers or he gets a lawyer to draw up an agreement.'

'So, it's a calamity we can't do anything about.' She shivered, and not only from the chill of the afternoon.

He got up abruptly, disappeared out of his office, and came back a few minutes later with one of his sweaters over his arm and a fresh cup of coffee. He gave her the cup and, as she sipped, draped the sweater over her shoulders.

'He's supposed to be buying a property for this development company?'

'Yes, but it seems clear he's doing it on the side so as to make himself a profit.'

'Hmm...' A pause. 'You know, I have some quite good contacts in the property market.'

'But only for sites in France and Spain.'

'That, chiefly. But the people I deal with abroad are often linked up with firms in this country, and some have departments for business property as well as private property.'

She was trying to follow his reasoning. 'What are you saying?'

'That I could put out a few feelers. Perhaps track him down.'

'Really?'

'Don't put too much hope on it, sweetheart. But the way I see it, he got this money out of your sister under six weeks ago. It can take quite a while to finalize a property deal in this country – searches have to be made for title deeds, planning permission has to be

433

verified. After all, a site for a casino is a big site. For instance, the land may belong to more than one person which would complicate matters.'

'Are you saying that he might still be in this country? Walt thought he'd have taken off for Brazil or some place.' Sighing, she set her coffee down on the desk.

'It's possible. He might have a solicitor to whom he's given power of attorney. But on the other hand, this is big money we're talking about and the whole thing's a bit tricky to say the least. Maybe he'd feel he couldn't trust anyone else with it, has to stay put until he can board the plane with the cheque in his hand.'

'Oh, if you could do anything to help us find him!'

'I don't want to raise false hopes. But I could try.'

'Jeffrey, you're such a comfort!' And, rising, she threw her arms about him.

They folded themselves together in a long embrace. They kissed then he let her go. 'I'll tell Alexis to ring for a taxi. Go home. Do your hair and change into something less damp. I'll collect you about sevenish, and we'll go somewhere handy for dinner and if it's raining we'll take an umbrella. And after that, we'll see.'

Laughing, she agreed to it all. It surprised her to find she was feeling greatly cheered.

As he handed her into the taxi he said, 'Don't mention any of this to your sister or brother-in-law. It may all come to nothing. But I'll spend a couple of hours making phone calls that might help.'

She carried out his instructions. When he called for her, she was looking and feeling better. When they had gone into the little local bistro and ordered their food, she asked eagerly, 'Did you get anywhere with your phone calls?'

He smiled. 'It's a bit soon to be asking that. But I chatted up a few old pals and they've agreed to make some discreet inquiries. That's as far as it can go at the moment, my angel. Offices are closed until the morning.'

'But did your old pals seem hopeful?' she insisted.

'None of them told me it was impossible. There are a few firms known to be engaged in helping possible casino developers. We have the guy's name and we believe the company he's working for is based in the States. It is an American company, isn't it?'

'Oh yes, I'm sure about that bit. It might even be based in Chicago, because that's where he was.'

'They're more likely to be in either New York or Atlantic City, but who knows, with the Native Americans opening up their reserves for gambling ... Well, try not to think about it for a day or three. All we can do is wait while the wheels go slowly around in the world of property dealing.'

She had so much trust in him that she was sure something would come of it. But, for the moment, enough had been said about Evie and her problems. They began to talk about themselves and how much they missed each other when they were apart. The night that followed was full of the love and passion that was the essence of their need for each other.

In the morning, he said over a quick cup of coffee, 'Would you think again about moving in with me, Karen?'

She gave a half-smile. 'I think about it off and on. But I don't really see how it would work.'

'But I was thinking ... I don't know what you'll say to this ... I was thinking we might get married.'

'Married!'

'Well, you know ... why not?'

She was so taken aback that she couldn't think of a reply. At last she said, 'Well, the obstacles would still exist, wouldn't they? What would Roly think?'

'But he knows people who are divorced do remarry. He understands that Louis is his mother's second husband, and quite a few of the kids in his school have parents in their second marriage.'

'We went through this before, Jeffrey.'

436

'But that was just about moving in together...'

'But I'd be Roly's stepmother?'

'Come on now, Karen, it's only in fairy tales that stepmothers are wicked.'

She was shaking her head. 'I don't know, darling. You know, when he talks about the set-up in Paris, he refers to his stepfather as Papa Louis. There's an awkwardness about it.'

'He'd call you Karen. He's always called you Karen.'

'Well, yes ... I suppose so ... Yet we don't really know what he'd feel about it.' She hesitated. 'Have you ever suggested such a thing to him?'

'No, I haven't. But I think I will, when I get the chance.'

She flung out a warning hand. 'Do be careful, Jeffrey. He's got problems enough without that.'

'But you're assuming he'd see it as a problem. He might like the idea.'

'I suppose that's possible.' Was it? Other children had to cope with step-parents – she'd seen many of them during her career in the travel business. Some seemed to cope with it quite well, but some were not adjusted. She'd had young travellers demanding not to sit in the same row as a stepfather or stepmother.

'What worries me is that I'd be here with

437

you all the time,' she explained, 'whereas he'd only see you once a month. He's almost bound to see me as a rival for your affections.'

Jeffrey sighed. 'It's clear you're not going to be convinced. At least think about it, angel.'

'Oh,' she said, laughing, 'now that you've put the idea into my head, I'll never be able to stop thinking about it.'

Later that day they were back to dealing with run-of-the-mill business. Jeffrey telephoned their troublesome client Mrs Dilliver in her Bordeaux hotel, to say he thought he should meet her to discuss her requirements. He could fit this in on his way back from Spain, where he was going almost immediately to deal with the damaged property.

Karen had paperwork to deal with at the office, which would take a day or two. After that she had a Paris assignment, a pair of apartment-hunters with very limited funds. It was arranged that she and Jeffrey would meet at the Hotel Babette at the weekend.

As usual she went by car ferry so as to take the faithful Peugeot. She felt she must drop in on Walt and Evie en route, to show support and to find out how they were faring. She arranged to arrive around nine, intending to take the boat early next day. She found Evie subdued. Walt on the other hand was trying very hard to be conversational, which was quite unlike him.

It was a windy, rainy day of late autumn. When it came time for Walt's evening cigar, he didn't go outside but instead betook himself to the old conservatory which Evie sometimes used as a studio. A glance and a nod at Karen alerted her to the fact that he wanted to speak to her in private.

Karen left her sister fussing with the children's clothes for next day. Walt was standing at the open door of the conservatory, directing cigar smoke out into the dark and rain. He turned as he heard her threading her way over the tiled floor towards him.

'Karen, I owe you a big vote of thanks.'

'What for?'

'That boyfriend of yours.'

'Jeffrey?'

'He rang me. Yesterday evening. From Spain, as it happens. Do you know he'd found out where that rat Ansleigh is holed up?'

'Good heavens!'

'Seems some pal was able to make guesses at the sort of company Ansleigh was supposed to be working for, and rang around saying he'd got a good site available and how could he get in touch. So, he was given his mobile phone number and passed it on to Lynwood.'

'Yes?' agreed Karen, blowing out a breath.

'And I know it was you that got him

involved in this so I want you to know, I'll be in your debt forever.'

'Well ... What are you going to do about it, Walt?'

'I got my secretary to ring the number this morning, to make an appointment to see him.'

'He agreed to see you?'

Her brother-in-law gave a grim laugh. 'She didn't give him my name. I told Millie I was making an appointment on behalf of an acquaintance of mine who actually does own an organic farm in Dorset. Ansleigh said his firm's receptionist had told him to expect a call like that. So Mr Chalmers is meeting Mr Ansleigh for drinks tomorrow at the Savoy Hotel with a view to doing some business.'

'Walt!'

'And the business will be to make him sorry he ever stole a penny from my wife.'

Twenty-One

In panic, Karen rang Jeffrey.

'Why did you ring Walt?' she demanded.

'Because it was Walt's wife that Michael tricked.'

'But he's going to meet him tomorrow at the Savoy.'

'That was quick!'

'You don't understand! He's in the mood to throttle him!'

'Good for him. If my wife had been taken in like that, I'd want to throttle him too.'

'But that's positively Neanderthal!' cried Karen.

'Nothing like a little tap with a Stone-Age club to make a thief repent of his misdeeds.'

'But it's the Savoy, Jeffrey! If Walt starts a fight, we'll be arrested.'

'We?' Now he was disapproving.

'I'm going with him, of course. To stop him from doing anything silly.'

'Stay out of it, Karen. You've done enough.'

'No, it's my fault Evie went on thinking Michael was Prince Charming. I can't make things even worse for her by letting Walt end

441

up in jail.'

'Stop worrying about Evie. She's got Walt to worry for her.'

'It's Walt who's chiefly on my mind at the moment. He's going to the Savoy and he's agreed that I can go with him. So I shan't be able to meet the Paris people tomorrow, Jeffrey.'

'You mean it's a done deal. You're not going to listen to me.'

'I can't, this time, Jeffrey. So can you arrange for someone to greet the clients...?'

'Oh, that's all right,' he said, though clearly with reluctance. 'I'll meet them myself. I'm flying to Paris on an early flight tomorrow.'

'Oh, thank you. I hate to let people down. So, I'll get the ferry as soon as I can tomorrow and I'll see you there in the evening?'

'Alas, no. I'll be on my way to Bordeaux to see the darling Dillivers.'

She sighed. 'Our life is like a railway time-table!'

'All the more reason why you should marry me and take up residence at Harkway Mansions. That way, our timetables would co-incide a bit oftener.'

'I'll think about that tomorrow, as Scarlett O' Hara said, after I've got Walt safely away from the Savoy bar.'

'If you're arrested, let me know and I'll stand bail.'

'I'm not going to be arrested. I'm going to

be in Paris on Friday and so are you.'

'Is that a promise?'

'I hope it is. Honestly, Jeffrey, I'm in such a tizzy I hardly know what I'm saying.'

'Say you love me.'

'You know I do. And when I say that I know what I'm saying. So, goodnight, sweetheart, and sweet dreams.'

'Sweet dreams? This is Spain! I haven't even had dinner yet! Which is why I'm so weak and faint I'm letting you go with that angry brother-in-law of yours tomorrow.'

'Weak and faint?' She laughed, and once again the magic of speaking with him seemed to make everything seem better. 'Well, then, *bon appetit*, darling.'

Next morning she and Walt drove separately to Dover Priory for the nine thirty to Victoria. Walt was wearing a business suit. Karen was in town clothes. They merged with the commuters in the crowded carriage and spoke little. Walt had decided to say nothing to his wife about the coming encounter. 'It'll only be something else for her to cry over,' he said.

When a taxi decanted them at the Savoy, they were in precise time for their appointment. To her secret annoyance, Karen found she was trembling.

Michael Ansleigh was sitting in a corner of the bar with a tall glass of something tawny on the table in front of him. The shape of a laptop satchel could be seen at his feet. He was gazing eagerly towards the door.

When he saw them enter, his mouth opened in a silent exclamation of surprise. He half rose, then sank back in his seat.

Walt strolled across the room, pulled out a chair for Karen then sat beside her, opposite their quarry.

'Good morning,' he said.

'What ... what—'

'What am I doing here? Taking the place of Mr Chalmers. He won't be coming.'

'B-but—'

'It was my secretary who made the appointment and the appointment was for me.'

'But how did you – how?'

'How did I get your number? Easy. It took us less than four days to track you down. So, you see, you're not a very good crook.'

'Crook? What do you mean, crook?' Michael had summoned some bravado, but his voice shook as he spoke.

'What else am I to call a man who tricks a woman out of a large sum of money and then disappears?'

'I didn't trick her! We made an agreement...'

'To which there were no witnesses and depending on a verbal promise to be in touch in a day or two. It's nearly six weeks now and not a word from you.'

'But I've been tied up. I've been in negotia-tion...'

'Over some piece of property, yes. For your own benefit, according to the signed agree-ment with my wife. She was to get her money back with interest.'

'And she will, she will! It's just that this thing is taking time.'

'And is a breach of your contract with your employers, Montigo Leisure Group of Atlantic City, operating by the good offices of DeMart and Rost of Chancery Lane.' Walt rolled this out with grim enjoyment.

Michael's face had been flushed with humiliation at Walt's first onslaught but now he lost colour. He stared at them in dismay. 'How ... how...'

Karen, studying, him, wondered if he had always been as shallow and weak as this. How could she not have realized?

'I told you,' said Walt. 'You're incompetent at this con-man stuff. Taking money from kind-hearted women friends, that's more your line.'

Michael swallowed with difficulty, unable to think of anything to say. Karen thought it was time she took part.

'You're on really dangerous ground, Michael,' she said. 'I know we can't charge you over that silly IOU, but double-dealing with your employers, that's really going to land you in trouble.'

'I don't know what you mean! I've done nothing wrong!'

'It's called flipping, isn't it?' Walt inquired in an interested voice, as if he were asking about the weather. 'Buying a piece of land and then selling it for your own gain and then reselling to – and perhaps taking a commission from – the original intended buyers. A double profit.'

'I'm not involved in anything like that!'

'But on that silly piece of paper you signed with my wife, it states that you're going to buy property and refund her investment with interest.'

'And she'll get her money – of course she will – when the deal goes through.'

'There's a hold-up?' Walt inquired, setting aside the matter of duplicity for the moment.

'Well, you know how it goes...'

'So you haven't handed over the purchase price.'

'Well ... no ... not yet. I had an option, which took up all my spare cash, and to complete the deal it just needed—'

'A donation from Evie. However, if it's still in your bank account, it can be refunded.'

'But if I have to refund that money, the deal will fall through.'

'What a shame. But at least if you hand it over, I might reconsider my decision to tell your employers about it.'

'What?' croaked Michael.

446

'They'd be very interested, I expect.'

'You wouldn't!'

'I certainly would. I'm in business myself, you know, Ansleigh. I don't like it when people behave unethically.' Karen saw her brother-in-law shake his head in a magisterial manner, and thought he might have made a good actor.

'I ... I ... If you would just let me—'

'You want to put things right by refunding my wife's investment?'

'You have no standing in our agreement,' Michael said, as if his brain had begun to function again. 'Evie's the one who should be handling this. I'll get in touch with her and arrange things.'

'I have the agreement of my wife to make this demand. Isn't that so, Karen?'

Karen nodded, although she knew very well that Evie had no idea what was going on here.

'So I'm acting as my wife's business agent, and can accept the repayment of her investment.'

'I ... I'll write you a cheque,' faltered Michael.

Walt gave a shout of laughter. 'A cheque?' he cried. 'From you? On some account that's probably got tuppence in it that you use for fobbing off your creditors? You must think I was delivered with this morning's newspapers, my friend!'

Others in the bar looked around, a little envious of the trio who were telling each other such good jokes. Karen smiled at them then turned her attention back to Walt, who was behaving much more cleverly than she had expected. But then, she kept on under-estimating him.

'No, no, chum,' he went on to Michael. 'I see you've got your dear little laptop with you.' As Michael tried to look uncompre-hending, he said, 'At your feet – got all your business information on it, including, no doubt details about the acreage you're trying to buy. Well, never mind about that. What you need to do is enter your password, call up your bank, give them your account number, and they'll ask you what service you require. You've done that in the past, I expect?'

Michael hunched his shoulders as if to protect himself from the heavy sarcasm, then bent to pick up the satchel. He got out the laptop, opened it, logged on, and soon had a screen with the conventional bank account display.

'Well done,' said Walt. 'Now, turn it so I can see the screen. You want to tell them to transfer £32,000 to the account of Walter Fenton, at the Kentish County Bank. Right. Now, if you'll just pass it over to me I'll type in the account number for you.'

He obeyed, as if under hypnosis. Walt

entered some figures then sat watching the screen. It blinked twice, gave a little mechanical beep, then the words 'Transaction completed' came up followed by 'New balance' showing the money had been subtracted.

Walt smiled. Still with one hand holding the laptop, he took out his cellphone and pressed a memory button. After a moment he asked to speak to a cashier. He gave the number of his account, then said, 'Have you received a transfer of money by Internet? You have? The amount? £32,000. Yes? Thank you.'

Michael, his hand trembling, made as if to take back the computer. Walt drew it towards him and closed the lid. 'Very efficient. Now I'm going to leave you, old son, and I'm taking the laptop with me. I'll leave it at the desk for you. But by the time you get to it, I'll have closed the account you just heard me contact and the money in it will be safely transferred elsewhere. So you won't be able to get anything out of it by telephoning and pretending to be me, if you had that in mind.'

Too shaken to achieve the hurt expression he was trying for, Michael swallowed and said in a low voice, 'It's all been sorted out now, hasn't it? You won't contact Montigo Leisure, will you?'

Walt was getting to his feet. Karen followed

suit. Walt said, 'You're a cheat and a chiseler, Ansleigh, and it'd be wrong to let you get away with it.'

'Please! You promised!'

'I did no such thing. On the contrary, I threatened. It might even have been blackmail.'

'Karen! Don't let him do it!'

She was startled that he should even think of appealing for her help. She shook her head at him. 'Why should I stop him? You hurt my poor sister so badly that she can hardly live with herself.'

'But you wouldn't want to see me sent to prison! You still have some feeling for me, Karen.'

'What? You can't really believe that. What happens to you doesn't bother me one way or the other.' She hesitated. 'But I don't want Walt to do something that would be a big shock to Evie. So—' she turned to her brother-in-law – 'take a minute to think about it, Walt.'

She'd given him pause. He knew his wife very well, and her soft heart would be injured if she heard that her once-beloved Michael had been arrested. It might make it even more difficult to sort out the problems they were already facing, and put some kind of barrier between husband and wife.

'I'll give you the weekend,' he said after a moment. 'On Monday, I'm going to ring the lawyers who stand in for Montigo, and I'm going to tell them what you've been up to. If you've any sense, by then you'll have reported to them about this site you've found and handed over the negotiations so they can put in an offer on behalf of Montigo if they want to. That'll give you the chance to tender your resignation and take off for the wide blue yonder before they start proceedings.'

He waited a moment for his adversary to react. But there was no response. Perhaps in an hour or two Michael might summon his resources and know what he should have said and done in this battle. But for now he was lost in no-man's-land, defeated at his own game.

Walt led the way out, the laptop under his arm. He handed it to Karen, who accepted it in surprise. 'Take that with you into the ladies' cloakroom, if you wouldn't mind. Give me five minutes. I'm going to phone my bank about closing that account.'

'Walt ... You don't really think he'd try to steal money out of your account?' she queried, wondering if he'd been too harsh.

'No sense in taking chances,' said her brother-in-law in a cold tone.

When she re-emerged from the cloakroom, Walt was standing by the way out. 'Let's go somewhere and have a champagne lunch,' he exclaimed. 'I think we've earned it.'

She glanced at her watch. Even allowing an

hour or so for this celebration, she ought to be able to catch an early evening ferry at Dover. 'I'm with you,' she said. 'Where shall we go?'

'Let's walk down to the Thames and eat on one of the restaurant boats.'

She thought it a strange choice, but she learned the reason when they were on the Albert Embankment. Her brother-in-law went to the balustrade and hurled Michael Ansleigh's laptop into the murky water.

'Walt!' she cried in amazement.

'Should've been him I threw in,' he grunted. 'Wearing concrete boots.'

Twenty-Two

When later Karen began her account of the episode, Jeffrey was listening with total seriousness. As she ended, he was chuckling aloud.

'I love it! A man after my own heart! I must get to know this brother-in-law of yours.'

'He said to tell you he wants to buy you a drink. You were such a marvellous help. So any time he can do anything for you, you only have to mention it.'

'No big deal, I only made a few phone calls.'

'But they were the *right* phone calls. Without you we'd never have got on Michael's track.'

'So Walt never actually did anything you were worrying about – never punched him on the jaw?'

'No physical blows. But I think he landed a few psychological knockouts.'

'I believe you. I especially liked it when he chucked the laptop in the drink.'

She gave a little grimace. 'I wonder if that was a bit harsh ... Perhaps all his financial and business stuff was on that.'

'Oh, he'll have a desktop computer at his digs with all that logged in, you can be sure of that. And what do you bet they're on hire and he'll skip without paying the bill?'

She could only shrug in acquiescence, recalling how Michael had left her with all the bills for hired office equipment when he first broke up with her.

'D'you think Walt means to call Montigo Leisure on Monday? Or was that an empty threat?'

'I think he'll do it. He's very angry. With Michael for playing such a dirty trick, and with himself for putting up with Michael so tamely.'

'Well, he's given him plenty of grace. I think Michael has already shaken the soil of England off his shoes. And Walt will get over all this. That glimpse I had ... they seemed such a happy household ... so settled and normal ... Wouldn't you think they'll sort it out by and by?' He sighed. 'I envy them. They have those kids around them all the time.'

Karen knew he was comparing Walt's children with the life of his own little boy. Roly's mother and stepfather were kind in a distant sort of fashion, careful for his well-being and generous with such things as pocket money. But the loving rough and tumble of the Fentons was a thousand times to be preferred to his lonely existence.

'Well, that's enough about me and my family. What happened with the Dillivers?'

'Ah, the darling Dillivers. I used my boyish charm on the matriarch. You remember that swimming pool on the shady side of the house in St Lotar?'

'Only too well.'

'I persuaded her to move it to the sunny side.'

'Move the pool?'

'It would only take about a month or six weeks. All be done by Christmas, they could have their first *Noël* in France.'

'But that would add to the cost...?'

'Oh, I know a couple of builders in Bordeaux, we negotiated a favourable price. Grandpa Dilliver got enthusiastic about that – he's the moneyman of the family.'

'But all the officials, the permissions and so on?'

'No problem, Kloss and his cohorts will see to all that, I've primed them for instant action. Now, how about dinner? I'm starving.'

They were talking in the little corner bar at the Babette. It was mid-evening on Friday. Karen had caught up with her office-seeking clients, and was to show them one or two more prospects next day. But after that they had the rest of the weekend to look forward to.

Although they spent the night together, they were so worn out by the stress of the past few days that they simply slept nestled in each others' arms. They slept late, so that they had no time to do more than kiss and part: Karen was going to collect her clients, Jeffrey had paperwork to deal with at the offices of Gustave Kloss. 'Tonight's still waiting for us,' he murmured in her ear before they went their separate ways.

For Karen it was a productive day. She 'sold' her clients on a charming first floor set of offices not far from the Left Bank. They had a late lunch in celebration, and agreed to be at Gustave Kloss on Monday to begin the legal business. She decided to ring and leave voicemail for the *notaire*.

She'd hardly finished the first sentence when the phone was picked up and Jeffrey's voice said, 'Karen! I was just going to ring you.'

'What are you doing, still there at three on a Saturday afternoon?' she demanded.

'Took longer than I thought. I had some money transfers to do – fees due to Kloss for two or three contracts. Listen, Karen, I just had a strange phone call from Louis. He's invited us to dinner.'

She was so astounded that she couldn't summon a word. He went on, 'He says it's something about Roly.'

'He hasn't run away again?' she burst out.

'No, that was the first thing I thought of. He says it's a long story and he wanted me to come to dinner this evening. I said I was meeting you, and he said he'd be delighted to see both of us. Nine o'clock.'

She waited a moment to think it over. Warning bells were sounding. 'I've scarcely heard from Roly recently,' she lamented. 'He used to ring me from time to time, but after the Mainz affair ... I think he was forbidden to ring me. And for my part, I haven't liked to ring him in case I'm still in disgrace.'

'Ye-es. You and I were regarded as a bad influence after Mainz. So if they want us there ... What does that mean?'

'Did you get any hints?'

'No, it was all politeness and good fellow-ship. I haven't recovered from the shock of the invitation – usually I'm only allowed there on the days when I have legal access.'

Karen had always seen Louis as the more tolerant of the couple, perhaps because he hadn't had the pain of wrangling over a divorce. In Karen's eyes, Hélène was too critical of the boy. Compared with Evie and her children, her relationship with Roly greatly lacked warmth.

'OK then, we're going to have dinner with the Dartieux,' she said. 'Pick me up in good time – I think we need a drink beforehand.'

'Good thinking. Seven thirty?'

That gave her time to have her hair done

and to buy a dress for the event. Why she should need to take these morale-building steps wasn't exactly clear to her. But when, after a long shower, she slipped the dress over her head and looked at herself in the hotel mirror, she thought she'd made excellent choices. Soft and clinging, the black silk jersey did good things for her. Her arms were covered to the wrist, but the neckline swooped at the back to expose quite a few vertebrae. Her dark hair gleamed from the ministration of the hair salon. She dabbed on a little Mimosa and told herself that though it had all cost quite a lot of money, it was worth it.

Jeffrey clearly thought so too when he saw her in the foyer. 'My word! If there's going to be an argument, I think you've won it already!'

She smiled, he helped her on with her coat, and they went out into the crisp Paris evening. They went to a bistro close to the Metro station, and as soon as they'd ordered their drinks were plunged into wonderings about what Louis wanted.

'He said he'd tried to ring me at the London office but the machine told him to try my mobile, which he did, and got me at Gustave Kloss just before you rang. He said he'd intended to make a trip to London tomorrow especially to talk to me.'

'Really?' That meant it was something very

important. What could Roly have done? She thought that over then said, 'I keep thinking that Roly's somehow to blame, but that's not really fair, is it? It might be something quite different.'

'What worries me is that it's about boarding school.'

'Boarding school?'

'Louis has threatened it before. When Roly's teacher says he's been inattentive, or insubordinate, or something, Louis begins to mutter about boarding school. I think he may have been a boarding-school child.'

'But there aren't many boarding schools in France, are there? I thought the French rather disapproved of that.'

'There *are* some, for the children of diplomats who have to go abroad and so forth. And there's a good one just over the border in Switzerland, so I hear. But as far as I'm concerned, that's not on. The poor kid has enough to put up with as it is. And it would make it even more difficult to see him every month, further to go, and so I probably couldn't bring him home to London.'

'And expensive fees, too – I suppose this meeting isn't about money?'

'I'm sure not. I pay a sum for legal maintenance, of course, through my bank, but Louis would think it beneath his dignity to squabble about money. He's got far more than I have.'

She nodded. She'd gathered that Louis had inherited money on a vast scale, and was moreover a financial wizard. Everything about the Dartieux way of living bespoke wealth. Although she chided herself for it, Karen had sometimes thought that the grandee lifestyle had been what attracted Hélène to Louis.

She brought herself to utter something that had occurred to her but that she'd suppressed. 'He's ... he's not ill, is he?'

'What?' He stared at her. 'That never occurred to me! He's always been such a spry little thing. Like a lot of kids these days he spends too much time at his computer so he's rather pale. But ... No, no, don't let's think that, Karen.'

'I'm sorry. I shouldn't have said it. But when I first met him, that time I brought him home from Cambodia, he was queasy – didn't like the idea of flying – but then, of course, that was a bad time for him, his mother and father had left him with – what was her name? Norah – Norah, the au pair who went off with her boyfriend.' She faltered into silence.

'He feels poorly on aeroplanes sometimes – that's why he likes the Channel ferry. As a matter of fact, his mother's not all that good as a traveller ... But she's always determined to be at Louis's side wherever he goes, so she doses herself with travel pills.'

They looked at each other and were at a loss.

They left their drinks unfinished. In the Metro there was little chance to discuss anything further. When they reached their station it was a short distance to Rue Lacharotte so they walked hand in hand, still trying to imagine what might await them. 'If Roly's in trouble again, I'm going to say it's their fault,' Jeffrey muttered. 'Attack's the best form of defence.'

'Go easy, love. Remember they have full legal authority.'

'We-ell ... If I start going over the top, warn me off, will you?'

In the lift on their way up to the apartment they exchanged a good luck kiss. When they stepped out at the second floor, the door of the apartment was already being opened – but not by Gabrielle. Louis himself was there, smiling a welcome.

It was so unexpected that they both hesitated. They'd taken it for granted that there was to be another scene, like the one over Roly's cross-Channel adventure. Angry looks, accusations ... But here was the head of the house welcoming them in as honoured guests.

Karen felt herself relax. Whatever was in the air, it wasn't any evil-doing by Roly.

'How nice to see you, mademoiselle,' Louis said as he ushered them in. Gabrielle stood

461

by, stone-faced, to take their coats. 'It's un-expected but very pleasing.'

'Thank you,' Karen murmured, at a loss.

They were taken into the drawing room. Hélène was there, in a dress of mulberry silk of exquisite simplicity, her only decoration the glint of diamond earrings. She was pale, but not with the air of exhaustion that had hovered around her while her son was missing in Mainz.

Roly was not in evidence. Of course, thought Karen, he's in bed asleep, it's nine o'clock.

They shook hands. They sat down. Louis bustled about pouring aperitifs. Karen accepted a *pastis* she didn't want but thought Jeffrey was glad to have a brandy.

'You're here on business, of course?' Louis said to Karen.

'Yes, clients looking for offices here.'

'I'm sure you dealt beautifully with their requirements.'

Jeffrey suppressed a smile at this stilted compliment. Karen looked into her glass and wondered how long this charade was to go on. Louis told his wife that Mademoiselle Karen was kind to spare time to take an interest in their affairs, and Hélène inclined her head gracefully.

'Roly's in bed?' Karen asked her.

'Yes,' with a glance at her watch that told Karen this had been a stupid question.

'How is he?'

'Quite well, thank you, although he's plaguing me because he wants to join a children's soccer team.'

Louis looked affronted at the idea and Jeffrey was about to ask what was wrong with it. But Gabrielle appeared momentarily in the doorway, so that Louis rose to conduct them to the dining room.

The room was so elegant that it was almost like something in a museum. The table was eighteenth-century walnut, the china was Marseilles faience, the silver looked as if it had been lovingly polished for generations, and the candles which lit the setting gave off a faint perfume of roses.

Karen was very glad she had bought herself a new dress.

The hors d' oeuvres were already on the plates. They took their seats. Gabrielle stepped forward to pour wine, then flounced out of the door. Louis smiled after her. 'My good old friend is a little put out because she has not done the cooking for this evening,' he explained. 'It was a last minute thing, of course. My intention was to travel to London tomorrow to see you, Jeffrey.'

'So you said. And you want to talk about Roly. So, can we get to it?'

'Oh, there's no hurry. We should enjoy our food, *n' est ce pas?*'

Karen could see that Jeffrey was about to

say something very uncomplimentary about both the food and his host, so intervened quickly. 'Louis, I think you have to understand that we're extremely anxious. We can't do justice to the food, however excellent, in a state of suspense.'

'Ah? That's true, I suppose. I hadn't thought of that. Well, my good friend,' he said, turning to Jeffrey, 'I relieve your suspense. What I have to say will, I think, be good news for you.'

'Good news?'

'First I must make an explanation.' He took up a forkful of guinea fowl *aux noisettes*. 'Perhaps you're aware that my government is about to send a trade mission to Argentina?'

Neither of his guests could make any response. They sat in silent astonishment.

'The titular head of the delegation will be a well-known politician – that goes without saying. But he will be unable to stay *en poste* permanently. He has to be here in the country for elections and votes in the assembly, you appreciate.'

Still no response from his audience. They were still wondering why they were being given a lecture on French politics.

'So, it is necessary to have a permanent head of mission, and I am proud to say that I have been offered this post.'

'Ah!' said Jeffery.

'Yes, now you see the situation. This is a

very, very important appointment. It involves much entertaining and social activity so that it is essential my wife goes with me. The economics of Argentina are, I suppose you know, in some trouble. They have been led astray by their dependence on the dollar.' He allowed himself a thin smile at that. 'My government has made a friendly offer to steer them out of their difficulties and my talents have been thought highly suitable. It will mean an almost permanent residence in Buenos Aires for at least three years, more probably, five—'

'You're not taking Roly to Argentina for five years!' Jeffrey said.

Hélène put out a hand. 'Don't get angry, Jeffrey.'

'If you think I'm going to let you take my son to the other side of the world where I'll never be able to get at him...'

'No, no, my friend, that is not the proposal at all. Hélène and I have talked it over for many hours and we have come to the conclusion that Roland should be given into your hands.'

Once again there was silence. Jeffrey looked as if someone had hit him in the chest. Karen knew that she looked just as astounded.

'We think it best,' Hélène said in a calm, neutral voice. 'Our first thought was to take him with us, I confess, but the educational problems are so great … So our next thought was boarding school—'

'No,' said Jeffrey. 'I would never agree to that either.'

Louis was nodding. 'We discarded both of those ideas quite soon. His education is important, and though there are some good boarding schools, it would have meant very frequent travelling for Hélène, especially if there was trouble at the school, as there has been in the past. And South America is a long way away.' He gave a fond smile towards his wife, who nodded and looked down. 'Travelling back and forth even two or three times a year would be too much for her. So, if Roland made trouble at the boarding school, it would be very difficult. I myself could not come, and to tell the truth I would be unwilling to part with my wife in such a stressful post even for a short time. Boarding school has severe downsides.'

The poor kid would be shut up with a horde of boys he probably would never make friends with, thought Karen. Judging by the day schools he'd attended, fitting in with others less bright was one of Roly's biggest problems. That was without taking Jeffrey's objections about access into account.

Gabrielle came in to remove the plates. If she noted that no one had eaten much of the first course she refrained from looking triumphant. She went out, then returned at once with *cul de veau Angevine*, followed by dishes of vegetables. There was a hush while she served the food. Louis took a restorative sip of wine and leaned back.

'It would be better if Roland were settled somewhere where he would be well handled while we are in Buenos Aires,' Louis went on. 'Hélène and I have our own exigencies. We have to learn the language – on Hélène's part, enough to get by, but I have to be able to argue on financial matters, so I am taking special courses immediately: what is called total immersion. So if we took Roland with us, we should at present be looking for a suitable school for him in Buenos Aires, and to do it long distance is not easy. It is a great distraction.'

A distraction, Karen said to herself. The poor kid is a 'distraction'.

'As you know, he is not an easy child,' Louis went on. 'He would have to learn Spanish—'

'That would be no problem,' Jeffrey said at once, then shook his head at himself. He was still struggling to catch up with the whole situation. 'Have you asked Roly how he feels about all this?'

Louis was surprised. 'Certainly not. We had first to make sure you would wish to have him with you on a semi-permanent basis.'

'Semi-permanent?' Karen repeated, perturbed. 'What are you saying? That when your stint at the embassy is over, you want to take Roly back?'

'Of course,' Hélène said.

'You must be mad! He's not a parcel to be left in a cloakroom until you feel like collecting him!'

'That's hardly a helpful thing to say,' Hélène said, with equal asperity. 'Of course I'd come and see him whenever it was possible, and perhaps take him on a holiday in France when Louis can do without me for a time or there's a gap in the trade talks and we both come back for a break.'

'But Louis has just said that the travelling would be hard on you.'

'My love, you must admit that you would not be able to make frequent trips,' Louis put in. 'It's never wise to leave financial discussions so I should very seldom return home.'

'That's true.' She hesitated. 'And I must be with you there. The important thing is that you should accept this post and have every help to do well, darling.'

'It *is* important,' he agreed. To Jeffrey he said, 'If I do well, I believe I shall be offered an embassy.'

'Ah,' murmured Jeffrey. 'You've always wanted that.'

'It's perhaps five years down the line, but my wife and I feel we must make every possible effort to succeed in Buenos Aires. For my country's political honour, and for my own advancement.'

'I see. And Roly's the stumbling block.'

'Well ... You choose a harsh word ... But in fact he is a big problem. I will confess that Hélène and I find him hard enough to handle here in Paris. Common sense dictates that we shouldn't add to our difficulties by taking him with us, and finding a boarding school where he'd be happy would prove ... well ... impossible.'

'So you want me to take him.'

'Yes.'

'For two or three years, perhaps four, perhaps five.'

'Yes.'

'And then you come back, almost perfect strangers by then, and take him away.'

'The legal situation—'

'The legal situation has to change,' Jeffrey said in a very cool tone. 'I want to have Roly with me – you know I do. But I won't accept those conditions. You don't seem to have considered him at all. All you want to do is have him stashed somewhere until you get back. If you really imagine I'm going to go along with that, you're crazy.'

'Jeffrey,' murmured Karen in warning.

'It's all right, Karen, I know what I'm saying.' He addressed himself once more to his host. 'Of course, I want to have my son

469

stay with me. But I'm not going to take him just to help you further your career! If I accept the responsibility for Roly I want it on a permanent basis. I want the legal agreement altered. I must be in full charge of my son, responsible for his care and his well-being. I'll agree to Hélène having access to him whenever she can get to London during your tour of duty in Argentina, but he stays with me even after all that is over.' He paused, then added: 'That is, if he wants it that way.'

Hélène gave Jeffrey a disbelieving stare. 'Good heavens, he's only seven years old! You can't seriously be saying you want the opinion of a seven-year-old boy.'

'Bet your life I do! Roly has his view of life, just as we've got ours. You tell me you haven't told him your plans. So you've no idea what he's feeling or thinking...'

'But a child can't make decisions of this kind, my friend,' Louis protested almost gently. 'If he were fourteen or fifteen – yes, then, perhaps.'

'But Roly is very grown-up for his age. Or hadn't you noticed?' Jeffrey challenged. 'He's very quick on the uptake—'

'I beg your pardon?'

'Quick to understand things. Once a thing comes into his ambience he wants to know all about it. He keeps a journal with all the things that interest him – he looks them up in books or on the computer.'

'Oh yes, the famous fish – he wanted to tell us a great deal about fish.'

'Don't make fun of him!' his father said protectively. 'He tries to talk to you about finance. You brush him off but he wants to discuss what you're doing – how many kids of his age even know what finance is? And I'm saying he's well able to tell us what he thinks, how he feels, where he should live and with whom.'

'Of course he'd say he wants to be with you,' Hélène said, sitting up very straight in her chair, 'because when he's with you, you spoil him shamelessly.'

'Hélène,' soothed Louis. 'Let us not be critical or unkind in this discussion.'

'By all means let us not be critical or unkind,' agreed Jeffrey, 'but let's apply some sense. You couldn't really have expected me to say I'd take my son for three or four years and then tamely hand him back?'

'Legally—' Louis began again.

'We're not talking law here. We're talking about what would be best for Roly. Are you saying that you want him to stay with me for a period of years, three or four or however many, and all the time we're going to be saying to each other, "When Maman gets back from South America, you're going back to live with her." Is that it?'

'I must say I see nothing wrong with that,'

Louis returned, although with some reservation in his tone.

'So he gets a complete change-around now, when he's seven, and another when he's ten or eleven...?'

'Children are resilient, Jeffrey—'

'Excuse me,' Karen said, taking them both by surprise. 'You're getting away from the main point, the one that Jeffrey made. Roly should be asked what he'd like to do. Even if he weren't such an exceptionally bright child, he'd still deserve to be consulted about his fate.'

'That's nonsense. The courts make decisions about the care of children every day, and they don't consult the child.'

'But Hélène, that's often because there's a doubt about the fitness of the parents, or money problems, or religious difficulties. None of that applies here and moreover Roly is *not* an ordinary child—'

'You keep saying that,' Hélène interrupted with irritation. 'He's just a rather difficult, rather conceited little boy—'

'Hélène!' said Karen, aghast.

'My dear, you don't quite mean that,' Louis put in. 'He's difficult, yes, and perhaps rather too keen on being noticed, but—'

'You don't understand him at all,' Karen cried. 'You don't have the slightest idea what he's really like! He's not difficult if you listen to what he's trying to say, and he's *not* conceited, he's quite the opposite – almost humble sometimes because he knows how much he still has to learn.'

Hélène rose from her place with icy dignity. 'What is this woman doing at my dinner table?' she demanded of the surrounding air. 'Interfering in my personal affairs, claiming to know more about my own child than I do myself?'

'Hélène...'

'No, Louis, I've had enough. You had no right to invite her without consulting me first.'

'But Karen is after all likely to be —'

'I'm going up to my room. When you've reached some sort of reasonable decision, let me know.'

'Sit down,' ordered Jeffrey. 'We're trying to work out what's best for Roly. You can't seriously say you're going to walk out on a thing like this.'

'If I stay I insist that this woman leaves!'

'No, I want Karen here.'

Karen was already getting up. 'No, Jeffrey, it's better if I go. I've no standing in this affair.'

'But you *will* have.'

'That's for the future. For the present you've got to see how to settle things so that Roly will be happy. So it's better if I leave.'

'But I'd rather you were here.'

'You'll do all right, love,' she said, touching

him on the shoulder as she went towards the door of the dining room. 'Let me know as soon as you get it worked out. I'll be up, no matter how late.'

She went out. Gabrielle was hovering outside the door, clearly eavesdropping shamelessly, but to what purpose Karen couldn't imagine since the discussion had been in English. The servant stood aside to let her pass but stayed at her listening post. Gabrielle too was facing a big change. It was certain she wouldn't want to go to South America with the Dartieux, and the apartment would probably be sold. As she let herself out and went down in the lift, Karen was almost sorry for her.

It was ten at night. She would have liked a good walk to clear her head, but to walk alone at this hour was unwise. She went home by Metro.

There was no point in trying to read. She changed from her dinner dress into jeans and sweater, hung everything up tidily, listened to her radio, and finally went out to a meal at the local bistro. She had need of something, for despite the lovely food that had been placed before her at the Dartieux, she'd hardly tasted a morsel. She made sure she had her mobile with her.

Jeffrey rang while she was in the restaurant. It was going on for midnight.

'We came to an arrangement. Briefly, it's

that you and I can talk to Roly alone tomorrow to tell him we're proposing that he should come and live with us.' He broke off. 'I'm right, aren't I? It will be "us"?'

She allowed herself a private smile at this. 'Are you using Roly to ensnare me?'

'Don't joke, Karen. Will you be there for Roly and me?'

'It seems likely.'

'He's to understand that it's semi-permanent. When Louis's stint in Buenos Aires is over, Roly's to be asked if he wants to go back to live with Hélène.' At that point he paused again.

Karen said, 'I think he's likely to say no to that.'

'And I think Louis understands that quite well. Hélène, on the other hand, seems not to have thought that far.'

She tried to look ahead to that point. Was Hélène's love for Roly strong enough to make her fight for him? There was no way of knowing, but she had the feeling that his mother might be happy to let the arrangement stand. All the more so if Louis got his embassy and she was picturing herself as His Excellency's wife. Some elegant building in a suitable country – Spain, perhaps, or Portugal – and a gathering of well-dressed people drinking fine wines...

'Are you too tired to come to the Babette?' she asked. 'And did you eat any of that gorgeous food?'

'Not a bite. I'm on the pavement at the moment trying to flag down a taxi.'

'I'll come to you, Jeffrey. We'll want to talk, and really my hotel room's not comfortable enough. And–' she was now laughing – 'what's more, I'll bring you a sandwich. I'm in a bistro at the moment where I can easily get one.'

She could hear him make a sound that was half a laugh, half a sigh. 'Practical as always.'

'You can scoff, but when I was working as cabin crew I learned the importance of food. I'll be at your place as soon as I can. See you there.'

When she got to his *pied-à-terre*, he was in his shirtsleeves. The smell of freshly made coffee was in the air. She offered him the carrier containing his sandwich but he put it down at hazard and took her in his arms. He buried his face in her hair. 'Thank God you're here. I'm nearly out of my mind with trying to keep my temper.'

'Poor love.' She held him close. 'Tell me all about it.'

'There's not much to tell, really. You heard their main proposal. We kept going round and round in circles. By and by I got the impression Louis was coming over to my side. He adores Hélène but he can see she's not really good at the maternal love bit.'

'You mean he doubted her notion that

476

after a long absence from her, Roly would be keen to go back to live with her.'

'He tried to make her see that she doesn't have much in common with the poor kid. She kept saying that Roly would grow out of his strange behaviour. "It's just a phase," she kept saying.'

Karen shook her head. 'Roly's behaviour isn't strange. It's *different* – because Roly is different.' She paused then added: 'But all the same, he loves his mother. I don't know what he's going to say when he learns she wants to go to the other side of the globe for several years.'

He sighed and let her go. 'As to the legal aspect, I agreed not to insist on a change of the custody order. They didn't say so, but they don't want to be caught up in a legal tangle while Louis is trying to learn Spanish and get ready for the negotiations. That was my bargaining point, and it worked. We're going to have an arrangement vetted privately by our lawyers, me to take charge of Roly if he wants to live with me and to have authority over his schooling and so forth. We're thinking of making an agreement for five years.' He sank down in an armchair. 'I hope and pray I'm making the right moves.'

She touched him on the cheek with a gentle finger. 'You ought to eat.'

'I suppose so. I made coffee.'

'Yes.' She retrieved the sandwich and went

in search of the coffee-maker. She put the sandwich on a plate and thought it looked unappetising, the filling dropping out of the stiff French baguette. She wasn't surprised when he paid it no heed, although he drank the strong black coffee eagerly.

She sat beside him on the small sofa. She drew his arm about her. 'What was the arrangement in the end? We're going to speak to Roly?'

'Tomorrow, after church. We're being allowed to take him out to lunch. Which, of course, means he'll guess something earth-shattering is happening. It's not one of my permitted visits so that will alert him. And the fact that we're going to lunch is strange in itself. He knows Hélène generally doesn't approve of what I let him eat. So, he'll be all keyed up.'

'Poor kid,' she sighed.

'Yes, it's very tough on him. Karen, you've learned to know him very well. How's he going to feel about Hélène going so far away and leaving him?'

'I wish they'd told him,' she said. 'It'll be a big shock when you tell him.'

But it was not. When they collected him next day from the foyer of the apartment block, they found him clad in church-going clothes – a miniature version of a charcoal grey suit, white shirt and blue tie. These were the kind of clothes that Karen's nephew

478

Perry wouldn't have been seen dead in, nor would his mother Evie have dreamed of buying them for him.

He seemed quieter in his greeting but there was nothing to warn them as to what was coming. In deference to Hélène's wishes about his diet they went to a specialist fish restaurant where they let him study the menu for himself. He asked for *brochet meunière*. 'Pike is a very fierce kind of fish,' he remarked. 'How annoyed it would be if it knew it was being served up on a plate in a restaurant!'

The grown-ups ordered sole. The waiter went away. Jeffrey began, 'We've something very important to say to you, Roly.'

The clever little boy couldn't resist showing off. 'I know, Daddy. About Maman and Papa Louis going to South America.'

Jeffrey was almost shocked. 'Maman told you?'

'No, but it wasn't difficult to know. Pierre – you know, my friend the porter? – he said Papa Louis was making arrangements to sell the apartment, and have some special pieces of furniture shipped out to South America. And then of course I'd seen tapes about learning Spanish on a table in the living room last week and when I asked about them Papa Louis said it was nothing important. But I knew it must be important because they're from a language studio that advertises special courses in the newspapers.' He gave an overbright little smile. 'After all, nobody would be doing that for no reason.'

The two adults looked at him in amazement.

'And, of course, if Papa Louis is going to take special courses and is sending some of his things to this place,' he went on, 'that means he's going to be there for a long time. And he wouldn't bother to take language lessons if he was only going for a month because he speaks a little Spanish already. I expect it's financial stuff he's studying – about how to talk about money in Spanish.' He ran a finger round a square on the checked tablecloth. 'And Maman always goes with him wherever he goes, of course. And they haven't said anything about it to me so that means ... that means...' He faltered into silence.

'What does it mean, Roly?' Karen asked gently.

'They're not taking me.'

It came out in a very small voice. He mouth turned down at the corners, but he blinked away the threatening tears.

No one said anything for a moment. The wine waiter came and poured Sancerre for Karen and Jeffrey, Coca-Cola for Roly.

'How do you feel about that, Roly?' Jeffrey asked at last.

Roly took a restorative sip of his drink and squared his shoulders in his little suit jacket.

'Well, in a way I'm sorry,' he said in a reasoning tone, 'because I think South America would be very interesting. But it *is* a very long way, and I'd probably be sick during the flight because it's so long, and then of course it would mean you couldn't visit me, Daddy, and I'd hate that.'

'Yes, go on.'

'On the whole...'

'What?'

'It's better if I don't go,' he stated. 'I thought it all out. There's all the trouble about schools. I don't know what the schools are like in South America. The picture books in the classroom have stuff about riding, like cowboys but it's not the Wild West, I think it's called the pampas. So perhaps I could've had a pony if they were taking me, and I could ride to school, but I don't know what the traffic's like and it would be a worry for Maman.'

'I think the traffic is pretty much like Paris,' his father supplied. 'They're going to a city called Buenos Aires. No horse riding, I imagine.'

'Are you sure?' He paused, summoning his thoughts. 'I looked up South America in my computer, you know. It said...' He tailed off, waiting until he'd managed to remember the exact words. ' "Largely agricultural", which means farms and things. And Buenos Aires – I looked that up, it's such a funny name, it said how to pronounce it and it means "good airs", so it can't have traffic like Paris, Daddy.'

'Oh, I think they gave it that name a long time ago, Roly. It's got a bit smokier since then.'

'Well, anyway, it'd probably be difficult finding a school for me. Maman hates all that. It never seems to work. So, it's better if I don't go to Buenos Aires. I might go later, though, when I'm grown up, because if they've really got people who ride horses a lot, it's an interesting place.'

'So if you don't go to Buenos Aires, what would you like to happen?' Jeffrey prompted.

'I don't want to go to boarding school,' Roly said with great earnestness. 'Papa Louis has said things in the past about finding me a boarding school, but you know, I don't seem to get on well with other kids.' He blushed momentarily then said, 'It's because I'm a geek.'

'A *what*?'

'A geek. Victor told me about it when I was there at the chess tournament. You remember Victor?'

'The one who spoke English with an American accent.'

'He's a geek too. It's American slang and it means you're interested in computers and chess and things other kids think are geeky. He says you can't help being a geek.' He sighed 'I think he's right. I don't *mean* to be geeky, but it just seems to happen.'

'It's nothing you need to apologize for,' Karen said gently.

'But it always seems as if I ought to – you know? People say things, and I say "Wait a minute, that's not right", and they get upset. Or I just let them say wrong things and then they say, "Don't look so smug", and I don't even know I'm looking smug. I don't know why it is.' A tear rolled down one cheek and he sought refuge in his glass of coke.

The waiter brought their food. In the interval that followed Roly managed to wipe away his tear without losing dignity. Karen fussed to ensure he had butter for his roll and enough vegetables. He heaved a great sigh and returned to his summation of life's problems.

'So if Papa Louis sends me to boarding school it might not work, because I'd just get on the wrong side of everybody. But he hasn't looked at any leaflets about boarding schools. He did that last year and I thought it was pretty certain, but that all went away. *This* time it looks as if he's not thinking that way, and I'm glad, 'cos it would all go wrong, I'm almost sure.'

'You've given it a lot of thought,' Karen observed.

'Yes, and I've been waiting for Papa Louis or Maman to say something. But they haven't.'

'What would be your solution to the problem?' Jeffrey asked.

'Oh ... well ... if I'm being asked, I'd rather live with you, Daddy, if that's what we're having lunch about.' He looked from one to the other, alert greeny-blue eyes assessing the result of this challenge.

Karen smiled. 'So this lunch is simply so we could put a big new idea to you, is that it? You've worked it out?'

'Not all of it. I wouldn't be having lunch with you and Daddy all out of the ordinary, unless it was something extra important, and the extra important thing at the moment is South America. So I guessed you and Daddy were going to explain it all to me. I expect there's a bit more. Is that right?'

'Not far out,' his father agreed. 'The chief point was that you were going to be given a choice to see what you'd prefer. But I see you've sorted that out for yourself.'

'Is it all right?' Roly asked, and a hint of anxiety showed in the frown lines between his brows. He looked first at one then the other for clarification.

Jeffrey looked at Karen. 'What do you think, Karen?'

'We have to explain that this might not be a permanent arrangement.' She turned to the little boy. 'Maman will come to visit you as often as she can. When Papa Louis ends his tour of duty in perhaps three years or so, you get to choose again – whether you want to stay with Daddy or whether you want to go to Maman.'

'Oh.'

'For the moment, you don't have to make that decision, Roly,' his father said to re-assure him. 'Maman and I are going to make a promise to each other – written out by lawyers, you know – that for five years I'll be looking after you.'

'How often will Maman come to see me?' His voice quavered on the question.

'We don't know about that. Maman will tell you how it's going to be arranged.'

'But Maman *doesn't tell* me things!' he burst out. All at once he scrambled down from his chair and ran across the restaurant, to an open door giving on to a patio at the back.

Karen rose without thinking what she was doing. She was off after the little boy before she remembered this was Jeffrey's son, not her own. She glanced back in uncertainty but he gave her a nod and she hurried on.

Roly was sitting on the broad plinth of a stone trough of evergreens, his face buried in his table napkin. She sat beside him and without a word took him in her arms. He pulled away for a moment – too proud to ask

485

for help, too accustomed to handling his troubles alone. Yet as she held him his body relaxed and he turned towards her. He sobbed for a while, then the sobs turned to sniffles. He sat up, blew his nose on the restaurant napkin, and looked at her with a wavering smile.

'What a baby,' he sighed.

'You're entitled to a tear or two, sweetheart.'

' "Tears don't produce anything except moisture",' he quoted.

'Who said that? Some big grown-up man who didn't know anything about it, I suppose. Tears make you feel better sometimes.'

'Well ... yes...'

They sat in silence. The patio was empty except for folded chairs and tables and a sunshade or two in plastic sheaths. The air was chill.

'Your pike *meunière* is getting cold,' she observed.

'But a pike is used to the cold,' he said, and gave a little smile at his own joke.

'I was thinking of it from your point of view. We'd better order something else for you – that's if you want to go back and eat.'

He let that suggestion go by. Then he said flatly, 'I don't think Maman will come and visit me very often.'

'What makes you say that?'

'She doesn't like flying very much and it's

486

an awful long way. I looked it up, you know.'

'That's true. But she'll come.'

'But not often.'

She didn't know what to say. He was too intelligent for any soothing yet meaningless promises. She took his hand and pressed it. After a moment he twined his fingers in among hers.

'We'd better go back to Daddy. He'll be wondering what we're doing.'

'OK, let's go. Would you like to dry your eyes first?'

He scrubbed at his face with the napkin. He then surveyed it ruefully. Karen smiled and said, 'We'll get you a clean napkin as well as some hot fish.' He made a little sound, half childish giggle, half sigh.

His father was sitting sideways on his chair watching the door as they came in. Roly went to stand close against him, leaning into his shoulder. 'I'm sorry I was such a baby,' he said.

'No problem.'

'Karen says I'm to have some hot fish.'

'Karen, as usual, is right.' Jeffrey beckoned the waiter, who came hurrying up with a face expressing anxiety and sympathy.

By and by they were all seated in their places and Roly was unfolding a clean napkin. 'So I can live with you when Maman and Papa go to Buenos Aires?' he said with great composure. 'And when they come back in the end, I get to choose what happens?'

'That's the proposal before the committee. But you don't have to make any decisions now. Papa Louis told me he thought they'd be gone for three or four years, perhaps more.'

'Oh, I'll be ten or eleven by then. I'll know a lot more.'

'About what?'

'Everything.'

'Well, that's true,' Jeffrey agreed peaceably.

A fresh serving of pike arrived and was placed before the child. He took a forkful or two and savoured it. 'It's nothing so awfully different,' he reported. 'I thought it might be sort of prickly to eat, since it's such a fierce fish.'

'Next time perhaps you can try shark?'

'Oh, Daddy, you can't eat shark! It's becoming an endangerous species.' Then, after a moment, 'Oh, that was a joke.'

'Not a good one, I gather.'

Roly gave a much more reassuring grin and went on with his food. Jeffrey said to Karen, ' "What do you think of the show so far?" '

'So far so good.'

Roly said, 'You're talking about me, aren't you?' and gave a little shrug. Then he held up a finger. 'Listen. Victor – you remember we were talking about Victor?'

488

'What about Victor?'

'He says there are schools for geeks. Have you heard about those?'

Karen and Jeffrey exchanged a glance. 'It seems to me I've heard something about it,' Karen said. And she had – she'd read an article in one of the broadsheets, about schools for specially gifted children.

'Victor said he went to one in Philadelphia. That's in America although Victor told me the name's from Greece, it means City of Brotherly Love. That's an even funnier name than Buenos Aires, if you ask me. But about those schools ... He says there are others, he's pretty sure, in London for instance. He told me he had to go to a shrink to be tested – a shrink, he said that meant a head doctor but it doesn't mean he puts on a bandage, I think it means a ... a ... that word that sounds as if it should begin with an "s"...'

'Psychologist,' Karen volunteered.

'That's it. When I'm living with you in London, Daddy, perhaps I could have a test and go to a school for geeks?'

'I think that could be arranged.'

'You have to consult an education shrink. I s'pose there's quite a lot of those in London.'

'I imagine so,' his father agreed gravely.

'So could we do that? See someone who would understand about being a geek and send me to a special school? Victor says that the one he went to in Philadelphia, they didn't just do sums, they did math, and I looked that up and it's really math-e-matics. That's sums where you don't just add up and take away, you use little letters as well. It sounds awfully interesting.'

'I think you mean algebra?'

'That's it! You *know* about it?' He gave his father a glance of admiration.

'Well, I did know about it but I've forgotten most of it.'

'Well, when I get to do it, you can do it too and help me because I don't really understand how you can add up little letters. And Daddy, can I join a children's football team?'

The wine waiter came to refill glasses from the bottle of Sancerre. Jeffrey stayed his hand as he was about to pour. 'I think, in the circumstances, we might have champagne,' he said.

'Certainly, sir. We have a very fine Mumm which we offer at a reduced—'

'That'll do, we'll have that.'

'Champagne?' said Roly. 'That's only for special occasions, Maman says.'

'I think this is quite a special occasion.'

'Is it? Then can I have some champagne too?'

'A spoonful,' Karen said.

Roly began to laugh. 'You can't drink champagne from a spoon! That would be ... wait, it's a new word I heard yesterday – *innommable*, that was it. But you know, how can something be unnameable? Everything has a name.' He began to scoop up the remains of the *meunière* sauce from his plate.

The tears of a moment ago were forgotten. It was as if the sun had come out for him. The silver lining, thought Karen. For all of us, not just for Roly.

The champagne came, there was the usual bustle associated with an ice bucket and the opening of the bottle. The wine was poured. True to her threat, Karen poured some from her glass into a dessert spoon and offered it to Roly. He giggled, but sipped it.

'And speaking of names,' he said. 'What am I going to call you? Mademoiselle Karen is going to sound funny in London. And if I translate it to Miss Karen, that's like a schoolteacher.'

'What do you fancy?' she asked. 'Auntie Karen?'

'That's what that boy at the big house said – the place where I got to ride the pony. Popcorn, that's the pony's name. The big boy called his mother Mummy. I call Louis Papa Louis. Do you fancy Mummy Karen?'

'How about just Karen?'

'Would that be all right?'

She smiled. 'We'll try it out,' she said. 'We've got plenty of time to try out lots of names.'

'We'll all three of us think up names for Karen. It'll be a team effort.'

491

'Yes, well, talking about teams, Daddy,' said the little boy quickly, 'you never answered my question. Is there a football team in London that I can join?'

'This is called "future planning",' Karen commented.

'I'll drink to that,' said Jeffrey.

They lifted their glasses to each other. The pledge they were making would keep them linked by their love, by the knowledge that after storms and trials they had found a lasting shelter in each other's arms, by their determination to become a family ready to face anything that life could set before them.